At the Crossroad

Sweet River Redemption Series

The Broken Trail
At the Crossroad

At the Crossroad

Sweet River Redemption Series
Book Two

By
Christa MacDonald

MBI

At the Crossroad
Published by Mountain Brook Ink
White Salmon, WA U.S.A.

The website addresses shown in this book are not intended in any way to be or imply an endorsement on the part of Mountain Brook Ink, nor do we vouch for their content.

This story is a work of fiction. All characters and events are the product of the author's imagination. Any resemblance to any person, living or dead, is coincidental.

Scripture quotations are taken from the King James Version of the Bible. Public domain.

ISBN 978-1-943959-36-5
© 2017 Christa MacDonald

The Team: Miralee Ferrell, Nikki Wright, Rachel Lulich, Cindy Jackson

Cover Design: Indie Cover Design, Lynnette Bonner Designer

Mountain Brook Ink is an inspirational publisher offering fiction you can believe in.
Printed in the United States of America

DEDICATION

To all the moms with more love than time, with more bills than deposits, and more problems than solutions; the world may not see you, but God does and He's always with you.

ACKNOWLEDGMENTS

First, thank you, mom, for being my first ever and most faithful beta reader. Oh, and for teaching me everything I know about being a mother. Thank you for being the best grandmother to my kids and for your unending support and love. I would not be the woman I am today if not for you.

I would like to thank my publisher, Miralee Ferrell, for her patience on this one. I had heard authors say the second book is harder than the first and they aren't kidding. It is. I appreciate her support and kindness more than I can say.

Thank you Rachel Lulich for taking this manuscript a piece at a time and helping me turn it into a book. I deeply appreciate your editing miracles.

Finally, I'd like to thank my husband for his steadfast support and encouragement. Thank you for being my rock when I am at sea.

CHAPTER ONE

ERIN SULLIVAN HUNG UP THE PHONE and resisted the temptation to kick something. Since this was the teacher's lounge and not her office, she closed her eyes instead and took a deep, hopefully calming breath. She could smell the mint tea that the guidance counselor stocked in the staff pantry, the leather of the lounge chairs, and the coffee pot left half-full on the beverage bar. The downside of being the athletics director at Sweet River Christian Academy was that her office in the gym was right in the middle of the action, but far from soundproof and definitely not private enough to make a call to a parent concerning their two sons. And especially not when those two sons were about to be kicked off the hockey team for yet again failing to attend practice.

The teacher's lounge was part of the administrative office, and since it had a door that could be closed, and so would be empty as a tomb at four in the afternoon, it was the spot Erin usually chose for these kinds of calls. Slowly exhaling, she realized that her calming breath hadn't done its job. She said a quick prayer, hoping that the knot of angst she felt in her stomach would disappear once her heart was emptied out and her head was clear. A soft knock split the silence, and she heard the door creak open.

"How'd it go?"

She didn't need to open her eyes to know who it was. Katherine MacAlister was both the director of the school and her friend, and Erin had briefed her on the continuing struggles with the Murphy boys. Katherine knew how difficult calling a parent could be and that a call to Claire Murphy would be that and more. The Murphys were a legacy family, with three generations having transitioned from students to donors. That was a boon for the school, but Claire tended to see it as a reason to receive special treatment. Erin didn't believe in giving anyone special treatment.

"It went awesome." Erin turned to Katherine with a wink. "Claire has resolved to make sure that her sons are at every practice from now on, and she's taking me to lunch tomorrow to celebrate what a fantastic job I'm doing."

"And without the sarcasm?" Katherine raised an eyebrow.

"About how you'd imagine." She ticked off Claire's excuses on her fingers. "It's not her fault the boys missed practice because her car was in the shop. Practices don't matter anyway. We always schedule them at an inconvenient time with little respect for the effort parents have to put into these things. She ended with a zinger though." Erin tried to imitate Claire's smooth diction. "I assume that a woman like you would understand." Erin mimed slamming a phone receiver down. "Dial tone."

"A 'woman like you'?"

"She said something about how her husband works so much she might as well be a single mom, and no one understood how hard she has it."

"That doesn't seem like her. She's normally on top of every detail. She heads a committee on the PTO and that's not a small amount of work."

"She seemed a little tense."

"Huh," Katherine looked thoughtful. "Could be it's as simple as not having a car."

"She picked them up today in one."

"Well . . . I'm trying to assume the best of Claire, but maybe it's too late in the day for soul calisthenics."

"Soul calisthenics?" Erin had to laugh. Katherine had a gift for odd turns of phrase. "I love that, but after today it would have to be more like soul boot camp."

"The Murphys are a challenge."

"To be honest, I don't really mind them. They're like most boys; they've got more energy than activities to occupy it. They're not bad kids, but they need structure. That reminds me, I've been meaning to ask you if we can add a morning PE elective. It would be before first bell, but after breakfast for the boarding students."

"What do you have in mind?"

"Nothing to get their heart-rates up, something to get their muscles stretched and their brains focused. We could start with the kids who seem to need it, and then open it up for others if it's a success."

"That's a great idea. I'll take a look at the schedule." Katherine began to leave, and then swung around. "Do me a favor though; send me an official proposal, because this is something that will need an okay from the board. It's your bright idea, so I figure you can do the paperwork."

"Thanks, boss," Erin called as Katherine walked away with a wave over her shoulder.

Erin left the lounge, calling goodnight to the admin staff as she headed back to the gym. The dance team was finishing up as she walked in. Tchaikovsky was playing over a set of small speakers propped up on the bleachers. The girls were all in a line, going one by one to do a series of steps that ended in a *grande jeté*. They spotted her and instantly begged her to join them. Although it had been years since she had studied ballet seriously, her body hadn't forgotten much. Erin toed off her sneakers and joined the back of the line behind the smallest girl who gave her a thumbs-up. The girl was tiny, but clearly talented, as she executed her steps well and had perfectly flat legs on her mid-air split.

Erin's *jeté* wasn't as *grande* as she would have liked, but it was fun all the same. "How'd I do?" The girls all cheered as if she had soared eight feet high with perfect legs. The teacher gave her a wink as she rounded up her students and then headed for the locker room. Erin waited until they left, then took a look around the gym to be sure it was empty. Satisfied that she was alone, she raised her arms and began to dance. She started slowly and then moved into a series of *chaînés*. Her hair swung off her shoulders and she could feel the wide smile form on her face as joy—there was no other word for it—filled her heart.

She didn't get the chance to dance very often. Her little house, while being perfectly lovely, didn't have a room large enough. Sometimes before or after school she would try to get in a session in the gym, but she was almost always interrupted. However, a night like this, with no one scheduled for at least another hour, meant that she could dance off the stress of that phone call in peace. In her mind she still heard the music playing as she twirled and circled her way across the floor. When she missed a step and had to catch herself before landing on her backside, she laughed out loud, her mood so different from when she started. She tried the *grande jeté* again and nailed it.

Clapping sounded from the corridor doorway, and she spun around to find Dr. Daniel Connors, pastor of Calvary Church, leaning against the door frame as if he had been watching, a slight smile on his lips. Erin's breath caught, and a thousand butterflies took off in her stomach. She hadn't seen him in a while since she had started attending New Day Baptist. When her daughter Brittany and husband Jake moved to Greenville, they started attending New Day Baptist since it was closer to their new house. Erin wanted to keep the whole family together on Sundays. It was tough leaving Calvary and driving to church rather than walking, but she felt her daughter needed the support and New Day Baptist had solid preaching. Not like Dan's, but it was good.

"I'm sorry I startled you. I was hoping to find you in your office."

Her stupid heart kicked up its rhythm, and if she wasn't wrong, the heat on her cheeks meant that she was blushing. Dan was in his usual suit, but he had taken off the jacket and loosened his tie. His hair was a bit rumpled too. For some crazy reason it only made him more attractive in her eyes. He looked approachable, not that she ever would.

"I'm afraid I'm not going to be at the meeting tonight. I meant to email you days ago, and it slipped my mind. It's been a hectic week. I figured I could tell you in person." He looked tired, like life had taken too much out of him today. If not for her screaming crush on him, she might have asked him what was wrong in case talking about it would help. Not that she would ever talk with the man. He had been the pastor of the church for almost four years, and she hung on his every syllable, but never said more than 'Hello' and 'Goodbye' to him.

"So . . . if that's okay with you."

Erin's tongue was still frozen in place. It was always like this when she ran into Dan unexpectedly. Or, truthfully, whenever she was near Dan at all. She had a full-body reaction to the man. Her brain froze, her tongue tied, her heart fluttered, and her stomach became a butterfly air show. No one else did this to her. She had been around men more attractive than him and hadn't suffered from paralysis. It was something about Dan.

Finally, she pulled her synapses together. "Sure."

"Okay." He stood in the doorway for what seemed like an unusually long time before he waved and then left.

Erin grabbed the stuff she had dropped earlier and all but ran back to her office. Of all the people she could be hung up on, she had to pick Dr. Dan Connors. He might be single, but he wasn't likely to be interested in her. What did she have to offer a well-educated church pastor who had traveled the world? The only place out of state she'd ever been was over the border to Canada and down to Florida. She was the widow of a man who'd dropped out of high school and whose only claim to fame was his beer chugging record at Flannigan's Bar. Half the town looked down their noses at her. No man of God would want anything to do with her and Dan was so far out of her league she would never stand a chance. If only her heart would realize that before it was too late.

Dan headed for the parking lot, his mind in a whirl. He needed a minute, maybe ten, to shake off what he was feeling. The image of Erin Sullivan twirling across the floor, her hair in a fan of gold around her, a smile like he had never seen on her face, was burned into his brain. As soon as she had spotted him she had turned into her usual deer in the headlights. Her shyness meant he had never gotten to know her despite her attending his church and running the after-school basketball program he had volunteered for. It was almost as if she was intentional in her avoidance, but that made no sense. He had never gotten the impression she disliked him.

"Any chance of a lift?" The husky, slightly distant voice called Dan back to reality. He looked up to find Pete Coleman, the local game warden, soon to retire after surviving a brutal attack from a suspect, slowly making his way out of the school toward him. Pete was leaning heavily on his cane as he walked, but otherwise seemed in good shape.

"Of course." Dan opened the passenger side door for him.

"You sure it's no trouble?" Pete gave him a quizzical look. "You seemed deep in thought."

Dan knew many things about Pete and paramount among them was his sage-like ability to look into a person's soul. Dan didn't want anyone looking into his soul today. It was a swirling mess. "I've got an hour before my next meeting, plenty of time to drive up to your place." He crossed over to the driver's side and got in, started up, pulled out of the parking lot and headed out of town, up the mountain where Pete lived.

"How are you doing, Pete?"

"Oh, can't complain. Well, I could, but it wouldn't do me any good." Pete settled his cane next to his leg. "Doctor says I'm fine considering the extent of damage the aneurism did. Therapy is harder than I thought it would be, not being able to drive is a pain, having my daughters fuss over me is getting old, but . . ." He took a deep breath and let it out. "That right there? Breathing in and out? Beats the alternative."

Dan was glad to hear it since the struggle back from brain injuries like the one Pete had suffered didn't always go well. Dan would know. He had been watching that struggle fail for years and living with the consequences.

Pete spoke, and it was like he had been reading Dan's mind. "I saw you at Brookings Rehab the other day. Figured you were vising your mom. How's she doing?"

The lead weight that always seemed to be in his gut got heavier. He knew the question was a kind one, but he would rather no one ever ask it again. Every visit with his mom produced the same mix of guilt, anger, and sadness. There was no way he would burden anyone with that. Each visit to Mom was a challenge to his natural optimism and a test of his faith. Since the day that he flew home to Maine in a panic, not knowing what the stroke might have done to her, he had watched his mother lay in her hospital bed or sit in her wheelchair and stare into space, maybe mumbling a few phrases if it was a good day, as the weeks, months, and now years went by.

"She's about the same," he offered flatly.

"And how are you?"

How was he? Useless. That was the honest answer to Pete's question. Only a miracle would change his mother's condition, and despite the thousands of prayers sent up, God had said 'No'. Each visit he made was fruitless and demoralizing.

"I'm about the same too, I guess."

"Hmm. Saw you signed up to coach basketball again. Were you up at the school to meet with Erin Sullivan?"

Dan's stomach did a strange flip. "Uh, sort of." The image of Erin dancing popped into his head only to be replaced by her expression of surprise and fear when she had spotted him standing there. "I'm surprised she chose teaching as her vocation. It must be a challenge with her shyness."

Pete looked at him like he had two heads and both were spinning. "Shyness?"

"Yeah, she's super shy. She doesn't say a word to me unless she has to. She's said more to me in an email than she ever has in real life."

Pete gave him an odd look, shook his head, and muttered, "Sometimes it's the bright ones . . ." But he didn't bother to explain. "Your best bet is to talk to Erin. See if you can make her more comfortable around you. Put a little effort in."

Dan didn't respond. He wasn't sure there was any point in going out of his way to befriend Erin. She was going to a new church so he saw little of her now. Strangely, that thought made him feel wistful.

As the minutes ate up the miles out to Pete's house, Dan thought about Erin. It made sense that she was a dancer since she had a fluid kind of grace. It was beautiful the way her hair moved with her. He imagined it was soft and silky. Immediately, he shook the thought off. Nothing good could come of contemplating the beauty of a woman so unsuitable for the kind of life he wanted. He wasn't sure how much longer he would stay in Sweet River. His heart yearned to return to India. Sometimes he would dream he was back at the mission, in the heat and the spicy air. When he woke from those dreams, it was always with a stab of disappointment that they weren't real.

Someone as shy and delicate as Erin wouldn't be able to handle a place like West Bengal. Besides the spiritual element, it took both emotional and physical strength to handle foreign missions. In the years that he had been home, he hadn't met anyone he thought was prepared for the harsh realities of the climate, the living conditions, or the work. He wasn't going to make a wife miserable for his own comfort, so he had stayed single, content with his current vocation. He never longed for anyone.

At least not until today, until he had seen her smile and her large blue eyes, and had suddenly felt that hit of desire—something he hadn't felt in a long time, if ever. Pete had to be nuts suggesting he talk to her. It would be best if he left her as alone as she apparently wanted to be. What would be the point of pursuing her if he ended up going back into missions anyway?

But later that night, long after he'd dropped off Pete, after he'd sat through his meetings, after he'd heated a frozen pizza and ate it watching a Celtics game, he could not get her out of his head.

CHAPTER TWO

ERIN STOOD WITH HER ARMS OVER her head, hair dryer in one hand and her roller brush in the other, while Katherine watched from the bathroom doorway. "Erin, you know we're going to the craft store and then to lunch, right?" Erin snagged another section of hair and coiled it around her brush, hitting it with the heat first and then the cool. When she pulled the brush out her hair fell in a perfect, bouncing wave.

"Patience is a virtue . . . besides, I'm almost done."

Katherine sighed and pulled out her phone. Erin went back to her hair. Having long thick hair was supposed to be a blessing, but to Erin it was a chore that she would almost rather not have had to deal with. Sure it looked good, she made certain it did, but it took a full hour from shower to shake-out. If she didn't blow it out she would have the frizzy-twisty nightmare that she had been born with.

When she was twelve, her dad had remarried and his new wife took one look at Erin's free-spirited style and decided to give her a makeover—her first lesson was how to conquer frizzy hair. Linda was a southern belle, and she arrived at their house with a trailer stuffed with her things and a list of beauty rules that she proceeded to metaphorically beat into Erin's head.

The first rule was that, fair or not, looks mattered, and a lady did not leave the house with ratty hair. To this day, Erin couldn't handle walking out of the house with wet hair or bare-faced. It felt almost sacrilegious. All the same, she never thought less of any woman who chose to go natural, in fact she admired it, especially at times like this when her arms were tired of holding a brush over her head. She switched off the hair dryer, shook her hair out, and took one last look. It would do. Throwing a lip-gloss into her purse, she turned to Katherine. "Ready."

"Finally." Katherine backed out of the doorway.

"No griping, that was only ten minutes."

"I suppose that's better than usual."

"Whiner." Erin followed Katherine down the stairs into the small foyer at the front door. "So who's driving?" She grabbed her coat and slid it on.

"Since I want to get there in one piece, me." Katherine took out her keys as the two of them headed out, Erin locking up behind them.

"I drive fine," she half-protested, but she followed Katherine to her Yukon anyway and climbed in the passenger side. It was just as well that Katherine wanted to drive. It was a week from payday, and she had slim pickings in the bank. The money would stretch through today's supply run, a trip to the market, and the electric bill—that was all. Filling her gas tank was not in the budget. The store they were headed to was an hour and a half away. Her old Explorer got about sixteen miles to the gallon. That added up to gas she really couldn't afford.

"You drive fine, yes, but your car doesn't have sat nav."

"Your phone has navigation . . ."

"It's not the same." Katherine began inputting the address of the shop into the navigation unit. "I like to have her comforting voice telling me where to go."

Erin rolled her eyes. "At least you have heated seats. Mine died last year. If I had the cash, it's the first thing on the old tank I'd get fixed."

Katherine looked aghast. "It's like, forty degrees."

"Yah, so?"

"You grew up in Maine."

Erin didn't reply. Instead she slid her sunglasses on and made a point of leaning over the console to turn the seat heater to high.

"New Englanders are supposed to be hardy," Katherine continued.

"I am hardy, but why pass up the blessing from God that is a warm seat? You've let that macho-man husband rub off on you."

Katherine shook her head, but Erin caught the slight smile on her face. She wasn't surprised Mac was rubbing off on Katherine. The two of them might have had a rocky time getting together, but their love was something beautiful to behold. Although, like anything so pretty, it hurt a little to look at it, especially when it was something Erin had always wanted and never had. Her marriage had been very different, almost the antithesis.

"So what's on the list for this trip?" Katherine checked her mirrors and pulled out onto the road.

"It's almost the Christmas fair season, and I'm low on earrings so I need beads, silver wire, and the rest. I only have a few weeks to get them done since the first fair is in November."

"I could help." Katherine turned to her with a bright smile before looking back at the road.

"Um…" Erin's brow furrowed.

"Not making them, you know I'm hopeless, like organizing your beads or something." Erin had tried to teach Katherine her art a number of times. It was surprising that someone who could sew and bake circles around her had not one iota of talent with wire and beads, an art that was second nature to Erin.

"I don't need a bead organizer, but if you want to keep me company while I work, you're more than welcome."

"Maybe." Katherine made a face. "Wait, that would require sitting in your basement. No offense, but it's a bit . . . creepy."

"It's not that bad. The workbench is in the daylight part. It's the storage half of the basement that's creepy. Luckily only the furnace guy ever needs to access that part, and it's mostly walled off. If the house was mine I'd convert the third bedroom upstairs for a workshop, but I asked the board if I could rip up the carpet and they said no. They want to keep it as is." She paused, a dark thought surfacing. "The cynic in me wonders if they're hoping I'll be out of there before the summer season."

"I could talk to them." Katherine glanced over at her, sympathy softening her face. "I know the school has owned that house for years, but maybe they would be willing to sell. It's probably Mindy that made the rule about updates. She's a whole lot nicer to work with now that Stephanie is gone, but she still likes to lord her power over people. If I give her a call—"

"Please don't," Erin cut her off. "After all the drama last year, I'm glad they renewed the lease, not to mention my contract. I don't want to rock the boat." Especially with her financial stability in it.

"Erin, they're lucky to have you. Why do you think your job is in jeopardy?"

"I'm the athletics director at a Christian school where my teenage daughter had to drop out after she became pregnant by another student. I mean it all ended happy and at the ripe old age of thirty-six I have a son-in-law I've learned to like and the cutest grandchild the world has ever known, but it wasn't exactly a good situation." Erin remembered the stress that she had lived with last year, and how she felt that she had failed Brittany; failed as a mom.

Katherine didn't know about the snide comments that Erin was still getting from the moms on the PTO, not to mention the anonymous notes in her mailbox suggesting that she was unfit and should take her 'trashy' family and leave. Even getting her contract renewed at the start of the summer hadn't eased her concerns. She half expected a call for her resignation at some point.

Erin couldn't help the feeling that even now there was a shadow over her, an asterisk forever beside her name, but it wasn't only because of Brittany. She had never been quite good enough, not for anyone.

"Don't take it to heart, Erin. There's always going to be people who can't see beyond a set of circumstances to the real person living them."

"Are you trying to make me feel better with rational facts and kindness?"

"Did it work?"

Erin took out her phone and hooked it up to the aux cord that Katherine had plugged into the car. "Okay, playlists available are: Work, Play, Pray, Relax, and my favorite—Shake it Off."

"That sounds good."

"It's mostly bad pop, so prepare yourself." Erin pressed play and the opening notes of a song began.

"Ace of Base?" Katherine's face looked pained.

"You were warned."

Katherine groaned, and they lapsed into silence as the car sped down the highway past tall pines and walls of rock. Like lost little sheep, her gloomy thoughts from earlier began to return. Erin's anxiety ramped back up again. It didn't matter that her daughter was turning out to be a model wife and mother, and it didn't seem to help that Brittany and Jake had already plugged in at their new church and town, quickly becoming well-liked and respected. It should. Erin knew it was stupid to give these thoughts room in her brain, but she couldn't stop it. She spent her life waiting for the other shoe to drop, braced for the next hit.

From the day Jimmy Sullivan had sauntered into the restaurant where she had worked and flashed her that good ol' boy smile, it had been one mistake after another. If not for her children, she would have thought that the ten years she had spent with him were nothing but darkness and sorrow. Even after he was gone, every time it started looking like they were out from under the cloud and the sun was shining again, something would happen and they would be back in the dark. Erin sat up in her seat. "Hey, would you mind if we change the list?"

"No argument from me."

Erin switched the music to the 'Pray' list. She had found that the only way to combat her dark thoughts was prayer or praise. Her mind was in no shape to pray, so she would praise instead.

"Oh! I love this one!" Katherine began to sing along. The music was folk-like and soothing. Usually Katherine went for classical. She had grown up wealthy, and so her taste in music was as refined as her taste in books, clothes, and even cars. She liked the nicer things, but wasn't the snob people sometimes assumed her to be. Erin had been guilty of that the first time they had met. She smiled to herself now thinking that Katherine's love of the jewelry that Erin made was a bigger compliment than she was giving her credit for.

Sing to Jesus began to play, and it was one that had never failed to calm her, so she began to sing along. God had blessed Erin with many things, but a good voice was not among them, so she kept it to a whisper. Closing her eyes she let the words fill her, pushing out the darkness.

An hour later, they pulled off the highway and over a short local road to the craft supply store. It was the largest in the region and had a selection of crystal beads that could not be beat. Erin ordered gemstones and other special items online, but the rest she found here. Every part of the process of making jewelry filled her with the kind of contentment that dancing did. Even picking up supplies was enjoyable. They pushed through the doors of the shop and were hit by the rainbow of beads lined up in their plastic bins covering one whole wall. The shop was about the size of a small grocery store, and it was packed tight with product.

"So much pretty," Katherine sighed. "I wish I was crafty."

"What? You craft."

"I sew," Katherine explained. "It's different."

Erin walked over to the wall of beads and picked up a tube of seed beads. "Then sew these onto something."

"Oh. I hadn't thought about these." Katherine took the beads. "I could make a beaded coin purse or maybe edge a scarf."

"There you go," Erin encouraged, giving her a little push. "Treat yourself to some pretty."

"I think I will. Mac finished my office-slash-sewing room the other day and I haven't had a chance to break it in yet. Did I tell you that?"

"Last I heard you were arguing with him about it because it was his office and you didn't want him to give it up. I believe you were feeling guilty."

"I was. I got over it when he said he wanted to do something that would make his house feel more like 'our' house. It was so . . . him." Her face was soft as she spoke. "And you should see it. He lined the walls with shelves for my fabric stash, set up this huge worktable with a cutter and layout space. Right in front of the window he set up this gorgeous French desk he got at the antique market with enough space for my laptop. It's beautiful."

"Good excuse for a new project."

Katherine agreed and headed for the fabric section at the back. Erin began perusing the beads, letting their shiny, bright colors help her push away any feelings of jealousy. Katherine had suffered enough in her life to deserve to be loved like that, to have that kind of security. Erin had known Mac for far longer than she had known Katherine, and well enough that she had no doubts about the depth of his love for his wife. It was a sacrificial love, a cherishing love, something Erin had never known. She absorbed the sting of that thought and then let it go. Grabbing a shopping basket near the register, she focused on buying her supplies instead of what her life was lacking. She was blessed with two beautiful boys and a daughter who had a lovely family all her own. That was enough.

An hour later they were at the Blueberry Bakery, a café in a little strip mall that looked iffy from the outside, but had the best food for miles around. As they were finishing their lunch at a table by the window where the late autumn sunshine flooded in, Erin was unashamedly dipping one of the bakery's soft rolls in the dregs of the soup that she had ordered, not wanting to miss out on a drop.

"Here, we'll share." Katherine broke the huge chocolate-chip cookies that she had ordered and held out a half.

"Whoa, that thing is huge."

"You have like, zero body fat. You need a cookie."

"That's not how it works," Erin laughed. "I keep telling you, every body is different, and yours is great the way it is, and if it wants a cookie it's perfectly okay to feed it a cookie. Mine does not need a cookie."

Katherine made a pleading face. "If you don't take this half I'll eat the whole thing. I need you to save me from myself."

"You are ridiculous; you know this, don't you?" Erin took her half of the cookie, broke it into two pieces and wrapped each in a napkin before stowing them in her purse. "James and Seth will save you from yourself. How about that?"

"Works for me." She popped a piece of the cookie in her mouth and closed her eyes. "Hey." Her eyes flew open. "I forgot to tell you, the board approved your new class. Do you want me to include it in Monday's announcements?"

"I've got to talk Claire Murphy into it, though. She's balked at anything that changes their schedule. I think I'll call her this weekend and see if I can get her to agree to it."

"Which will be tough."

"Ah, but, I have a clever plan." Erin gave her an exaggerated wink.

"What are you up to?"

"Okay, you know how the Murphys live in that development that's attached to the resort?"

"Sure do. It's part of the property that Mac has to patrol. At least twice a week he gets a call from one of the residents complaining about something."

"Not surprised. The townhouses there go for half a million. Anyway, remember Claire said she didn't like the practice schedule and getting the boys to and from was too difficult?" Erin waited while Katherine nodded her acknowledgment before she went on. "Did a bit of research and it turns out that the resort shuttle bus has a run from the welcome area right by that development at 6:30 A.M. into town, and it unloads, guess where?"

"Right in front of the school. I've seen them before."

"Exactly. And the return bus at night is at 4:45, which is plenty of time for the boys to catch it. If they take the bus instead of their mom dropping them, they'll be early enough to school to take my new class and have a ride home after practice. It's perfect."

"But, every season? I mean, when it hits mid-winter will they still run the bus on that schedule?"

"I spoke to the resort manager, and he said those two runs are all year round."

"Nice. If you can get her to agree that would solve their tardiness issue, too."

"They've been late?"

"Twice last week. I was about to give her another call."

Erin felt her jaw drop open. Claire was always so on top of everything. It wasn't like her to let her kids be late. She was a leading member of the PTO, heading up the Harvest Party fundraiser at the end of the month, which was a huge task. "Are you concerned at all?"

"Not really, but it's something to keep an eye on."

On the long drive home, they listened to classical music, and Erin tried not to fall into a carb coma.

"Hey." Katherine interrupted the quiet. "Are you free for dinner on Friday night? My mom is coming to stay for a few weeks, and I'd like to introduce all my favorite people to her."

"Your mom is driving?" Erin was surprised since Katherine said her mom didn't like to drive to the corner store.

"Oh, no, one of her art students is driving her in exchange for her lessons. I guess she has family up here she'll visit while mom stays with me and then will drive her back down."

"Well, that's handy. It's someone your mom trusts?"

"Mom trusts everybody, but the driver is fine."

"Meaning Mac checked her out."

"Well…he had a friend run her license—just in case."

"I wonder if that's weird for him."

"He says he's content, and I've learned to take him at his word." Mac used to be Captain MacAlister, the local policeman and chief of detectives for the county. He was well known and widely respected, but he had quit for Katherine. They had a 'Gift of the Magi' sort of story. He had given up his life-long career in law enforcement to follow her, but she had signed on as director of the school to stay for him. But it had a happy ending. Now he was the chief of security for the Sweet River Resort & Lake Houses.

"If there's one person you can take at his word, it would be Mac."

"Yes." She sounded thoughtful, so Erin waited her out. "But he seems preoccupied lately."

"Have you asked him what's up?"

"I haven't. I'm not sure I want to know."

"Katherine," Erin scolded. "You know he loves you. Whatever it is, you know that it's not that he's not happy with you. If he says he's content, he is."

"You're right. I'm a coward."

"No, you're still skittish. You haven't been married a year yet. I know it took time for you to trust him and there's probably a part of you that still holds back. While you do, you need to be open. Talk to him."

"That shouldn't be hard, but it still is. These old habits die so hard. I have to keep reminding myself I am a new creature in Christ and in Him all things are possible."

"Well…" Erin was out of good advice. Katherine and Mac would have to figure it out for themselves. As far as she was concerned, Mac was about even with Dan Connors in the 'Men Who Were Too Good for This Earth' competition. But she wasn't married to him.

"Hey, you didn't answer my question though. Are you free?"

"Of course. What else am I going to do on a Friday night?"

"Seriously?" Katherine shook her head. "You're gorgeous. You could hit the grocery store and without lifting a finger you'd have every single male there eating out of your hand."

"No thanks."

"Okay, so not the grocery store. How about the Smooth Moose?"

"A bar?"

"They have food too."

"Katherine, I love you, but I do not need advice on where to go to get a date. First, because your suggestions are terrible, and second, because I don't want one. I'm too busy for dating right now."

"Have you, though?" Katherine gave her a sharp look. "Dated?"

Erin pressed her lips together, reluctant to admit that it had been seven years since Jimmy's death and no, she hadn't dated. The first few years she was too busy dealing with the chaos that their lives were thrown into, then she had to focus on helping her kids come to terms with their grief, and then she had to tackle her own confused grief. There was all the fallout from Jimmy's family, too. They had never believed how bad things were at the end, and some of them still treated Erin as if she had driven his car into the tree for him. Even now, she couldn't imagine a man, a good man, wanting to deal with all her baggage.

"Okay, that long pause probably means no, and I—"

"I'm fine." Erin interrupted. "I don't need anyone." This was half true. There were moments she wished she had someone to lean on, to not always be alone in every decision, every crisis.

Her friend shook her head, but thankfully didn't try to convince her that she was wonderful and any man would be glad to have her. Erin heard that enough in the calls she got from her dad and step-mom in Florida. They were more than a thousand miles away and somehow they still knew by only hearing the tone of her voice that she wasn't seeing anyone.

Katherine pulled into the driveway in front of Erin's house and sighed. "I still love your house. It's the cutest in town." She wasn't wrong. It was a Victorian painted butter yellow with white trim, a wrap-around porch, and a white picket fence enclosing a cottage-style garden. The garden was mostly done for the year, but the mums were lovely and the frost had held off so the foliage stood out.

"It's about a third the size of yours and has almost no storage."

"It's still cute." Her stubborn tone made Erin laugh as she grabbed her bags from the back seat and opened the door. She jumped out then leaned toward the open window. "Hey listen, don't worry about me. I'm fine on my own, I always have been."

"But, why be lonely when you have options?"

"Lonely?" she scoffed. "Girl, I'm too mean to be lonely." She smiled, but Katherine didn't return it. "Relax. I really am fine. I'll see you tomorrow." She shut the door, waved goodbye as she ran up to her front door, and let herself in. The house was quiet, which meant the boys were still at their friend's house. Erin took her purchases down to the basement and put her new supplies away.

Since she was in the basement anyway, she stopped to put a load of laundry through, but found that James had not put the wash in the dryer like she had asked him to that morning. Most of the time James was her rock, always doing what he was told, always eager to please, but lately he had been huffy when told to do a chore. She wasn't sure if that was him turning thirteen or if there was something else to worry about. She would have to add it to the list. Reaching into the washer she pulled out the cold, damp clothes and stuffed them in the dryer. It was mostly jeans, so she set it on high and shut the door.

As she grabbed the waiting basket of dirty clothes and started to load the wash, a screeching mechanical sound from the dryer echoed through the basement. She reached across and whacked the OFF button. The noise ground to a halt, but her nose picked up the telltale smell of burnt rubber. "Seriously?" she shouted at the now silent appliance. "You are not in the budget!" Tugging the door open she pulled out the damp clothes and piled them into a basket. Now she was going to have to find a way to get a repair guy out or…

Across the basement she spotted the drying rack she used for her delicates. It would have to do for now. It was a bit spindly to carry jeans, but she didn't have a whole lot of options. Hauling the rack upstairs with the basket, she set it up in a sunny corner of the kitchen, figuring they would dry quicker there than in the basement. Setting the rack up was easy enough, but the socks tried to slip over the rails and the jeans didn't want to fit.

To her surprise, the prickle of tears began in the back of her throat. Before she could stop them, they came and not only a single, graceful tear. It was too hard. Living paycheck to paycheck, worried about everything, always alone. Why couldn't anything be easy? She took a shaky breath. "Pull it together," she said aloud into the silence. After a few more straggly breaths, the storm passed. Today she had let it all overwhelm her, but she wasn't going to stay down. Her boys would be home soon, and they didn't need to see her a mess of self-pity.

She would find a way to get the dryer fixed. She would find a way to keep her job, even if the women of the PTO were lined up against her, and if she didn't, there would be a way to find another job. There was always a way to get by. Leaving the laundry where it was, she climbed the stairs to fix her face and change into comfy clothes. Dinner needed to be made, life was moving ahead, and it was up to her to get on with it.

CHAPTER THREE

DAN STOOD SHIN-DEEP IN THE river, his waders protecting him from the rush of cold water all around him. It was the kind of day that only autumn seemed to produce; a sky impossibly blue, scant clouds, warm sun, but with a bite to the air that reminded all that winter was coming. Dan reserved Saturdays for the outdoor pleasures that he rarely had time for during the week. If he wasn't on the river fishing, he was hiking one of the state park trails, or if the mood struck, down east on the coast walking the rocky beaches. Maine was beautiful almost any time of year, but nothing beat the autumn. Even now, the trees stretched overhead halfway out into the river, the sun filtering through the bright red, orange, and yellow leaves.

His soul felt more settled when he was surrounded by God's creation in all its glory. With a satisfied sigh he cast again, aiming his lure at the reeds on the far side of the river. The fly soared in a low arc to flick against the water and then back before he deftly tugged the lure enough to see if he could tempt any trout to take a bite.

"Any luck?"

Dan closed his eyes in a silent plea for patience as he turned to face his friend Mac, standing downriver on the shore, his line in the water, a bored look on his face. They had only been at it an hour, but it seemed that was Mac's limit. Dan should have brought Pete. Then again, if he had, Pete would want to start some soul-deep conversation, and Dan wasn't up to it. He had had a tough week. The three funerals were rough enough, but his final visits to Margaret Jackson in Hospice had taken a toll. He'd been there for her last moment, and he'd never seen anyone fight that hard to live. After consoling her husband and children, he knew why. Deaths like that challenged his faith like nothing else. There was a powerful temptation to ask God how he could take a mother from her kids, a wife from her husband, especially when the soul leaving earth was such a generous and beautiful one. Fishing was supposed to be his release. He was preaching tomorrow and didn't need to get wound up on his one day off. Reeling in, he started wading to shore.

"Hey, are we calling it a day?" There was no mistaking the relieved tone in Mac's question.

"Yep. I guess they're not biting today." Dan hid his smile as Mac immediately sloshed his way to shore. By the time Dan had stowed his rod Mac was already back in his camp chair, his feet up on a boulder, and one hand rummaging in the cooler. He pulled out a wrapped sandwich, set it in his lap, and went digging again.

"Y'know, Mac, the object of fishing is to keep going until you catch something."

"Yep. Caught something. Pretty sure it's a case of 'this is boring'." He pulled out another wrapped package. "Have a sandwich."

Dan took the sandwich from Mac and sat down on the other camp chair. Dan peeled back the wax paper to find cheese, lettuce, and tomato on whole wheat.

"I reminded Katherine you don't eat meat, so yours is missing the roast beef." Mac took a huge bite of his sandwich and closed his eyes as if in ecstasy. "Mmm. Meat."

"Oh shut up." Dan kicked dirt on Mac's boots and took a bite of his own sandwich. It was delicious. He wasn't surprised, since Mac had frequently shared what a good cook his wife was and how lucky he was to have met her. Mac was still in the newlywed stage and, if allowed, would sing his wife's praises at length. It was a good thing and normally Dan didn't mind, but his head was cluttered and he had been looking forward to emptying it by spending a few hours on the river catching up with his friend. Having to listen to Mac's joyful boasting took a bit more patience than usual.

"Speaking of which"—Mac balled up his sandwich wrapper and chucked it back in the cooler--"did you go vegetarian when you were in India? Out of sympathy for the culture?"

"No, high school." He felt the familiar nudge of grief before explaining. "My dad died young–heart attack. Turns out heart disease runs rampant in my family. Decided I could do without red meat. Then found I could do without pork. I eat chicken occasionally, but I love fish. It's good for the old ticker."

"I lost my dad pretty young too, but as a result of the job."

Dan felt a rush of sympathy. "He was a detective as well?"

"Patrolman. It was a domestic disturbance. He was stabbed. Died almost before he hit the ground." Mac said it point-blank, no dressing, which was his style, but Dan knew from experience that it didn't diminish what he had suffered.

"Wow, that is rough. And you still followed in his footsteps?"

"I always knew I would go into law enforcement." Mac shrugged. "Never doubted that." He laughed. "Didn't know finding the love of my life would mean I'd end up in private security after leaving it, but when you're following God's will, life doesn't work like that. This might not be the job I've always dreamed of, but I'm content in a way I never was before."

"That's impressive, Mac. Not a lot of men can say they're content even when they have everything they want. Managing to feel that way after leaving a career you loved?" Dan shook his head.

"Worth it." Mac gave him another satisfied smile. "Besides, I've been thinking about another change lately."

"Really?"

"Yah." He paused as if he was reluctant to get into it. "It's something I've wanted to run by you."

"Me? You considering ministry?"

Mac laughed. "No, but sort of yes. You know Jake and Brittany finished that house in Stonebridge and moved out of mine, right?"

Dan nodded.

"Course, you'd have to know since they decided to join that little church over there. Can't think of the name."

"New Day Baptist."

"Right. Erin and the boys are over there now, aren't they?"

"Mac." Dan shook his head and laughed a little. "Why are you asking me questions you know the answer to?"

"Sorry, old cop habit. I was trying to see where you stood on the Sullivans decamping to another church."

"I make a point to never take someone leaving personally, unless on their way out they say it was me that pushed them out the door." He shrugged. "I never asked why they were leaving."

"Erin was pretty active at Calvary, but she often felt like an outsider because she was one of the only single moms there. That and, well, Katherine's said that some people were still upset about how Brittany and Jake got together, that somehow them getting married and having their baby was all well and good, but that the church had a responsibility to punish them so no other teens would get the idea that what they did was okay."

"Right, because being publicly called out and forced out of school wasn't enough for Brittany, and being dragged before the school board and formally punished wasn't enough for Jake." Dan sat back and scrubbed his hands through his hair, trying to release his frustration. "They confessed their sin, accepted the consequences, and got married. By all accounts it's a loving, strong marriage and they're good parents. What more do people want?"

"Scarlet letters," Mac answered, his voice gruff.

"Surely not."

"You're a better man than I am, Dan, so you assume the best of people. I'm working on that, among my other faults, but some of the people in those pews cannot forgive. I'm not surprised Brittany didn't feel welcome. As for Jake, he's got a quick temper where his wife's happiness is concerned. He couldn't have put up with her being mistreated."

"I wish they had said something. I suppose Erin left to support them?"

"She didn't say as much to me or to Katherine, but we got the feeling that was the case."

"Walter Brunner is the pastor at New Day. He's a good man, solid theologically. I think they'll do well there, but I'm sorry to see them go." Erin and her kids had sat in the same pew every week, left side, two up from the last. The first few Sundays after they left it was almost unsettling to look out and not see them. It made no sense, but whenever her name was mentioned he would feel a tug in his chest. If he caught sight of her or got an email about the basketball team from her, that feeling would be even stronger. It wasn't like the nudge he would feel when the Holy Spirit was moving him to talk to someone or the prod to pray for one of his parishioners. This was different.

"They'll probably come back after Jake and Brit get settled."

"So you and Katherine are back at your house and settled in?"

"Yeah, my place has plenty of space, but it's a bit remote, so Katherine misses her short commute. When I built the house I was thinking of it as an investment, so I built it to make the most of the market. Then I decided to stay and fixed up the stables and barn. Then came the animals. It wasn't the plan, but now I've got a six-bedroom house and a ranch which hardly makes sense for a couple who works full time." Mac paused and Dan got the sense that they were coming to the real reason Mac had suggested they get together today. It certainly hadn't been his love of fishing. "See, I've been feeling…led to something." Mac was staring down at his shoes. "Maybe God has another plan for all those bedrooms."

Dan leaned forward, surprised at the turn in the conversation. "Are you thinking about adopting?"

"Fostering. I haven't said anything to Katherine. You can probably guess why."

He definitely could. Mac's wife had been in a car wreck years before she had met him and lost her baby as well as any chance to have another. He couldn't even imagine the emotional minefield Mac would have to navigate to bring up foster parenting.

"It's been on my mind for a long time, Dan. It's like a voice in the back of my head. Lately, that voice has been a whole lot louder." His face became pensive, as if he couldn't put into words what he was thinking. "I feel like my life is about to change. I don't know for sure what it might look like, but I'm trying to be open to whatever God has in mind for me. I'm also no fool. I'm not exactly young, although Katherine's younger. We'd still probably have some hurdles to jump."

"I think any agency would likely fall all over themselves to place kids with a decorated police officer and a nationally known education expert."

"Ex-police officer. I'm a rent-a-cop now."

"The work must be really different. Do you mind the change?"

"Not a bit." The confidence Mac appeared to have in those words was almost palpable and Dan experienced a twinge of envy. He could start a fire with the resentment still smoldering inside him over having had to leave the mission in India. He had been fighting it for years, and it had barely abated. How could Mac be free of his so easily?

"There are days, though—I can't lie—where I'd rather not be working security." Mac dug into the cooler and pulled out two water bottles, offering one to Dan. "But depending on how things go… God's in control. I'm ready for whatever He decides."

A mix of admiration and jealousy hit Dan. He had to take a minute to center his thoughts and expel the emotion. He had prayed on a daily basis to feel like that, to be able to let go and surrender to God's will joyfully without reservation. He had prayed for peace, for direction, but none had come. "I'll pray for you, brother, but I can see God working already. I'm a little jealous."

Mac seemed surprised and Dan realized how much he might have revealed with that honesty. "Do you have regrets? About leaving the mission field, I mean?"

"I do." He sat back in the camp chair, taking a moment to separate his thoughts from his emotions so he wouldn't download all his confusion and misery on Mac. "When I got on the plane to come home, I told myself it would be a six-week furlough. It was supposed to be enough time to get my mom on her feet while taking a break and doing some fundraising. But I was not prepared for how bad off she was." The memory of his first visit with his mom after the stroke popped into his head, choking off all other thoughts. He had never seen her like that, so broken, close to death, and utterly helpless. His chest tightened with the all-too-familiar guilt, but he forced his way past it. "I wanted to get right back on the plane."

"I get that." Mac's voice was quiet and the sympathy in it made Dan resent his own weakness even more. He didn't deserve Mac's pity. A better son would have accepted what was and worked harder to make peace with it, and he definitely should have visited more often, or at least not felt gutted when he did.

"It's tough on Mom, not on me. I'm lucky that the position of pastor was open at Calvary. If it hadn't been, I'm not sure if I could have found work up here to continue supporting myself. I love the church, love the people, but being a pastor is very different from being a missionary. Everything is different, to be honest. It was a hard adjustment coming back and leaving everything behind. The mission was my life for a decade."

"You going back?"

Dan shrugged, unable to answer the question that had been plaguing him for months as he watched his mother slowly decline and as the words of her doctor changed from hopeful, to cautious, to consoling. He was utterly alone in this; with no family to share the burden, it was just him and his mom. There were many days that he didn't know what to do. Even after three years of being stateside, he felt like a half-stranger. Leaving India was like being ripped away from family, only no one knew, so he had had to suck it up and act like he was fine. He knew that he was blessed to have his job, but no one seemed to understand what he had lost when he took it.

"But, hey, foster parenting. That's awesome, Mac. You'd be a natural, and whatever support the church can provide, we'd be happy to. I understand there's a shortage of foster homes willing to take sibling groups, so if you're serious about those six bedrooms that might be something to consider."

"That's what I was thinking. Foster to adopt. I thought we'd sign up for the classes, jump through the hoops now, and see if God sends us a family."

"That's how that call works, you know." Dan focused on being glad for his friend and ignored his own conflict. "All you have to do is raise your hand and say 'here' and God responds."

"Thanks, Pastor. I've been carrying around these thoughts for a while. It's a weight off my chest to say them out loud."

"Happy to help, Mac. Anytime. I mean that."

A chime sounded and Mac pulled his phone out of his pocket. "Ah, the Mrs. is reminding me that I'm supposed to invite you to dinner on Friday night. Her mom's in town."

"Friday . . ." His mind scanned the most recent memory of the calendar on his desk. "Pretty sure that's good. I'd be happy to come."

"Great. It's at six." He began thumbing over his screen in what Dan assumed was a return text. "She's also reminding me that I promised we'd go for a ride this afternoon. The horses are restless."

"Hey, don't worry about me. I'm perfectly content to sit out here all day." Dan gestured to the woods around them.

"Okay, if you don't mind."

He smiled as he watched Mac pack up and hurry home to his wife. It was true, 'It is not good that the man should be alone'. Dan didn't feel alone, although technically he was. He had never questioned the decision that he had made back at seminary, to stay single and devote himself to spreading the Gospel. It had felt right. He had written the words of another missionary, William Borden, in his Bible as a reminder of his commitment, 'No Reserves. No Retreat. No Regrets.'

But what felt easy and natural while serving overseas lacked the same power now. He wasn't questioning his choice, but he was wondering if someday he might make another one.

CHAPTER FOUR

ERIN DROVE UP THE LONG DRIVE to Mac and Katherine's place and parked to the side of the driveway so she would be able to leave early if she needed to. Not that she expected to have a bad time, but it had been a long day and she wasn't feeling super social. She walked to the front entry, an open porch of sorts made out of squared-off logs. The house itself was made of the same logs and looked like a classic chalet, only bigger. The front was almost modest, but it was built into the side of the mountain to take advantage of the view. She knocked on the door and a moment later Mac opened it, a warm smile on his face. "Hey, stranger."

"It's been a while, hasn't it?" She walked in and he shut the door behind her before giving her a hug.

"No boys?"

"Brittany and Jake decided to be brave and take them on tonight."

"Good, gives you a break."

"Yup." She snuck a look into the kitchen where Katherine was furiously stirring something with Pete sitting on a stool nearby talking to her in what sounded like soothing tones. "I see Katherine is . . . what is it that she's doing?"

"I don't know." Mac looked over his shoulder at his wife. "But it's making her tense. I think it's something fancy. How about we slip past her into the family room?"

"Seems wise." Erin followed him through the great room noticing subtle changes from when Brittany and Jake rented his house. The big dining table with its benches instead of chairs was still in the same nook by the front of the house, but the wide, open living space was now organized into what looked like a formal seating area with a piano and another, less-formal area around the fireplace that had cozy-looking armchairs and a Scandinavian-style area rug. Other than that, the floors were still wide-plank and stained the same warm color as the logs in the ceiling and some of the walls. Erin loved the look of it. It was homey, but almost elegant and matched both Katherine's and Mac's styles.

"I like what you've done with the place." She half-shouted it in Katherine's direction and got a wave of acknowledgment in return.

Walking down the short set of stairs to the family room she could see it was still very much Mac's style. It had the traditional peaked ceiling and huge glass windows to take advantage of the view and the light available. It was mostly trees since they weren't at the top of the ridge, but it was stunning in the daylight. The sun had long since set, but the sky wasn't fully dark, so a bit of the view was still visible.

The family room had one new item, a big, sectional sofa, dark-brown leather, but it was strewn with red and denim toss pillows so it looked almost bright. It was centered on the floor-to-ceiling fieldstone fireplace and the low mantle sported a huge flat-screen TV instead of pictures or art. A small fire crackled merrily away in the grate. *Okay*, Erin thought, *this was where she was going to spend the party tonight.* "Mac, this place is amazing. Have I told you that before?"

"Glad to have you here." Mac turned to look down the left side hallway as someone drew near. "Lauren." His smile was welcoming and warm. "I'd like you to meet someone very special to Kate and me." He turned back to Erin. "Lauren, this is Erin Sullivan. Erin, this is Kate's mom, Lauren."

Erin held out her hand, but Lauren lunged forward and pulled Erin in for a hug. Erin was not a hugger, but she had been prepared for this, since she knew Katherine was and suspected the woman who raised her was probably one too. She patted her back awkwardly and gently pushed away, but held onto the woman's hand. "So glad to finally meet you. Katherine talks about you all the time."

"Oh, I hope it's not too annoying." She cringed.

Erin smiled to set her at ease. "Not at all."

"Shoo . . ." Lauren mimed wiping her forehead with her hand. Then her expression grew excited. "You're Erin the artist, aren't you?"

"Oh, well, I don't know about 'artist'."

"Yes, you are! I've seen your work. That ring you made Mac for Katherine was some of the best work I have ever seen. Such detail, and those gemstones. What were they?"

"Tourmaline. Mined in Maine."

"How lovely."

Erin was struck by how dissimilar Katherine and her mom were, and yet at the same time, how alike. Katherine shared Lauren's coloring, but not her body type or height. Not even their features were similar, but when Lauren smiled, Erin saw Katherine in it, and when she spoke, Erin perceived Katherine in her tone and the way she gestured and moved.

"Careful there." Mac was moving towards the stairs as Pete was descending them, leaning on his cane to steady each step.

"Quit fussing, Mac." Pete poked Mac in the shin with his cane. Mac shied out of the way while Pete took the last two stairs.

"It'll be a good day when you're stable on both feet and you lose that cane." Mac rubbed his shin.

"I may keep it. Now are you gonna get out of the way so I can lead these nice ladies to the couch to have a visit? Or do you wanna keep standing around until dinner?"

"I, for one, would love to sit." And with that she plopped down on one end. "I'm almost positive Katherine is responsible for the toss pillows, but I have to give you props for this couch. It feels super comfy." Pete and Lauren made their way a little more slowly, and Erin couldn't help but notice that they sat on the same side, right next to each other and proceeded to take up a conversation that sounded as if they had started earlier. Erin looked up at Mac, who seemed to have noticed the same thing. She raised an eyebrow at him, but he only shrugged and headed back to the kitchen.

Erin stayed right where she was, even though she knew she was breaking all of the 'best friend rules' by not joining Katherine in the kitchen. She was probably breaking a few 'lady guest rules' as well, but it couldn't be helped. It had been a tough day. Between the PTO hassling her into volunteering for things she had no time for and the students deciding Friday was a good excuse to be horrible, she was exhausted. It was what made her decide to leave the boys with Brittany rather than drag them along. This was what she needed, a cozy sofa, a roaring fire, and pleasant company completely ignoring her. She watched Pete pull out all the stops in charming Lauren, and it looked like he was doing an excellent job.

It was a nice thought, Pete and Lauren. Pete had lost his wife a few years ago, and being only sixty-five, had a lot of love left to give. Katherine's dad had abandoned the family and divorced Lauren a long time ago. If Pete wanted someone to appreciate his love, she couldn't think of a better person. Erin kicked off her shoes and tucked her feet up under her. Normally this would not be dinner party behavior, but Katherine, Pete, and Mac were practically family, and she was too tired to worry about being perfect tonight. It wasn't long before the warmth of the fire and the softness of the couch enveloped her, and she closed her eyes to rest them for a second.

"Hey, you're here!" Katherine pulled the door open wider and motioned for him to come in.

"Thanks for inviting me." Dan stepped inside. He almost closed his eyes and sniffed the air, it smelled that good. Instead, he shrugged out of his coat and hung it on one of the hooks in the wall behind the door. He'd been to Mac's house enough to know his way around. Katherine motioned him into the dining area.

"We are about to sit down to dinner, but . . ." She looked over at the table and seemed to be counting heads. "We're missing someone."

"She's asleep on the couch," Pete explained, taking a seat on one of the benches at the table beside a woman Dan didn't recognize, but assumed was Katherine's mother. "Didn't have the heart to wake her up."

"Oh, well that's… she'll be annoyed if we let her sleep through dinner." Katherine glanced into the kitchen. "I've got to get the rolls. Dan." She turned to face him, grabbing his arm and towing him further into the house. "I need you to very carefully go wake Erin up and tell her it's time for dinner. Do not scare her," she warned and then rushed off into the kitchen before he could answer one way or the other.

Dan wanted to ask why Mac couldn't go get her, but maybe she'd picked Dan because he was already standing. This was no big deal. He would just go down there and tell her it was time for dinner, and then she would wake up. He crossed the room and hit the stairs to the family room and felt it—that weird tug—the moment he saw her. She was curled in a ball, her feet tucked up, her head on the back of the couch with her hair covering part of her face. "Hey, time for dinner."

But she didn't stir.

He got close enough to hear her soft breathing, to see the peaceful look on her face and repeated it. She didn't stir.

He had the urge to brush her hair off her forehead, but stopped himself since that seemed somehow . . . creepy. She would probably freak out. Instead, he leaned down and gently shook her shoulder while calling her name. Her lips quirked in a lop-sided smile that was plainly adorable. "C'mon," he urged, shaking her shoulder again as gently as before. Her eyes flickered open, and when they focused on him her smile broadened for a second before disappearing altogether.

"Hey, you fell asleep before dinner." He laughed a little. "I was sent to fetch you. I hope I didn't scare you."

"What?" Her expression was confused and then embarrassed before it shut down altogether. "I cannot believe I did that." She swung her feet down and stuffed them into her shoes, her cheeks flushed and her manner hurried. "Thanks. Sorry." She all but ran up the stairs to the table.

He felt like kicking something.

Dinner was nice, all things considered. He was seated opposite Lauren, who must have been an old hand at dinner parties since she moved the conversation past any awkward silences or topics. Pete seemed to be at ease, his usual humor shining bright. Seated on his right and across from Mac was Erin and, despite having several openings, she had nothing to say. She smiled at all the right spots and laughed along, but that was about it. She even begged off early, leaving right after dessert as everyone else lingered over coffee.

Mac suddenly looked up from his now-empty plate of pie. "Hey, did

Erin leave?"

"Where were you?" Pete gave him an incredulous stare.

"I went for seconds." Mac pulled his phone out of his pocket. "I've got to call her before she gets home."

"Why?" Pete asked.

"I told her I'd be over tomorrow night to fix her dryer, but I got a call from work saying they're short staffed and can't spare me."

"I can do it." The words were out of Dan's mouth before he knew it. *Wait…what am I thinking?*

"You sure?" Mac raised an eyebrow as if to suggest that he doubted Dan's ability.

"In India we didn't have repairmen. I wouldn't trust myself rebuilding a car engine, but general appliances? We had to find creative ways to keep those working."

"Well, okay. If you're sure you have the time."

"I can find it. What's wrong with the dryer anyway?"

"She says it's a belt. She picked one up this week, so you shouldn't need to bring anything other than your tools." Mac gave him a side-eyed glance. "You got a toolbox?"

"Yes, I have a toolbox."

"I know I seem protective, but it's with cause. She doesn't have anyone up here to lean on but us and Pete. Her dad and step-mom live in Florida, and Jimmy's family…well the less said there the better. With all she's facing up at the school, it's been a tough time."

"What's going on at school?" Considering that he was at the school twice a week coaching basketball, he should know if something was up, and he hadn't heard anything. Sweet River Christian Academy might be a tightly run ship, but people were people; they talked when there was something to talk about.

"Some of the members of the PTO aren't happy her contract was renewed." Katherine shook her head. "They were fond of the old director and didn't like it when I moved Erin into that spot last year. Some were hoping she'd get fired after what happened with Brittany and Jake. Or I guess it's more accurate to say they felt she should have been let go."

"That . . ." He stopped himself before saying something he would regret. "I barely know Erin, and I know she wasn't in any way responsible for her daughter getting pregnant. It could happen to anyone's kid."

"When does rational thought enter these things?" Lauren asked rhetorically, a wistful note to her tone, and Dan was reminded of her daughter's own story.

"None of this is because of the job she's doing," Mac added. "It's because of who she is. A single mom. A woman who had a kid when she was only eighteen herself, never mind that she was married at the time. That's strike one and two in some people's books. The parents up at the school are wealthy, college-educated types who can't grasp getting married right out of high school even though there are plenty of kids who do. Especially up here. Rural Maine isn't a progressive sort of place; it doesn't have the same rules, but Erin is getting judged by them all the same. In fact, she thinks that's why the old director got rid of her before. People say she would be gone again if it wasn't for Katherine."

"But, Erin's a widow. It's not like she chose to be single."

"I'll say this since it's public knowledge and I don't feel we're gossiping about a friend, but you should know, she left Jimmy before he died. Had to." Pete nodded his head when Dan's mouth dropped open.

"He was a drinker, and a bad one. She tried, years she tried. She took the worst he dished out, but when he turned it on the kids, she left. He didn't take that well. Spiraled out of control and ended up wrapping his car around a tree, high as a kite." Pete shook his head. "Unfortunately, there are some who feel that she pushed him over the edge, that she didn't do enough to stop him."

"They hold his alcoholism against her?" Dan couldn't believe it. He wanted to track down whoever was saying stuff and set them straight, but that wasn't his place. Even if he was still her pastor, that wouldn't be his place. All he could do was feel the burn of injustice on her behalf.

"I'm not sure what they hold against her, but it goes without saying that with Brittany and Jake doing what they did, anyone who already had it out for her got new ammunition."

"I had no idea." When he had thought of her in the past, he had imagined that she was still single because she had loved her husband too much to try to find love again with anyone else. Now he knew the truth, and he couldn't believe the weight she carried.

"I think the people that hold those opinions aren't likely to voice them around you." Mac was right. No one wanted to let the pastor see their bad side, or leave their dirty laundry hanging in the breeze. Better to keep it in on Sunday.

Dan took a breath, letting his anger ebb. "We're all so quick to see the sin in others and pounce on it, calling people out. It makes us feel better about the mess we're in. I wish we had more empathy for each other. This world is hostile enough as it is. Why Christians can't be merciful, can't exhibit grace…I have real trouble understanding that."

"It's that whole 'pluck the plank out of your own eye before going at the speck in your brother's', isn't it?" Pete asked. "Seeing your own sin is far harder than seeing someone else's."

"'My sin is ever before me', as the psalmist said." Dan confided quietly. "I think sometimes we go after another's because it's easier, not because we don't see our own."

"You're the expert." Mac stood and stretched. "Kate, let me help you with the dishes."

"I ought to get going." Dan stood as well, climbing over the bench.

"I'll call Erin's and let her know that you'll be over in my place tomorrow. She'll be expecting you at six."

"Six works for me." Dan said his goodnights and headed for the door. Before he could close it, he heard Mac shout, "Don't let me down, now. I don't want to hear you blew up her dryer or something."

Dan shut the door to the sound of Mac chuckling at his own joke.

CHAPTER FIVE

ERIN SLID THE TRAY INTO THE oven feeling a bit guilty for resorting to chicken nuggets and tater tots, but she wasn't up to the prep work that a healthy meal would have required, and the boys deserved a treat. She hadn't had great sleep last night, too busy reliving her embarrassment from dinner at the MacAlisters'. She would have like to have taken Pete's cane to whoever sent Dan over to wake her up. When he had said her name, she had ended up working him into her dream. She had been at the beach, laying in the sun, waiting for someone and suddenly he was there. Not only was he there, but he was hers. When he had awakened her the second time, she had opened her eyes and found him there, then smiled up at him like a loon. Mortifying. All through dinner she was so worried about making a fool of herself she didn't utter a word to him—or anyone else. He probably thought she was nutty.

At least today had been productive. She had woken up irritated and knew the only cure was to spend some energy tackling a big project. Since James had run out of clean pants twice that week—she still hadn't worked out how that was possible—she had decided that it was time to clean out the closets and change out the seasons. Winter was in and summer was out. The boys had groaned and complained, but once she had hinted that new snow gear might be in it for them they had cooperated. Thus, the reward of 'Nugget Night', the boys' favorite meal. The living room was now covered with piles of clothes destined for Goodwill, the rag pile, or out-of-season storage, but their closets, dressers, and even the foyer were spotless and organized.

Her little house was close to perfect, despite what she had said to Katherine. The gardens were gorgeous from April through October, looking like something out of an English countryside. In the summer she could sit in the swing on the porch and smell the lavender lining the brick walkway leading to the front steps. Inside, the original wood floors gleamed, the small kitchen was bright and sunny, and the bedrooms upstairs were cozy and warm.

The charm of an old house meant living with its tiny closets. Her boys weren't into clothes, but at eleven and thirteen, their growth spurts had her buying new jeans and sneakers every few months. Now that she had all their stuff organized, she had a list of things they needed. She'd have to find room in the budget for new clothes before Christmas, an unexpected expense, but it was always something. Too bad boys never seemed to produce decent hand-me-downs after the age of ten. James' jeans all had ragged knees, and it was rare she'd find a shirt he grew out of that didn't have a rip, tear, or hole somewhere in it.

Erin took a deep breath to avoid a spiral into self-pity. "You are blessed." She whispered aloud, trying to focus on the good and not let the bad drag her down. The doorbell rang. Erin turned to the hall, not sure if she should answer the door. She was in yoga pants and a ratty tee. Her hair was up in a bun that was now probably more mess than anything else, and she had not one iota of makeup on her face. Checking the time, she saw it was five of six. She decided that she could relax. It was probably Mac coming to fix the dryer. He had said he would be there at six, and he was always punctual. Better yet, he wouldn't notice what she looked like, or if he did, he wouldn't care. They had been friends long enough that he had seen her at her worst.

She pulled open the door with a smile on her face and felt it freeze in place. It wasn't Mac on her top step with a toolbox in hand and a polite expression. It was Dan Connors, the man she made a fool of herself in front of on a regular basis. Of course it was Dan, but why was it Dan? Erin's brain seized, and the seconds ticked past as she stood staring.

"Hi." He gave her a lopsided and completely adorable grin. "I'm guessing you didn't get Mac's call?"

She fumbled for her pocket and pulled out her cell. There was a voicemail there. "Dang. I missed it. My phone is ancient. Sometimes I don't get calls…" She closed her mouth to end her babbling explanation. It wasn't an excuse. She should have replaced her phone a long time ago, but it was another monthly payment that wasn't in the budget. That wasn't something she was keen to share.

"Well, I'm his replacement. He ended up getting called into work."

"His replacement?"

"To fix your dryer?" He held up his toolbox.

"Oh, duh." She smacked her forehead. "Of course. C'mon in."

Dan followed her into the entry hall and shut the door behind him. Almost immediately she saw him glance into the living room with its piles, bags, and boxes of clothes. "Wow, I guess you've got a lot waiting on that dryer."

This evening was getting worse by the minute. "We were sorting out our closets. Ha, probably a stupid time to do it, but I wanted to get the boys' old clothes out and donate them. Winter stuff, y'know. It's getting cold and all."

Dan didn't respond, but he did turn to her and she watched as his eyes swept up to the top of her head. He gave her a soft look she didn't quite understand until she reached up with a hand in her hair and the light dawned. She had left a stack of sparkly, pink and purple headbands up there. She'd found a stash while cleaning out the spare bedroom that used to be Brittany's. With full hands, she'd stuffed them on her head planning on adding them to the donate bin when she reached it. "Ha, I must look ridiculous."

"No." He was still giving her that soft look and the butterflies in her stomach began to test their wings. Seth picked that moment to rush down the stairs and greet Dan, saving her from saying anything stupid.

"Hey! Pastor Dan. What are you doing here?" Seth stood about a foot from him and machine-gunned questions. "Is that your toolbox? Are you here to fix something? Is it the dryer? Mom tried and gave up. She said she's not 'mechanically inclined'. Are you staying for dinner?"

"It is Nugget Night, after all." James had come down after his little brother, and he hung back as if to create a mature example against Seth's puppy-like excitement.

"Seth, give him some room to breathe." Erin pulled him back.

"Can we show Pastor Dan where the dryer is?" Seth gave her a pleading look. It was rare that they had visitors, and when they did they were rarely men. She needed to spend more time on their manners. They had the basics, but she wanted them to know how to behave in any situation.

"Okay, but don't get in his way."

Seth grabbed Dan's arm as if he meant to pull him the whole way. She tried to give Dan an apologetic smile, but he was already following the boys to the door leading downstairs. She could hear him chuckle as they descended. Their voices floated up the stairs from the basement. Dan seemed amused rather than annoyed with Seth's running dialog. Hopefully Dan's sense of humor would survive. She closed the door to the basement, bringing herself face to face with the hall mirror mounted onto the back of it.

"Drat," she snapped aloud, pulling the sparkly headbands out of her hair and smoothing it down. She found an open donate box and pitched them in. For a second she was tempted to run upstairs and try to brush her hair out, or put on a bit of lipstick, maybe even change clothes, but then Dan would know she had done it for him. Which would be weird. She was stuck, as-is.

A few minutes later she went to the oven and checked on dinner. Nugget Night was usually stress-free. Maybe Dan wouldn't take the boys' invitation to stay for dinner seriously. Rummaging through the fridge, she found enough ingredients for a salad and hastily put it together in case he decided to stay. It wasn't a thing of beauty, but it had plenty of leafy greens and veggies to make up for what it lacked in presentation. She set the table with real plates, not the paper ones that she had planned to use to avoid dishes.

Footsteps pounded up the basement stairs, and the door banged open. "Good news, mom," Seth shouted as he ran into the dining room. "Pastor says he can stay for dinner. We told him Nugget Night is like the best thing you cook." She cringed inwardly, but gave her boy a smile anyway and added a place setting for Dan. Seth took this in then ran back to the door to the basement. "All set, Pastor Dan. Mom's even got real plates out. She's gettin' all fancy."

Erin rolled her eyes to the ceiling and almost laughed. It was all too ridiculous. It didn't really matter what Dan thought of her. It wasn't like she had any reason to impress him. She would never be anything to him other than a sort-of colleague. *Shake it off*, she told herself, almost wishing that she could turn her playlist on and dance for a bit to kill her anxiety, but she had seen enough sitcoms to know how that would end.

Back in the kitchen, she pulled out the trays and filled the bowls with chicken and tots. The boys continued to chatter as they came into the dining room. Gathering up napkins and condiments, she headed to the table, expecting to see Dan's less than enthusiastic reaction to dinner. Instead, he was sitting at the end of the table listening to Seth going on about a TV show that he had seen at a friend's house. The boys had taken seats on either side, leaving Erin to sit at the opposite end. Seeing Dan seated at her table and talking with her boys was all too close to her secret wish, the one that she refused to nurse into an actual hope. Dan wasn't ever going to be hers, and she needed to get over it. She set the ketchup and barbeque sauce down and took a seat.

"I'm sorry you've caught us on junk food night. We usually eat better than this."

"To be honest, I never cook, so your 'junk food' is better than anything I'd make myself."

"What, not even tater tots?"

"The most I do is nuke a cup of ramen."

"Seriously? But you seem so healthy."

"Takeout from the better places. And that gourmet grocery store in town. I can microwave with the best of them."

"How can you afford that?"

"Well, it's only me, and I don't cost much."

"Right. I'm so used to the way the kids eat. I can't imagine living on takeout."

"We never get to eat out." Seth grumbled. "Mom won't do fast-food, so the only time we get to eat anywhere but home is on Sunday afternoons at Maria's."

"Which is eating out, buddy," Erin corrected.

Her son shrugged.

She shook her head. "You're so deprived."

"Whatever," Seth grumbled and popped a tot in his mouth.

"Hey, grace first." She took Seth and James' hands, and they in turn grabbed Dan's.

It was James' turn to say grace, and he got right to it. "Lord, bless this food to our use and us to Thy service, and make us ever mindful of the needs of others. Amen."

Dan gave James an approving smile, and Erin felt the butterflies stir at the sight. Mentally kicking herself, she dug into her food. Nugget Night might not make the top ten healthy meals list by any stretch, but tater tots were as close to perfect as a potato gets and well worth the calories. Dinner went quickly, with Seth keeping up a running dialog between bites of food. Dan was patient with him, letting him ramble on about everything from why he hated math class to the raft he and James had made. That last subject was a sore one for Erin.

A fast-moving stream ran behind the school property, which was an easy walk from their house. Sure, it wasn't an actual river, but it was deep enough in some places for two boys to get into trouble and drown. She wanted to ban them from playing anywhere near it, but she knew that it would only make the place more attractive. Instead she had insisted on ground rules, like no body parts in the water. They could float what they liked on it, but they better not get caught being on that float. The first few days she had even spot-checked and found that they were obeying her rules to the letter, so she had let it go.

"You're not putting that in the river though, right?" Dan's eyes narrowed.

"No. The stream behind the school," James clarified.

"Buddy, that runs into the river. You guys know that, right?" Dan looked from Seth to James, and it was immediately clear that they knew, and they didn't care.

Thing was, Erin didn't know. She thought it was totally separate. That did not make her happy.

"It's low right now, but when we get a heavy storm that thing gets fast. You put in a homemade raft up by the school, you're going to be clinging to scrap by the time you get through the rapids in that stretch behind the gas station. From there you've got about a dozen yards before you're straight into the Sweet."

"How do you know?" James was not the kid who talked back, ever, but clearly Dan questioning him got his back up. She tried to catch his eye to give him the 'you better not use that attitude' look, but he was staring defiantly at Dan.

"That doesn't even touch the fact that Warden Moretti would probably cite you both if he saw you put something like that in the water."

"Oh, come on!" James scoffed. "It's a raft. What's the big deal? You're worse than Mom, and she wants to cover us in bubble wrap as it is."

"James." Erin said it warningly, shocked that he was taking it this far.

"Okay, then think about your mom for a minute." Dan gestured to her, but kept his eyes on James. "How would she feel if you guys got into trouble and couldn't get to shore? No big deal then?"

"That's not going to happen." But James looked less sure of himself. Seth was following the back and forth, his face scrunched in worry.

"It's a moot point because the boys have been told that not one single part of their persons gets in the water. I don't care what they float on the water as long as it's not garbage or something, but they can't go floating along with it." She said this to James and Seth, searching their faces, worried that they might have been breaking the rule all along.

James nodded and she believed him. He didn't lie to her. The two of them had an agreement. He'd get into more trouble for lying about what he had done than he would've for doing the thing in the first place. Lying wasn't only a sin, it was a betrayal of trust. They had been over this, and Seth did what James did. They were pretty much inseparable.

"Glad that you guys are obeying your mom. If you want to do some actual boating, I can take you out on the lake. Might even get some fishing in." Dan quickly looked to Erin. "If that's okay with you."

The boys wasted no time in pleading with her by giving her their 'puppy-dog' eyes. Erin wasn't sure if it was a good idea. Now she was going to feel like she owed him something for taking the time to keep James and Seth from drowning themselves. It was too late, though. Once he'd offered she was on the spot.

"If you promise to behave and not to cause Pastor Connors any trouble."

Seth immediately nodded his head. James gave her a little salute, his sarcastic way of answering yes. He was getting old enough to push his limits, but always managed to do it in some wiseacre way that half the time she found funny.

"You're in luck guys, I save Saturdays for stuff like fishing, so I'm free this weekend."

"Awesome. What kind of boat do you have? Is it as big as the ones the wardens use? Does it have a motor?" And Seth was off, peppering him with questions again. Dan fielded each one good-naturedly until Erin asked her son to save it for Saturday and put an end to it.

Then she asked the two boys to clear the table. As usual, they groaned, but being the decent kids they were, they did it anyway. "And the dishes while you're at it," she said over her shoulder.

Dan had an indulgent smile on his face when he turned to her and said quietly "You're doing a great job with them. They're good kids."

Her heart soared, but she immediately tried to shoo his compliment away with a wave of her hand.

Dan ignored it and went on. "I'm not an expert, by any means, but I can see it's harder when you're on your own. No one to be the bad guy."

Usually that was true, but tonight she'd had Dan backing her up, and it was something she'd liked far too much. Erin needed to shut this down. The temptation to take this for more than it was—to let his words settle in for her to build castles in the clouds with—was too great. She knew what happened to cloud castles. "We get by." She stood, trying to give him the subtle hint that it was time to say goodnight. But rather than putting him off, it seemed to draw him in. He got up as well, stepping close to her, his eyes sweeping her for a moment.

"I can see that you do, but I'm still sorry it's hard. I know things have been rough lately."

"What?"

"Mac said you've had some trouble at the school."

Erin turned away as a stab of shame hit her, and her face began to heat. If Mac had been standing next to her, she would have kicked him, hard. He had no business talking about her troubles to Dan.

"Hey, don't be mad at him for sharing." Dan reached out and put his hand on her shoulder, gently tugging her back in his direction. Reluctantly she looked up and met his eyes. What she saw there was surprising. Instead of the pity she feared, he seemed to be angry. "Nobody should be bad-mouthing you over what happened between Brittany and Jake."

"Yah, well . . ."

"Did you set no limits? Let her do what she pleased?"

"Of course not."

"Well then, I fail to see how this is your fault. Don't forget it was me who counseled Jake after it was all said and done." He shook his head. "No one should be judging you by their behavior."

"That sounds nice, but even in the Bible you're judged by how your kids behave. Like, you can't be an elder if your kids are running wild."

"Nicely paraphrased." He said it approvingly, but she rolled her eyes anyway. "I'm sorry, you're right, I get it, but Brittany wasn't running wild. It was sin, plain and simple. They sinned, handled it poorly at first, but in the end repented and did the right thing, and anyone holding it against you is wrong."

"You're awfully nice, Pastor Connors, but the fact is that as a teacher I'm a role model for my students, and they all know what happened with Brittany. It makes it seem like I'm permissive, even when I'm anything but. Just ask the boys." She waved a hand towards the kitchen where she hoped they were actively working and not listening. "It doesn't matter anyway. It's only a matter of time."

"Do you think they'll fire you?"

"I think in the end they'll ask me to resign. I was surprised when they renewed my contract."

"I know that feeling."

"You do?"

"Sure, my first few months here I was convinced I'd be a goner. My sermons stunk, the church secretary thought I was a moron, and I was terrible with the hospitality committee, always getting the dates of their shindigs wrong."

"No way. Your sermons were amazing, and the ladies on the hospitality committee love you. They love everyone. I think you're a little full of it."

"I'm serious. I got notes from an elder every week letting me know where I was falling down. It was painful."

"I can't believe that." And she couldn't. His early sermons might not compare to what he delivered now, but they'd had a huge impact on her. She wanted him to know that but wasn't sure how to say it without it sounding like some throwaway compliment.

"It's all true. Even now I disappoint people. There's too much they want me to show up for. I'm constantly late to meetings, missing stuff I shouldn't, like that meeting for the coaches the other day."

"Oh, that's nothing I can't catch you up on."

"But I hate letting you down." He said it so earnestly it made her heart squeeze, and she was about to tell him not to worry about it when an alarm rang, and he dug through his pocket. "Speaking of missing stuff..." He pulled his phone out and swiped the screen. "Luckily modern technology lets your alarm clock follow you wherever you go. I've got to polish up tomorrow's sermon. I should probably head out."

"Yes, and thanks again for fixing the dryer and for putting up with my kids. If you don't have time next weekend, that's okay. I can let them know."

"No, it's not a problem. I promise." He returned his phone to his pocket and followed Erin to the front door. She held it open for him and gave him what hopefully looked like a friendly smile and not a dopey grin. One corner of his mouth lifted. "Thanks for the tots."

"They were literally, almost nothing so . . ." Erin trailed off and waited for Dan to say something, or leave, but they both stood at her front door caught in a moment that was awkward and yet, strangely exciting. Finally, Dan broke the silence.

"This was nice." He still didn't move to leave. "I've wanted a chance to get to know you better, but I was beginning to think it was impossible."

"Why?"

"You have a tendency to bolt."

"Oh. Right." This was the moment. If there ever was time to kill her stupid crush and turn it into the possibility of a real friendship with this man, now was the time. "You intimidate the heck out of me."

"What?" He reeled back as if surprised.

"You're super smart, you're all...holy." She waved a hand at him. "I am…not."

He shook his head as if he couldn't take that in. "I . . . that's . . ." He furrowed his brow, and she wanted to laugh. He looked adorable when confused. "Okay, I'm not going to take that as your final answer. Instead…" he stuck out his hand. "Friends?"

She took his hand and shook it. "Friends."

"Done." He stood straight. "And now I and my holiness are going to finish my sermon." He gave her a wink. "I'll see you next Saturday, if not sooner."

She nodded and waved before shutting the door. "I am a loon." She said into the silence.

"Yes, yes, you are." James was standing in the kitchen doorway.

"Eavesdropping?"

"No, looking out for my mom. Humph." He stuck his nose in air and turned on his heel. Erin laughed out loud.

CHAPTER SIX

"HOLD THAT POSE." ERIN LOOKED OUT over the crowd of kids, twenty in all, who had showed up for the first day of 'Morning Motion' class. She walked between their yoga mats as they stretched into the downward dog pose, most of them doing it perfectly. When she'd planned the class, she had picked the poses that she thought the students would both be able to hold and enjoy. Yoga wasn't her thing, and she only held a minimal certification in it, so she'd started the class with warmup drills and only added a few poses at the end. Hopefully, it would be enough to get them calm before classes began.

"You guys are going to love this next one. It's called the 'corpse pose'." With minimal giggling, the kids managed to lie on their backs in a neutral position pretty easily. Even the Murphy boys, who had showed up on time, held the pose. She was glad they were getting into it. When she'd called their mom, Claire had readily agreed to them taking the bus, but warned that she didn't think the class would be their speed. Surprisingly, the boys seemed to like it.

When time was up she spoke softly. "Okay guys, grab your stuff and head for home room. Nice job everyone. I'll see you tomorrow."

"Hey, coach!" One of the students waved and pointed behind her. Erin looked over her shoulder to see Dan approaching. She felt the quick thrill at the sight of him, but it died a quick death when she got a good look at his expression. It was thunderous. She wondered what had ticked him off this early in the morning.

"Hi." She kept her tone friendly. Dan was in his 'preacher' uniform of trousers, button-down shirt, and tie. His hair was a bit of a mess, but it usually was. Dirty-blond and curly, he rarely cut it short enough to be manageable, and today was no different. It was almost scandalously long.

She was tempted to offer to cut it for him. After a second she realized that while she'd been staring he had been talking. "Sorry?"

"You didn't hear me?"

"Um. No."

"I asked why you were teaching yoga. It's never been part of the curriculum here has it?"

Erin checked quickly behind her to ensure that all the students had filed out. "This is a new program. It's for the kids who need something to transition successfully into the school day. Yoga is only one of the things we'll be doing, but the idea is to help them release their stress and center themselves. The poses are light exercise and—"

"Yoga is a spiritual practice," Dan interrupted. "Not an exercise program."

Erin didn't appreciate being interrupted, and she didn't like his tone either. "There's nothing spiritual about yoga as we'll be doing it. The poses are devoid of any spiritual reference. This isn't 'real' yoga."

"Real yoga? Any yoga is 'real' yoga."

"Not the way I'm teaching it."

"Any way you teach it. You can't dismiss the spiritual nature of it by ignoring it. This is a religion. There are millions of people in India who practice this religion. It's as sacred to them as Christianity is to us."

Erin took a breath and tried not to let her temper rise. Dan was acting like this was personal in some way, as if it meant a great deal to him, and she didn't understand why. She wanted to cut this off and reminded him that she was the director and that he was welcome to his opinion, but she was going to do what she felt was best anyway. However, she decided to find out what was going on in his head.

"Why are you making a big deal out of this? The senior citizens program that meets at the church does yoga, and so does the community center. I've never heard you complain before."

"I have. Dozens of times to the elders, and I've been told to shut up every time."

That came as a surprise. "But, if we're not teaching the spiritual meanings behind it, isn't it just stretching?"

"It's a religion. Every movement is devotion to a pagan belief system.

To an entire culture, it's all sacred."

"That's ridiculous. You can't put a religious stamp on a motion."

"It's the whole package."

"But I'm not doing the whole deal."

"It's impossible to truly separate—"

"Wow, you're really hard-lining this, Dan. You're taking what's an incredibly healthy and beneficial exercise and pretty much demonizing it."

"The only 'hard line' is between the truth and the lie that this is—" Dan stopped in mid-sentence and his expression softened as his anger seemed to drain away. "I'm sorry, Erin. I'm doing this all wrong. I jumped all over you without explaining it well."

"Well . . . kinda."

"Let me do this the right way." He looked around and then motioned to the bleachers. "Will you sit with me for a moment? Let me try to explain it better. It's important to me that you understand what I'm talking about. I'm not being uptight about this. It's something I feel strongly about."

She nodded her agreement, followed him to the first row of bleachers, and sat. For a moment he didn't say anything, like he was considering his words very carefully. Then he sat down as well, right next to her, and her heart sped a little faster. He leaned in a little, and she caught the scent that seemed to be his alone; wood smoke, soap, and tea. It was weird, but she liked it.

"If I could take you to Tamil Nadu…" He trailed off with a slight smile. "Can you close your eyes for me?"

"What?"

"I've got an idea. Go along with me for a minute or two. I promise it will make sense." He held up his hand in a boy-scout salute.

"Okay." She closed her eyes.

Dan began speaking in a soft voice. "I'm going to take you to India. First, imagine it's warm, and not only warm, but muggy, like the muggiest, hottest day you've ever experienced. You woke up sweaty and you know you're going to stay that way all day. You go to the window and the compound outside is already up. The kids are at their lessons, staff chattering as they work. Outside the gates the city has been up for a while.

The streets are full of people. There are women in colorful saris and vendors selling everything you could imagine; the air is spicy in places, smoky too, and rank in others. You head for the temple down one of the main streets where you buy breakfast off the same street vendor that's there every morning and you try to speak to her in Tamil. She jokes with you about your terrible accent. This city is small enough that it doesn't see the mobs of tourists that come to this part of India to see the Hindi temples or to stay at hotels on the coast.

"In the city, they don't like you very much. You stick out like a sore thumb, and they know why you're there. They'll tolerate the mission up on the hill with the orphans nobody wants, but when you come to town people watch you. There are Christians throughout the state, but they're scarce in the city. They don't want you bringing any in, either. Someday they may come for you, so you do your best not to appear threatening. When you talk, you choose your words carefully.

"At the small temple in the center of town is the one man who is probably ensuring your safety. He's a yogi, old and weathered. His skin looks like bark, but he's quick in body and sharp in mind. He finds you funny for some reason and lets you sit with him and talk. He listens politely while you try to share the gospel. When he explains his spiritual traditions to you it's clear he lives and breathes his faith; it's ingrained in every action, part of every thought. Slowly you realize that how you've approached him has all been wrong. He might have heard what you had to say had you taken the time to understand his faith rather than dismissed it."

"Open your eyes." His words were soft. When she opened her eyes, she saw his expression was warm. "I sat with that old man for weeks. The day I had to leave I went to him and explained I'd be going home because my mom was ill. He seemed moved, like my pain meant something to him, but then he said I would not be coming back." Dan took a deep breath. "And he was right. The mission was closed a few months later. We relied on local staff and they left shortly after I did. The yogi knew his people better than I did. But that's not really my point. When I think of yoga, I think of him, his devotion. It's a spiritual practice, and it belongs to India. What we've done in the States... it's like what the modern world has done to Christmas. We stripped it of all meaning and made it about buying gifts and being nice to people. If anyone should respect a religious practice and not participate in its commercialization, it should be Christians."

"I honestly never thought of it that way." No wonder Dan was so ticked. "I didn't get it before, and I'm sorry for being so defensive."

"Don't apologize, I burst in here like a jerk, ordering you around. I deserved it. I should have taken a breath first."

"That's the story of my life," she joked.

"I find that hard to believe."

"I'm not as nice as I appear. Anyway, don't worry about the class. Yoga wasn't the only thing I was going to do. I've got barre exercises, and I may just teach them ballet."

"Makes sense." His expression was admiring. "You dance beautifully, so I can only assume you'd be great at teaching it."

"Oh, right. You saw me the other day." That day was still mortifying. "It's good for stress relief." She thought that sounded like a sensible reason to be dancing and laughing like a loon in the middle of the gym.

"I fish."

"What?" Obsessing over his impression of her, she couldn't follow his train of thought.

"Or hike. Sometimes I run. For stress relief. There's nothing like fishing to help you chill out. You have to be calm or you're not going to catch a thing."

"The boys are looking forward to Saturday with you. I think they're hoping they'll get to fish."

"Then I'll make sure that happens." He smiled like he was looking forward to it too, but Erin worried that he didn't know what he was volunteering for.

"But remember, if something comes up or you're too tired by Saturday—"

"Not a chance. I'm counting on dinner afterwards. I figure we'll bring home what we catch, and I'll clean if you cook?" He held out his hand, and she shook it.

"Okay, then it's a date." She felt her eyes widen. "I mean, it's a deal or whatever." Her cheeks began to heat, and she wished a hole would open up under her so she could disappear.

"Oh, don't do that." Dan held onto her hand.

"Do what?" She was tugging on her hand ever so slightly, but he wasn't letting go.

"Get shy on me again."

"I'm not shy."

"Okay." He let go of her hand. "Then don't get however it is you were before when you never spoke to me and generally avoided me."

"It's a hard habit to break." The bell rang, echoing through the gym. Erin looked up to the clock. She had only a few minutes before her next class.

"You've got to go?"

"In a few minutes, there will be a flood of seventh graders coming through those doors."

"I'll get out of your hair then, but I want to thank you. For being willing to change the class. It means a great deal to me." He held his hand over his heart. The gesture was a small one for the impact it had on Erin. Her brain stalled out for a moment before she recovered.

"Thank you too. I mean for telling me that story. India is a mystery to me. You miss it, don't you?"

"Like you wouldn't believe." The moment the words were out he seemed surprised, as if he hadn't meant to say them, or maybe not out loud. For a moment, she felt the urge to touch him to show her support in some way. It was a brief, vulnerable moment, but it made a heavy impact on her.

"Why don't you go back?"

"I don't feel the call. And it's hard to admit that." There was more than a little ruefulness in his tone. "I keep waiting to feel it again, and it's not there."

"Do you feel the call to be here?" She braced, not sure she wanted to hear his real answer. Dan wasn't the kind of person to lie to make someone feel better. Whenever he spoke, he seemed to speak the truth.

"It's complicated. I came home because my mom had a stroke. I never thought I'd be here this long. I'm up for renewal again actually. I've been wondering if it's time to consider staying for real, putting down roots. With things the way they are, I don't see leaving any time soon." There was something in his expression when he said this, a kind of regret mixed with hope that she didn't understand, but she wanted to.

"I'm sorry about your mom. I know that kind of brain injury can be tough to deal with."

"One day at a time." The words sounded rote.

"It must be hard on you, being alone in this."

He seemed to struggle for a moment before nodding. Erin wondered what it was like when the person everyone usually counts on to comfort them, to counsel them, needs help himself. Dan really didn't have anyone. People probably thought as the pastor he didn't need anyone, but she could feel the power of the emotions rolling off him like a wave. She wanted to pull him into her arms and tell him it was all going to be fine, but she could hear the kids running down the stairs. They were out of time.

"You don't have to be. Alone that is. You have friends willing to help bear the load." She gave him a smile he didn't return. "I mean that in the real way, not the socially appropriate, nice way where you say you're there to help, but you're hoping they never call you."

"Oh good." He laughed. "Wouldn't want you to be nice."

"You know what I mean." She stood up and he followed, turning for the door. Then he stopped and swung back.

"Thank you." He leaned in close, his face inches away. "And I mean that in the real way, not the nice way." He backed away as the doors to the gym banged open and the kids poured in.

CHAPTER SEVEN

Sunlight filtered through the atrium windows to cast a warm glow in the otherwise antiseptic space where Dan sat with his mom. He'd wheeled her in, hoping the change of scenery would do her good. A beam of light glinted off the wheelchair and split into a rainbow on his pant-leg. He stared at it while listening to his mother's soft conversation with herself. The words didn't make any sense to him. They were strung together like odd-shaped beads on the same necklace, pretty enough on their own, nonsense when put together. Part of him hoped the words made sense to his mom and part of him didn't. The idea that she was still in there, but lost down some twisting, turning corridor of her injured brain was hard to take.

When he'd arrived, she had noticed him, but there was no recognition. There never was. Ellen Connors' son sat beside her almost every day, and she had no idea who he was. He wondered what she thought of the people that came and went around her; the orderlies, the nurses and doctors, the visitors. Who did she think they were? What roles did they play in her world now?

When he was a kid, his mother had been the bright light in his life, and his father had been the bright light in hers. When his father had died, he watched his mom's light dim, but it hadn't gone out. Not until the stroke. He looked up at her now, shoulders slumped forward, gray hair hanging in her face. Frowning, he stood.

"Hey, Mom, let's take care of this for you." He took the barrette stuck uselessly in the side of her hair and used it to pin back the hank of hair covering her face. She looked up at him with watery brown eyes and smiled. He felt the answering smile on his own lips, but it ended as she dropped her gaze to her lap and went back to her uneven string of words.

By the few he could catch it sounded like she was fixated on coffee of all things. She didn't drink coffee.

"Do you need something to drink?" He waited to see if she'd react. She didn't. Her gnarled hands lay limp in her lap, her eyes stared out the window and her muttering went on, unchecked. Dan got up and headed out into the hallway. Dr. Fellows said he'd be by with an update over thirty minutes ago and still hadn't showed. Dan walked down to the nurse's station and found Dr. Anderson there.

He liked Anderson; the man didn't have the removed and superior tone that Fellows did, like Dan was stupid for even asking a question. He wasn't precisely friendly, but he was open and warm, which made him approachable.

"Dr. Anderson, do you have a minute?" The man looked up and recognized him. He smiled and stuck out his hand for Dan to shake.

"Good to see you, Dr. Connors."

"I was hoping to meet with Dr. Fellows today, but it appears something has delayed him. Is there a possibility you could give me an update on my mother instead?" Dan watched as Anderson put down the file he was holding and reached back for another.

"Sure, how about we head to my office. I've got a few minutes." Anderson led him along the hall and into a small but cheerful office. He motioned Dan to one of the two chairs in front of the desk. Dan took a seat and waited, trying not to hope for good news. The doctor opened the file, thumbed through a few pages and then looked up.

"Do you remember when your mother was first admitted?" Dan nodded and Anderson sat back in his chair, tenting his fingers together, elbows on the armrests of his chair. "You'll probably remember me saying that there were several challenges your mom had. We talked about recovery rates for patients who have suffered a massive stroke and the factors in her favor; she'd been in good health, active for a sixty-two-year old."

"Right, you said it wasn't hopeless. You said we'd see progress."

"Yes, I said there'd be gains, but we couldn't get our hopes up for a rehabilitation that might not come."

Dan felt his heart fall to somewhere near his stomach. He'd known this was coming, but hearing the hopeless tone in Anderson's voice was tough to take.

"At this stage what we're likely looking at is a refocus of our goals. We need to shift to focusing on keeping those gains Ellen has made and maintaining her quality of life as it is."

Dan had to force himself to stay in his seat and not get up and walk away. He forced down the wave of disappointment that filled him and the anger that chased it. He waited it out, knowing he had no right to feel angry. He hadn't been lied to, and he should have been prepared for this. When he felt calmer he spoke. "Her quality of life is not what I was hoping for."

"No, of course not," Anderson agreed. "No one hopes for this kind of outcome, but it's far better than the alternatives. She has the ability to feed herself with adaptive utensils, to stand without support, to walk short distances: these are all goals for people who have suffered the kind of brain injury your mom has. There are patients here who don't have the ability to use the toilet. I know that sounds like nothing, but it makes a world of difference. I know it's difficult to deal with the memory loss she's suffered and the dementia that has persisted, but she has regained her ability to speak in these last few months and that is a significant gain."

"But it's all nonsense."

"Not always. She can respond to questions with a yes or no answer."

"But she's not lucid." Dan pressed, trying hard to hold it together, to keep it polite and professional when all he wanted to do was shout his frustration, fear, and loss until the windows shook. That's what it felt like—loss. He lost his mom that day she fell to the floor of her little house in a heap. She would have died right there if not for her friend Martha, who had gone to the house when Ellen had failed to show for a lunch date. It was a thought that haunted him, followed by the thought that the life she was living hadn't gotten better, and that she didn't deserve any of this.

"I wish I could tell you that will change, but with significant damage this may be the best we can hope for."

Dan nodded in acceptance. He needed to be patient, to accept that this might be as good as it gets for his mom. Fighting against what he saw as her fate was making him miserable and not doing a bit of good for her.

"Thanks for your time." Dan stood and headed for the door.

"Wait a moment." Anderson got up from behind the desk. Dan had the door open, but he shut it again. Anderson drew level with him. "This doesn't mean we stop trying. We still do the current therapies, then we try new ones. If there's a treatment I think will help, I'll suggest it. This isn't me telling you to give up. This is me telling you to adjust your expectations. You never know what lies ahead." He stuck out his hand and Dan shook it.

He left the office but didn't return to his mom's room. Instead he went down to the cafeteria and got her a cup of tea and himself a coffee. Maybe he could interrupt her thoughts on coffee and get a reaction. Maybe it would spark some synapse and she'd be able to make sense. In his heart, he knew what he really wanted. He wanted her to look up, even if only once, and see it was her son sitting with her, her son caring for her. Any small sign that somewhere in her confused mind she remembered who he was and that she loved him.

Erin spotted Katherine hunched over the laptop open on her desk. One of the things she admired about her friend and boss was that rather than use the former director's opulent office, she'd turned that room back into a classroom and taken a small office in the administration area instead. It spoke to her humility and her good sense. Katherine was one of those people who was deeply intelligent and yet practical as well. She knocked on the open door of the office. "Got a minute?"

Katherine looked up and waved her in. Erin took a seat. "Don't freak out, but I had an argument with Dan today."

"Dan Connors?"

"One and the same."

"Over what?"

"Yoga. Or rather my cultural appropriation of yoga for the morning program."

"Ah." Katherine sat back in her chair, her face a study in conflicting thoughts. "It's open to interpretation, but I guess he'd feel pretty strongly about the whole topic since he spent so much of his life in places where it's spiritual."

"Yes. That's the way he explained it." Erin thought back to him asking her to close her eyes and then describing it like she was right there. It was an intimate moment, and she wasn't sure she wanted to share that.

"Spill." Katherine was giving her a sharp look.

"What?"

"Don't play innocent with me. Something he said has you all . . ." She waved her hand in Erin's direction "I don't know what it is, but you've been quiet today, and that's not like you."

"I can be quiet. Besides, it's normal to be thoughtful after having an argument with a friend." But that wasn't necessarily true. A friendship of sorts had started, but she didn't know the rules yet.

"Are you friends now?"

"I think I'm over my crush. No, honestly." She spoke over Katherine's attempt to interrupt. "I still have feelings for him, but they're going to grow into friendship. He needs a friend right now. The stuff going on with his mom seems to be weighing him down. He has no one to help him. I want to help, but I can't do that if I'm still hung up on him."

"So you're going to be his friend."

"That's the idea."

"Good luck with that."

"Hey!" Erin picked up the little squeeze-ball Katherine kept on her desk for agitated students and chucked it at her. Her friend batted it away, and it bounced out into the hall.

"He probably likes you. If you start spending more time together the obvious will happen and friendship might turn into something else. Are you ready for that?"

"I don't know."

"So…that's the reason for the moodiness."

"Maybe." Erin sighed and then stood up. "Dan's taking the boys fishing on Saturday, and then he's staying for dinner."

"Whoa."

"Yeah. I'm going to have to be careful with him about boundaries and the boys. They can't get the wrong idea, or they might get hurt." It was hard enough protecting her own heart, but she had to cover the boys as well. Seth was only a baby when Jimmy died, James not much older. They'd never had a father, only father-figures. If Dan started spending time with them on a regular basis, they'd form bonds that would snap like twigs if he went back overseas or moved away. She couldn't bear to think about how they'd handle that loss.

"Dan would never let whatever might happen between the two of you hurt your boys."

"No, of course not intentionally, but the boys could get ideas all on their own and then managing those expectations would be tough. I wish I knew the rules about being friends and not-friends and everything in between. Men are impossible to sort out."

"Mac gave me the rules on our first real date." Katherine shrugged her shoulders.

"Hilarious. Of course he did." That was so Mac, straightforward and to the point. "How's he doing anyway? You said the other day you were worried about him. That he didn't like the new job."

"He's tip-toeing around me, and I'm not sure why."

"Maybe he needs to know it's safe to talk about something you might not like."

"Why?" Her voice sounded hurt. "He knows he can talk to me about anything."

Erin chose her next words carefully. When she and Katherine first become friends, it was in spite of Erin's own bluntness. Katherine had braved Erin's temperament, and Erin was deeply grateful for that. Their friendship was one of the best things in her life, and Erin wanted to protect it. Not at the cost of the truth, but she could be diplomatic in telling it. "Your reaction can be kind of intense when you don't like an idea."

"Well." Katherine rolled her eyes. "That's everybody."

"You're in a class by yourself, girl."

"Really?" She frowned as if she wanted to deny it, but realized she couldn't. Erin had known Mac long enough to guess what he was feeling.

"And then there's your history together, all the false starts, the drama. He's probably afraid you'll do a runner if he fouls up or suggests something for your life together that you're not going to like."

"That's depressing. He shouldn't feel that way." Her expression was troubled. "He's made me feel safe. I want him to feel the same."

"I think it's going to take time for him to trust the bond you have enough to tell you something you don't want to hear. He won't want to risk the happiness you two have. It was too hard won."

"I guess so." Katherine sighed. "Still, I'm going home tonight and getting it out of him."

"Be honest and straightforward with him, and I think you'll be fine."

"Thanks." She sat back in her chair for a moment, then leaned forward and grabbed a short stack of papers. "Back to our earlier subject, the morning program already has generated a few happy calls from parents. I even got a call from Claire Murphy saying her boys will be joining the early class daily and will be using the bus for transportation. Looks like you worked a miracle. I think that was her way of saying you're doing well."

"Oh, wow, from her that's high praise. And it's good news. Those kids need the extra time, and now they're on time every day to boot."

"She was a little worried we would be adding a fee for it, so I let her know it's included in the tuition, no fees."

"I'm surprised she was concerned." Erin had been to their house once for a PTO meeting. It was huge and gorgeous. "They seem pretty well off. You know where they live, right?"

"You never know what's going on with people, not unless you really get to know them. Sometimes the most desperate of circumstances hides behind the windows with the best curtains."

CHAPTER EIGHT

"People, can we get down to it please?" Claire Murphy tapped her water bottle on the desk like a gavel. Erin managed not to roll her eyes as Claire swept the crowd with a disdainful look. The woman was in her element with the entire PTO assembled before her, ready for her to dole out the Harvest Party assignments. Technically, Erin was not on the PTO party committee, but Claire had sent out an email demanding all parents attend since the Harvest Party was one of their two largest fundraising events. Pulling off a successful Harvest Party should be relatively uncomplicated, but Claire was treating it like a military campaign.

The parents assembled were mostly the moms, as usual. The husbands of the committee members were there, although it looked like Paul Murphy had escaped duty. Claire said he frequently traveled for business, so Erin guessed he must be out of town. *Lucky for him*, Erin thought.

Claire picked up a clipboard and started reading off the sub-committees and announcing who would be assigned to them. Decorations was up first, and of course the A-list moms were on it. They were in a line of chairs at the front of the crowd, and as Erin watched they turned to each other as if silently congratulating themselves on being awesome and getting the good gig.

Claire ran quickly through the rest of the choices—food, promotion, music, games.

Erin was hoping to join that last one, but it sounded like she was going to be punished yet again.

"Okay, clean-up. I know no one likes this one, but it's a necessary and important part of a successful event, so I'll be putting Erin Sullivan in charge of that. We're out of parent volunteers, so you'll need to round up some students or community ones." Erin entertained a very brief fantasy in her head where she got up out of her chair, told Claire to stuff it, and marched out in a huff. Taking a breath, she unclenched her jaw and smiled back at Claire.

"Oh, I should add we don't have janitorial staff on this one. Last year the Barn charged us $300 for set up and tear down, so we'll be doing it ourselves. It's hardly effective as a fundraiser if we're paying for things we can do ourselves."

"Right. 'We'." Erin mumbled under her breath and was surprised to hear a commiserate giggle beside her. One of the other moms was giving her a smile. It was so rare that anyone in the PTO interacted with her that Erin didn't know how to react. It took a second, but she returned a smile of her own, even if it was a bit wonky.

"I bet if you bat your eyes and look helpless you'll get the dads to help you with the tables and the rest of the heavy stuff," the woman whispered.

"You think?" Erin was trying not to take offense at the idea that she'd ever 'bat her eyes' at anyone. Ever. She did not play games. If she needed help, she asked for it, like a normal person.

"Well, you know . . ." The woman gave her a sly look. "A woman like you can wrap the average man around her finger with a wink. I'd give anything to be thin. Blonde I can pull off at the salon." She pointed at her blonde, highlighted and layered hair. It was beautiful and clearly she took time with it and her makeup. "But this body was made for birthing babies and little else."

Erin saw that she was a little heavy, but nothing out of the norm. "Your body was made to hold your soul, and little else," Erin whispered back. "We come in different shapes, and that's totally okay."

The woman drew back as if surprised. "You wouldn't say I need to lose weight? That I need a trainer?"

"I'll tell you what I tell every woman and girl I work with: the only person offering an opinion on your weight should be your doctor. If you're happy where you are and your doctor says it's healthy, you're good. No worries. Who cares what some guy thinks?" Erin watched while her words seemed to sink in. "God didn't put us here as window dressing.

He put us here to work for His glory."

"Oh right. Sure." The woman nodded her head and turned back to the front with a thoughtful expression. Erin sent up a quick prayer that what she said was what the woman needed to hear. She often felt the impulse to speak about what she considered 'big' truths in situations that called for small talk. It was hard to tell sometimes if it was her being her somewhat acerbic self, or if it was Spirit-led. All she could do was pray that she hadn't blown it and hope for the best.

The meeting wrapped up with handouts detailing their assignments. Erin looked at the sheer amount of work listed on hers. She was expected to ensure that all decorations were removed, the chairs and tables broken down and returned to the school's storage area, all trash removed, the floor swept, the parking lot policed for loose trash and put in the dumpster in the back with the rest. She was also in charge of ensuring that the leftover food was packed up and delivered to the church so the hospitality committee could decide if any of it could be donated. It was insane to think she could get all of it done with no volunteers assigned with her.

This was par for the course in her dealings with the PTO. Despite her efforts to make peace with them, they stuck it to her every time they got the chance. Even after she'd gone out of her way to help Claire, she assigned her the worst job and arranged it so she'd have no help. That was a move for an enemy, not even a neutral party. Erin was tempted to rush up to the front and demand to know what it was she'd done to deserve their hatred. She wasn't anyone's enemy. All she did was try to get through life with the hand she was dealt. No one deserved the grief she got from these women. No one.

Instead of causing a scene she grabbed her purse, said a perfunctory goodbye to the people around her, and left. Her phone chirped in her purse. Pulling it out she read a text from Dan. He and the boys were done with their day on the lake and back at the house with fish. Great, Erin thought. Now she was going to get to cook a meal she had zero energy for and try not to embarrass herself in front of a man she was still half in love with. "Ducky," she said aloud as she walked home.

Dan turned around as the front door opened and Erin walked in. She had a stormy look on her face as she hung up her purse, but it vanished as Seth ran to greet her, flinging his arms around her waist to give her a hug. He leaned back and peered up at her. "We had the best time!"

She held his cheek and smiled down at him. "I'm glad to hear it. Did you catch any fish?"

"Yeah, I got a brook trout! Pastor Dan says I'm a natural." And so he was. Seth had taken to fishing immediately, which he hadn't expected. For a kid so full of energy and so talkative, he had worried that standing at the river's edge and casting a line in the quiet of the morning would be akin to torture. But the only one who seemed tortured that morning was James. Although he was too polite to admit it, the boy showed all the classic signs of being bored to tears. Luckily, Dan had prepared for that since he'd thought it would be Seth he had to entertain. They'd only fished for a few hours, and the rest of the time they tooled around the lake in the bass boat he'd borrowed from Pete.

"James didn't catch any, but Pastor Dan did. He got two rainbow trouts." He let his mom go and turned to Dan. "Do you say trouts? Or is it just trout."

"Just trout, buddy."

"Well, anyway, we got three fishes." He picked up the cooler they'd used. "Don't worry." He handed it to his mom. "We gutted them all. Which was super gross, but kind of cool. Pastor Dan says all you have to do is cook them."

Erin took the cooler from Seth and peeked inside. "Hmmm . . . nice fishes, boys. What shall we do with them? Fry, grill, bake, broil?" Erin gave Dan a playful look, but behind it he could tell she was tired.

"If you've got a grill, I think that would be my choice. I can even do the cooking."

"No grill, but I do have a broiler in the range that's pretty good. We can upside down grill them."

"Can you make that sauce to go with them?" James stepped around Dan. "The spicy stuff?"

"Sure. Now you two go get cleaned up and then set the table while Pastor Dan and I work on dinner, okay?" The boys headed upstairs, and Dan followed Erin into the kitchen.

He liked her house. She had little touches here and there that marked it as her space. In the kitchen it was the sunshine-yellow dish towels, the bright green curtains on the windows, and the row of glass canisters on the counter with chalkboard labels in curly-cue writing. Her appliances were like the ones in his apartment–purely utilitarian, but in good shape. Her fridge was covered with funky magnets, pictures of the boys, various schedules, and coupons. *Signs of life. Signs of a family.* Erin took a paper out of her pocket, unfolded it, and slapped it onto the fridge with a magnet that featured a fifties horror-movie style heroine in mid-scream.

The paper looked to Dan like it was for the Harvest Party. "So they roped you in too?" He nodded towards the fridge. Her expression darkened.

"Yup. What do they have you doing?"

"Chaperone." He looked closer at her paper. "Wow, they stuck you on trash duty." When he read through the list of tasks he whistled. "Do you have a crew big enough to help?"

"I have no crew. Apparently, I'm either to do this myself or find my own volunteers."

"That's nuts. This is a huge task. They know you work full time, right?"

She nodded. "It's okay. I'll find a way. Maybe I'll bat my eyes and help will appear." She'd muttered the words, and he wondered if he'd heard right.

"Bat your eyes?"

"Oh, never mind." She took the cooler and set it on the counter. Rummaging through one of her lower cabinets, she pulled out a broiling pan. Dan took it out of her hands and turned her to face him.

"What's up? Why would they assign you this without help? Is it part of the stuff that's been going on at the school?" Her eyes slid to the side, and he could tell she didn't want to answer him. "How about I help you make dinner, and once it's done the boys clean up while you tell me what's going on."

"I don't want to lay everything on you." She was still not looking at him, her eyes fixed on her toes.

"Hey. It's what I do for a living. Listen to people's burdens. Let me help."

She looked up at him, and he watched while fleeting glimpses of hope and fear filled her eyes. He wondered what in her life had made her so cautious of accepting help. That was something he meant to find out.

"Okay. You asked for it." Her lips quirked with the smallest hint of a smile. "Are you any good in the kitchen if you don't ever cook?"

"Oh, no, my mom raised me right. I've got all the basics down. Tell me what to do." For the next half hour they worked together in her kitchen grilling the fish and mixing a lemon garlic sauce that seemed incredibly easy, but tasted like a gourmet creation.

"It's the chili oil." She explained when he'd asked why it was spicy. "I only put in a little, but it gives it a kick." To go with the fish she made broccoli and rice, using a countertop appliance that Dan had never seen before.

"I cannot believe this thing. You can cook perfect rice and steam veggies at the same time. I need me one of these."

"And don't forget..." She did a split Vanna White/Don Pardo impression. "The steam basket is good for fish as well. It's a lazy man's dream." She laughed. "Not that I think you're lazy. You're busy...and not culinarily inclined."

"I'm not sure that's a word."

"Sure it is." She picked up the serving bowl of rice and broccoli. "Get the fish, would you?" He picked up the tray of broiled fish and joined her at the table.

An hour later they were sitting on the small back deck, mugs of tea in hand, Erin bundled in a thick wool sweater. Despite the mildness of the day, the night had the unmistakable bite of winter. Dan didn't mind it since he'd layered up knowing he'd be outside all day. Erin had fingerless gloves to go with the sweater and still seemed cold.

"We could always go inside."

"Thin walls, big ears." She shook her head. "Better to stay out here. Besides, it's not that bad."

"Okay, but tell me if you change your mind." When she nodded her agreement he wondered how best to start the conversation. There was so much he wanted to know, and not all of it was how things were going at work. He wanted to hear her story, but he wasn't sure if she was up to it. "So, stuck on trash duty without help. I'm guessing you made someone on the PTO angry?"

"Honestly? I think the simple fact that I exist makes them angry, or rather that I exist enough to have taken the job of the guy they liked, even though he was a mess. Then of course, there's the fact that I'm not one of them."

"What do you mean 'one of them'?"

"We have all the big stuff in common: motherhood, womanhood, faith. But it's the small stuff that seems to matter more to them. I don't have the free time to do Pilates at the fitness center, and I don't get my hair and nails done at the New Leaf Spa. My kids don't hang with theirs because I can't afford a membership at the Resort activity club, and when we go out to dinner it's Maria's, not the Lake House Grille. My kids don't have multiple pairs of sneakers they can choose from every day. They get one pair of sneakers, boots, church shoes and whatever they need for the sport they are in and that's it. They don't have North Face jackets. I never bought UGGs for Brittany."

"But that's all material stuff."

"Sure, and a few of them don't look down on me because I'm only getting by, but that's not the worst part. I'm single, and some of them look at me and see either a failure or competition. As if I'm a loser because I didn't remarry or they think I'm going to get close to them only to seduce their husbands. It's gross. I hate it, but what can I do? It's been years and I haven't changed a single mind in all that time."

Dan took a deep breath and let it out slowly. The picture she painted was grim, and he didn't want to believe it was that bad. He knew parents chose to send their kids to Christian schools for various reasons, not always because they themselves were believers. That might account for some of it, but not for all. It was disheartening to think that some of these women were Christians but still treated her this way. He saw some of them in church every Sunday. Erin could be reserved, but would that warrant this attitude towards her?

"I know what you're thinking."

He looked up at her and her expression was locked down, but he heard the defensiveness in her tone. "I'm thinking that the way you've been treated is terrible."

"But you're also thinking I must be exaggerating? That if I just got to know them better they would like me and we'd be friends? That I'm too standoffish?"

"I don't think you're standoffish. I only thought you were shy. Now that I know you're not, I do wonder if you're assuming they think these things about you because others have in the past." He watched as Erin shifted on her chair, her body twisting away from him, and he sensed she was angry. It was amazing how different she was from what he'd assumed. This was part of the point he was trying to make, but he was doing it badly. "We often show each other one version of ourselves, but another, truer one lies beneath. Rarely do we ever take the time to figure out who someone really is. That's why I'm so glad you're willing to talk to me." Erin shifted back slightly, and he realized he needed to tread lightly. "I'm glad to get to know you, but the side-effect of that is you get to know me as well, and sometimes I'm a jerk." A rush of happiness filled him as a smile bloomed across her face.

"You're never a jerk."

"But I have a bad habit of speaking before considering who I might hurt."

"I wasn't hurt, I..." She trailed off, her lips pressed together, her eyes looking away again.

"You were what?"

"Frustrated. My step-mother loves to tell me that if I could be a little more friendly, go out of my way to be nice, I'd have no troubles anymore."

"Maybe she was thinking about that passage in First Corinthians? 'Love assumes the best . . .'."

"What?"

"I was paraphrasing. It's, 'Love bears all things, believes all things, hopes all things, endures all things'."

"That would not be me."

Dan laughed. "It isn't any of us. It's the goal, though."

"And you think if I cozy up to these chicks, pretend to be friendly to them, suddenly I'll stop getting nasty notes in my mailbox, the board won't get formal requests for my removal, and I won't get stuck hauling garbage at every event?" Even with his limited experience with women, Dan could tell Erin was angry and it was not only with her situation.

"No. I don't. Obviously, there are people involved with the PTO who are acting against you. I didn't mean to make it sound like you were being—"

"Don't worry about it." She looked crestfallen, but only for a moment before she straightened in her chair. "So, thanks again for taking the boys out. I really appreciate it. They don't get enough time doing 'guy stuff', y'know? I'm trying to be better about that, arrange for Mac and Pete to take them hiking or riding. They're waiting for the snow, since Mac promised to take them out on his snowmobile. Before you know it…" She stood up as if going back into the house, "…they'll be asking for their own, but I've seen the stats on accidents, and I think we'll wait on that." She gave a little laugh that was utterly fake. As she reached to open the door, he leaned a hand against it.

"Sign me up."

She looked up at his hand holding the door and then to him. "What?"

"Sign me up. Garbage duty. I'll get a few volunteers from the church, and we'll knock that out for you. You can direct us."

"I can't ask you to—"

"You're not asking. I'm offering. Actually, I'm insisting." He gave her a smile.

"It's a lousy job. Why are you volunteering for it?"

An honest answer might be that he wanted to make her smile, or that he didn't like the idea that one finger on her perfectly lovely hands had to touch garbage at all. Another honest answer might be that, at that moment, he was desperate to make her happy. "I have to chaperone anyway, why not help with cleanup? Besides, the Calvary hospitality ladies love me. They'll be happy to help us out. Trust me." Dan waited for her to answer, and when she didn't he added, "Let me do it to make up for having been a jerk a minute ago. That's twice I've told you what to do. I'm sorry." He watched while her expression softened slightly.

"Okay. You want to do garbage, who am I to say no?" She passed under his arm and into the house with the briefest of glances back at him.

It was hours later, when he was back home re-reading his sermon notes and looking over his schedule for the week that he realized something. He was tired, but in a good way. Normally a long day would leave him feeling emptied out or used up, but he felt filled. The time he'd spent with Erin and her kids made him feel a part of something and it fed his soul in a way he'd never experienced before. It was as if a part of him had been neglected for years. Only now that it was being filled did he even notice he had the need at all. He was in unfamiliar territory, but it didn't feel alarming or dangerous. On the contrary, it felt like his feet might finally be on the right path. He wasn't sure how Erin and her children fit into his life, but he knew God had placed them there and he was willing to wait and see what the reason might be.

CHAPTER NINE

A FEW DAYS LATER, DAN MADE his way up the dirt and gravel driveway dodging the worst of the ruts, but the car still managed to bottom out. He winced and hoped he hadn't lost his muffler on that one. Stopping the car a few feet from the house, he climbed out and took a quick look underneath. At least nothing was hanging down. As he headed up the path to the house, he couldn't help but notice that the siding that was bulging a few weeks ago was now hanging off. Rob had not called the Rural Relief fund for help, after all. They would have fixed that siding, and the roof leak that was causing it. Dan stepped up onto the porch, mindful of the soft spot to the left of the post and knocked on the screen door. He could hear the dogs barking and someone shouting until finally Rob pulled open the door.

"Hey, what's up?" Rob looked out over Dan's shoulder as if checking if he came alone. Dan was struck by how much Rob had changed in a short amount of time. He'd lost weight, and he wasn't a big guy to begin with. There were dark circles under his eyes, and he seemed to be dodging Dan's gaze.

"It's Thursday, buddy. Didn't see you at the meeting, couldn't get you on the phone, so I thought I'd drop by." Dan watched as the expression on Rob's face grew guilty. Dan pushed his way in as Rob corralled the dogs into the side room. He knew from experience that if he stayed on the front step he'd eventually get a door slammed in his face. Rob's manners weren't the best, but if Dan was actually in the house, or better yet, at a seat in the kitchen, he wouldn't throw him out. Dan headed there as he did on most visits. Rob followed behind.

The house smelled like the dogs had been peeing in the corners and somebody needed to take out the trash. It didn't look like the kitchen had been touched since the last time Dan was there. He couldn't be sure, but the same dishes might have been in the sink. Rob sat down at the small dinette and Dan joined him, pulling out a folding chair and sitting down. The surface of the table was sticky and a juice box, lying on its side with a pool of dried goo underneath it, seemed the source.

"So, how's it going?"

Rob snorted and ran a hand through his hair. He didn't look great. Between the lived-in jeans and the stained white tee, it was a safe bet he hadn't been out of the house much.

"Got fired."

Dan felt his stomach sink. Rob had barely managed to get by on his job as it was. Without it, he'd lose the house. It wasn't a great house, but it was all he and his kids had.

"Have you thought anymore about—"

"Don't get on me about rehab." Rob reached into a pocket and pulled out a pack of cigarettes, lighting one up and tossing the rest of the pack on the table. He had one leg crossed over his knee, his foot bouncing. Dan prayed for discernment as Rob's agitation increased. "And I don't want to hear about AA either. Never did a thing for me."

"Did you hear back from your aunt?"

"Yeah, she won't take 'em. Says she works too much already and doesn't need another hassle. That and she knows I wouldn't be able to pay her enough."

"Maybe I can—"

"Nah." Rob read Dan's mind and cut him off before it got any more awkward than it already was. He lifted his chin to blow a puff of smoke over his head. "She's on a tear about how I've messed up everything my dad gave me. You callin' will make it worse." Rob dragged on his cigarette again, the end turning an angry, bright red.

Dan fought his mounting frustration to try and focus on the problem at hand, where to put Rob's kids so Rob could finally get into rehab. He'd been counting on the aunt to take in the kids. Now they were back at square one.

"It's Felicia's fault. If she hadn't run off on me…" Rob's words trailed off and Dan knew from experience what would come next. Once the man got on that track he'd run through the same thoughts each time. "We were together since junior year. Did you know that?" Dan nodded and waited for Rob to finish. "Loved her. Gave her everything. Never gave me any trouble until that guy started coming around." Rob's expression darkened.

"I know, buddy." Dan cast around for anything that might derail the rant he knew was coming, the one where Rob railed at his unfaithful wife. "Hey, where are the kiddos?"

"Uh." Rob sat up like he was finally paying attention. "Around. You know how they are."

Dan knew they were six and eight and shouldn't be 'around' a house in this condition and a yard that backed up on a wood with a good-sized creek running through it without an adult who was watching out for them. "How about I go say hi?" He got up from the table and started for where they usually hid when their dad was drinking or high.

Once in the backyard, he headed for the shed where Rob kept his tools and where the kids had created a play house. He knocked on the door first and then opened it with a smile. He found Kayla and Dylan, dirtier than the floor they sat on, faces filled with concern.

"Hi." Dylan shifted slightly in front of his sister. A defensive move that made Dan's chest ache because he knew it was probably a knee-jerk reaction. Dylan was all Kayla had between her and the danger in the world all around them and it was clear he knew it.

"Hey, kiddos." Dan smiled in what he hoped was an encouraging way. "Whatcha up to?"

"Playing." Dylan did the answering, per usual. Kayla looked up at him with big brown eyes. Her hair was a messy ponytail, and the ruffles at the end of her pant legs hovered at least two inches above her ankles. Her shirt fit a bit better, but it was on the borderline of too-small as well. Dan looked up and saw Dylan watching him closely. He hadn't missed Dan noting his sister's less-than suitable attire. The boy stood stock-still, a slight tremble in him that likely had nothing to do with the cool air of the shed.

"Did you guys go to school this week?" Dan tried to make it sound like a light, throw-away question.

"Dad says Kayla doesn't have to go."

"Have you been going?" Dan used his 'preacher' expression, trying to ensure the answer he got from Dylan was a truthful one. He was a good kid and he wanted to do the right thing, but there wasn't much in his life to encourage him in it.

"Couple days." Before Dan could say a word Dylan came to his own defense. "I wanted to go, but I missed the bus and dad...couldn't drive me."

"Maybe we can work something out with a neighbor? I can talk to your dad—"

"No." Dylan immediately answered, an edge of panic in his voice.

"Dylan, we've got to work something out. You can't miss too much school."

"I'll make sure I get the bus. You don't have to worry about it."

"Okay." He was worried though. There were now too many signs of neglect to overlook or explain away. Not to mention that from the moment he'd opened the door it was clear Rob was either drunk or high. Again. He'd have to report it to DHHS. There was no dodging that now. "Hey, you know what I have?" The kids looked up at him. "I brought you guys a surprise."

"A present?" Hope, like the morning sun, dawned on Kayla's little face, and his heart squeezed in response.

"Yup. C'mon out to the car and I'll get them."

"Them?" Dylan got up off the floor and pulled his sister to her feet. "We both get something?"

"Sure."

Dan led them out to the driveway and got the two gift bags out of the back of his car and handed them to the kids. Grabbing the cooler that the hospitality committee had packed for the family, the three of them went inside. The kids flopped on the couch in the living room and dumped out their bags, squealing over the various toys and personal-care items that came spilling out. The ladies who ran the committee knew exactly what the kids needed; matchbox cars, a stuffed pink cat with purple ears, a small hairbrush with hair ties attached to its cardboard package, toothbrushes, flossers, even travel-sized soaps and shampoo.

A movement at the doorway to the hall drew his attention. Rob was standing there and he didn't look pleased. "What's all this?"

"A few gifts from Calvary." Dan braced, hoping that Rob's better nature would prevail, and he'd let the kids keep the stuff. Then he remembered the cooler and the food packed inside it. Not having to feed the kids dinner might help. He picked up the cooler and headed into the kitchen with Rob following. "Are you guys hungry?" He set the cooler down on the counter and started to unload it. "I've got some good stuff here."

"We aren't a charity case." Rob's voice was quiet, but there was no mistaking the anger in it. The kids, probably knowing what would come next, headed into the living room. From where he stood in the kitchen he spotted them a moment or two later in the hallway, their gifts stuffed into their bags.

"We'll be upstairs." Dylan called as both kids headed for the stairs, dragging the bags up with them. Knowing the kids were moving fast to probably hide their stuff and avoid their dad dumping it or getting angry about it caused a wave of frustration and anger to wash through Dan. His hands balled into fists at his sides, his teeth clenched and he had to take in a long, steadying breath to stem the tide. Returning to the counter he continued to unpack the food while he prayed for patience, for understanding, and for God to soften Rob's wounded heart. Only when he felt calm did he face Rob, who had slumped into his chair and lit another cigarette.

"You're not a charity case. You're a man with a family who needs some help. That's what the church is for. We like helping. We're glad to do it."

"I don't want any hand-outs from a bunch of stuck-up, holier-than-thou people, talking about how I'm a lousy dad and my kids are a mess, and my life is…" His face contorted before he hunched over, his body wracked by sobs. It was a pitiable sight. When he was sober and healthy, Rob was a mountain of a man, well over six feet, cannons for arms, but the booze and the drugs had beaten down his body just like they were destroying his mind. Swinging from one emotion to the next, Rob was no longer his own man.

Dan sat down, laying a hand on Rob's shoulder. "Rob, can I pray with you for a minute?"

Rob threw his hand off and surged to his feet. "Get out." He pointed at the front door; his face contorted and flushed red.

"I promise." Dan stood up, holding up his hands to show he meant no harm. "I am not here to judge you. I'm here to help."

But Rob seemed past the point of reason. He took a step closer to Dan who at six-one was not short, but nowhere near as tall. He leaned over and with his face inches away from Dan's the smell of alcohol was overwhelming. "I'm not your friend. I'm not your buddy. I'm nothing to you and you're nothing to me. Now get out!"

"Okay. If you need me to leave, I'm gone." Dan slowly backed up. "But you are something to me and to the church." From the look on Rob's face, Dan had only a few seconds left before Rob started answering with his fists. "We want to help."

"Nobody wants to help," he scoffed. "You all think I'm a loser."

"Rob, look at me. I'm on your side. What if I could find a family to take the kids in while you get yourself on your feet? I know this couple—"

"No! I've told you, I'm not doing rehab. It's a waste of time. I'm fine. My kids are fine, and we don't need your charity." He picked up the soda can on the table and hurled it across the room. Dan batted it away, and it exploded in a wet thud against the wall. Rob swore. "Don't you see, you're making it worse!"

"I'm going." Dan began backing down the hallway. "But God loves you, Rob. He's holding out His hand. You only need to take it."

Rob laughed out loud, fell against the wall, and slid down to a crouch. "What a crock." His laughter, a broken and ragged sound, followed Dan out the door.

Thirty minutes later, Dan was walking up the shrub-lined path to the entrance of his office, knowing he had to make the call and dreading it all the same. The office was in his living space and normally a place where he felt settled and content. He'd lucked out that the Calvary Christian Church didn't use their parsonage for the pastor. All of their previous pastors had owned their own houses in the town, so they'd converted it into a duplex and used it for visitors and emergency housing for members of the community. When Dan arrived without the means to even rent a house, let alone buy one, they gave him one of the other properties they owned, a converted barn right in the heart of town. It had been a blacksmith shop at one point and, although small, it had the open feeling and high ceiling of a barn, at least on the bottom floor. The loft had a sloped ceiling, but was still large enough to hold a small kitchen and a studio-like space for his bed and living room.

His favorite part of the barn was the huge, multi-paned glass door in the front where the sliding barn door used to be. It was not warm, by any means, but it let in light and so much of the downtown scenery that it made up for its lack of weatherproofing. As a single male pastor, it helped that his office was completely open to view as well. If anyone wanted to know what he was up to, they could come on by. He had an official office at the church, but the church secretary shared the space, and he didn't like to invade her turf. He'd made the mistake of asking her to hold off on her calls or make them quietly while he was writing an email one afternoon. He needed quiet to think. Instead, he got her huffy sighs and staccato typing. Ever since then he'd used the first floor of the barn as his office.

When he'd first started, the church had apologized for the accommodations, and he'd nearly laughed. After years spent in temporary housing of every sort overseas, having an entire barn to himself was an unexpected luxury. The walls were made up of naturally-aged barn board, the wide pine floors worn down over the ages to a honey-gold color.

He opened the man-sized door on the side of the building and walked in. Throwing his keys on the side table, he took a deep, cleansing breath. With it came the smell of home—old wood, paper, and leather. The familiar, comforting smell helped settle his ragged emotions. He ought to go upstairs to the loft and get something to eat, but he wasn't up to it. Instead, he flopped into the chair behind his desk, rolled it forward, and rested his elbows on its glossy surface. He loved this desk. It had been a dining table in a previous life, but wasn't a bit spindly. It was art-deco in design and sturdy in construction with warm-toned walnut wood. No modern table would be made as thick, or if it was it wouldn't be something a man like him could afford. Another unlooked for, but deeply appreciated, luxury.

Across from the desk sat three wooden chairs arranged for visitors. Beyond that was another of his favorite areas: across the room sat a leather sofa facing two wing-back chairs, and in between them an oriental carpet still in pretty good condition for its age. None of the furnishings were new; they were all out of someone's attic or basement, but they were luxuries to him nonetheless. He might not own any of it, but even having use of it felt decadent.

Dan never had the drive to own things. Other than the clothes in his closet, his laptop, and his fishing gear, he didn't own anything. The car was his mom's, the barn the church's–even most of the books lining the huge bookcase on the far side of the room were borrowed. He'd never been in a place long enough to accumulate much beyond a Bible and a few concordances and commentaries. The rest he had borrowed. His mother had nicknamed him 'the nomad'.

Shaking his head, he tossed away the thought, unwilling to let his brain jump from the memory to Mom's current condition. That was the last thing he needed on top of today's disaster. He opened his laptop and googled the DHHS hotline number. His hand hovered over the desk phone, ready to dial, but still reluctant to call, fighting the very real feelings of guilt. "Don't be a coward," he said aloud. Picking up the handset, he dialed the number and waited for an intake rep to answer. When she did, he related the details of what he'd seen this afternoon.

"He's a good dad." The woman on the other end of the call had no reply. "He's having a rough time since his wife left him."

"Okay, so they're divorced?"

"I'm not sure if they made it official, but she's in New Hampshire. In a new relationship."

"So she's a non-custodial parent? Do you have her contact information?"

He gave the woman the last known number he had for her, but he didn't think she'd still be there. Felicia had hooked up with a rough sort of guy who had no real occupation and seemed to drift from place to place. Dan suspected he was a dealer, or else worked for one.

When Dan finally hung up he felt like a traitor. Rob needed rehab, and his kids needed a loving family to take them in while he got that help. DHHS wasn't likely to screen his call. Most likely they'd be showing up at the ramshackle house later this week. But Dan knew how that would end. The kids would wind up in the system unless Felicia decided to care that she had two children in Maine or the aunt changed her mind.

Dan sighed and checked his voicemail. There was a message from Beth Russell, an old friend from seminary, about helping her with fundraising for a new refugee mission she was going to direct. "Dan, this is right up your alley. I know you've been state-side for a while, but wait until you see what we've got planned. It's really exciting. I'm going to be in New England for a month. I'd love to add your church to my swing through Maine. Call me." Then she paused. "I know it was a real let down when your project ended, and I've heard your mom's not well. Call me if you need to talk. I'm here for you." That was a bit odd. Beth wasn't the type to want anyone to cry on her shoulder. It was kind of her to think of him, though. Instead of calling, he wrote down her info as a reminder to put her on the schedule of guest presenters at Calvary.

The only other message was from the chairman of the board of elders. It was a friendly reminder about his contract renewal. They were pressing him to sign for five years, not only one as he had before. In five years he'd be forty. That seemed so old. He had been asking God, begging really, for some kind of direction, a new call, and none had come. If nothing did, he supposed he'd sign the contract and resign himself to life as the bachelor pastor of Calvary Christian Church until he was an old man.

"Oh, shut up." He spoke out loud to head off any more self-absorbed wallowing.

What he needed to do was work on his sermon. Although he'd had a few ideas earlier in the week, he'd never fully developed them. If he didn't get a good head start on it this afternoon, he'd have to spend all of Saturday working, and that thought was depressing. He liked to spend it outside, weather permitting, not hunched over his desk in a panic. He pulled his Bible out from underneath a pile of papers and flipped to the passage he'd been reading when he'd gotten the idea.

CHAPTER TEN

ERIN CHECKED THE TIME ON HER phone before stuffing it into her coat pocket. She picked up her purse and started to head out of the administration department.

"Hey, you're here late." Katherine had her briefcase in hand and was shutting the lights off in her office.

"Coaches meeting."

"Heading home?"

"Maybe... Dan missed the meeting. I was thinking I might drop by his office. Talk to him about taking this year off. He's really busy, and I'm pretty sure I could get another volunteer."

"Oh so you're at the 'dropping by' friend level?"

"Hush. Why are you here so late?"

"The usual nonsense, but I was hoping to talk to you." Katherine leaned against the door jamb. "Do you remember the other day when I said Mac was sort of tip-toeing around me?"

"Right, did you talk?"

"Sure did." Katherine's expression was hard to read, but it looked like she was happy. "Mac wants us to be foster parents."

Erin gasped and then smiled wide. "That's a great idea!" Then she realized her friend might have mixed feelings. "Are you okay with that?"

"At first I worried that he was saying we weren't enough, that somehow our life was lacking, but he explained he felt a calling from God." Katherine folded her arms in front of her. "It hits some soft spots in me, but after we talked I prayed about it, and a real sense of peace came over me. I think it's the right thing to do."

"That's awesome. I couldn't be happier for you. You are going to make a great mom."

"*Foster* mom."

"No, take it from someone who has a biological mom and a step-mom and loves them both. A mom is a mom."

"Well, now you need to go away because you're going to make me cry."

Erin knew what her friend needed, so even though it wasn't her way, she reached out and pulled Katherine into a hug, squeezing her tight and then letting her go. "Love you, Katherine."

"Love you too, Erin." Katherine dug into her purse and pulled out a tissue. "Now, you're off to see Dan?"

"Yes. I think it's probably best to drop by his office."

"Rather than a phone call?" Katherine's eyes danced with mirth.

"Quit it." Erin started to leave and then turned back. "Tell Mac I'm really pleased for you both."

"I will."

Erin left thinking that Mac and Katherine as foster parents was definitely good news. What she needed now was news from Dan. At the meeting, she'd planned to make sure he meant what he said about helping her with the cleanup at the fundraiser. Also, she had been stung by some of the things he'd said. Actually, she'd felt convicted, but she didn't want to admit it. She was too quick to assume the worst of anyone's actions towards her, but now she was doing the same thing to Dan, double-guessing his intentions. He said he wanted to help, but she wanted to be sure that's what he meant, not that he felt sorry for poor, pathetic Erin after she'd unloaded all that stuff on him. "Stupid." She repeated aloud the thought that had been banging around in her head for days.

On the short walk from the school to Dan's house Erin noticed the shops lining Main Street had swapped their window boxes of bright annuals and trailing vines for autumn-hardy mums and asters. A few had gone the extra mile and set out pumpkins as well. Erin headed down the gravel path that cut through the end of town square where trees lined both sides. The setting sun filtered through the leaves overhead intensifying their color. She decided the sugar maples were her favorite since they were like a slow firework show turning from green to yellow and then to red. Though there was something to be said for the paper birches too. Their peeling bark and bright yellow leaves stood out against the boring oak trees on the far side of the square. Erin kicked her way through a small pile of fallen leaves as the path led up to Dan's street.

The barn that made up his office and apartment sat slightly back from the sidewalk and behind a little hedge, but she could still see the big window in front. As she walked down the path to his side door she spotted Dan bent over a pile of papers on his desk. Her steps faltered as she debated disturbing him. In the end she decided a break might help anyway, so she knocked on the door. She had to knock again before she got his attention and the door finally opened.

"Hey." He looked a bit rumpled despite being dressed in what she thought of as his 'on duty' clothes, dress trousers and a button-down shirt. He'd rolled the sleeves of the shirt back, but if he'd had a tie on it was gone now. There was a slightly puzzled look on his face, but he smiled at her as if he was glad to see her.

She was suddenly struck dumb, overwhelmed again. Why couldn't she think straight around this man? Finally, she blurted out, "Guess what day it is?"

"Uh, Thursday?" He stepped back to allow her into the room.

"Do you remember what was happening at 3:30 today?" She smiled as he walked back to his desk and took a seat, motioning for her to do the same. "Maybe a meeting?"

Slowly the look of understanding dawned on his face, and he closed his eyes. "I can't believe I forgot." He threw a hand out at the mess of papers, books, and notebooks scattered on his desk. "I've been wrestling with this week's sermon, and I completely spaced it." He rubbed at his forehead, his expression pained.

"Don't worry about it. The guys you rounded up to man the clean-up crew at the Harvest Party all showed, and we went over what each person needs to do. That leaves you, and I wanted to be sure you really had the time for this and—"

"Seriously, Erin, I'm sorry for missing that meeting. I did intend to come." His eyes on hers were intense, and she believed what he said, but she saw something else there as well. Dan was troubled. He looked weary and yet tense.

"No worries." She looked down at the chaos on his desk. There was only one clean spot, directly in front of him. The mess spread out in a rainbow of clutter around him. "I'm not surprised the meeting slipped your mind. Your desk is a disaster."

"It is." Dan shuffled a stack of papers in what looked like a vain attempt to put it in order. "I've never been great about the paperwork aspects of this job, or of any job."

"Did you finish it?"

"What?"

"Your sermon." She took her purse off her shoulder and set it down on the chair in front of his desk.

"No." He looked defeated. "I'm stuck." He started pawing through the papers on his desk. "There was this quote I read the other day that gave me a great idea, but I can't find my notes, and I haven't been able to recreate that same idea."

"Can I help?"

"I don't really write like that."

"Not with the sermon, genius." She gave him a quick smile to take out the sting of her teasing. "With the desk. Let me see if I can restore some order for you and you can get that sermon done."

"I'm not sure you can, to tell you the truth. It's pretty bad."

"Well, you're helping me at the party, so I'll help you clean up here, and it will feel a little more even." She looked down at him, hoping he could see this was hard for her. "I'm not good about accepting help, even when I need it. It makes me feel indebted, and I'm always afraid the bill will be too high in the end."

"I would never—"

She held up a hand to cut him off. "Of course you would never. How about you help me and I help you? I know you're giving without wanting a thing back, but it would make me feel better to give you something in return. A clean desk."

"If you feel up to it, I am not going to say no."

"Okay. Then scoot." She shooed at him with her hands and he stood. "You take a seat on your couch." She pointed over to the leather couch in the seating area. "Read or whatever, and I'll tackle this."

"Um…"

"I'll be super careful and only sort out your stuff." She reassured him. "I won't toss anything that's not trash. Then you can get back to working. I honestly like doing this sort of thing." This was mostly true. "I've got nothing better to do for the next hour." This was absolutely true.

"Okay, I trust you." He picked up a pen, notebook, and his Bible and started walking to the couch, but stopped next to her. He gave her a long, searching look. She wasn't sure what he was trying to see.

"Shoo." She waved him away.

"Okay, boss. It's all yours." He moved to the couch and sat in the corner, facing away but watching her out of the corner of his eye.

"Stop worrying." She smiled at his flinch. "I'm organizing, not judging. I promise not to look at anything personal. I'll put it all in a pile for you."

"Right." He opened the Bible on his lap, and when she checked back a minute later it appeared he was actually reading and making notes, not worrying about what she was up to. He was right, the desk was probably the worst disorder she had ever seen, but he had no drawers, not even a filing cabinet, so it was to be expected. The desk was a beautiful antique, and huge—but without some kind of storage system he was going to be lost. Under one pile of random papers, she found a tiered inbox with nothing in it. She set that aside.

Once she started to sort through it all, she could see it did have a system of a sort. He had put like with like, but they'd all merged into a chaotic mess when the piles fell over and combined. After about ten minutes she had all his mail in one pile. She took it and a waste bin she'd found in a corner and marched it over to him. "My advice? Chuck the junk mail without opening it. Separate anything you need to respond to in one pile, and everything you want to hang onto but aren't sure what to do with in another pile, and the rest in that basket." She nodded down at the wicker basket on the low table in front of the couch. "I think that was put there for magazines, but I'd repurpose it for now."

"Okay." He smiled up at her, and a warm feeling bloomed in her chest.

"I'll leave you to it." She headed back to the desk. There were a few books in small stacks so she went hunting in the book shelf for something that could be used as book ends. She found a small marble globe and a cast iron teapot that looked vaguely Asian. It didn't seem to be an antique, so she figured it was free game. Using those, she created a bookshelf of sorts on the end of the desk, spines inward so he could grab what he needed. She removed a desk lamp that wasn't needed since he had track lighting overhead, and then uncovered a desk-blotter sized calendar that looked like it was a good idea he just didn't keep up with. She removed the months already passed and left October on the surface.

By now she was entirely into the project, and if she'd had her special markers, she would have gone to town on the calendar with color-coding, but she checked herself. This was his. She did put down the next coach meeting, though. There was only one meeting left in the month anyway.

Halfway through the last pile of loose papers, she called out, "Got it! Or I think I do." She walked over to him with a small stack of papers. "You've scribbled 'sermon' in the corner here. Would these be your sermon notes?" She held the papers out to him.

He eagerly took them out of her hands, read them over, and let out a relieved sigh. "This is it. Thank you so much. I was thinking I'd have to work on Saturday to finish. You saved my day off." The look he gave her warmed her from the inside out. "And you saved the congregation from having to listen to what was probably going to be a mess."

"I doubt that." When he seemed ready to argue she admitted, "I still listen to your sermons."

"Really?"

"When I have downtime, I go to the Calvary website and listen. I've always enjoyed your teaching."

"Thank you." There was a slight flush on his cheeks like he might be blushing. "I appreciate you telling me that. Sometimes I'm not sure if I'm reaching people."

"You are, Dan, you definitely are." Was he doubting himself? She wondered how a man so clearly gifted could question whether he was doing a good job. The size of the congregation alone should let him know how well he was doing. Calvary had doubled in size since he took over. Dan's teaching had drawn people from all over the county. She'd always assumed he knew how good he was. He seemed so confident. Something was up with him, and it didn't seem like it was work, or not the work he had at hand. "Is it the sermon that's got you in this state or something else?"

Dan looked up at her and, although it still made her uncomfortable, she held his gaze and was struck again by how tired and burdened he seemed. He looked like a lost little boy, his hair a mess, a clump of it falling into his eyes. Unable to stop herself, she reached out and brushed the curls off his forehead. He closed his eyes at her touch. Time seemed to stop.

CHAPTER ELEVEN

ERIN HAD CROSSED RIGHT OVER A line and she knew it, but neither of them reacted. Slowly, he opened his eyes, and it wasn't Dan the pastor staring back at her. No, it was the man, in all his vulnerability and strength. She felt his draw kick in. The attraction came close to overwhelming her common sense.

"Do I look that pitiable?" His smile was a weak thing, and somehow it broke the spell. She moved back a little, stuffing her hands in her pockets so she wouldn't be tempted to touch him again.

"You look tired, or maybe more. Can I help?"

"You just did." He got up and walked to the desk. "Wow."

Erin smiled as he sat down and took in her efforts. She'd set up the center of his desk with the calendar for a blotter and a handful of pens and pencils in a low tray she'd found that seemed dedicated to the purpose. His laptop she'd moved slightly to the side so he could swivel his chair and type. The phone was in easy reach, as was his inbox, and the empty space between each ensured that he didn't feel closed in.

"I set it up as if it was mine. I hope it works for you too."

"Erin, this is perfect. I can't believe you did this in the time you had."

"Oh well…" She didn't want to confess she'd enjoyed thinking of him sitting at a desk she'd set up for him, or that even the idea that she'd made his life easier set off the butterflies in her stomach.

"How do you do it? You're probably as busy or busier than I am and yet you have a beautiful home, a perfectly neat desk at school, absolute order everywhere. And you have the boys! I know from experience that boys are disorder personified, but you've got it all together. How?"

"I don't really have a choice." She said it with a laugh, but it was true. She gave him her brave smile, but he seemed to see right through it.

"It must be hard to be on your own."

"It was harder when Jimmy was alive." She regretted the words almost the moment they were out. They were too honest, too real. Who says life was harder with their husband alive? But it was true. "It's a terrible thing to say." She looked down at her toes, unable to meet his eyes. "But, by the end...the drinking was tearing us all apart. It was..." She couldn't think of the right words.

"You know where I was today?"

She shook her head, still not looking at him. "Visiting a parishioner. He's got the two cutest kids you could imagine. Good kids." His voice was quiet. "And he's drinking himself to death." Erin looked up in shock. Dan nodded his head. "It's a terrible thing, like you said. His kids are taking care of themselves, and not doing it well. He's maybe a week or two from destitute, and he can't pull himself together enough to care." He leaned closer. "I say all that because I can see how it would've been harder when Jimmy was alive. I'm sorry you went through that."

"Long time ago now." She dismissed his sympathy with a wave of her hand. She didn't want to talk about Jimmy with Dan, especially now that Dan seemed to be talking about what was troubling him. "I'll pray that your parishioner sees the light before it's too late."

"It's probably already too late, but he'll need the prayers either way."

"It's hard when you can't stop someone from destroying themselves, isn't it? You can see the train coming down the track from a mile away and you're jumping up and down, waving flags, shouting, and they stand there and let it mow them down anyway."

"Was that what it was like?" It appeared Dan didn't want to let the subject of Jimmy go.

She tossed her hair over her shoulder and stood a little straighter. She didn't want him to think she needed pity or even sympathy. It was what it was. "We married too young and too quick. I wanted freedom." She shrugged. "Typical teenage stupidity. I thought my step-mom hounding me about dance lessons and homework was oppressive." She added finger quotes and rolled her eyes remembering her own silliness. "We got into some real knock-down, drag-outs and Jimmy Sullivan, the original good ol' boy with his laid-back attitude to match his laid-back life looked like freedom to me."

"Didn't turn out that way?"

"Great…until Brittany came along. Then he had to get a real job since we couldn't live off my tips anymore. With that came resentment, a new crew of friends who liked beer a whole lot better than their wives, and the slow slide into alcoholism." She mimed the downward spiral with her hand. "It got bad, I kicked him out when Brit was only two. Went back to school part time. Jimmy realized I wasn't taking him back as-is so he quit drinking and came home."

"But that didn't last?"

"That's the thing." The familiar grief settled in her chest. "It did last, for a while. Long enough for me to finish my bachelor's, to have James and then Seth. Jimmy seemed… cured."

"There's no cure for addiction." Dan said it softly, almost like he didn't want to interrupt.

"Don't I know it." Erin shook her head. "One night he ran into one of the guys from his old crew, had a few beers, and that is all she wrote. We were back on the downward slide. He got mean again, lost his job again, and I kicked him out again." She rushed on, wanting to get it all out and then, hopefully, never have to talk about it again. "But I had to let him go because he wasn't safe anymore, not for me, not for the kids. When he drank he became someone else. Someone who didn't love us." She met Dan's eyes and could see that he understood. "His family asked me to take him back again. I said no. They said he might kill himself and all I could think was, better him than us." She closed her eyes, hating how it sounded out loud, like she didn't care.

"You made the right call, Erin. Don't let the choices he made leave you with guilt you don't deserve."

"The night of the accident he'd called me. I let it go to voicemail."

"Ah," He nodded his head. "So you feel responsible."

"He was drunk as could be and still got in his car and drove to our house. He had a stack of presents with him." She paused for the ache, but for once it didn't come. "It was a week after Christmas. Jimmy was all about grand gestures." She fought off the tears that threatened to clog her throat. Pity, swift and fierce, flooded into her chest, making it hard to breathe. He'd tried. Whatever had happened to kill his love for Erin, Jimmy had never stopped loving his kids. Right up until the end, and that made her ache for them, for what they'd lost.

"That must have been hard on the kids."

"It was *all* hard on them." She reached up and ran a finger under each eye, catching the tears before they could really fall. "His mom was…" Erin shook her head. "She sold the house and moved. We don't see her, she doesn't call, doesn't take my calls."

"I've seen that happen. Death can pull people together or divide them. There's always hope, though, but you probably know that." His lips lifted slightly.

"It's why I still call," she admitted. Arleen might never accept them back into her life, but Erin was determined to keep a space waiting for her. "My mom, not my step-mom, came to the rescue. She'd only recently moved back home, but she opened up her place to us. We lived with her until I found a decent job. She did everything she could to give the kids 'normal'. That was huge. I know it sounds weird, but making their lunches for school, making sure they got to little league or dance lessons, that stuff doesn't seem to matter when your world crashes in, but you need it."

"I was a lot older than them when my father died, and his death wasn't tragic, but I went back to school after the funeral and told my buddies to shut up about it. I didn't want anybody to talk to me about him or how I was feeling. It was my way of pretending it never happened."

"I didn't know that you lost your dad so young."

"Not that young, I was seventeen."

"I'm sorry."

"Like you said, long time ago."

"Right." Dan probably meant what he said, but his eyes held a different story. There was pain there and Erin wondered if he'd fully dealt with his dad's death. Did a child have to deal with it forever? And now he was dealing with his mom's ill health. Erin hadn't known his mom very well before the stroke since she'd only moved to Sweet River a year or two before. What she did know about her was all good. She was a cheerful, active woman, friendly to all, volunteered for everything at church. She was sweet and kind and didn't deserve to have that light put out.

Dan began to pull away, maybe seeing the empathy in her eyes and mistaking it for pity. He held up the paper with his notes. "Thanks for this." He laid them on his now tidy desk. "And thanks for this too."

"Anytime, Dan. I mean that. If you need help…" She pressed her lips together, not sure how to say what she really meant, that she wanted to ease his troubles, that she'd do almost anything for him. "Well, I should head out." She turned around ready to go, but Dan grabbed her hand and gently pulled her back.

"Wait."

There was something different in his tone and a look on his face that she couldn't believe was for her. It was warm, almost affectionate. He hadn't let go of her hand either. A shiver moved through her as she felt his thumb stroke her fingers ever so softly. She almost stopped breathing. The seconds ticked away and neither of them spoke. With only his presence and his gentle touch, it was like he had surrounded her in warmth. She let it soak in while she absorbed the shocking thought that Pastor Dan Connors might actually be fond of her, maybe even more than fond.

A knock sounded at the door. Erin jumped a bit and Dan rolled his eyes. "Don't go anywhere." He headed for the door then swung it wide. "C'mon in."

Erin spun around and tried not to look like she was embarrassed about anything, since she shouldn't be. Should she? The door opened and Pete walked through.

"Hey Pete." She gave him a little wave. He looked both pleased and puzzled to have found Dan and Erin together. She braced for Dan to explain it all away, to tell him not to get any ideas, that they were just friends. He needed to be careful in his position, and she wasn't anything to him anyway, but Dan didn't say a thing. He stood next to her while Pete took a seat in one of the hard-backed chairs set in front of the desk.

"I'm sorry Pete, I didn't notice the time. That's twice today I've forgotten a meeting." He winked at Erin. She managed not to let her jaw drop open in shock. "But now that I'm all organized…" He gestured towards the surface of the desk.

"I thought this looked better than usual." Pete looked the desk over.

"Erin straightened me out." He nodded at her.

"Really?" Pete looked up at Erin and raised an eyebrow. She could feel the heat creep across her cheeks. She needed to get out of there.

"She's a miracle worker." The look Dan gave her was definitely affectionate and she wasn't ready to process that in front of Pete. All her brain could think was 'escape,' so she did.

"I've got to get going." She pulled the strap of her purse off the chair so quickly it swung wildly and nearly clocked Pete on the head. "Oh, sorry. See you later." She turned her back on both of them and marched out the door, shutting it firmly behind her.

It was truly dark now. The cold air was bracing and she hoped it would help her get a grip. Her thoughts and feelings were in a whirl, buzzing too quickly and frantically for her to sort out. She'd basically spilled her guts to Dan about Jimmy's death, something she never talked about, and that was embarrassing and made her feel vulnerable, even if he hadn't been outraged or horrified. She didn't know what he wanted from her. Remembering how he held her hand was a serious hit to her determination to get over her crush. She was scared to hope he might want her for something other than a friend.

Dan sat at his desk and watched Erin walking away. Something had happened between them today. It felt like the start of something. It was as if that pull she had on him only got stronger, and he realized that he wanted something more than friendship with her, as good as that friendship was. As soon as that thought surfaced it seemed to fit like a puzzle-piece inside him. The idea of having something more, something like a real relationship, felt right. It never had before. "So." Pete had an odd expression on his face, like he'd been watching Dan and could read his thoughts. "Erin seemed right at home here. You two getting close?"

Dan couldn't stop the smile that broke out on his face. He liked the idea of her feeling at home around him. "I've been helping Erin and she's been returning the favor. Friends. For now."

"Well, I approve." Pete smiled wide. "In case you cared, but I doubt you do."

"Actually, I'm glad to hear it. I've never had a relationship, and I know that when I took the position of pastor I repeated my intent to stay single. I'm wondering now if that might change. I'm not sure if that changes how the elders feel."

"Never fear. There's not a member of the board who wouldn't look at you finding a wife as anything other than a good thing."

Dan felt a stab of alarm at the word 'wife', but then the idea settled in his mind, and he liked it. Not that long ago he thought her delicate and shy, but now that he knew her he sensed her strength. Could she handle the mission field? Then again, God had not called him back there. Right now, Erin would be signing on to be a pastor's wife, although not everyone was suited to that either.

"Hypothetically speaking at this point of course."

"Hmm?" Dan had been lost in his thoughts. He backtracked to what Pete had said. "Hypothetically, of course."

"Speaking of the elders, you can probably guess what I wanted to meet about."

"The contract?"

"You seem to have some doubts."

"Typically it's for a year."

"Well, we can't help but notice that you've stuck around for a while now. We're thinking you might be putting roots down." He waggled his eyebrows. "That means you'd be able to give us a longer commitment. It helps us budget, helps the congregation feel settled. We want to think you're keen on staying."

"I love Calvary and I am grateful for how flexible everyone has been, but…," he trailed off. The words wouldn't come. "It's hard to know what to say when I'm not even sure what I'm thinking or feeling. Signing the contract means I'm saying no to missions, at least for a while."

"This is a mission, Dan."

"You know what I mean, Pete."

"I do. But I think sometimes you assume you're up there preaching to the choir. Those pews are filled with some second and third generation families, but God doesn't have grandchildren. Each person comes to Christ on their own. Sure, their family helps, but you can't raise a Christian. A parent, no matter the strength of their faith, cannot ensure their child has a saving faith in Jesus Christ. There's only one way that happens, and we need good teaching, a good shepherd in the pulpit to help. There's as much need here as there is anywhere."

"I know that. I do believe that. It's just hard to let that old calling go."

"Ah, there was glory in it, wasn't there?" Pete tapped the picture frame Erin had unburied from the clutter on his desk to display. It was a photo of a crossroads Dan had taken while he was in Tibet. The main road was wide and even, the cross road was ragged, more a goat trail than anything else. He'd felt it was the perfect vista, so he'd scrawled his life's quote across it: No Reserves, No Retreats, No Regrets.

"'Glory'?"

"Sure. Reminds me of how I felt about the Army when I joined up. Was gonna see the world, fight for God and my country. No guts, no glory. Granted, you're working for God's glory over there, but I see some of those bits of ego peeking out once in a while when you're telling a story. You went to spread the gospel, but you were still a young man looking to make his way. Some of that probably still calls to you."

Dan had never considered it that way, but part of what Pete said felt true. He had been after glory in a way. He was definitely arrogant when he first went overseas, until the reality of missions knocked him down enough times that he learned to be humble. His last few years in India were different. He was in charge of the entire mission. There was pressure, sure, but there was also some glory in that as well.

"On another topic, I heard you were scheduled to visit Rob Foster today. How'd that go?"

"He didn't hit me when he threw me out of his house. Put it that way." Dan rubbed his chin. "Had to call DHHS."

Pete sighed. "I expected as much. Haven't seen them in church in weeks. Heard he got fired again."

"It's the drinking." Dan shrugged. "And it looks like drugs too. He's self-medicating. When Felicia left, it really tore a hole in that man."

"I've seen it a dozen times. Woman cheats and leaves, guy crumbles from within. Either they end up drinking, or taking up with a woman half their age so they can soothe the hurt. Seen more than one man's faith suffer that way."

"Pride, that's what it comes down to. It was a hit he couldn't recover from and he's been in a downward spiral ever since. It's the kids I'm worried about now. You should've seen Dylan today, playing the part of protector. Makes me wonder who's been in the house lately."

"You did the right thing."

"That will be a small comfort when those kids enter the system."

"Yah, there's no sugar-coating that. Maybe Felicia will come to her senses?"

"I'm praying she does."

"Something else to add to your prayer list. Talked to Mac today. He and Katherine are starting classes to become foster parents. Probably too late for Rob's kids, but it's a done deal. They're gonna need support."

"That's great. I'm so glad they're going forward with it. I'll do anything I can." If only Mac had started the process a few weeks ago, they'd be ready; they were the perfect couple to take on Rob's kids. Dan knew better than to question God's timing, but he did it anyway. Even knowing that God ordered the steps of all those who walked with him, his mutinous heart seemed to hold a grudge.

CHAPTER TWLEVE

"MOM?" SETH ASKED AS HE SLID into the booth. "Can I order off the regular menu? I'm so hungry, the kids' one won't cut it." Seth's appetite for food was like his appetite for conversation, unending. He could out-eat James and that was saying something.

"Sure." Erin handed him a menu although with how often they'd been to Maria's, he probably didn't need it. During the week they normally wouldn't be eating out, but Erin had spent too long at Dan's office to come up with dinner. Or it might have been that her thoughts were too confused to pull it off. She'd opened the fridge, seen nothing inside that looked like dinner, and shut it again.

"Did you see how many games he had? And that's his back-up system. He said he usually plays the PS4 the most." Seth was talking a mile-a-minute as usual. He and James had spent the afternoon at the Resort activity center as the guest of a friend. Wes MacMillan was the son of Penny and Ward MacMillan, solid, salt-of-the-earth folks, even though Ward made a ton of money as a financial advisor. Erin knew them from hockey, and Penny was one of the few moms at the school who didn't fit the stereotype. For one, she was petite, left her hair its natural medium brown, and never wore yoga pants, fitness wear, or anything that lacked a skirt. Even the one time she'd been forced into fitness wear for a parent/child field day, she'd worn skirted capris. They were perfect and perfectly her. Penny did not mess around with other people's expectations.

"What are you guys talking about anyway? I thought you were at the activity center. Were you playing video games there?"

Sensing danger, James jumped in first. "No, don't worry. There were other kids there that had brought their own games to play on the center's system, but Seth and I stuck with Wes. Mostly we played foosball. Evan Murphy brought a whole bag of his own games. That's what Seth was talking about."

"It's ridiculous to even own that many games. I mean he's never going to get any use out of that Nintendo U. He should sell it."

"Yah, I'd buy it." James shot his mom an apologetic look. "Not really. I mean if he was giving it away…" Erin rolled her eyes. She was dog tired of the video game battle. Most days she was tempted to give in and get them a system, but then she remembered how she'd have to police which games they bought as well as how much time they spent on them. That was too much work.

"Did you guys have fun?"

"Yah. Sure." James shrugged. The only time Seth let James speak for him was when he didn't know what to say or a lie was required.

"Really? You seemed pretty glad to leave. Weren't they playing with you?"

"You say that like we're all little kids or something. We aren't." James' tone wasn't exactly respectful.

"Okay, then as a grown man of 13, level with me." Another look passed between her sons. Now she was getting downright alarmed. "What's going on?"

"The last hour Wes wanted to play Xbox, too. It would have been no big deal, but while we were waiting our turn we heard some stuff."

"What kind of stuff?" Her mom radar was on high alert.

"Did you know today was Evan Murphy's birthday?" Erin shook her head and James continued. "He says his mom forgot."

"Forgot?"

"Yah, she told him she'd make it up to him. Have a birthday party next month, but he said that's going to be tough with his dad out of town again. He said his dad has been out of town a lot."

"Well, I think he has a demanding job."

"No, mom." James leaned forward as if willing her to work it out. "Like, a lot. Like he hasn't seen him in weeks."

"Oh." Erin sat back in the booth. With excellent timing the waitress cruised by leaving menus and glasses of water.

"Do you want to put your drinks in?"

Erin ordered, since she knew what the boys wanted, and the waitress left.

"He was complaining about how his dad calls, but his mom gets upset, and they never end up getting to talk to him."

"Yah, and when she came to pick them up she started yelling at them to hurry up for no reason. She walked in the door and went off on them. It was..." Seth seemed to be searching for the word.

"Awkward," Erin said.

"Totally." James nodded. "And after they left, Wes said that there was a rumor the Murphy's were going to have to move out."

"I hope you guys didn't join in on that gossip."

"No, we heard it, but we didn't like, mean to. It was an accident." Seth's forehead scrunched.

"Evan and his brother have been kind of a pain at school." James was looking at Seth as if waiting for him to say something. "Haven't they, Seth?"

"C'mon, we said we wouldn't—"

"Hey, whatever's going on, you know that you can trust me helping, not freaking out. I do not freak out." Erin looked between the two of them, but they were still acting shifty. "Are they picking on you?" She directed the question towards Seth since he was smaller.

"I don't think they're singling me out, since they've done it to other kids too. It's stupid stuff like bumping into me in the hall, knocking my lunch out of my hands. Sometimes the other guys pile on, but I can hack it." Seth jutted out his chin and crossed his arms over his chest.

"I think they're jealous." James' eyes shifted from his brother's defensive posture to his mom. "Seth is the best forward the team has ever had, skates faster than anyone, and is a year younger. Last week, the middle school team beat the freshmen, and those guys cannot handle losing. All the talk from the senior varsity squad through the freshies has been about how Seth kicked... um, how well Seth did."

"So they're knocking you into lockers because they're jealous of your hockey skills?" Her eyes narrowed on Seth. "Not because you've been talking trash?" The slight change to Seth's face confirmed that he probably had been talking trash, but fourteen-year-olds shouldn't be knocking eleven-year-olds into lockers anyway. "I suppose you do not want me to talk to them about this? Or their mom?" Seth and James emphatically shook their heads, and Erin sighed. "We'll give it a week." She pointed at Seth. "No talking about this at school. But I'm telling you, if this keeps up, we're going to have to make it official and I'm going to talk to their mom."

"Okay. I'm sure they'll cool off. Maybe their dad will get back and things will smooth out." When James finished speaking, Erin felt a swell of pride. Her son was wise beyond his years. He seemed to understand that while getting beat on the ice might make them angry, their home situation was at the root of it all. She wondered if losing his own dad had given James an extra degree of empathy.

The waitress arrived with their drinks and they ordered. Erin kept them busy by talking about their plans for the rest of the week while they waited for the food. Once it arrived, the boys dug in. Erin was lost in her thoughts while the boys ate, and the sounds of the diner filled the silence. All was not well with the Murphys, she was sure of it now. But without any kind of real relationship with Claire, how could she offer to help? If what she suspected was right, Claire was going to need someone to lean on. Would the other A-list moms on the PTO step up? Maybe they already had but Erin hadn't spotted it. She should be willing to give them a chance.

"Hey! Got room for one more?" She looked up. Pete stood by their booth. She slid over, pulling her barely-touched dinner with her.

"Of course, since it's you."

"Good to know I make the cut." Pete smiled at the boys. They were still pretty much inhaling their burgers and fries. "Those look good, but I think I'm going with the soup." He looked over his shoulder, nodded to someone and a minute later a cup of black coffee, a glass of water, and the soup of the day were placed in front of him. "Why, thank you. That's some service." He gave the waitress a wink as she hustled back to her next table.

"I think it may be a sign you're here too frequently when you can nod at a random waitress and get your order filled to perfection." Erin gestured at his dinner.

"Nonsense. I'm here three nights a week, just like always."

"Didn't the nutritionist talk to you about how restaurant food has high levels of sodium and that—"

"I'll stop you there, Ms. Bossypants."

Her boys snorted, trying to suppress their laughter.

Pete held up a hand. "I eat my oatmeal in the morning, my rabbit food for lunch, and every other night of the week it's the veggie stuff she assigns me, but I am allowed to eat out."

"Okay, I'll quit bugging you."

"Good. Cause it isn't only you doing it. I hear it from my daughters, from Katie, and even her mother Lauren's gotten on my case."

"Lauren?" Erin grinned. "So, um...have you and Lauren been spending a lot of time together?"

"Who's Lauren?" James looked puzzled.

"You know her as Mrs. Grant, Ms. Katherine's mom. She's been staying with Mr. Mac and Katherine for a few weeks." She turned to Pete. "Actually, it's been longer than that now. I thought she was only visiting?"

"Turns out she likes the place. Extended her visit." Pete said it like he wanted no questions asked and there was no way she was letting him off the hook.

"Is it the place she likes or the company?"

Pete turned to her, slung his arm over the bench seat and fixed her with a patented Pete stare. "To answer your question, the one you're asking without asking, Lauren and I have formed a friendship. But let's leave that aside for another time. I hear that other folks in town have recently formed a friendship. Should we discuss that instead?"

"No." Erin turned away and forked up a tomato out of her dinner and stuffed it in her mouth.

Pete pivoted back to face front and took a sip of his coffee. "That hits the spot. So how are things going, boys?"

"Pretty good. The Harvest Party is tomorrow night though, and Mom says we have to go. Which is lame because it's mostly for high schoolers, and there's dancing." James rolled his eyes.

"Why do they have to go?"

"Because I'm on duty, and it's going to be a late night. Katherine's on as well. Brittany and Jacob would take them, but the baby is teething and giving them fits right now. I don't want to burden the kids."

"I'll take 'em. They can spend the night at my place and in the morning they can come with me to the men's breakfast at church. All you can eat pancakes, boys. Not. To. Be. Missed." Pete tapped the table with each word. One look at Seth and James showed they definitely approved.

"Wouldn't you need a ride, though?"

"Nope. Got the new car this week—drove it here, as a matter of fact. It took a bit to get used to driving again, not to mention no shifting. I haven't had an automatic transmission in . . . actually, I don't remember the last time I bought an automatic. This one's a beaut too."

"Does it have a DVD player?" Seth leaned forward in excitement. "Or a sunroof?"

"It's got a sunroof, sat-nav, heated seats, a third row fit for passengers of your stature, and a tow hitch."

"I thought you were buying a nice, sedate sedan. Didn't you say that was befitting a man in his retirement?"

"With the weather up here?" Pete shook his head. "Got an Explorer. Oh!" He turned back to the boys. "I forgot, it's got satellite radio, but no TV. Don't want too many good things all at once. Makes you spoiled."

"Satellite radio is cool." James seemed to approve.

"Men and their toys." Erin muttered under her breath, which earned an eyebrow lift from Pete. The boys went back to polishing off their fries.

"Boys, now that you're done, hit the bathroom and wash your face and hands, okay?" Erin watched them run off. "Why can't a child keep ketchup on their fries and not on their faces?"

"You and Dan, that new friendship you're forming. How's that going?"

"Listen, I know we probably looked all cozy when you ran into us today at his office, but we're barely even friends. I mean, he's come over and we've chatted, but it's more him helping me and me returning the favor."

"Right." Pete nodded and Erin could tell by his tone he wasn't buying it.

"Okay, so maybe there's something else there, but we are not exploring that. We're two friends helping each other out. He's bringing a crew tomorrow night to help with the clean-up at the party."

"Heard that. Seems you got stuck with the job and he offered to help *you* out." Pete pointed at her in emphasis.

"Yes, it's to help me, but as a friend."

"You've been stuck on clean-up before and he hasn't offered to help."

"That's because we're friends now . . . of a sort." She watched Pete's eyes narrow and had to fight off the impatience that rose. Pete was the soul of kindness, and with her own dad over a thousand miles away in Florida, she appreciated the role Pete took in her life. She just didn't want to talk about what Dan was to her or what he could be. What they had begun felt so fragile that speaking some of her thoughts or feelings aloud might break it like new ice on a pond; one step and the whole thing cracks.

"If that 'sort of friends' turned into sort of something else, no one would be happier than me." Pete set aside his coffee and turned to face her. "It would be something to see you with a good man, someone who would be a real partner to you, someone who would understand you and love you for who you are."

"You're going to make me cry, old man." Erin looked down and away from him, but he lifted his hand and gently pulled her chin up so they were eye to eye.

"I love you like my own daughter. So, in that love, I'm telling you to be careful."

Her eyes widened as he dropped his hand to the table, picked up his coffee and took a long sip.

"Dan is at a crossroad in his life. Everything he has been and everything he thinks he wants to be is meeting head on. His life is gonna change soon, one way or the other. You tie yourself to him, you'll feel that tug. Maybe he ends up back in India, or China, or some other place at another mission, or maybe he puts down roots and builds a family right here."

Erin sat back in the booth and stared ahead. What Pete said made sense. She'd seen that Dan was conflicted, troubled by something. "Does he not want to be the pastor?"

"I'm not sure that's the question to ask."

"Does he really want to go back overseas?"

"That's the one, and I don't know the answer. He doesn't know the answer. I've got a feeling he's been stuck staring down these two roads for a while now. He might say he's waiting for God's call, but I think God's been calling him to something for a while and he hasn't heard. Maybe God's waiting for Dan to listen."

"What should I do?" She expected Pete to give her an esoteric answer, but he didn't.

"Be you. Keep doing what you're doing. He needs someone like you in his life."

Erin embraced the warmth those words gave her. There was nothing she wanted more than to be what Dan needed, to be in his life and have that be a good thing. She knew how life worked though, or at least how it did for her, so she braced for the 'but' and didn't have to wait long.

"But be careful. Who knows which road Dan will choose?" Pete finished off his mug of coffee and set it down. "It may be a bumpy ride."

"Cool, you're not done. Does this mean we can get dessert?" Seth slid into the booth, James behind him.

Erin shook her head.

"Tuck in." Pete nodded at her dinner.

Erin stared down at her plate as the boys began to pepper questions to Pete about his new car, the state of his fridge, and if they'd be allowed to both watch TV and get pizza when they stayed over. Soon, she was lost in her thoughts again, navigating unknown territory.

CHAPTER THIRTEEN

THE WEATHER IN OCTOBER, AT LEAST in the state of Maine, seemed to be a toss-up, Dan reflected as he walked across the short foot-bridge over the brook that ran between the parking lot and Harper's Barn. There were often warm days with blue skies, but by the time Halloween arrived it was almost always cold. Tonight it wasn't too bad. The short walk to the barn where the Harvest Party was just getting started was almost pleasant. Dan looked up to see the stars peeking out amongst the treetops like little lights flickering on and off when the wind swayed the branches. He could hear the music as he approached, and soon enough he saw the light coming through the open barn door. It must be hot inside, but they'd slid the door open a few inches.

He walked in, nodded to the teacher behind the ticket table, and made his way around the crowd. It was early, so the kids were in boy-girl mode, with the girls generally keeping to themselves while the guys raided the refreshment tables. In the center of the room on the parquet dance floor a few brave girls danced to what sounded like pop songs with Christian lyrics. It wasn't his thing, but the kids seemed to love it. There were teachers here and there chatting to each other or watching the kids, smiles somewhere between genial tolerance and genuine mirth on their faces.

He searched for Erin and found her at the punch bowl. She must have been conscripted into service since that wasn't the task she'd been assigned. Her hair was up in a sort of knot that looked complicated but pretty. Her long bangs were pulled to the side and pinned. She was wearing a dress, something he rarely saw her in. It was olive green and to the knee. With it she wore knee-high boots. A smile broke out on his face. "Fancy seeing you here." He watched as her lips quirked in an off-center smile. Trying not to stare at her he added, "You look lovely." Erin blushed and Dan decided that looked good on her as well.

"Nice to see you too." Her eyes swept over him. "I like your suit."

"Thanks." He was pleased she liked it since he'd picked it with her in mind. He'd bought it a few days earlier. He'd put it on at the store and thought it was too modern, too sleek, but the ancient tailor there had offered, "A man like you, probably this is too much, but maybe you need 'too much'." Dan had no idea what that meant, but he had bought it anyway. Tonight, he was glad he did.

"But you're going to get messy." Erin cocked her head to the side.

"Nope. The crew is bringing aprons, manly ones, they've assured me. Gloves too. Not those elbow-high 'June Cleaver' jobs—proper work gloves." She laughed and he nodded in approval.

"Do you watch a lot of *Leave it to Beaver*?"

"No, honestly, I don't think I've seen a single episode, but I've heard enough sermon illustrations using the show that I feel like I've watched it."

"What always got me was Mrs. Cleaver doing her housework in a starched dress, crinoline, and pearls. My step-mother is as lady-like as any human I have ever met, and she did the housework in an old track suit with her hair up in a bandana. Although--" she raised a finger "—she wouldn't answer the door that way. In fact, if we had a caller and either the house or she wasn't presentable, she'd pretend we weren't home."

"Would she make you hide behind the couch?"

"No, but we had to sit very still until they went away."

"Your step-mom sounds hilarious."

"Now that I'm an adult I can see the humor in it, but of course when I was a bratty teenager it was all drama."

"I can't see you being a dramatic teenager."

"I over-reacted with some regularity."

"Like slamming doors, throwing fits?"

"Like getting married the minute I turned eighteen to a man I barely knew, thinking I'd be able to escape my 'oppressive' parents."

"Ah."

"Hey, do you want a bottle of water or something?" She pointed down to the bowl of colorful liquid with floating islands of what looked like ice cream. "You do not have to drink this punch."

His eyes darted up and met hers. They were smiling.

"Seriously, you would not believe what goes into this. It's three jugs of ginger ale, rainbow sherbet, and cranberry juice. I fear for these children's insulin levels. One cup of this and you'll want a nap."

"I like sherbet."

She wrinkled her nose and Dan thought that was possibly the cutest thing he'd ever seen. "Gross."

He picked up one of the cups she'd filled and chugged it. "Ah, chemicals and sugar."

As Erin was laughing at him, one of the PTO leaders approached them. Dan couldn't remember her name. She was dressed to the nines, but had a clipboard in her hand. "Erin?" she asked while her eyes were still on Dan.

"Hi, Claire." Erin's tone was guarded.

"I am so sorry to interrupt . . ." Claire's eyes darted between the two of them. "But Rebecca didn't show, so I have no one refilling the snack tables, and the entire class of junior boys is going through what's out at an alarming pace. Can I get you on the snack tables?"

"Of course."

"Hey, I'm pretty sure I can man the punch bowl and chaperone at the same time. If that would help," Dan said.

"Oh . . . yes. That would be great." Claire scratched something on her list and then turned to Erin again. "Are you all set with clean-up tonight?"

"Yes, Dan was kind enough to get together a group of volunteers to help." Erin nodded to Dan.

"That's great." Claire sighed in what seemed to be genuine relief. "I was worried . . . it's a big job and I said I didn't think one person should be stuck . . . whatever." She waved a hand through the air as if dismissing the thought. "I'm really glad." She reached out to Erin and held her arm for a moment. "Really glad you have help." She looked back to Dan and then smiled. "This is good." Then she sort of shook herself and waved goodbye as she bustled her way back through the crowd.

"'Curiouser and curiouser'," Erin quoted.

"What's up, Alice?" Dan whispered to her.

"Things are not what they seem with Mrs. Murphy." Erin inclined her head towards Claire's retreating form. "I'm thinking I had her all wrong."

"And that's a good thing?"

"Yes." Erin motioned for him to come behind the table, which he did. "Okay, staff and adults get the big bottles of water, kids can choose between the small bottles or punch."

"And if the punch runs out?"

"Armageddon." She said it deadpan and Dan wondered if she meant it, but at the look on his face she laughed. "I'm kidding. Snag a passing kid and tell them to find me. I'll help refill."

"Got it, boss."

With a smile and a wave she left him to it. He watched her leave thinking that nothing about her outfit was particularly alluring, but it left him weak in the knees anyway. His head and his heart were suddenly on the same page, working out the math, trying to decide if it could work, could she be his, should he be hers. That ache to belong to someone was almost enough to take his breath away. But why not? Why not let it loose, let it off the chain and let Erin in? No more 'maybe' about it. Nothing felt as right as having Erin near. It was past time to make it official.

It was almost the last dance, the time when they'd shuffle the kids out the door and home before spending what would probably be at least an hour cleaning up. Erin's feet hurt, which was her own fault. Her boots were super-cute, but what they did to her toes was criminal. She'd give anything to sit down and pull them off so she could rub her feet. Her thoughts immediately jumped to how nice it would be to have someone to go home to, someone who might offer to rub her tired toes. She gave that selfish thought a moment before shoving it aside and assessing what work there was to be done. As she was counting tables with the remnants of food and drink to be cleared, she felt someone approach. A smile broke out on her face as she looked up into Dan's face. "Hey."

"Hey, yourself." He gave her a soft look that made her feel a whole lot less tired.

"All done?"

"Almost." He looked away to the stage area where the DJ, one of the dads of the PTO, was playing the music, then asked. "Dance with me?" When she failed to answer since she was recovering from shock he added, "I mean, these kids. The dancing is horrible. What gives with that?" He nodded over his shoulder at the few kids on the dance floor jumping around. She could feel a blush heating her cheeks.

"You dance?" She blurted out the question without really thinking.

"Mom taught ballroom." He didn't seem to be offended by her question. "She used me as her assistant from the moment I hit five feet tall."

"Your mom was a dance teacher?"

"Yes, among other things. She was a librarian, dance teacher, herbalist..." he trailed off. For a second she saw the conflicted feelings pass over his face.

"She sounds amazing."

"You actually remind me of her in that way—multi-talented." His expression grew serious. "I'm sorry you never got to know her when she was . . . well, herself." He reached out and took her hand. "She would've loved you." Erin wanted to tell him that there was still time, that his mom might recover, and that he shouldn't lose hope, but she knew that, at least in that moment, he didn't want to hear it. A new song started, one that she didn't recognize, but had a slow, sweeping rhythm. He tugged on her hand ever so lightly. "How about this one?"

Erin gave him a nervous look. "Can we dance to this?"

"Let's show them how it's done." Dan pulled her into his arms, a respectful distance still between them, and started leading her around the dance floor. He did know how to dance. She didn't have to do the work, just followed his lead, her steps falling into easy harmony with his. Whatever Dan was thinking of their dance, he was keeping to himself. His eyes hadn't left her face, but they weren't telling his secrets either.

She was memorizing every bit of this moment, how his suit felt under her fingers, how her hand fit with his. She didn't want to step out of place and blow the beauty of this moment. He whirled her around the room and she watched as a smile slowly dawned on his face. She wanted to do whatever it took to keep it there. Until that moment, she hadn't realized how infrequently she'd seen it. Life was too hard on him.

I could make it better. The thought ran through her mind and settled in her heart. She liked that idea; perhaps too much since it was chased by *He could be mine. I could be his.* She shook it off. Dan wasn't offering that, and she certainly wasn't asking. No, they were going to be friends and she was going to help him by being a good friend.

The song ended. Dan let go of her and slowly stepped back, albeit seemingly reluctantly. With a flourish, he bowed to her and she snickered before dropping a graceful courtesy. Applause erupted around them. Erin could tell her cheeks were flaming again as she motioned the kids to be about their business. She could almost feel every eye in the room on them. Dan didn't seem to care. He bowed over her hand and kissed it. A strong rush of tenderness filled her, overwhelming her sense of surprise.

"You do know—" Erin looked up to see Katherine standing next to them, her eyes almost bugging out "—that the editor-in-chief of the Sweet River Lowdown is staring at you two like you're tomorrow's front page." Katherine gaped at them. Erin immediately looked around at Elaine, the school secretary and owner of the Sweet River Lowdown blog, standing against the wall giving them a wave. Dan waved back, but Erin ducked her head, tucking a strand of hair behind her ear, not sure what to do.

"I couldn't care less." Dan smiled down at Erin and then turned to Katherine. "I hope she got pictures. Erin dances as gracefully as she does everything else."

"Well." Katherine began, and then stopped only to start again. "Well. I guess I'll be going."

"You *should* care," Erin told him as she watched Katherine walk way. "Elaine has a habit of blowing things out of proportion. One little dance will be us dating."

"Would that be so bad?" He leaned closer, every word setting off an explosion inside her. "What if it wasn't only one dance? What if it was the

CHRISTA MACDONALD | **111**

start of something instead?" Her mind was blown, mush, incapable of rational thought or replying. She must have looked like a pole-axed cow.

"How about dinner, next?"

"Next?" she managed to ask.

"Here's my plan. Dinner. We swap stories and talk politics and see if I don't completely bore you. Then we see a movie and hit the Moose afterwards and talk about what we did and didn't like, and you can decide if I have terrible taste or not, and if I do, if you can live with it. Then, maybe we spend an afternoon at my fishing spot. That definitely has to wait for the third date. It's not like I show anybody where that is."

Her head cocked to the side and her eyes narrowed. "You're serious."

"Absolutely."

"People are going to talk."

"Let them." He truly didn't seem to care.

Could this be real? She was afraid and excited all at once. Finally she managed to nod her head. "Okay." She drawled the word out. "Dinner I can do."

CHAPTER FOURTEEN

DAN LEANED HIS HEAD BACK AGAINST the concrete wall and closed his eyes. Hospitals all seemed to smell the same—that mix of disinfectant, plastic, and something that he suspected was human desperation. Emergency rooms were the worst. The lobby was filled with people either bored and waiting or agitated and wounded. At the moment, he felt like a mix of both. It had been an hour since he'd received the call that Rob Foster was found unresponsive in his car outside the grocery store, Dylan and Kayla in the back seat. In his wallet had been his ID, a few dollars, and Dan's card. The cops had called him when Rob was brought in.

Dan opened his eyes and checked on Dylan and Kayla. They were each in their own chair, but Kayla was curled into Dylan as if cuddling for warmth. Dylan had moved in his sleep and now his body was turned to hers as well. It was a pathetic sight in every sense of the word. Even though the hours had wrung most emotions out of him, his heart still responded. If Rob was in front of him in that moment, he might have done the man harm. Dan wanted to save them. He'd made the call to child protective services thinking he'd done the right thing, that the state would intervene where he'd failed and keep what was bad from turning worse, but there hadn't been enough time.

Soon the social worker would arrive and Dylan and Kayla would be off to part two of their nightmare. Dan prayed that whatever family they were placed with would have the patience and the compassion to understand what they'd been through and, God-willing, love them. If only Mac and Katherine had started their foster parent classes sooner he could have arranged for them to be placed with people he knew and trusted. He tried to beat back a rush of impatience and anger that filled his heart. God's Providence was perfect, he knew that. For years he'd trusted in it, felt safe in it, but lately . . .

Thoughts he didn't want to acknowledge and anger he had buried began to surface in his mind, telling him this was exactly like being pulled away from his life's work to come care for his mother, only to watch her decline in a living death while his mission in India failed. All for nothing. Dan closed his eyes this time to pray. "Father in heaven, have mercy on me, forgive my doubts and strengthen my faith. Have mercy on these children, on their father so desperately lost, please cover this entire situation with your grace . . ." Dan looked up as someone called his name.

"Here, sorry, I'm right here." He stood and got the attention of the police officer standing in the hallway. "I'm Pastor Connors."

The man walked towards him, his face softening ever so slightly as he looked over the kids. "Social worker says she's going to be here soon. I called her a few minutes ago and gave her an update, so she knows what she's dealing with." His expression was now carefully blank and his words barely above a whisper.

"News?"

The police officer nodded his head at the nurse's station and Dan followed him to it. "Their dad didn't make it." Dan hung his head, his eyes on the floor. The officer went on. "The EMTs said he'd been out too long. The stuff they use to bring them back? It didn't work. He was dead in the ambulance, basically."

Dan's head shot up. "Does that mean those kids were with him like that for hours? Sitting in the car with him passed out?"

"Yeah, it's likely." He looked back over at Dylan and Kayla still huddled together. "I'm hoping that maybe they thought he was sleeping. You know them real well?"

"Kayla might have believed he was asleep, but Dylan . . ." Dan shook his head. "He told me they had no food in the house and their dad was leaving, so they asked to go with him. It was already late by then, but I get the idea the kids were a bit desperate. I'd left food there for them about two weeks ago. I tried to go back, but he didn't answer the door. I think, from the state of things, that might have been the last time they had something decent to eat."

"We think he had the kids in the car with him when he met his dealer, and then he went to the store. Probably meant to get them some food, but decided to shoot up first."

"Why'd he OD, then?" Dan couldn't understand it. "He had the kids right there."

"They don't do it on purpose. Sometimes they get bad stuff, it's too potent, sometimes it's mixed with tranqs, sometimes they mess up and do too much. I doubt it's ever really intentional." The glass doors of the emergency room whooshed open and an older woman rushed in, unlaced sneakers on her feet, her coat barely buttoned and a distinct look of sleepiness on her face. "Okay, this is her." The officer waved, and she made her way to them. As she walked over to them her eyes swept the lobby, seeming to stop on the children for a moment. When she looked back at Dan, he could see it in her eyes. She might have been to dozens of emergency rooms in her career for scenes like this one, but she too could feel the particular sadness here.

With a degree of professional efficiency that seemed to impress even the police officer, Nancy, the social worker, took charge. In short order the officer went home, and Nancy was asking Dan to gently wake the kids and explain to them that their dad was dead and they were now wards of the state. "There is no easy way to do this. Some would even question doing it tonight, but if Dylan is as sharp as you say, it's better to do it now. He needs to know that as his case manager, I'm worth his trust, and I won't get that if I start this off by lying to him. It's great to have you here. Usually I have to do this myself, and no one wants to hear this from a stranger."

"Okay." Dan nodded and took a seat in the chair beside Dylan while Nancy stayed standing. He gently shook the boy's shoulder and Dylan instantly woke, his eyes fearful, then cautious. He took a long look at the social worker and then back at Dan.

"Dad's dead, isn't he?" His little face hardened, and he reached over to Kayla, taking her hand in his. "We stay together." He looked up at Nancy. "We'll be good. I'll make sure of that, but we stay together." Kayla woke, her eyes darting around between them. "It's okay." Dylan turned to face her. "'Member what I said in the car? We'll be okay."

Dan looked up at Nancy and saw the impact Dylan's words had on her. It was only for a moment, but she wasn't any more immune than Dan. "Buddy, this is Nancy. She's here to help you and Kayla. I promise you . . ." He stopped long enough to clear the clog in his throat. "Promise. She is going to take good care of you and your sister. It's going to be okay." Dylan nodded and Dan stood up.

Nancy held out her hand to Kayla. "How about we get something to eat, for starters? It's pretty much breakfast time—well . . ." She looked out at the smudge of gray lighting up the otherwise dark sky. "Bird breakfast time, but that counts." She smiled at Kayla who still looked as scared as she did the moment she opened her eyes, but she did take Nancy's hand. "Do you know that there is a McDonald's right down the road? They have the best breakfasts."

Later, Dan climbed the stairs to his loft and crawled, fully-clothed, into bed. He turned to face the wall, away from the sunlight streaming through the windows opposite the bed. It was noon. Luckily, it was also his day off so he could sleep for a few hours.

"Erin," he said aloud when he remembered that tonight was their first date. After all the night's drama, all the morning's shared sorrow and concern, he was emotionally spent. He prayed that God would restore him. He wanted nothing more than to show up at her front door unencumbered by all his baggage, not only Rob's death and the chaos that went with it but his own struggles. Erin didn't need him ragged and wounded. She deserved better than that.

"It's not that bad." Erin heard Katherine's words, but she couldn't get past the all-powerful cringe she was experiencing while reading the latest edition of the Sweet River Lowdown. She was sitting at her kitchen table with her laptop open in front of her, Katherine reading over her shoulder. Her friend had arrived to babysit for the evening so Erin could go on her very first date with Dan. At eleven and thirteen the boys could stay by themselves just fine, but she couldn't trust them to cook dinner, and she didn't like leaving them too late in the evening. After reading the blog post, Erin wasn't sure Dan would still show.

"'A Dance to Remember'." Erin read off the title, turning to look over her shoulder at Katherine. "Seriously?"

"Shush, I haven't finished reading yet."

"Fine." Erin looked back at the screen and read the rest.

If you weren't at the SRCA Harvest Party fundraiser on Friday night, let the Lowdown fill you in on what you missed. As the party was winding down and the kids heading home, a certain church pastor decided to ask someone to dance. That's right, single ladies, prepare to have your hearts broken. Pastor Dan Connors may be off the market. We witnessed this one first-hand and couldn't be happier to report that his partner for that slow dance was none other than Erin Sullivan. Points to both for their skill on the dance floor. Who knew the pastor could ballroom? And what's even better, a little photographic evidence that these two were meant to be together.

The picture was of them dancing in profile. Erin could plainly see that she was smiling. Dan's face was pointed down to hers, but she couldn't make out his expression.

"There's no denying it. You look good together." Katherine pointed to the pic. Erin didn't want to agree. She hadn't wanted to talk about it either, even with Katherine. It was too new, too precious. She wanted more time to turn over the events of the last few days in her head until they felt real, until she felt they weren't going to disappear in a puff of smoke. Being with Dan was like a dream. That probably wasn't a good thing since dreams have the distinct tendency of ending.

"I'm still going to have a few words with Elaine." Erin clicked the window closed and shut her laptop. "That blog is a menace."

"You didn't think that last summer when Elaine posted all those pics of Stephanie Campbell tripping on the hem of her dress, going right off the dock and into the lake." Katherine stood back as Erin got up to put her computer away in the living room.

"No, well that's what she gets for wearing six-inch spike heels and an evening gown to a boat race."

"It was a regatta."

"Fancy-pants for 'boat race'. Seriously, it was at the lake, not Newport."

Katherine laughed, taking a seat on the couch and pulling her phone out of her pocket. She slid the screen open. "You're bad for laughing at that, and so am I. Stephanie has mellowed a bit since then, though. She said hello to me downtown last week. Didn't even spit on me."

"Don't be a drama queen, she'd never spit on you."

"I was kidding!"

"So the boys should eat pretty much the minute they're done upstairs. They'll try to convince you they can eat in front of the TV; they can't."

"I remember the rules."

"Have you and Mac talked about setting your own house rules now that you're going to be foster parents?"

Katherine looked thoughtful. "To tell you the truth, I hadn't thought about it. I think it's going to depend on the ages of the kids they place with us. We started the classes, but that sort of thing hasn't come up yet. Maybe I'll ask at the next one."

"Good idea."

Katherine thumbed over her phone screen and then looked up in alarm. "You do know it's already six, don't you?"

Erin turned her head to see the clock on the wall so quickly she almost pulled a muscle. "Ouch." She rubbed her neck. "It's okay. I've got a half hour before he gets here." Looking back at Katherine, she tried to remain perfectly calm. "That's fine. Totally fine." Even though it didn't feel fine. Her stomach was in a tight knot.

"You look like you're about to pass out." Katherine shooed a hand at her. "Go get dressed now. You'll probably have a clothing crisis and need to change anyway."

"What? It's like you don't even know me." Erin headed for the stairs, but turned back around. "I had already mentally identified and evaluated ten different outfits by eight this morning. I lined up accessories, shoes, and handbags about an hour later. I do not have 'clothing crises'." She tossed her hair over her shoulder. "Really!" She climbed the stairs listening to Katherine's laughter. It was true, though. She'd never had any trouble putting together outfits or deciding what to wear. Linda had trained her better than that.

Upstairs, she got into her black palazzo trousers and cap-sleeve, silk blouse with the cute bow at the neck. The color of the blouse was what made it date-worthy. It was pearl-white and slightly shimmery. Instead of any elaborate jewelry, she wore a gold bangle on her left wrist and a ring of her own design on her right ring finger. It was one of her early pieces, a strand of gold wire tied in a bow. To complete the theme, she pulled a pair of black heels out of her closet that had a gold bow on the toe. Like most of her wardrobe, she'd gotten these on consignment. It was another of Linda's rules: smart ladies do not pay full price.

She headed to the bathroom to check her hair. With it mostly down—just the front swept up and pinned to the side—she didn't bother with earrings since no one would see them. Her makeup she'd kept soft and subtle. She liked that her whole look was understated, like she wasn't trying too hard, even though she was definitely trying hard. On the way downstairs, she grabbed the purse she had switched her stuff into making sure she had added her lip gloss.

"You look fantastic!" Katherine was still sitting on the couch but had leaned over to see Erin at the foot of the stairs.

"Thanks." Erin opened the closet door and pulled out a short, black trench coat. "This is so weird." She walked back to the living room and tried not to pace. "I haven't been on a date in . . . I can't even do the math." She shifted her coat to hang over the arm holding her purse and then back again. "I don't know what to do with my hands."

A knock sounded on the door and she froze in place. Katherine looked at her and then back at the door before jumping up. "I'm going to get the door while you remember how to breathe." She winked at Erin and opened the door. "Hey, there." She greeted Dan and then stepped inside. "C'mon in."

Erin bobbled her coat and purse one more time before standing still as a statue and smiling for Dan. When he caught sight of her, she watched his eyes dart from her hair to her outfit to her hands, obviously trying not to be rude and give her the usual guy toes-to-hair once-over.

"Hi." It was one little syllable, but the way he said it was enough for the butterflies in her stomach to take off.

"Hey." She waved and then immediately scolded herself for being an idiot for waving at him. "I'll get my coat on and we can go."

Dan lurched forward and took her coat, holding it out for her to put on.

She almost passed out. When she'd slid her arms inside the coat, he settled it on her shoulders, his hand lightly brushing her arm on the way down and then taking her hand. It was a smooth gesture. If he kept this up she'd have to be carried out of the house.

They said their goodbyes to Katherine as Dan walked her out to his car. He opened the door and waited for her to be completely settled in before shutting it. It didn't seem forced with him either; it was as if being a gentleman was an extension of his natural personality, almost ingrained.

When he was in and the car started, she asked where they were headed.

"I made reservations at Seasons."

"Whoa. Nice." Seasons was seriously fine dining. The food was refined, complicated, and expensive. The atmosphere was at the extreme end of posh. Although she was sure her outfit could stretch even to Seasons, she would have probably gone a bit fancier had she known that was his plan. But while she was thinking that, she was also watching him. As he drove, she could easily spot that he was tired, but something else was up. There was a tension in him that she didn't usually feel. "Hey, when you left last night I didn't get a chance to say thank you for the help. Your crew set a record for clean-up. We were done in an hour."

"You're welcome. No need to thank me. They were happy to help."

"It was great because I got to bed at a decent hour. I'm well-rested for once, unlike you." She gave him a quick look. "Am I right about that?"

"Good to know I look as tired as I feel."

"I didn't mean anything bad by it, I—"

"Please don't worry about it." He reached across the center console and took her hand in his, giving it a quick squeeze before letting it go. "I had a . . . pastoral emergency last night."

"Everybody okay?"

"No." He sighed. "In fact, it was about as bad as it could be. Rob Foster OD'd last night. His kids got picked up by the state at the hospital."

"That's . . . I'm so sorry."

"I got a message from the case worker tonight that they're with a family in Palmer now. The family usually does emergency placement for infants and toddlers, but the state is having trouble keeping up with the sheer number of kids entering care because of this opiate epidemic. It's not ideal, but I'll be praying that the parents fall in love with those two kids so they don't have to go through another upheaval. It was a rough night. I was hoping a few hours of sleep would be some kind of cure."

"For fatigue, yes. For the rest of it?" She shook her head.

Dan pulled the car over to the side of the road and turned to her. "Have I completely blown our very first date?"

"No, but how about we pick a place that isn't so . . ."

"High-stakes?"

"Yeah. I'd be fine with anything that doesn't have an audience of our neighbors at the other tables or fast food. I'd even do the Moose."

"We don't have to resort to the Moose. Do you know the pizza place past the resort?"

"Um, know it." Erin admitted. "Every once in a while, Katherine and I call for take-out for lunch at school. Don't tell Maria, but they have the best chicken parmesan I have ever tasted."

"Great." He sounded relieved. "They also have a corner booth that's nice and quiet, and if we're lucky it will be vacant."

"Then let's go."

It was after they'd stuffed themselves silly with Italian food, after they'd taken a walk downtown to work it off, and after they'd stood on her front porch for long enough that the moment became the tiniest bit awkward that she said, "I forgot to ask you."

"What?" He was standing so close she could see the freckles he had on his cheeks and over his nose. They were adorable, and she was tempted to tell him that, for about a second.

"I can't ask you now. I meant to ask you the second you picked me up, but I got distracted."

"Erin, you can ask me anything."

"Okay." She braced. "Did you read the Lowdown?"

His lips curved into a self-satisfied sort of smile. "I did."

Erin immediately hid her face in her hands.

He reached up and pulled them away. "And I copied off the pictures of us dancing. The post was a bit . . . over the top, but I don't mind."

"See, here's the thing. You know that I'm not naturally a shy person, but I had this crush on you, and sometimes I still feel sort of unsteady around you and—"

"Does this help?" He leaned down and she closed her eyes in time to feel his lips touch hers, soft at first and then confidently firm. Erin leaned into him, completely boneless, utterly undone, thinking *I, Erin Marie McKenzie Sullivan, am kissing Dr. Daniel Connors!* How was this even possible?

Dan seemed to have no doubts at all, one hand to the back of her head, his fingers gently threading through her hair. His other hand firmly held her waist, like he wanted her to stay put. Erin wasn't going anywhere. Her hands were on his shoulders, and she was holding on for what was the best kiss of her life. He was taking his time, responding when she responded, and eventually ending with a soft touch of his lips, his forehead resting on hers.

She was a bit breathless. "That's much better. We should do that more often, and I think I would be less uneven."

Dan was chuckling. "That was pretty nice, and I think repetition is a good idea, but we may want to save it for a night Katherine isn't standing at the front windows watching."

"Typical." Erin rolled her eyes.

Dan's mouth moved to her cheek, and she felt his lips smile before he placed a kiss there and mumbled, "Friday then? Pick you up at six?"

"Okay." It was more a sigh than a word. He pulled away and walked backwards down her steps.

"Goodnight," he called softly. She opened her door and stepped inside, but looked back at him as she shut it. He was still walking backwards, down the path. When he hit the sidewalk he continued backwards towards his car, raising a hand to wave as she shut the front door, giggling at him.

"Did you just giggle?" Katherine snorted out a laugh from her spot on the couch. "I guess your night went well?"

"Shut it." Erin picked up a pillow from the chair and chucked it at her.

CHAPTER FIFTEEN

"HOW BAD IS IT?" DAN WATCHED his mother draw in a breath. It looked like a struggle. The machines around her were lit up like a Christmas tree, but nothing about their lights and sounds made sense to him. The doctor finished tapping something into the tablet she carried and glanced up at him.

"We'll know more after the tests come back, Dr. Connors."

"You can call me Dan." He had told the staff this about a dozen times, but they always defaulted to protocol and called him what the next of kin box stated on the chart. "Do we know what this is?"

"We don't, which is why the tests are so crucial. We should know by tomorrow at the latest."

"Guesses?" He wanted something to go on.

The doctor sighed. "Pneumonia is what we're worried about, but it could be a simple virus, so I'm reluctant to make any guesses."

"Pneumonia sounds pretty serious."

"It is, Dan. In her condition it could be fatal."

Dan closed his eyes and absorbed that word, 'fatal.' He was not prepared. It didn't matter that he'd already spent three years knowing she might never recover; he wasn't ready. He might never be ready.

"Let us do the worrying. You do the praying." The doctor gave him a small smile and Dan tried not to resent words that sounded so flippant to him, but he knew she meant to be comforting. He'd been at enough bedsides and gravesides to know there were few words that helped truly alleviate the kind of clawing unease and concern he was now feeling. It followed him out of the hospital and back to his office. He sat at his desk, ignoring the blinking voicemail light on his desk phone, trying to order his thoughts enough to pray.

He heard his text sound and reached into his pocket to pull out his cell. Erin had texted a picture to him. He opened it and stared at it for a full minute with no idea what it was. 'What is this?' he sent back. She sent him another pic, a better one, and now he could tell he was looking at a bug of some sort, so he sent 'I'm not an entomologist, but if that's life-size, I'd run.' She sent back a few laughing emojis and then 'Not life-size, but is on my workbench. It's gross.'

'Squash it.' He sent back.

'I do not kill bugs.'

'Do you need me to come kill it for you?'

'That would be a level-up in our relationship. Are you ready for bug-killing duties?' That was interesting. He wasn't sure what level bug-killing was, but he was fine with leveling up.

'Be there in five.'

Erin almost dropped her phone in surprise. She'd been kidding. If she needed to kill a bug, she would just do it. Sure, it would have been nice for Dan to be there to kill a bug for her, but she hadn't planned on summoning him. First, she was yet again in her yoga pants and a tee, this time because she was working on her jewelry in her basement workshop. James was at his friend Nathan's house supposedly working on a group project for school, but Erin suspected he was playing Overwatch since a new character had come out that week. Seth was doing his homework. The house had been quiet, and she hadn't felt inspired, so when the bug crawled onto her bench she'd decided to text it to Dan.

Deciding there was nothing for it, she climbed the stairs and quickly checked her appearance in the hall mirror. At least she still had her makeup from earlier in the day in place. Her hair was up in a knot on the top of her head, and it didn't matter what it looked like, since she could hear someone walking up to her door. She opened it before he could knock. "Hey." She pulled the door wide so he could step in. He was wearing jeans and what looked like a hand-knitted sweater. In casual clothes, he always seemed more earthy, less the untouchable pastor. It left her a bit tongue-tied.

"I'm here for the bug." He smiled.

Her lips curled upwards in response. "Be prepared. It's scary."

"I can handle it."

She led him downstairs to her workbench and looked until she found the spot it had crawled to. "Right there." She pointed to it and gasped when Dan picked it up with his bare fingers, crushed it, and after looking around a second, dropped it in the trashcan she kept in the corner. "Eww." She laughed as she said it.

"You should see the bugs in India. That thing was a joke."

"I don't doubt it." She took one of the hand wipes she kept on her bench and passed it to him. "That was very manly, but very gross."

He took it and cleaned his hands while he seemed to examine the work area. "Is this how you make your jewelry?"

"Yup. This is where the magic happens." She took a seat on her stool and handed him the pair of earrings she'd finished before staring off into space and getting bored. They were simple silver drop earrings with bright, blue glass beads. He held them up to the light.

"Wow. And you sell everything you make?"

"Most of it. Sometimes I make things as gifts, or there's a few things I keep for myself. I have to sell at least thirty percent of what I make to break even after paying for the space to sell, like a table at a craft fair. The rest is profit. It makes a nice Christmas savings account. Gotta buy all that boy swag."

Dan smiled at her use of slang. "Action figures and the like?"

"Yes. Although the older they get the higher the price tags go. Now it's gaming systems, tablets, laptops. I've held off so far, but James is going to need either a tablet or a Chromebook for school next year, and Seth is right behind him."

"So, a bit more expensive than action figures." Dan handed her back the earrings. "Doesn't the school have a supply they hand out?"

"Yes, but they're first come, first served and . . ." She began to wish she hadn't gotten into it. Usually she wasn't upfront with her financial challenges. She'd end up bracing for the eventual offer of assistance of some sort. Not that it was a bad thing for a friend wanting to help, but it got a little old having to always tell people she was fine, and she'd ask if she really needed it. There were plenty of times she'd had to swallow her pride and do exactly that. "If you're a kid who is always the one in class without the newest, shiniest, coolest stuff, it can put a wee little chip right there." She pointed to her shoulder. "The boys have had to grow up with a lot of hand-me-downs. I really hate to do that with the school stuff, too." She shrugged. "So, I sell pretty stuff to buy cool stuff."

"I . . ." Dan began, but he didn't finish, instead he pulled her up to him and kissed her, hard, before letting her go. "You are a great mom." The way he said it seemed intense. "Don't let anyone make you feel bad for working so hard to raise your children. There shouldn't be any chips on your shoulders."

"Okay." She was blinking up at him, not sure where all that feeling was coming from.

"It's like that stupid thing with the PTO. You don't get half the credit you deserve, Erin. I had no idea you had this entire side business to support your family. That's pretty impressive."

"Well, it's not really a business, and you'd be surprised how many moms have to work two jobs, but—"

He reached out and took her hand. "Nope. No need to clarify or diminish. You're pretty great, Erin Sullivan."

"Okay." She took a long look at him, not letting herself be distracted by how nice it felt to be close to him, to have his fingers wrapped around hers. "And now we're going to talk about what happened today." She watched as his face fell. "Dan, what's wrong?"

"Is that perception of yours a 'mom super-power'?"

"Maybe? But the only adult it seems to work on is you." Her eyes widened as she realized what that sounded like, but, instead of freaking out about revealing the depth of her feeling for him, she watched his reaction. He closed his eyes, and his shoulders slumped a little like he'd been holding something back and had suddenly let go. "Hey." She shifted places with him and forced him to sit on the stool. Taking his chin in her hand she lifted his eyes to hers. "Whatever it is, I can help."

"My mom . . . she's struggling with some kind of virus or infection. They're doing tests, but . . ."

"Oh, Dan." She didn't say anymore. His face said it was serious, and what could she say to that? Any infection for a person in Mrs. Connors' condition could be serious. Erin wrapped her arms around him and held him close. "Do you want me to pray with you?" She felt his answering nod, so she did.

"Thank you." Dan pulled out of her arms and rubbed at his face when they'd finished. "I was sitting in my office trying to pray when I got your text. God knew what I needed." His lips twitched like he was trying to smile. "I better hit the road, though. I've got a sermon to finish, and more emails than I know what to do with."

"Ah, one of those will be from me."

"Basketball?"

"Yup. I found a volunteer for the JV squad if you really want to take a break this year." She hoped he would. As much as she loved having him as a coach, she wanted to make things easier on him. "Believe it or not, it's the new game warden, Alex Moretti. He played ball all through high school and college. Pete suggested him."

"I hate to give it up, but if this guy is available I probably should do it."

"It's settled then. You get a break this year, and we get to try this new guy out."

"You'll tell me if something changes, though?"

"Yes." She laughed a little. "We are sort of seeing each other so . . ."

He rolled his eyes. "You know what I mean."

"I do, but I also like teasing you."

"I'm glad." His expression became serious. "I'm glad we're past all that . . . I mean I'm glad you're 'you' now and not shy around me." He got up. "I should get going." Together they headed for the stairs. When they hit the top he swiveled toward her. "Hey. Friday. You free for a movie?"

"I think I could be." Erin wondered if they were moving too fast, but couldn't bring herself to say no.

"Right, and we can go to the Moose afterwards and you can let me know what you think about my taste in movies."

"Works for me." They were standing at her front door, and he seemed to be waiting for something. "What is it?"

"I was doing the math on kissing you when there is a distinct possibility one or more of your children might be watching."

"Hmm…. Fair point. I'd rather the boys didn't . . . Not that I don't want to tell them—"

"No, I get that. I agree." He dropped his voice to a whisper and opened the door. "Friday—six."

Dan walked home feeling a lot better than when he'd headed out. Being with Erin was exactly what he needed. She was a quixotic mix of strength, humor, heart, and a womanly characteristic he couldn't even define, but knew he liked. It was like she was soft inside, but only for him. It was something she hadn't shown the world. His head wanted him to sit down and quietly examine every detail, turn it over again and again until he was certain of what he'd found, but his heart told him to shut up and enjoy it. For tonight at least, that's what he planned to do. He felt light, like someone had taken a weight off his shoulders that he hadn't known he was carrying. He could fly if he wanted to. Laughing to himself he headed up the path to the barn.

"Sounds like you had a good night."

He stopped dead in his tracks. He knew that voice. Out of the shadows the small porch to the side door created, stepped a tall, slender woman. He couldn't quite see her face, but the voice and the form could only be one person. "Beth?"

"So you do remember me." She came forward with her arms out and enveloped him in a hug. He patted her on the back trying to figure out why she was there, and then it hit him. Beth had contacted him weeks ago about coming up to speak at Calvary while she was fundraising in Maine for her new mission. It was about the size of the one he'd run in India so she needed substantial support. She'd asked for his help in finding a place to stay and setting up presentations. He'd put her in touch with Rachel, Calvary's secretary and then with so much going on, he'd completely forgotten she was coming.

Dan let her go and took a step back. "I never forget old friends. I knew you were coming up, but I guess I lost track of when."

"Oh, no that's fine. I arranged everything with Rachel. I didn't tell her until yesterday that I was coming up for sure. So many organizations waited until the last moment to confirm. I've got the next three weeks scheduled with events from Kittery to Caribou. I hope you have some free time in your schedule, because I could really use some help."

"I should be able to move some stuff around."

"Great. And Rachel arranged for my housing as well. I guess you have a furlough apartment for ministry peeps in your parsonage so she made sure it was free, and now, here I am." She gave him a bright smile. "Y'know, I called you about five times this week."

"I haven't checked my voicemails. Crazy busy this week. Sorry about that."

She waved a hand as if to dismiss his apology. "Hey, I know how it is. I've been flat-out for the better part of a year now."

"Right, I'm looking forward to hearing the details. You're going to Africa, right? Lodestone Missions?"

"See, you do pay attention." She smacked his arm playfully. "I've got another six months left state-side to get more support, and then I'll be heading to Mozambique." She reached behind her and picked up the bag she'd left on his step. "Right now I need to find my apartment, though, because I am exhausted. It's a long drive up here."

"Sure. I can walk you over."

The walk was a short one, since the parsonage was right next to the church. When they arrived, Dan waited while Beth dug through her purse for the key that Rachel had sent her. He looked down at her. "It's wild seeing you here."

"It's always strange being home." She paused as if choosing her words carefully. "I know you've been back for a few years now, but you must still feel a bit out of place, a stranger in a *familiar* land?"

Dan nodded his agreement.

"I feel most at home when I'm not actually home. It's good to be with someone who gets it." Beth gave him a warm smile.

"Well . . ." He wasn't sure what to say. "I guess we'll have the chance to catch up tomorrow."

"Definitely." She leaned in and kissed his cheek before opening the apartment door and heading inside. "Good night." She shut the door and Dan turned away, heading home. He was feeling slightly off-balance. He didn't love surprises, but thinking ahead to the next few weeks he could probably make time to give her whatever help she needed. Soon the fatigue he'd felt earlier in the day returned with a vengeance. Once he was home, he headed up to the loft and to bed hoping a good night's sleep would empty his head.

CHAPTER SIXTEEN

ERIN PUT HER CELL ON THE table and got up to check on the boys in the backyard. James was running, twisting backwards to catch the ball her son-in-law Jake was preparing to throw. Jake waited a hair too long, though. Seth tackled him from behind. Jake had about two feet on the kid, but he went down to a knee anyway. Seth knocked the ball out of his hand and strutted around the yard doing some end-zone dance. Football was one of the common languages of men. Even if they didn't like the sport, they'd still toss the ball around, still have an opinion on the best teams. Erin was a baseball fan, football she could take or leave.

Walking away from the window she picked up her cell to check for a text, a call, an email . . . since he was now officially a half-hour late, she'd accept a smoke signal if he sent it. Nothing. He hadn't returned her text or answered when she called. She tried to assume the best, maybe something had come up, but why wouldn't he have called? What was making it worse was that she hadn't heard from him since the night he'd come over and squashed the bug. Granted, that was only three days ago, but was that normal for him? There was no way to know. They were so new. Despite her best efforts to remain positive, a little voice in her head kept whispering this was the brush off. He was standing her up, and tomorrow he'd email or text with an excuse and there would be no second date in the end.

Was she too real with him? Did she overshare? Was she clingy? "Oh, shut up!" She'd rather know one way or the other than sit there all night and worry about it. She pulled open the back door and called out to the guys. "Hey, I'm out of here. Be good for Jake. I'll be back soon."

"Have a great time, Erin. Don't worry about a thing." Jake tossed the ball to Seth and gave her a half salute, half wave, and she managed to smile. She'd grown to love him. She still didn't appreciate the way he'd become her son-in-law, but the way he loved and cared for Brittany, the baby, and his nephews had more than made up for it.

"'Bye!" The boys called out to her as she shut the door.

With her stomach in a knot, she pulled on her coat, belted it tight, and headed out the door. "Assume the best." The advice she was giving herself sounded good, but for someone who spent the better part of her life bracing for the next hit, it was tough to follow. "He probably has a really good reason for being late. Give him a chance." This advice also fell flat. The walk from her house to Dan's place was only about five minutes. Soon enough she turned the corner onto his street and felt a rush of relief. His car was in his driveway, and she could see the lights on in his office. He was home. She knew he was working right up until their date, so he probably got lost in some tricky passage of scripture and didn't realize the time. She could see him doing that. That made total sense. Her heart felt about ten times lighter the closer she got. She'd been stupid, letting herself believe that this was the other shoe finally dropping, the dream ending.

When she reached his front walk she spotted him through the large, paned window that had replaced the original barn door. He was sitting behind his desk, his head thrown back, laughing. Her feet froze in place as her eyes took in what she was seeing. Dan was not alone. Sitting in one of the wooden chairs in front of his desk was a woman . . . a pretty woman . . . a young woman. Erin didn't recognize her from church or around town. She had thick brown hair that had a slight wave. It looked like she was telling him a story, her hands waving animatedly. Erin had never seen him laugh like that.

A wave of anxiety hit her, and it took all her strength not to turn and run. There had to be an explanation. Dan was not the kind of man to stand her up and suddenly start dating someone else. This woman could be a long-lost cousin--although he said he didn't have any. Maybe she was someone his mom knew, someone that came by to cheer him up, and he'd lost track of time. The only way she'd know anything was if she could get her feet to move the rest of her to the door. Taking a deep breath, she let it out slowly, forcing her heart to stop racing. Erin walked the rest of the way to the door and knocked.

The door opened, and Erin's heart fell as the expression on Dan's face turned from surprise to what looked like disappointment. "Erin." He definitely did not look happy to see her. "What's up?" He didn't sound upset, but he didn't sound glad either. He also didn't sound like he knew he was standing her up.

"It's Friday." She said it as quietly as she could to avoid his companion overhearing them. "Remember?"

He still looked clueless.

"We had a date?" She watched as it dawned on him.

"I thought that was tomorrow. I must have mixed up the days. Something came up this week and I . . ." He looked back inside at the woman sitting at his desk, her face turned towards them.

Erin felt a pang in her heart when she got a good look at her. She was lovely, and she looked like what Erin imagined was his type—petite, delicate, sweet.

Dan spotted her staring at his friend, and instead of introducing her, he walked out onto the stoop with her and shut the door behind him. "I can't believe I forgot. I'm so sorry." He stepped closer, his words gentle.

"No worries." Erin backed up a step. "It's totally fine. You're super busy. It's no wonder you forgot. I mean, it's not like it's a big deal. It was movies and the Moose." She laughed awkwardly. "Listen, I'll go and you can get back to . . ." She waved in the direction of his office and the woman waiting for him to return.

"Wait—I mean." He turned around to the shut door and then back to her. "Are you sure it's okay?"

"Of course!" She took another step away. "Why wouldn't it be? You've got a guest and I'm . . ." *Going to cry if I don't get out of here.* She spun on her heel and walked down his path. "See you later." She spoke over her shoulder, adding a wave.

"Hey, rain-check?" he called after her.

She made a kind of non-committal sound because it felt like her heart was in her throat. She double-timed it back up the street and out of his sight. She was a block in the opposite direction before she stopped and took a deep breath. It hitched halfway through, but she refused to stand in the middle of downtown Sweet River and sob. Erin Sullivan did not cry in public. Linda would hear of it, march up from Florida, and blister her ears if she did. Right then she wanted nothing more than to call her step-mom and bawl. Linda had never been the 'tell me all about it' type of mom, but she'd understand what Erin was feeling right now.

Calling Linda was out. Calling her mom was out too since she was on the road somewhere in her RV. Even calling Katherine was out since she and Mac were busy. Instead she walked home. Once she got to the house she knew she couldn't face going inside and explaining why her date lasted five minutes. Instead she took her car keys out of her purse, and got into her car. She started it up and drove down the interstate to the shopping plaza. There she browsed, pretending that she hadn't been stood up, that Dan hadn't forgotten her because of the pretty woman with the kind eyes in his office right now.

The night had been a disaster of epic proportions, and it fed into Erin's insecurities. Part of her wanted to text Dan and ask him who that was sitting in his office and how he could forget their date? The rest of her wanted to block his number and forget he existed. Neither was the right response, so she chose to do nothing. He'd eventually contact her with an explanation, or, if he didn't, she'd have one all the same.

CHAPTER SEVENTEEN

DAN STOOD BEHIND THE PULPIT, HIS expression warm and welcoming as he looked out over his congregation. "With us today is Beth Russell, a program director for Lodestone Missions. You may have heard me talk to you about them before. They have programs throughout Africa." The congregation craned their necks to where Dan was gesturing in the audience. Beth stood and waved. Dan went on. "She's going to be giving a presentation on the organization's efforts and the new program they have planned for Mozambique. Ms. Russell will be staying with us for three weeks so, for those that can't attend this evening, we'll have further opportunities during her visit. Please feel free to seek her out if you have any questions or an interest in her work. Next Sunday we'll be having our semi-annual International Missions luncheon. Come try the cuisines of many nations, and stay to hear how Christ is working in them.

"The hospitality committee would like me to remind those with culinary talents that there is a signup sheet in the vestry if you'd like to provide a dish. Never fear, I promise to go nowhere near it." This got a laugh, as his inability to cook was well-known. "Okay, folks, let's sing hymn number 146: 'Great is Thy Faithfulness'. Standing as we sing." The congregation got to their feet as the pianist began to play. Dan stepped back a bit from the mic to avoid his amplified voice drowning out the rest. Instead, he relished the sanctified sound of many voices raised in praise as it washed over him. He closed his eyes, knowing the words by heart, and sang in concert with them, worshiping the God that was his all.

"You looked so natural up there. Do you feel that way?"

Dan looked up to where Beth was standing at the vestry windows watching the kids play a pick-up game of soccer on the town green. He was sitting at the small conference table waiting for Rachel to meet with them and discuss the upcoming schedule of events. Rachel was a bit late, but that was hardly out of the ordinary. Coffee hour was the time everyone at church caught up with each other and Rachel was a social soul. Dan had been appreciating the silence when Beth had broken it.

"I'm not sure I'd say I feel natural, but I feel comfortable. My first few weeks were rocky, but Calvary is a patient church. They gave me time to find my way. Half the battle is in your head, anyway. If you get up there thinking your sermon is garbage and they're going to hate it, you're setting yourself up for a bad time even if you're MacArthur."

Beth laughed. "That's how I feel about these fundraising events I'm facing. You remember those." She had turned around to face him. Like most of the time they'd spent together this week, Beth was playing 'do you remember'. They had a shared history, one he didn't have with anyone else. They'd met in seminary, ended up at the same language school, and worked for the same mission until Dan had left it to run his own. He hadn't kept in touch with many people from college or seminary. Beth had done the heavy lifting in their friendship. She was a faithful correspondent, sending emails from wherever she was working.

Having her in Sweet River was great, but it was reminding him of what he'd lost. Beth was on fire about her new project, confident in her calling. Dan was confident in nothing. There were times he suspected she saw his struggle and was either resigned not to ask him about it, or was biding her time. And how would he answer her questions? He felt like he was wandering in a spiritual desert entirely alone, that no one could understand what he was going through. But the truth was Beth was one person who might. He couldn't broach the topic, though. She was too happy with her new mission. He didn't want to bring her down. What he wanted to do was talk to Erin. In person. He wasn't going to call or text her and risk another misunderstanding. Between visits to his mom, dealing with the everyday kind of crises his parishioners had, and working with Beth, he hadn't been able to find a time to track her down. He'd tried at the school twice, but she'd either just left for the day or was in a meeting. Every time he thought of dropping by her house it was either too early or too late. The longer he waited, the more he worried she'd misinterpret his actions.

He stretched in his seat to loosen the tightness in his shoulders. It had been another bad night for his mom, and he'd spent most of it sitting at her bedside before the nurses kicked him out.

"Oh, I remember fundraising. Those were the days. Now I wait for the quiet criticisms or the phone call from an elder with suggestions for next week."

"Do your parishioners do that?"

"Not so much anymore. I think my sermons have gotten better. I only get calls about what I'm not doing lately and they're all from the elders."

"Like what?"

"Signing my new contract."

Her eyebrows lifted in surprise. "Sounds serious."

"They're looking for a five-year commitment."

"And you're not sure." She sat down in the chair next to him.

"My mom's health is not great. You probably guessed that from me spending most of last night at the hospital. Even before this crisis it wasn't good. The stroke caused significant damage; she has dementia, so when I am there she doesn't know it's me. It's made it hard to justify the point in staying other than the guilt I'll feel for leaving her and that's almost . . . selfish. Once this crisis passes, and the doctors now say they think it will, should I stay or should I go? Will it matter if I only come to see her every six months instead of every other day? Would she even know the difference? Am I being selfish in wanting to leave? God has not weighed in on this one."

"Oh, Dan." She took his hand in hers, giving it a squeeze. The gesture was kind, but unexpected. Beth wasn't very physically demonstrative, and they'd never had that kind of friendship. She seemed to realize this as she let his hand go and sat back. "I'm sorry you're in this position. Sorry for you, and if I'm honest, sorry for me. I was kind of hoping to talk you into coming to Mozambique with me."

He was stunned into silence for a moment. "To work for Lodestone?"

"Yes, I need a co-director. We're growing fast, and I can't handle the work load on my own."

"Why not hire an assistant?"

"I have an admin, but what I need is a partner. I need someone with experience in foreign missions, someone who's run a program before and is someone I can trust. Some of the people I thought might be a good fit turned out to be interested in taking over more than working together. I don't want to end up in some big conflict any time there's a decision to be made. I know you and I see eye to eye on a lot." Her gaze was fond as it settled on him, her expression warm. "We went through some pretty extreme situations, and I know we work well together."

The door at the far end of the room opened and Rachel rushed in, stopping abruptly when she saw them. Dan watched her eyes flit back and forth between them and saw her do the mental math, coming to the wrong conclusion. "So sorry for interrupting."

"You're not interrupting." Dan shifted away from Beth a bit, and she withdrew her hand.

"Okay, I'll get my notebook out if we're all ready to start?" Rachel had a bright smile for Beth as she took a pencil out and they began their meeting. The two of them seemed to have formed a fast friendship. That was a good thing, but Dan would have to be extra careful with Beth's tendency to show him friendly affection. Rachel was a good person, but could be a bit of a gossip. The last thing he needed was for her to get the wrong idea about his relationship with Beth and then start sharing it with others.

ERIN CLOSED HER EYES AND LET the music play, listening until she could feel the itch to move. Opening her eyes, she began to sway and then let her body take over entirely, moving with the sound. She spun in a series of *pirouettes* before launching into a jump, loving the feel of gravity trying to hold her down. She moved quickly, her steps exaggerated in the open space. Dancing in the gym on a Sunday afternoon meant guaranteed privacy and the ability to use the whole space. She could spin from one end to the next, crank the music high, risk looking like a fool if she got too ambitious and fell. This was what she needed, the ultimate in stress relief, the best way to rid her head of the Dan drama. More than once in recent days, Pete's words of caution rose up and nagged at her. She hadn't been cautious; she'd jumped right in with both feet. Now her heart was a mess, and she had only herself to blame. There was nothing she could do about her heart, but at least she could clear her head.

There was a noise in the background that she ignored for a few minutes. Slowly it pushed its way past the music and started nagging at her. Finally she had to stop. She listened carefully, but between her own labored breathing and the music she couldn't make it out. She had to head over to the bleachers and turn off the portable speakers connected to her phone. When she did, she got a good look out the windows of the gym to where the sound was coming from. Down on the playground a group of boys were circled around something, and they were cheering.

"Oh, no, you don't." Grabbing her phone and disconnecting it from the speakers, she bolted out of the gym and sprinted down the lawn to the crowd. There was only one reason a group of boys would be on school property after hours, huddled in a circle and cheering.

"Hey!" She shouted as she reached them, but only the boys at the back heard her. They were smart enough to run for it. She had to pull a few away that she recognized as middle-schoolers before she got to the combatants trading punches in the center. They'd fallen on the ground and were beating the stuffing out of each other in the dirt.

"James!" She reached down and grabbed his collar and his belt and hauled for all she was worth. Once she had him up and on his feet she saw Evan Murphy, bloodied and bruised, lying on the ground and checking his front teeth.

"Somebody better have some answers for me right now or you are all suspended."

"What?" Evan's face had gone white.

"You are fighting on school property. What did you think would happen?"

"It's the weekend." James offered and Erin, still clutching his collar, gave him a shake.

"Do you think the school magically disappears on the weekend? This . . .!" She pointed to the ground. ". . . is school property! You're technically trespassing. You were definitely fighting. I . . ." She looked skyward, praying for God to check her anger before this got out of hand. "James." She searched the crowd and spotted her other son. "Seth. Up to the gym, right now. Not one word out of either of you until I get there." She let go of James's collar and the two boys slunk away, her tone enough to keep them from risking even one word of defense. She scanned the crowd again and spotted Evan's brother Nate.

"Don't move." She pointed a finger at him. "The rest of you. This is your first and only warning. I see any of you here again, it's a demerit and a formal letter home. Do you understand?" The remaining boys nodded in agreement. "Go home."

"Evan and Nate, come here." The boys shuffled forward looking mutinous, but they obeyed. "I don't want to know who started it or why. I want to know it's never going to happen again." She gave them both a long look, one they didn't back down from. "How did you get here today?"

"Mom brought us to church." Evan mumbled his answer from a rapidly swelling lip. Erin fought off a sympathetic wince. He'd bought that fat lip.

"Is she still here?"

"No. We wanted to stay, so she said we could catch the shuttle bus back."

Erin pulled out her phone and called Claire, but got no answer. She debated leaving a message, but decided she'd sort out what happened and then take them home. "Okay, well, I'll be taking you home. Come up to the gym." She led the boys up the hill and into the gym. There James and Seth were sitting on a riser of the bleachers looking miserable. James, she noted, didn't have a mark on him other than bruised knuckles. She wasn't sure what to make of that. "All right. I'd like to hear what went on between you all that ended up in a fight."

"Evan said all this . . . stuff about you and then about Brittany. It was nasty." Seth looked between James and a noticeably pale Evan. Erin guessed it was nasty stuff since Seth wasn't willing to use the words.

"Okay. Who threw the first punch?"

"It was James." Evan pointed at her son who was looking defiant.

"James." She said his name softly.

"No one talks about my family like that. I'm not about to let somebody run their mouth about us." He raised his chin. "I don't care if I get expelled."

Erin realized that she should have been paying better attention to James's protective streak. She should have been guiding him to use the natural desire to protect his family in ways that didn't involve his fists. It was time to give him a reality check. "Expelled might be only one of the consequences, James. Hitting someone is called 'battery', and is very serious. If the circumstances were different, if I hadn't caught the both of you fighting, you might be talking to the police instead of me." She caught the barest of flinches from him. "You and Seth need to go home and stay there until I get back. We're not done."

"Evan and Nate, wait right here while I lock up." She hit the lights, locked the door, and then had the boys follow her to the front. She watched her sons walking to their house and then locked the front doors of the gym and took the Murphy boys to her car.

"Into the Explorer, boys." She watched as Nate's lip slightly curled. She knew her car was hideous with its Bondo-covered holes and rust spots. "Any commentary you might be tempted to make can probably wait until you aren't in the most trouble you've been in since you started at SRCA." Nate's lip quit curling, and the boys climbed in. Erin pulled out of the parking lot knowing that James would likely be expelled since he started it, and she wouldn't be far behind.

CHAPTER EIGHTEEN

ERIN TOOK A DEEP BREATH AS she knocked on the door. She was still holding back an almighty tide of anger and, if she didn't calm down, it would be washing right over Claire Murphy in about ten seconds. There was no answer, so she knocked again, this time closer to pounding. She could hear shuffling behind the door, as if someone was moving stuff aside, before it was opened the smallest amount and a sliver of Claire appeared.

"Erin, this is a surprise." Claire took one look at Evan's face and threw the door open wide. She rushed out onto the step with them, almost knocking Erin aside. "What have you done?" That was a shocker. Erin had expected her to fawn over Evan and ask what had happened. Instead she started shouting. "You've been fighting again. What have I said? Didn't I tell you what was going to happen if you kept at it?" Evan tried to defend himself, but she talked right over him. "I don't want to hear it anymore. Do you know what this means?"

Evan shook his head, but Nate seemed to understand. "He's going to be expelled."

"Public school. That's what this means. I can't afford to send you anywhere at this point. I've already paid. We'll lose that money, and for what?"

"Mom, you don't underst—"

"Don't even start with me," Claire began, but Erin heard the waver in her voice and knew what was coming next. "The amount that *you* don't understand about what's going on . . ." Claire lowered her face into her hands and burst into tears.

"Let's go, guys, inside." Erin all but shoved the boys past Claire and into the house, and then she gently guided a weeping Claire in behind them. "Go to your room while your mom and I talk. Stay upstairs until you're called down, okay?" Miraculously the boys nodded and ran upstairs.

"Claire, let's sit . . ." Erin looked around and took in the state of the place for the first time. Claire's house was a disaster. Her front entry room, which should have been a formal hall like the rest of the townhomes in the development, was instead a wasteland of piled coats, boots, backpacks, hockey equipment, loose grocery bags, piles of mail, and stacks of papers on a console table that looked ready to collapse under the weight. Claire walked towards the back of the house and Erin followed. They passed the great room, which held a large sectional sofa covered in piles of clothes, and a huge entertainment center that was curiously empty.

Erin followed Claire into the open kitchen. A pile of dishes in the sink resembled the Leaning Tower of Pisa, threatening to topple at any second, held up by some miracle of gravity. Otherwise it was bare, no snacks on the counter, no fruit bowl, no cereal boxes. Considering the state of the rest of the house, an almost empty kitchen seemed a red flag.

"Have a seat." Claire gestured to one of the bar stools at the kitchen island. Erin parked herself there, her mind spinning. Every assumption she had made about Claire was cracking like glass. Claire leaned on the kitchen counter opposite the island, a hollow but defiant look on her face. "So, go ahead." Her chin raised ever so slightly. She was waiting for Erin to let loose, but Erin's anger was gone, chased out by the signs of chaos all around her. Something was very wrong in the Murphy's world.

"What's going on, Claire?" Her words were soft, and she hoped they sounded sincere.

"What does it look like?" Claire laughed as she gestured at the mess all around. "I'm the worst mother ever, obviously."

"I don't think that's what's going on. Did something happen? Are you okay?"

"Don't pretend that you give the slightest—"

"Wait." Erin held up her hand. "Don't finish that, because I do care about you and your family. I really do. I'm angry that James and Evan were fighting, but that doesn't mean I can't see that something is wrong, and I want to help."

"Why?"

"Because I know what it's like to need help and not have it." Erin tried to be careful with what she said next. "I think, maybe, when you said earlier this year that Paul was away a lot on business, maybe you meant that he wasn't coming back?" She watched as Claire winced and it answered her question. "How long has he been gone?"

"Three months." Claire slumped forward to lean her elbows on the counter, her head hanging down. "But to be honest, he's been gone a lot longer, it just took me a while to realize that his 'business trips' weren't for 'business'."

"And the boys know?"

"He took them for a weekend last month. Told them he had met someone else. They knew we had separated, but not the worst of it. The papers came on Monday. But those two don't miss a thing, you know? They seem like these big bruisers, but they have the softest hearts . . ." Claire's voice trailed off, and Erin knew she was close to tears again, and she had to head that off.

"He took the TV?" She guessed the empty space wasn't an accident.

"Turns out Paul never thought through how expensive having two households was going to be. He said he'd bought the stuff himself, and he was going to keep what was his. The boys still have a TV in their room, but . . ." She waved at the rest of the empty space. "He took the car, too. It's all in his name. I tried to rent a car, but it got too expensive, then I tried borrowing, but I've pretty much spent any good will this neighborhood had." She was quiet for a moment. "They liked Paul, they tolerated me. I have no friends here."

Claire's words were a kick to the gut. How many times had Erin felt that way herself; un-liked and barely tolerated by people who thought she was nothing. She searched for something to say without sounding like a motivational poster or a greeting card, but came up empty. Instead, she focused on what she could do to help. "Okay, well, we need to find you a cheap car so you can get around without bumming rides."

"Erin, there's no money. I'm completely broke."

"Isn't he giving you child support?"

"Yes, but it's never going to be enough." She walked out of the kitchen to the front hall, grabbed a big manila envelope off the console table and walked back to Erin. She pulled out a long, legal document and tossed it on the counter. "He says he has no savings other than his 401k, and that his salary isn't enough to give me more than a grand a month." She huffed out a laugh. "That won't even cover rent on this place."

"But I thought these were all owned?"

"That was another nasty surprise. He told me he bought it, but he was only renting. He told me we were in the black, flush with cash, but that was another lie. I never did the banking. He used to give me cash when I needed it. I have no credit history, I have nothing and nowhere to go, and they're going to kick us out of this place soon. I don't know what to do." Claire's face twisted as she broke down again. "My parents won't help. They said this is my mess." She was barely getting out the words. "We're running out of food and I can't . . ." Claire shook her head, the tears flowing free.

Erin knew in that moment that Claire needed an intervention. As angry as she was with James, she couldn't help but be glad he'd forced an opportunity for Erin to be right where she was and finally able to help. God in His infinite wisdom had known Claire would never reach out for help on her own. Erin sent up a quick prayer asking God for help and got to work. "Okay, this is bad. No question. But this isn't impossible, and you are not alone."

"What?" Claire lifted her face out of her hands.

"Honey, I have been there, done that, and I've got this T-shirt in every size and color."

"You're making no sense." Claire managed to sound snooty even through her tears, and for some reason this made Erin smile.

"I've been out of money, out of options, about to be evicted more times than I can count. I might be financially stable now, or at least for the time being, but I've been through this kind of thing before. This I can handle." Erin stood up off her stool. "First things, did you already sign? Is this your copy?" She pointed at the papers on the island and Claire nodded. Erin pressed her lips together rather than say she really should have gotten a lawyer. "Okay, that's done. We have a thousand dollars from him per month for you to live on so you're going to need a car, a job, and a new place to live."

"I can't—"

"No, but we can. For starters, how about we call Pete about his Jeep? He hasn't been able to drive it since he was injured because he can't drive a stick shift. He got a souped-up SUV a few weeks ago. I bet he'd be willing to let the Jeep go for cheap."

"It could be months before I could pay him for it."

"He might be flexible. Let's see."

"It's too much." She shook her head, and Erin saw that the first thing they were going to have to tackle was Claire's reluctance to admit she needed help, and then accept that help.

"We have a saying in our family. 'We practice our humility so that others can practice their charity'. It's not easy, but you've got to kill that pride. It's clear your husband has decided not to be a decent man and provide you with enough for your kids. Now you're going to have to do that yourself. That means killing that pride."

Claire didn't seem convinced. "The PTO, I tried to ask for help, but they—some of them acted like it was my own fault. No one wants to help me, Erin. They want nothing to do with me."

"Were they giving you trouble with volunteering at the Harvest Party?"

"Spotted that, did you?" Claire rolled her eyes. "Things went really downhill. I trusted the wrong person to confide in. Instead of supporting me she began pushing me away, like she was embarrassed to know me." Claire looked around her house. "I'm a little embarrassed to know me right now."

"Whoa, don't let yourself start thinking that way. You are not your stuff."

"Well, I know that." She waved a hand.

"Do you really? Your standard of living is about to radically change, and it might be hard to deal with at first. That's something I didn't go through, not really. Jimmy was pretty broke when I married him, and more broke when he died. I grew up middle class, but I never had this." She pointed to Claire's granite kitchen counters. "You're going to need to downsize. You ready for that?"

"No. I'm probably going to be a big baby about it, actually." Claire sat down heavily on one of the kitchen stools, her shoulders slumped in defeat. "He was the one who had the affair. He left me. Why do I have to pay the price?"

"He's paying his too. He'll never have the same relationship with his kids. Even if he bribes them with stuff every time he has them for the weekend, it's not the same. He made his choices thinking he was getting an upgrade, but what he did was downgrade his family, and they'll notice."

"This is all so sordid, so hateful."

"Let me help."

"I'm too broke to say no." Claire's expression was glum.

"You need to let the church help too."

"What? No way. I'm not putting up with people looking down their noses at me."

"You sound like me when I first moved here. I thought I had everyone convinced that I was fine on my own, but they barged their way in anyway, and I'm so glad they did. I can't imagine my life without friends like Pete, Mac, and Katherine." Her expression grew serious. "If it wasn't for Calvary Church, I'm not sure I'd be a Christian. I'm not sure I would have survived it all."

"How can that be? You are . . . You always look perfect."

"Looks are deceiving. I walk out the door every day braced for the hate."

"No one really hates you, Erin. The other moms . . . Honestly, it's probably jealousy. You may not know this, but you're gorgeous, you have a great job, you have the respect of the people who really count, not who want to count, but don't. Like Dan Connors. Not a single woman in this town could turn his head, but you sure did. It made them resent you more."

Erin's stomach twisted at the sound of his name. She'd gone from blushing anytime he was mentioned to feeling sick instead. There was a swirling mass of anxiety in her gut that he'd put there, and she still didn't know what to do with it. Maybe she'd give it another day and go see him.

"Oh well. I'm not sure Dan and I are going to end up—that is, he's thinking about leaving and there's this friend of his—"

"Nonsense." Claire waved a hand through the air dismissively. "You mean that Beth Russell person? I saw her in church today. She's pretty, I'll give her that, and she seems nice, but she's not you. Besides, if he was going to marry her he would have done it by now. They've known each other for what? Ten, twelve years?" Claire seemed to register the surprise on Erin's face. "You didn't know that? They went to seminary together. They're old friends." She hopped off her stool and stood in front of Erin. "I may not know how to pick a man myself, but I can look at a couple and know if they're going to make the distance." She nodded her head enthusiastically at Erin's doubting expression. "Jennifer and Bill Pyke? Called it," Claire sing-songed. "A full year before they broke up. I'm telling you, I have the gift. I can see who's right for each other too—even if they're not together, like our librarian and that new warden." Erin tried to interject, but Claire was on a roll. "Oh, I know he's not Mr. Personality, but I can tell. I was in her bookshop downtown when he walked in and kapow!" She flicked her fingers like fireworks going off. "Sparks. Serious ones."

"Annie doesn't seem—"

"I know, you'll tell me she doesn't seem like his type since he's all outdoorsy, fit-guy, active and she's a bit, well, round, but—"

"Claire!"

"I didn't call her fat. You're a fitness guru. Wouldn't you tell her to lose weight?"

"First of all, unless she hires me as her trainer I have no business saying anything about her weight. Second, even if she was my client, I'd tell her that if she and her doctor are fine with her weight then she's all set. You can't look at someone's outside and make judgements like that." Erin tried to keep the stern out of her tone, since Claire hardly needed a lecture, but the woman seemed to pout a little anyway.

"Moving on." Claire stated. "I appreciate everything you said, I really do. I probably needed the intervention."

"We all have our moments. Now, it's time for a game plan."

"Can't we do that tomorrow? Today has been very emotional. I'm exhausted." She flopped forward, folding her arms on the counter and laying her head on them.

Erin gave her a hard stare. "If we don't stop right now and plan your next steps, you're going to close that door after I go and sink right back to where you were."

Claire huffed out what sounded like, "Fine."

Erin pulled out her notebook and flipped to a blank page. "First things first—new apartment. I happen to know of a building that has a vacancy. They're all two-bedrooms and the place is top notch, well-kept, parking lot is big and always plowed." When Claire made a face, she explained her new reality. "Here's the thing. You're about to down-size in a serious way. It's going to stink. There's no question about it. What you're about to move into isn't going to aesthetically please you. It will probably have white appliances and laminate countertops. You'll be lucky to get wood floors. You won't be able to paint the walls, and you're almost guaranteed popcorn ceilings, but it will be a roof and four walls, and that beats a shelter." Erin waited while Claire absorbed that. She looked like a deer in the headlights. "You're going to need to put on your 'making the best of it' face for your kids. You're going to have to find a way to make this move fun."

"Are you serious?"

"Claire, they're worried about you."

"They're good kids." Claire's voice sounded strangled, and Erin felt a surge of sympathy, but she had to get through to the woman that things were going to change and she had to change with them.

"Yes, they are. I've always thought that. Moms of boys are lucky. We get these fierce little protectors, our mini-knights in shining armor, but we have to be sure they know they are safe, they are loved, and that their mom is the grown-up, and God is looking out for us. Sure, Dad has left and things are grim, but God hasn't left us. God is right here." She reached out and took Claire's hand, giving it a squeeze before she let go. It wasn't an Erin thing to do, but it felt like the right thing.

Claire nodded, took a breath and let it out slowly. "Okay. What comes after the new apartment?"

Erin smiled as she returned to the notebook. "Step two, a job." She turned back to face Claire. "What did you do last?"

"I graduated from Boston College with my MRS."

"That's not a degree."

"Um, yeah. I didn't finish. I was three years into an Art degree when 'Mr. Right' came along." Claire shrugged. "I didn't think a degree mattered. Paul was already in grad school by then, and he said it would be too expensive, too much trouble for me to finish, so I waited tables until he got his first real job."

"Okay, but waiting tables is something."

"It's been ages."

"Trust me, it's not something you forget, but, if you could do anything, what would it be?"

"I wanted to be an artist." Claire said it shyly, as if she expected Erin to scoff. When she didn't Claire went on. "Pottery. Don't laugh."

"Claire, I make jewelry for a living. No joke. Every Christmas for the last ten years has been financed by my stuff selling at craft fairs, art shows, even some of it online."

"Why didn't I know this?"

"I guess you wouldn't unless you frequent craft fairs."

"I mean, why don't you advertise? Tell the parents at school?"

"I . . ." It was hard talking about this since these ideas had been formulating in the back of her mind, but she hadn't worked them out yet. "I've always assumed I'd get a negative reaction." She shook her head. "But let's talk about your pottery. Is it something you could sell?"

"Maybe. I haven't done it in a really long time, but I still have my wheel, my tools. Maybe?"

"How about this. We get you an apartment, a job that pays, and then a car. You coast for a bit and then we see about stage two, which would be trying to get a side business together with your pottery."

"Okay. I think I can handle that." Her eyes slid to the front hall and the piles of papers, the mess of coats and boots. "Moving is going to be hard."

"Not with friends. The Calvary Hospitality Committee is chock full of ladies waiting for a call."

Claire gasped aloud. "No way am I letting any one of them through the front door with the place like this. What are they gonna think?"

Erin almost smiled. Claire almost echoed Linda word for word. Actually, Claire reminded her of a Yankee Linda, but with a whole lot less steel in her spine.

"They're not going to judge you."

"Right. You left that church when Brittany got married because you were worried about what they'd say."

"Not really." Although Claire was more right than wrong. "I wanted to support Brittany and Jake in starting a new life, and that meant going to their new church. I could have come back a while ago but, yah, I assumed I'd hear some stuff I didn't want to. That's on me, though. I should have given them a chance. My calling them to let them know they have a parishioner in need will be a good first step towards getting back to normal."

"Parishioner?" Claire let out a sardonic sort of laugh. "We're barely more than Christmas and Easter at that church. I doubt they know our names."

"I can guarantee they love you just the same," Erin insisted. Claire ducked her head, eyes to the floor and Erin saw her shoulders shake. Erin knew what this felt like; to be so low and to have someone hold out a hand was overwhelming.

CHAPTER NINETEEN

WHEN MONDAY MORNING CAME, ERIN RELUCTANTLY emailed Katherine the official account of the fight.

"With regret, James has admitted that he threw the first punch. He was upset by taunts from Evan regarding our family. He acknowledges that no words said by a classmate justify his actions. He deeply regrets those actions and is willing to accept whatever punishment you deem appropriate." She didn't envy Katherine's position. The school had a zero-tolerance policy regarding fighting. The only mitigating factor was that it was not during school hours.

"While Evan did respond to James' punch with his own, and I did find them actively trading blows, I think it's important to note that Evan is going through a difficult time. I believe that it is in his best interests, and that of his family's, if he is able to remain enrolled. The school has a moral obligation to do what's right for its students and I truly believe this is the correct action to take." She finished off the email with an appeal. "I realize that if James is allowed to remain it might appear as favoritism on your part because of my status as an employee. If it needs to be one of us going so that the other can stay, I will offer my resignation immediately."

Financially, she had no business making that plea, but she knew that there were those on the board who wanted her gone. That might be enough to change their minds about James staying. If he was expelled she could probably homeschool him to finish the year, like she had done with Brittany, but he'd have to go back to public school next year. That meant the regional high school. She was afraid he'd get lost in the shuffle among kids he either didn't know or hadn't been around since grammar school. That, and the high school was poorly funded, with limited offerings, huge classes, and a party-culture reputation.

She hit send on the email and tried to think about the next few classes she had to teach rather than the ball of anxiety sitting in her belly. Not that she had heard from Dan. As much as she wanted to call or text him, she waited. He had to know that it was up to him to explain things to her. She checked her schedule. The morning program was up next, and the kids had really taken to the barre stuff she had introduced, so she wanted to focus on that. Hearing the bell, she got up out of her chair, shook off her gloomy thoughts, and got down to doing what she did best: surviving.

By the time the afternoon bell rang, Erin was feeling better. There was something about working hard at what she did well that filled her with a kind of contentment. It didn't mean she was suddenly worry-free, but she felt less jangly, stronger, like she could handle whatever hit came next. In her office she checked her email, but had no reply from Katherine. That wasn't a surprise. When Erin had called her to warn her about what had happened she said she'd probably have to discuss it with the board. SRCA didn't have a traditional structure where the director made all disciplinary decisions. If it was one of the few that required expulsion, the board usually weighed in.

"Hello, there!" She looked up to see Pete smiling at her from her doorway. He was leaning heavily on his cane.

"Hey. How are you? How's the leg?"

"Still attached." He winked.

"Doing the therapy though, right?"

"No, don't start. You're as bad as my new trainee, Alex." Pete stepped inside and sat down on the folding chair in front of her desk.

"Really?" Erin's eyebrows rose.

"Beneath his stoic exterior beats the heart of a mother hen."

"I'll take your word for it." Erin looked at the slightly pained expression on his face and felt her own inner hen start clucking. "You shouldn't be having pain at this point, Pete. Stiffness yes, but pain, no. Did you overdo it?"

"A wee bit." He lifted his boot and balanced it on a crate full of tennis balls nearby and then rubbed his knee with both hands. "It's not the leg anyway. It's my knee. I twisted it."

"Did you ice it? Is it swelling?"

"We're not getting into my medical history. I've got an appointment with the doc on Monday, and he'll probably tell me it's arthritis or something and bug me to retire for the fifteenth time. I'm done next year. And bum leg, bad knee, or questionable head, I'm finishing on time, not early."

"Okay. I'll shut up. For now."

He shook his head. "Anyway, how are you doing?"

"Great as always."

"See, I've been hearing things." He squinted at her. "Someone told me about this dance the school put on and how Dan had showed up to chaperone, but ended the night by whirling you around. Seems I heard you two were seen out to dinner the next night. I thought they had to be wrong. Couldn't be you. If it had been you, why, you would have called your oldest friend and let him know."

"Pete—"

"There's more. It seems that, despite that rather nice start, suddenly there's drama!" He spread out his hands in the air. "Some old friend of Dan's is here, and now you're not talking to him?"

"That's not—"

"There's more. Your son was caught kicking the pants off some kid out on the school playground. Then I hear that you're best friends with the mom of that kid. That you even petitioned the church to help her move into a new apartment because her husband abandoned her and her kids. We're all supposed to meet the two of you on Saturday and move her into a new apartment."

"That part is true."

"You've been busy." He didn't sound pleased.

"Life comes at you fast, old man." She gave him a smile, but he didn't seem to believe it.

"Sweetheart . . ." That one word, or the gentle way he said it, almost brought her to tears. As if he sensed how fragile she was, he kept his voice soft. "Call him. Get things straight."

A surge of anger flooded her chest, and she shook her head. "*He* needs to call *me*. I know that's selfish, but what he did hurt. It took a lot of trust to let him in to begin with and to get hit with that, no explanation, no call, no email, no text, nothing? For days? No, he needs to call me."

"That boy . . ." Pete rolled his eyes to the ceiling. "He doesn't know what he's doing, Erin. That's all I'll say."

"And I know you warned me and I didn't listen. You're nice not to say 'I told you so'."

"Not really. You didn't listen, but I'd never say that, because I'm hoping you two will work this out."

"Okay." She sorted through a few papers on her desk waiting for her emotions to settle down.

"Got a call about the fight. The board is discussing it on a conference call tonight."

"I figured." Erin felt her stomach sink, that ball of anxiety returned and now it felt twice as big.

"You ready for what they might do?"

"Do I have a choice?" She heard the warble in her voice and regretted it instantly. Pete stood and she looked up. "Don't do it. If you hug me, I am going to cry like a baby, and I can't do that right now. I've got to get home, make dinner, and somehow not let on how bad it is to James, who is feeling so guilty he's practically bent in two." She took in a shuddering breath. "Then I have to tell my heart to stop wanting Dan to come and make me feel better, because that's what I'd gotten used to. We might have only been friends for a few weeks and then something else for a few days, but I liked it. I got used to it, and I didn't want it to end." Pete reached for her anyway, pulling her up and into a hug. Predictably, she burst into tears.

Everything that she'd been holding inside let loose as if his arms around her were the crack in the dam holding back her emotions, and a flood of them started spilling out. She was safe with Pete, so she let all of the hurt, the sadness, the stress, and the fear surface and then let it go. He held her all the while, gently stroking her hair.

"When did I get so weak?" She tried to joke.

Pete let her go. "Weak? You're the strongest woman I know." He pulled her close again and gave her another quick squeeze. "Do you have a plan if the board decides to expel him?"

"Yes. I'll homeschool him for the rest of the year, and then next year send him to the regional high school in a 'Jesus is Lord' tee shirt to keep the party crowd away and a bag over his head to discourage any girls from talking to him." She huffed out a laugh. "Maybe I'll draw pimples on his face and make him wear head gear so none of the cool kids will like him and he'll come home without a single party invitation all four years."

"You've raised him right, Erin. Even if he was tossed into that crowd, he'd do okay."

"You, sir" —she pointed at him—"are an optimist. I am a realist."

"No, you're a sweet, kind, loyal woman who's taken too many of life's slings and arrows, and now thinks she's all hard when we know she's soft."

"I wish that were true." Erin was thinking of Beth who did look sweet and kind. Most people probably thought Erin looked irritated and acerbic. That was her rep after all.

"You are too down on yourself."

"Oh, Pete, I don't want to be mean to you, but today I can't do the spiritual gymnastics required to have a good attitude. I'll be better tomorrow, but today I can't do it."

"Okay, honey." He started to leave and then nodded to her. "C'mon. I'll walk you home. Let me talk to James. See if I can help." Erin breathed a sigh of relief and followed him out.

Dan picked up his phone and checked the time. It was 8:00 PM, not exactly the polite time to drop by someone's house, but he didn't have a lot of options. He couldn't let one more day go without talking to Erin. He'd almost called or texted a dozen times, but he was resolved to see her in person. Between trips to the hospital to see his mom and Beth needing his help on her presentations, appeal letters, and proposals, he still hadn't found a time. Working with Beth, being surrounded by her enthusiasm, was filling a spiritual need in him. His struggle to hear God's will for his life hadn't suddenly disappeared, but in focusing on the work, he'd found inspiration and a bit of peace.

But he missed Erin. In the short time they'd grown close, he'd developed a need for her that he couldn't explain. There was something about spending time with her that soothed his soul in a way nothing else did. There was also a voice at the back of his head telling him that if he didn't get things sorted out, all they were building together might be over. That voice was practically shouting at him, so here he was, knocking on her door at an unsociable hour, hoping she was home.

He had to knock again before he saw through the glass that Erin was coming down the stairs to the hall. She opened the door, and he instantly knew from the look on her face that he was in far more trouble than he expected.

"Hey, I know it's late, but—" was all he got out before Erin put a hand in the middle of his chest and pushed him out of her doorway, off the porch and down the steps. He assumed she was getting him out of earshot of the boys, but it wasn't a great start. He tried not to panic; he could fix this.

"It's late, Dan."

"I know, and if you'd give me a second I'll explain." He realized that was probably not his best answer since she planted her feet and crossed her arms over her chest. Dan took a breath and let it out slowly. "I wanted to explain about the other night, but I wanted to do it in person, not over the phone. I would have done it already, but I've been very busy."

"Obviously." She put a world of censure in that one word, and he flinched. This was definitely not going well.

"That didn't come out right. What I'm trying to say is that I'm sorry for forgetting our date."

"It wasn't that you stood me up. You get that, don't you?" Her eyes were squinting at him.

"It was a little awkward having you show up when Beth and I were meeting, I realize—"

"Awkward? For you?" She slapped her palm to her forehead. "I should have called first to make sure you weren't meeting with someone during the same time you had scheduled a date with me, you're absolutely right. So glad we worked this out." She spun on her heel and headed for the house. Dan ran to get in between her and the front steps. He opened his mouth to apologize again, but she cut him off. "No. You do not get to come here at this hour and give me a ham-fisted apology so you can feel better about standing me up for your friend. No way."

"But that's not—"

"I don't know what you're doing, Dan, but it feels . . ." She closed her eyes, and he could see the hurt written on her face. He wanted nothing more than to go back in time and not foul up. "I can't handle this on top of everything else. What you're doing –"

"I don't know what I'm doing." He threw his hands in the air, at a complete loss. "That's what I'm trying to tell you. I have no idea how to do this." He was relieved when she didn't bolt inside. "I've never dated anyone seriously. I've never had a romantic relationship as an actual adult. My high school girlfriend dumped me after two months, and then my dad died and everything changed. My next date was in college, and every one of them, and they were few, was half-hearted and not repeated. Not until I met you." He watched as her shoulders seemed to relax and the hard look in her eyes began to fade, replaced by something softer. "I'm going to make mistakes. It's almost a given." He took a step nearer, relieved when she didn't retreat since that meant she might let him fix things.

"Then lesson one on dating is that when you forget a date, and the woman you're supposed to be with shows up at your office and sees you with another woman, you do not wait five days to explain the situation."

"See, when you say it out loud . . ." He shook his head. "I am so sorry. I was looking forward to seeing you, and when Beth arrived out of the blue I spent hours scrambling to move things around so I could help her, and I got the day mixed up. Never for one minute did I forget you or how I feel about you. These last couple of days I've wanted to call, and I realize now that it was completely stupid not to, but I was determined to explain it in person. I also missed you and wanted to see you when we talked. I blew it. I am sorry for hurting you; that is the last thing I wanted to do." He searched her face for some indication that she might forgive him. "Do I get another shot?" He waited while she seemed to think it over. Her expression was impossible to decipher, but she didn't look pleased. He felt his heart contract in pain thinking she might cut him loose.

"I've seen your calendar myself. Now that you've explained it, I'm not surprised you mixed up your days, but it didn't feel good, Dan. It hit some soft places in me that I've tried hard to protect. Yes, I want to try again, but I need you to promise you're going to communicate with me. Don't leave me in the dark again."

"Never, I promise." Relief and guilt warred in his gut. He leaned forward and kissed her softly, needing to show her he meant what he said. He would have to remind himself to go carefully. She might be strong, but she wasn't made of iron. He ended the kiss with a brush of his lips against hers, which twitched in a smile.

"Well, at least with that you know what you're doing."

"No, actually I don't." His experience was about as limited as could be. "I've been following your lead."

Erin looked up at him in surprise, and then a sly look crossed her face. "Well, I am a good kisser." She rolled up on her toes and gave him a light peck on the cheek. "I'm really glad you came over tonight, and it feels good to have talked, but you need to go. They boys are going to get curious and wonder what I'm doing out here. James considers himself my protector. If he spots you, he might haul you inside and demand to know your intentions."

"I'm happy to tell him that my intentions are to spend more time with a woman I like very much and to see where this might go." He took her hand in his. "I'm not experimenting with dating, or playing around here, Erin. This relationship might be new, but it and you mean a lot to me."

"You mean a lot to me too, Dan, but I've got more to lose than you do." She gestured at the house, and Dan understood that to mean her boys. "It feels good to hear you say that. I need your actions to match."

"They will." He held her gaze while he raised her hand and kissed it. "I promise." He watched as some of the wariness seemed to leave.

"Thank you."

He pulled her into his arms and held her for a long moment before whispering goodnight in her ear and letting her go. She responded in kind before turning away and heading toward the house. Suddenly, he didn't want to leave it there. "When can I see you again?"

She turned around. "How about Friday night? You can come for dinner."

"Great. Dinner. Yeah. That's great. I can totally do that." Dan realized he was practically babbling. "I'll see you Friday." He started to walk away before he made a fool of himself. He could feel the huge smile on his face. Erin gave him a wave and headed inside. Dan walked home feeling like a new man. Erin didn't hate him, she'd forgiven him, and they were on track again. He marveled at how quickly it had begun to matter to him that she was happy. *Does love start like this? Maybe it does.* That idea should have made him apprehensive, but it didn't. It didn't feel unreasonable to be thinking this might be love.

His experience with love had been limited to family, friends, and God. Romantic love was a bit of a mystery. His parents had loved each other. They were over thirty when they met and married. Their love might have come later in their lives than others, but nothing he'd seen before or since had been stronger. He remembered how bad it was in the days after the funeral. He had been only fifteen, so he had a teenage boy understanding of grief and pain and few skills to help his mother through it. Instead, he'd spent every minute he could with her. Even his choice of college was made with his mom in mind so he could come home every weekend. He'd never regretted that time, not for a moment, and he didn't now.

No Reserves. No Retreats. No Regrets. The words surfaced in his thoughts, and he wondered if he hadn't betrayed them. They'd been his driving force for nearly two decades. He wanted to give his all, leave nothing behind, and die in hope of hearing "Well done, good and faithful servant." *What had changed in the last few years that has dimmed the fire inside me? Am I getting soft? Am I falling victim to the weakness of my flesh?* For a moment he felt a stab of doubt, thinking his pursuit of Erin might be about what his body wanted, not what his soul needed. But then he remembered how she made him feel. It wasn't about kissing her or holding her, it was about feeling uplifted, supported, cared for. That wasn't lust. That felt like love.

CHAPTER TWENTY

"IT'S RIDICULOUS." KATHERINE SLAMMED HER FILE drawer closed, the sound oddly muted in the small office. Erin sat and waited for her friend to get a grip. Katherine had called her to the office at the end of the day to give her the news about how the board had decided to deal with the fight. "The full board doesn't need to meet on this. They could have handled it with a phone call. This is not how Greg would have handled it."

"He's not the chairman anymore."

"And it shows." She slammed her desk drawer shut. "Why that man had to retire to Arizona of all places, I do not know."

"Dry climate. Remember? Don't be mad at him for having bad lungs." She tried to smile, but her heart wasn't in it. "It's okay. I knew this was one option they might choose. It'll be fine."

"Erin . . ." Katherine's eyes met hers, and Erin could tell she'd moved from anger to sympathy. That really didn't help, but it felt nice. Erin had been relieved when she heard they'd be issuing Evan Murphy a formal warning only, and she hadn't been surprised when she learned that James would not be getting off so easy. He was suspended pending the full meeting of the board, which wouldn't be until the following Monday. It was the absolutely worst outcome for them. This gave time for the story to circulate and for those who wanted her gone to let the board know it. It also meant that Erin got to fret and worry for an extra six days. That was stress she did not need.

"God is provident," Erin stated, half for Katherine, half for herself.

"Well, of course He is."

"We say it like we believe it, but when push comes to shove . . ." Erin shrugged a shoulder. "I'm trying to remember that God is in charge, He loves us and, whatever happens, we're safe in His hands. I want to feel it though, you know? I want to feel calm, like when it's late at night and someone else is driving you home and you can close your eyes and go to sleep, no worries." She wanted someone to hold her hand and promise it was all going to be okay.

"You're right to be worried." Katherine shook her head. "I hate to say it, but I'm concerned too. They may choose to use this incident against you. And I'll admit that part of what's got me so angry is that I have little say in it. I made my recommendation, and they rejected it. You know I'm not exactly the poster child for 'letting go and letting God.' Quite the contrary."

"Yeah, you're still a control freak."

"Hey!"

"I'm joking." But it was close to the truth. Katherine was an executive by nature. She might have found her way back to God last year and even learned to share space with her bossy husband, but she still liked to be in charge. Because of that, Erin didn't think Katherine really understood what she was feeling. Erin wasn't struggling with wanting to push God aside and run her own life. She was tired of being the boss, making every decision on her own, never having anyone to lean on, no one to step in when she couldn't handle it anymore. A small curl of resentment unfurled inside her like a springtime fern, but she beat it down. It was horribly selfish. She had the Author of the universe in her corner, she didn't need anyone else.

"I need to work on that—holding on to God when things start to get ugly. And I need to work on not assuming the worst. Although . . . it's handy when the bad stuff comes. I feel like I'm prepared, braced for impact."

"I've never thought of you as a pessimist." Katherine lifted her purse out of her office drawer and set it on the desk.

"I'm not really. I've just gotten into the habit of thinking of the worst-case scenario so I can be prepared for whatever happens." Erin stood and Katherine followed suit, picking up her purse and getting into her coat. She flicked off the lights as they left the office. It was dark in the administration department since the rest of the staff had long since left. It was the season for weak afternoon sunlight as well. It barely lightened the hallways despite the huge front windows of the building. Once they were outside, Erin felt a blast of November chill and wished she'd swapped out her cute but thin trench coat for something puffy involving down and nylon.

"What is it, November seventh or something, and it's this cold?" Katherine asked.

"It's Maine."

"You keep telling me that, but then we have a warm summer and I forget."

"We're inland too. That makes more of a difference than you'd think."

"That reminds me. We sold the beach house on the Cape."

"What?" Erin stopped in her tracks, a stair above Katherine, and stared down at her. "But that was your house. You loved it. It was close to your mom."

"Believe it or not, she's moving here." Katherine continued walking down the stairs and Erin rushed to keep up.

"I feel like I'm missing something. Spill." Erin grabbed at Katherine's jacket, and she stopped. She had a smile on her face when she turned around.

"Good news and better news, which first?"

"Good news."

"Mac is letting mom have the cabin until she decides if she wants him to build an in-law apartment onto the house. We want to give her time to settle in, since she might end up living somewhere else close by." Katherine gave her an exaggerated wink.

"Pete." Erin barely whispered it. "Did it get serious between them that fast?"

"About as fast as two others I know."

"Nope." Erin shook her head. "Not going there today."

"That is not fair. I gave you all the details of me and Mac."

"Uh, no, I'll remind you that you tried and I told you I didn't want to hear it. I didn't get involved until he was stupid enough to leave you for your own good."

"And I'm glad you did." Katherine moved in for a hug and Erin didn't even fight it. She wondered at her newfound ability to be cuddly and if it had anything to do with Dan.

"Wait, you promised better news."

"Yeah, I did." Katherine's face lit with some secret emotion. "DHHS called. Said normally they wouldn't choose a family like ours because Mac and I have never been parents, but considering our backgrounds and the sheer number of hours we've spent around kids . . ."

Erin drew in a sharp breath, waiting for her to finish, guessing what it might be.

"It's a sibling group. Five kids. Parents died in a car accident a year ago. The kids have been living in a residential program because the state couldn't find any relatives willing to take them all on. We're their last option. If they can't make it work with us they'll be forced to split them up. The youngest is two and the oldest is twelve."

"Oh, Katherine, that's . . ." Erin didn't have words for it. After all her friend had been through, this was a blessing, but it would also be the challenge of a lifetime. Katherine didn't look like she minded the challenge at all. Her eyes were shining. Erin felt the prickle of tears start. "I think I'm going to cry."

"Don't, because I've cried about eight times already and Mac is beginning to worry."

"I have no idea what has made me so soft." Erin pawed through her purse for a tissue. "Are you going to resign?"

"No. We've talked it over, and we're going to see if we can get the older kids enrolled. With me working here, it would be easier to handle any issues that came up. The five-year-old has another year before kindergarten because of the way her birthday falls in the year. We've got time before we decide what she needs."

"Boys and girls?"

"Youngest is Harry; next is Emma, then twins Noah and Matthew. Olivia is the oldest, and they told us that she's very protective of her siblings and has given the staff at the home fits."

"You're going to have your hands full."

"Which is why mom is moving up. My sisters made some noise, and then I reminded them that they'd had her grandma services all to themselves for about a decade and they needed to share."

"Your sisters are a hoot. But that's really great about your mom moving up here, and who knows, maybe the kids will get both a grandma and a grandpa eventually?"

"It's so weird to think my mom is dating Pete, but there you go. They hit it off the moment they met." Her expression turned thoughtful. "There was none of that dancing around either. No dramatic tension, no warring sides. They said hi, shook hands and it was off to the races. Who does that?"

"Normal people? I wouldn't know." Erin started to head for home, but she turned around to say. "I couldn't be happier for you and Mac. I really couldn't. And you know, I'll be there. Whatever you need."

"You always are." Katherine waved as she got into her car.

Dan drove through downtown and past Erin's street feeling a strong desire to turn down it. Spending the evening with Erin and the boys was all too tempting. After the day he'd had, what he probably needed was having dinner that wasn't microwaved, tossing a ball around in the backyard with James and Seth, and then sitting on the couch with Erin. They weren't at the 'drop by for dinner' stage yet, though. Dan hoped that would be soon. He'd have to wait for Friday night and her actual invitation. Instead, he drove the rest of the way home feeling like the weight of the world was on his shoulders. Funerals were hard enough. Funerals for people he barely knew and strongly suspected weren't saved were far more difficult. His exhaustion was more spiritual and emotional than physical. He knew spending the evening in reading and prayer, or maybe running and prayer, was the way to go.

He pulled into his driveway—someone waiting for him. It didn't happen every day, but it wasn't unheard of. Having his residence over his office meant that his 'on duty' hours were pretty flexible. When he looked closer, he realized it was Pete.

Getting out of the car he greeted Pete. "Hey, were you waiting for me?"

"I was. Sorry it's on the late side, but I need a few minutes of your time."

"No, that's fine. C'mon in." He let Pete into the barn and headed for his desk, dropping his briefcase and keys. "Do you want a cup of coffee or something?"

"No. This will be quick."

Dan felt a twinge of apprehension. Pete's tone was all business with none of his usual humor. "Okay, have a seat. I've got plenty of time." He sat down, but Pete didn't take a chair.

"I'm gonna get straight to it, because I'm not happy with you."

Dan felt his previous twinge of anxiety return in force. His gut tightened.

"See, a few days ago I had a chance to talk to Erin. I told her straight out that I was pleased you two had begun seeing each other and I was hoping for the best." Pete's jaw was tight. "I told her she needed to be cautious. I didn't think I'd need to tell you the same. I didn't think I'd need to tell the pastor that he should be careful with someone's feelings. She didn't tell me what happened between the two of you, but when I saw her yesterday, she was hurting. It was easy to see that you were the cause. I am not going to get in-between you two, but I am going to ask you to treat her heart like the fragile and precious thing it is." Pete finished and Dan's gut twisted even harder with guilt. Being called on the carpet by Pete was demoralizing. It was like having Erin's father come to his office and tell him off. He needed to fix this.

"I did hurt her. I hurt her badly. It wasn't intentional, and I've seen Erin since and we've talked it out. I've apologized, and she's forgiven me."

"Of course she has." The words were scathing. "That's what she does. She's the mother of boys and they require extra grace, so she's all too used to forgiving easily. I assumed as much, and I'm not here for that." Pete pointed a thick finger at Dan. "You've got a lot going on right now. I know you're struggling with something on top of dealing with your mom's health and your contract renewal, and that friend of yours dragging you all over the state to help her fundraise. I can see it and I sympathize, but you need to get your head on straight or you'll hurt her again."

"No. Pete, you don't understand, it was just . . . a misunderstanding, and it's not going to happen again. I will be careful with Erin. She means a lot to me."

Pete put his hands on his hips. "Son, you're not hearing me. This isn't about Erin, it's about you. I'm not sure what you need, an epiphany or a kick in the pants, but you need to get yourself right or you will blow this. Erin needs and deserves a husband who has his stuff sorted out. That's your end game, right?" Pete asked and Dan nodded. "Right now? That's not you."

He felt the anger rise, but immediately put it in check. Pete wasn't wrong. Dan was struggling with his purpose, his lack of direction, the silence he was getting from God. He should be seeking out counsel, not getting ticked off when an elder offered it. This warning might sting, but it was justified. "Okay. Message delivered."

"I hope so. Right. That's done, now how is your mom?"

"I'm going to see her tomorrow. Couldn't get there today with the Devin funeral."

Pete sighed. "I forgot that was today. Meant to be there. I knew Frank years ago, but we'd lost touch when he retired. How's Bonnie?"

"I don't really know. She was a bit of a brick wall. We only met twice and both times she told me she didn't want any 'bells and whistles' and to keep it simple. Today though . . ." Dan trailed off thinking of Mrs. Devin's quiet strength in each of those meetings compared with her unvarnished grief at the graveside. It was as if seeing the coffin lowered finally made it real for her. She'd broken right there, tears coursing down her face, her two daughters holding her up. Dan shook his head. "It was grim."

"I'll drop by next week. See how she's doing."

"I think she'd appreciate that. I also let the hospitality committee know so they can see if she'd be up to accepting meals. She was adamantly against it when I first brought it up, but maybe that's because it was me. The committee speaks 'Yankee' better than I do."

"Too many years away?"

"Too many years among people with nothing who were desperate for any help no matter who was offering. Of course, those last years in

India, not so much. Resentment was building. That's one of the reasons Beth's project in Africa sounds so appealing. The population she plans to serve is a welcoming one. There's security concerns due to political conditions, but that's anywhere in the third world. The town she's going to has asked for help. It's not her team rushing in where they aren't wanted."

"You thinking of joining them?"

"What? No. I mean it would be right up my alley, but this isn't great timing."

"Probably not. Couldn't help wondering, though, with you putting so much time in on helping her with it. Folks might have the wrong impression about your feelings there."

"No worries. I'm not going anywhere, and if anyone asks, that's the answer."

"Right. Well, I'll be praying for you." Pete started to walk away, but stopped at the door. "Contrary to what you might assume, I'll be rooting for you too."

Dan watched him leave, both encouraged and troubled by the meeting. He opened his laptop and answered a few emails before locking up and heading upstairs. He should eat, but his stomach was telling him not to. Instead he got a water bottle and sat on his bed, trying to sort out his emotions. They were a swirling mess. Picking up his phone, he texted Erin a quick message letting her know he was thinking of her and wishing her good night. He smiled when her return text was a string of emojis with the last one being a kiss. Something about her playful answer struck him, and he knew Pete was right, he needed to get his head on straight. He also needed council that didn't come attached to his paycheck, someone neutral. He texted Mac with a request to meet for coffee. Mac was Erin's friend, but he was also Dan's. Of anyone, he was the most levelheaded and even-handed of those he could trust. Dan needed that kind of calm in the middle of his storm.

The next day dawned bright and cold. Dan walked to the coffee shop Mac had suggested with that morning's Bible reading on his mind. The text had been Proverbs 3 and verses 5-6 were still echoing in his brain. "Trust in the Lord with all your heart and lean not on your own understanding; in all your ways submit to him, and he will make your paths straight." That's what he needed, a straight path. Hopefully, bouncing his thoughts off Mac and getting his in return might lead him there.

The coffee shop was new, but it didn't feel that way since the owner had not cleared out the old bookstore before she moved her operation in. Instead, she had absorbed it, shelves and all. The center of the space had all the shelves removed and was filled with tables and chairs. The back had the coffee counter and baked goods, but the walls were still lined with books for sale. The shop had a rack of the daily newspapers as well, which drew in the local old guys. Sure enough, as Dan entered he spotted Mac and Stuart Bell, one of the parishioners at Calvary, at two tables by the front windows reading the papers with cups of coffee. He greeted Stuart with a wave before putting his order in at the counter and joining Mac.

"Thanks for meeting me."

"No worries. It's perfect timing, since I was going to call you and let you know about my news."

"What's that?"

"Got a call from the State. It's not final, but it looks like they're going to place a sibling group with us."

For a second, Dan felt his hopes soar, but he already knew it wasn't to be. He'd gotten a call from the social worker at the end of last week. Rob's kids were in the system, already at a group home while they were being evaluated. The social worker suspected PTSD at the least, and that would require a very special family to take on. The MacAlisters were the sort of special family that could easily handle them, but they were too new, too inexperienced.

"Parents are gone, no relatives to speak of, none to take them on, anyway. Five kids. Ages range from two to twelve."

"Wow, Mac that's great." Dan suppressed his feelings of resentment. If only God had ordered it differently. A rush of guilt filled him when he realized he was questioning God's timing yet again. Where was his trust?

"I'm really happy for you and Katherine. Five kids. That's going to be a handful. Please let me know when you're ready for the church to know. I can guarantee you, folks are going to want to help out with clothes, beds, whatever you need."

"We've got the basics sorted, beds, dressers, that sort of thing. What we'll need is prayer. Katherine and I might love kids and have worked with them, but neither of us have been parents before. We'll be getting them all at once, and it's going to test us in ways we can't imagine. We haven't been married that long, either. She's still getting used to me, and to some degree I'm still being careful not to annoy her." He laughed. "She might not see it that way, but I have."

"I'll be praying for you both." Dan looked up at the sound of his name and hurried up to the counter to collect his coffee. When he was seated again he asked, "Are you planning on adjusting your work schedule at all? You work some crazy hours now."

"I've decided to quit."

Dan drew in a surprised breath and then tried to cover it, but failed.

"You sound like Katherine." He smirked. "She was stunned. Heading up the security team at the resort paid very well, but it was just that—a paycheck. If we can get by without it, I'd rather spend my time being a father."

"How would that work?"

"I'd be the primary care giver for the two and five year olds. Katherine wanted to look at preschools, but I felt . . ." He looked out the front window of the shop at the quiet street beyond, his face impossible to read. "I've waited a long time to be a dad. Why waste a second of it?"

"Financially it will all work out?"

"Katherine's loaded." Mac laughed at Dan's surprised expression. "If I was going to get hung up on Katherine having more money than me, we would never have got past the first date. She comes from money, made piles of it over the years, and has royalties from her books, investments that even I don't fully comprehend. She's even got a personal assistant who handles all that stuff."

"I had no idea."

"She's very low-key about it since that's what she's used to."

"And it doesn't bother you? I mean the idea that she'll be the breadwinner?"

"Well, I'll be making a few crumbs. I got an offer. Part-time deputy back at my old station. Mostly filling in on vacations and emergencies. It will fit in nicely around what the kids need. It's amazing how this has all fallen together. We have a need, it's filled. God is ordering it all, and we're in His hands."

"That's . . ." A strong surge of jealousy choked off his words. "I'm jealous. I really am. I want nothing more than to know that my feet are on the right path and that I am in God's will, headed in the right direction."

Mac sat back. "I'm thinking we're getting around to what you wanted to talk to me about."

"Yeah." Dan took a sip of his coffee to give his mind time to form the right words. "You know that Erin and I are seeing each other, right?"

"Yup. Katherine is pretty pleased. She likes the two of you together."

"What do you think?"

"I'm trusting you to take it slow and treat her respectfully."

"I've already blown it at least once with her, and she's had to forgive me. Pete's on my case to 'get my head straight'." He explained with air quotes. "And he's right. I feel like I've been treading water for three years waiting for God to throw me a life preserver. I hate admitting that out loud." Dan shook his head. "But I need to. Spiritually, I am not in concert with God. It's like I'm singing my heart out, but it's all off-key. It's never felt this way before. I'm used to being on fire for God, consumed with my mission. 'No Reserves, No Retreats, No Regrets.'"

"Ah, I know that one. William Borden. You've preached on that before, haven't you?"

"Yes. It's been my life motto, but lately, dealing with my mom's condition on top of everything else has got me dragging. And, this is harder to admit. I'm second-guessing God. Some of the things that have happened recently, I'm feeling resentful. My prayers seem to be falling on deaf ears. I can't get this stone out of my heart."

"It's anger. You've left it there long enough for it to get bitter, and it's coloring how you see God's work in your life and the life of others."

Dan sat back, surprised by Mac's answer. "I'm not angry."

"But you are. I know because I was the same for years. You need to do some soul searching, Pastor. You need to find out what it is you're holding onto and let that go. It's like a wall, and it's standing between you and God."

Dan didn't think that was it. How could that be it? He didn't feel angry. He'd never struggled with anger or bitterness. Sure, he was upset about his mom, but he wasn't angry at God for what she was suffering.

"You need to take a few days off. Go fishing. Be on your own for a bit."

"I wish I could. With my mom ill and now Beth in town taking up the time I'd have free it's impossible."

"And Erin filling in the spaces between, I hope?"

"I have to move heaven and earth to see her. It's driving me crazy. Yesterday was rough, and last night all I wanted to do was to drive to her house and see if she'd let me spend the evening with her and the boys. There's something so restorative in being with her. It's like nothing I've ever experienced. I should be more tired when I leave her house, but it's the opposite. I feel better, lighter."

"Hmm . . ." Mac finished off his coffee and set the cup down. "You two are moving fast."

"We've known each other a long time; I think that's part of it."

"Or, she's the one." Mac slid back in his chair, and that comfortable silence that oftentimes happens with good friends allowed Dan to mull over that idea while finishing off his coffee. When they finally headed outside, as Dan buttoned his jacket against the chill of the autumn air, his thoughts started to coalesce, and a picture of sorts began to form.

"Hey, Mac," He said to his friend's back as he walked to his truck. "I think she's the one."

Mac smiled. "Then be sure to treat her that way."

CHAPTER TWENTY-ONE

"DR. CONNORS, THIS MESSAGE IS TO let you know that your mother's temperature was normal this afternoon. We will continue to monitor her closely, but we wanted to be sure you knew of this improvement in her condition. Please call with any questions." A surge of relief swept through Dan. He hadn't made it to the hospital yesterday and was worried she'd declined further. This was the first piece of good news on her condition in a while. He was planning on visiting her today before his meeting with Beth to do a video conference with the executive team at the organization that funded her. She'd asked him to be there for moral support. He'd been trying to be more conscious of how much time he spent on Beth's work so that she didn't rely on him too much, and so that no one would get the wrong idea about why he was helping her. He didn't need anyone else jumping to wrong conclusions.

When he arrived at his mother's room, he found her sitting up. "Hi, Mom." He got close and kissed her forehead. "You look great." She still looked ill, but far better than before. The nurses had also braided her hair, probably to keep it from knotting. It reminded him of how she used to wear it when cleaning house.

Surprisingly, she looked up at him as if she'd heard and knew to respond.

"I like your hair. Reminds me of when you used to make us spend Saturday cleaning up." Dan's heart contracted with a powerful emotion as she slowly smiled in response. "It's so good to see you, Mom."

"You smell like Henry."

Dan's jaw dropped open. It was rare she'd speak to him directly and rarer still that her words would make sense.

"Henry smells like coffee."

"Dad . . ." Dan swallowed around the lump forming in his throat. "Yeah, Dad smelled like coffee, he sure did. Drank the stuff all day long. You remember that?"

"Well, of course." Her eyes slid away as if remembering something. She didn't share whatever it was. Dan was so glad she'd spoken to him that he didn't mind sitting in silence with her. He held her slim hand with its papery skin and waited, hoping for more, but praising God that at least she was conscious. He'd been around for each improvement, each setback, so he knew not to let his expectations get ahead of him.

By the time Dan left to meet with Beth, his mother seemed stronger. She'd managed to eat most of her lunch before nodding off. The nurses were encouraged, and Dan felt like walking on air. The next few hours passed at a snail's pace. He ended up checking the time so frequently Beth asked what was up.

"I'm having dinner at Erin's tonight. I don't want to lose track of the time."

"Oh, right. You don't need any more misunderstandings there, do you?" Her tone was light, but something about her body language told him she wasn't happy.

"I haven't seen much of her with how busy we've been."

"Right, well I'm helping her friend tomorrow. Erin was looking for volunteers to move her friend out of her house and into an apartment and I signed up." Beth began to pack up her papers, shoving them into her bag with less care than usual.

"Was the friend Claire Murphy?"

"Yes. Rachel asked me to help out."

"That's great. I'm so glad you found the time."

"It's Saturday morning. I figure we can put in a few hours before we head to Portland." She paused. "You didn't forget, right?" He hadn't, but he didn't want to go with her to Portland, and he'd been pretty clear about that. She didn't need him at that meeting, and he was planning to take Erin out to the movie they'd missed, a kind of do-over.

"You know you don't actually need me for that."

"I need you for all of these." Beth countered. "This church is super conservative. If I go on my own, they'll listen, yes, but they may not actually hear me."

"Do you really think they'll 'hear' better if it's coming from a man?"

"I have no doubts." She laid her hand on his. "I know I'm taking up practically every free moment you have. I wouldn't ask if I didn't really need the help." She stood and shouldered her bag. "And there's something I'd like to talk to you about on the drive."

"You could talk to me now."

"No, it's five already. I don't want to keep you any later. Have a good night. We'll talk tomorrow." Her smile was a little lop-sided, and Dan wondered what on earth she had to talk to him about that would both take hours and make her anxious. After she left he took a shower and changed into casual clothes in case there was time before or after dinner to play ball with the boys. He wanted to get to know them better. After all, if everything worked out how he hoped it would, they'd be his stepsons. Suddenly, as if his heart finally caught up with his brain, he felt a lump form in his throat at the thought of being a father. He hadn't even realized his heart yearned for that, but now that it might be a possibility, he knew he wanted it. He wanted to be a husband, to take care of a wife and children, to belong to a family. It was a strange feeling, but a good one.

"Hey guys, can you set the table for four? Pastor Dan's coming for dinner." Erin watched while Seth got to it, but James hesitated. There was a brief look of calculation on James's face as if he was adding up the number of times Dan had visited recently and coming up with a conclusion. Erin decided to wait until he was ready to talk about it. She had a feeling that would be soon enough. When Dan arrived, James got the door.

"Hi, James." Erin looked down the hallway and saw Dan stick out his hand for James to shake. Her son shook his hand and then let him into the house. Erin ducked back in the kitchen and finished the salad, bringing it out as Dan and the boys were taking their seats.

"Hi." Dan gave her a little wave from his end of the table.

"Hi, yourself. Have a seat everyone." She put the bowl down and sat. "Whose turn is it for grace?"

"I think Pastor Dan should say grace. If I'm counting right, it's his turn." James gave Dan a look that was part challenge, part assessment.

"You got it." Dan bowed his head. "Thank you, Lord, for this food, and bless the hands that prepared it. In Jesus' Name, Amen." He looked up and caught Erin's eyes as she did the same.

A slow smile formed on Dan's face, and Erin felt her heart flutter. More proof, though she didn't need it, that this man meant more to her every day. She was relieved and grateful that they had worked out their communication fiasco. She reached over and passed the salad to James who was staring at Dan, his eyes cautious. When he turned to her, having spotted her holding the bowl in mid-air, his expression changed again, and he seemed to be doing his best to pretend nothing was wrong.

Seth missed the silent drama, launching into a long story about a toad he'd found under the oak in the backyard last summer. It was a healthy distraction. He managed to keep up a stream of conversation through most of the meal, usually directing his words to Dan while James sat thoughtfully silent. After dishes Erin sent the boys upstairs. Seth got going on his homework right away. Erin headed with James to the spare room where she kept her bookshelf of kid-appropriate books. "Since we don't know if you're going back to school on Monday or not, I'd like you to pick a book and start reading with an eye to doing a report. Gotta keep your brain moving. I know Brittany said you were doing your online stuff over at her house, but nothing beats reading for homework. Pick one." She gestured to the shelf, but James didn't browse the stacks of books. Instead he shut the door to the room.

"You and Dan?"

"Dan and I what?"

"Are you and Pastor Connors together now, like boyfriend and girlfriend?" His expression was hard to read. She couldn't tell if he liked the idea or not. Considering how much he liked to spend time with Dan, she was hoping what she said next would make him happy.

"Yes. How do you feel about that?"

"I like him. It's kinda weird to think of him as anything but the pastor." James shrugged. "I get it though. You're probably tired of only having Seth and me to hang out with."

"No, that isn't it." She reached out to him and pulled him into a side-hug, generally the only kind he'd allow. "I love hanging out with you and Seth. Our times together are super special. You two, Brittany, Jake, and the baby are my world. I'm not with Pastor Connors because I don't want to be with you."

He ducked his head and bangs swung down over his forehead, hiding his eyes. She let go of his shoulder to take his face in her hands. She tipped it up so she could look him in the eye. "Nothing is further from the truth." She brushed the hair off his forehead, marveling that he was almost eye-to-eye with her. He was such a boy-man. "I'm making more room in our world for someone new. Someone I care for. It might be that we realize we're not right for each other and stay friends instead, or it might turn into something else. Either way, nothing changes what I feel for you. Nothing." She gave his shoulders a quick squeeze and he gently pushed away.

"Okay, enough with the hugging. Gross."

"Right, then pick a book out and get to reading. Make sure you have your stuff packed up for when I drop you off at Brittany's tomorrow too."

"Got it." He gave her a salute as she left the room.

When she made it to the living room she found Dan asleep on the couch. It wasn't a light doze either, he was out. She laughed quietly as she covered him with the afghan off the back of the couch and sat down next to him. Looking up at the clock, she decided she could give him an hour before waking him. She curled up next to him, pulling some of the afghan her way, and read a book on her phone while the house settled around them.

The hour passed all too quickly. She slid out from under the afghan and stood, missing his warmth. "Dan." She must have called his name too softly since he didn't stir. "Dan." She lightly shook him, and his eyes blinked open. "It's getting late, mister." He looked up at her in confusion for a moment before that cleared away and he seemed to remember where he was.

"Man, I can't believe I fell asleep like that." He sat up and rubbed his eyes.

"Your body must have needed it."

"It did. I barely slept last night. Couldn't shut my head down." He stood and kissed her forehead, a mere brush of his lips, but she still waggled a finger at him.

"None of that." She grabbed the cardigan she had hanging by the door and slipped it on. "I'll walk you out." When they were safely on the front porch she let him know about her conversation with James. "He's a sharp kid. I should have guessed he'd figure it out."

"It seems he's okay with it, so that's good."

"Yes. We have one more crisis to get through, though—the school deciding if he can stay. After that, I'm hoping James goes back to being my adorably reliable first born who is never, ever a source of trouble or difficulty."

"What do you think is going to happen?"

Erin sighed. Her pessimistic side said she'd be fired and he'd be expelled. The rest of her was too afraid of hoping for anything. She shivered a little, her sweater too light against the cold night. "I'm trying not to think about it. It's in God's hands."

"Best place." Dan reached out and rubbed his hands up and down her arms before pulling her against his chest. He hadn't buttoned his coat, and Erin pressed herself into his warmth. "I'm a jerk to keep you out here. But, we're on for Saturday night right? We'll give that movie a go?"

"After moving furniture for Claire all day? Uh. No. I'll fall asleep."

"Oh, wait," He made an aggravated noise in the back of his throat. "I'm driving Beth to and from an event in Portland. We'll never make it back in time for a movie anyway."

"You sound annoyed."

"I am. She doesn't need me there. There seems to be a lot of tension between her and the missionary board funding her because she's a single woman. I guess they've always funded men or couples. She thinks she needs me at these events as some kind of 'male covering', which is ridiculous. Women outnumber men in the mission field. And since Beth is the best, they'd be shortsighted to object to her status."

"Well, I guess if it helps to have you there . . ."

"That's why I'm still going. She said she has something she needs to discuss with me on the way back too, so there's that."

Erin swallowed down a stab of jealousy. It was so ridiculous to be jealous of Beth, but she was all the same. She didn't like her having long car rides or long discussions with Dan. Another involuntary shudder ran through her that had nothing to do with the cold. Dan wrapped her up in his arms again and kissed her tenderly.

"I'll call you when I'm done tomorrow. Maybe we'll get back early and you and I can have a late dinner?"

"We'll play it by ear." She pulled away, and he blew her a kiss as he walked away.

Erin pulled her car into the parking lot outside the Murphy's new apartment building, noting that the moving truck was already open and she could see people headed inside with boxes. That was encouraging. It was moving a lot faster than she'd thought it would. She'd stayed at the old house making sure nothing had been left behind and turning in the keys so Claire wouldn't have to. The boys had helped a ton, so she'd dropped them off at Brittany's instead of asking them to help her with the second shift. As she headed in, her phone rang and she fished through her purse for it, catching it before it went to voicemail. "Hello?"

"Erin, you need to get here as fast as humanely possible. Wait, *humanly* possible. Whatever, just get here."

"Claire, what is going on?"

"I'm going to push that woman out a window in about a minute."

"What? What woman?"

"That Beth person. She's driving me crazy. When we got here she was already waiting with the crew of volunteers, which was nice, but since the moment she got up here she's been ordering everyone around, rushing like we've got some kind of deadline. She also overrode the kids' bedroom picks. The boys have to share, and I wanted them to have the biggest room, but while I was in the kitchen unloading boxes, she told the people to set up their beds in the second bedroom, not the master like we'd discussed. Now they're ticked, and I don't know how to tell these nice people to change it, but seriously, it's two of them, one of me. I don't need the big bedroom."

"Okay, I'm coming up the stairs now." Erin ended the call and threw her phone into her purse. Running up the two flights of stairs, she had to dodge people coming back down. When she got to the apartment the tension was palpable. "Hey," she spotted Rachel, the church secretary. "How's it going?"

Rachel pursed her lips. "I know that Claire's having a hard time, but she's also being really difficult to work with. She's kind of pushy, frankly. I'm not sure how we're going to get people to stay and help when she's being so ungrateful, asking people to move stuff around multiple times. It's not okay."

"I'll talk to her." Erin didn't have to track Claire down. She came storming out of the kitchen, spotted Erin, grabbed her arm, and dragged her out into the hallway. "What on earth is going on?"

"Beth. I told you. She's acting like the boss on a work crew and wouldn't listen when I asked her to stop."

"Rachel said—"

"Apparently Rachel thinks rainbows and baby bunnies follow Beth wherever she goes. I tried to ask her to intervene—I've known her for ages—and instead of helping, she got in my face." Claire waited while two men came up the stairs with a couch and entered the apartment. "You need to help me fix this."

"I'll see what I can do, okay?"

"I think I'll go down to the truck and help unload for a bit. I really can't take one more—"

"I'm on it." Erin cut her off and headed back into the apartment. She went to the big bedroom and found Beth there, directing the placement of furniture. Claire had every right to be upset. This was not Beth's apartment. She shouldn't have a say in where the furniture went or who took which bedroom. "Hi!" Erin stood in the doorway. "Could I get a second of your time?" Beth looked up at the other people in the room.

"We're super busy."

"This will be quick."

"Okay." Beth followed her into the bathroom where Erin was hoping they would not be overheard.

"Today is a difficult day for Claire. To say she's 'downsizing' is an understatement. After life dealing out some pretty big hits, she's sensitive, broken. I'm sure you can understand that having some degree of control over what happens to her is really important."

"I'm not following." Beth had a slight Midwestern accent and a softer voice than Erin expected. It went with her sweet and mild exterior, but at the moment it didn't match with her behavior.

"She's had her whole life altered against her will. Today she's starting over, and being able to decide which bedroom her sons are in and where their stuff gets put is part of that. For this to feel like her home, she needs to be the one making decisions about where their things are put."

"Well, we tried that, but Claire was having trouble making up her mind. We only have a few hours, so I had to step in." Beth used a tone Erin tended to reserve for children who weren't getting it the first time, patient and yet annoyed.

"I appreciate that some folks have limited time to volunteer, and it's totally fine for someone to leave early if they need to. But Claire and her family need to feel comfortable and secure here. She's grateful for everything you're doing, but—"

"She has not been acting grateful. She's been difficult to work with."

"Claire has . . . you do get that her husband cheated on her, left her, took all their savings and bought a new house for his new girlfriend and has essentially abandoned his wife and children to their fate? He even cleaned their place out of electronics, took their car . . . she's had it rough."

"That's not rough on the grand scale. That's a blip. She's a well-educated, white woman in the United States. She has resources that women in other parts of the world can't even dream of."

"That's not the issue here. Claire—"

"Needs to get over herself."

Erin stood back in disbelief, her mouth hanging open.

"Her bed is big so it goes in the big room. Her boys have a bunk bed; it fits in the second room. This is not rocket science, and if she'd take a breath she'd see that we are setting things up really nicely for her. She would be grateful instead of tossing her hair and giving everyone a hard time."

Erin took a breath to avoid doing or saying anything stupid since a dozen really stupid ideas were flying around her head, and most of them involved shouting for a start. Erin needed to understand where Beth was coming from in order to deal with her, but she was having trouble engaging her own empathy. She thought about her comment 'tossing her hair'. Claire was naturally pretty, but she was a woman, like Erin, who made sure she didn't leave the house without her hair done and makeup on. She'd worn fitness clothes to handle the move today, as Erin had, but Claire's were designer while Erin's were Old Navy. Claire looked like money. She also looked pampered. Beth had probably taken one look at her and written her off as a spoiled housewife, and any empathy she had disappeared.

As Erin was gathering her calm to try again, Dan walked in.

"Hey, ladies." He seemed to be in a good mood. He gave them both a broad smile before looking around the apartment. "Place looks great. Really nice job."

Beth gave Erin a look that was all innocence. But Erin was not having it.

"We'll need to make some changes in the bedrooms, though. Claire wants her stuff in the middle bedroom instead of the large one. She set that aside for the boys, since they'll be sharing."

"Her bed is too big." Beth folded her arms over her chest.

"If she doesn't mind having little floor space in there, that's up to her." Erin kept her tone carefully neutral.

"It isn't a good use of space."

"That may be, but it's her decision."

"Okay, so now we have to swap everything out? She won't even try it this way? That's not only ungrateful, it's wasting the time of people who gave up their Saturday to help her."

"Y'know what—never mind." Erin stomped out of the room and into the kitchen/living room area where most of the people were working. "Hey, folks, can I get your attention?" They stopped and looked up at her. "If you need to leave because you're on a tight schedule, don't worry a bit. We're totally okay. I don't want anyone staying if they need to be somewhere else. We're very grateful for your help. Again, any time you need to leave is okay, please don't feel any pressure to stay. "

"Nah, we're good," a tall man with what looked like his two grown sons answered.

"I just got here, so I'm fine," another person said.

"Great. Thank you. If you have any questions about where something needs to go, you can ask Claire. I think she's down with the truck. Okay?" The crowd nodded or smiled their assent. Erin turned around and saw Dan holding Beth's hand and speaking softly to her. Erin felt her stomach drop about the same time her heart clenched in pain. Dan was leaning close to Beth who had a hurt expression on her face. Erin had a moment of doubt that she'd done the right thing. That was replaced quickly with irritation that she told herself was not jealousy. No, definitely not. Dan looked up and saw Erin watching and came out of the room with Beth trailing. "Beth and I need to get on the road to Portland."

Beth and I? The words cut into Erin. She nodded her assent even though she was not okay with his use of "Beth and I" as if they were a couple. At least it would get Beth out of the apartment.

"Beth, why don't you head down and I'll catch up to you." Dan solicitously guided her out of the room, his hand at the small of her back. Something about that gesture stuck the knife in Erin's gut even deeper and twisted. Dan watched Beth leave and then turned to Erin, maneuvering her into the bathroom, shutting the door part way. "What was that about?"

"Your friend doesn't like Claire much, and she was letting it show."

"I don't think so. That's not Beth."

"How well do you really know her?" Erin waited for Dan to answer.

"I'm not sure that's the right question to be asking."

"So, you're going to take Beth's opinion of the situation instead of trusting mine?"

"I know Claire is your friend."

"She's become a friend, yes. Watching her go through this trial, I can't imagine anyone not wanting to be a friend to her. Your girl seemed to have a problem with that, though."

"She's not 'my girl'. I've explained it."

Dan's tone was impatient, and that hurt. Erin took in a quick breath to try and find her calm. It was long gone. "No, you really haven't. Not the soft words and holding her hand, not the 'Beth and I' way you speak of her, not the fact that you're letting her take up every spare moment you have. None of that you've really explained. But you seem to expect me to put up with it all the same."

"What have you had to put up with?" He had gone from impatient to annoyed.

"Seriously?" Erin had been so patient with him, and he wasn't giving her even an ounce of that in return. With all she was facing with the school meeting on Monday, she couldn't have this relationship be rocky too. She needed to know he trusted her and that she could put her trust in him, but at every opportunity to show it, he'd failed. She'd been failed too many times before. It was making her feel ragged and exposed. "I'm done." She stated it flatly.

"Okay, there's a ton of people here, I'm sure they'll be fine."

"No. I'm done with this." She waved a hand back and forth between them. "You need to get your head straight. I know you're dealing with a lot between your mom and the contract the church wants you to sign. I wanted to help you, I wanted to make it easier, to be . . ." She almost said 'helpmate', but she checked herself at the last moment. "This hot-and-cold thing you do, I can't take it. I'm not built that way. I guess I'm too insecure or something, but I can't do it."

"Wait, are you ending things between us?"

"Yes, because clearly to you it was only ever a 'thing'." She closed her eyes, willing him to walk away before she got any sadder. "You have no idea what all this back and forth does to me." She opened her eyes and he was still standing there, looking surprised and unhappy.

"Erin, don't do this. Give me another shot."

"How many are you going to need?"

"I don't know." He shook his head. "I told you, I don't know what

I'm doing."

"I don't think that's it. You're struggling with something bigger than a relationship, bigger than a new contract. I don't know what it is. I want to be there for you, but for some reason the normal hits—stuff that would have bounced off me if it was someone else—because it's you, it kills." He reached for her and she backed out of his arms. "You need to go. I . . . I need you to go."

Without a word, he did.

Erin was in turmoil. Her head was telling her it was the right thing to do while her heart was aching. She was sick to her stomach, half prepared to run after him and take it all back. Instead she counted, waiting for some kind of calm to return, one she could put on like a mask so she didn't walk out into that room with what happened written all over her face. After a minute she found it and then left the room and got to work. It looked like Rachel had left with Beth and Dan, and that was for the best. Apparently, she had picked her side, so to speak. A while later, after they'd switched the bedrooms around, which no one minded doing, Pete arrived and Erin pulled him aside. "I need to tell you something and not have you mention it to anyone, but also sort of run interference for me."

"That's a tall order."

"I broke it off with Dan today, please—" She held up a hand to stop him from asking why. "I know you want to know why, but I can't get into it. All I know is that he is in no way ready for a real relationship. I'm not sure what's up with him, but I can't keep letting him in only to have him work me over. The sad thing is he doesn't even know he's doing it."

"I'm not surprised he doesn't. It seems that man is at odds with himself. He still hasn't signed his contract. He's been working with Beth Russell for the last two weeks on her mission project, and I wonder if maybe she isn't trying to recruit him."

"Oh." The light dawned. Beth didn't want Dan romantically, she wanted him professionally. She was worried that she'd lose her funding without a male partner. That must be why she was occupying all his time, trying to remind him of his first calling, get him to go back into missions with her. "Do you think he'll go?" Asking the question opened up a crater in her stomach. If he left . . .

"I want to say no, because I believe he belongs here, was called here, and should stay here, but I don't know." Pete looked concerned, and if Pete was worried, there was a real possibility that Dan would leave. The idea of him moving overseas, of maybe never seeing him again was so painful, she couldn't breathe. She had to walk away from Pete, had to empty her head of the thought of Dan leaving so she could take a breath again.

Dan stared at the road ahead, willing the minutes to eat up the miles. All he wanted was to be alone, but they were still an hour outside of Sweet River. Beth had been silent so far, sensing his mood. The presentation had gone fine, exactly as all the others had that she'd dragged him to. Once again, she'd deferred to him a dozen times when she didn't have to, but if that helped her, he'd do it.

"Dan?"

He turned to acknowledge Beth calling him and then looked back at the road again.

"You seem distracted. I have something I'd like to talk to you about, but if you'd rather have your thoughts right now . . ."

"No, my thoughts right now are not happy ones."

"Erin?" She guessed and he nodded. She sighed. "That's my fault. I was impatient with Claire. She was acting like such a pampered princess that I lost my temper and started ordering people around. I ought to apologize."

"No." He couldn't imagine a scenario in which Beth apologizing to Erin would help him out. *He* needed to apologize to Erin. "It's something the two of us have to sort out. I haven't been the greatest boyfriend, and she's been patient enough. It's time I got my head together."

"It's not together? Why??"

"The contract. No, it's not the contract, it's that I don't know if I truly want to be a pastor, if this is what God wants. It feels like He's been silent for so long. I feel like a failure." It was hard to admit that to Beth, but she didn't seem to think less of him for it.

"We all go through that. Are you kidding? Sometimes it's because we're being stubborn goats and He's waiting for us to catch on, sometimes it's impossible to tell the reason. I don't want to sound like your mentor, but have you been reading? Not for work, but actual study for you, one-on-one time."

"I've been slacking, honestly."

"Start there then. And something to take to your one-on-one time . . . I want to make you an offer."

"Really?" He felt apprehension start to settle in his gut.

"Lodestone needs a co-director. I'd like that to be you. I wouldn't need a time commitment." She added quickly. "We could consider it temporary if you really wanted to, until you felt it was where you wanted to be, but . . ." She trailed off.

He turned to look at her and she was biting her lip. A tell of hers he remembered from their seminary days. She was nervous. "I could really use your help there."

Dan was about to open his mouth and turn her down when she raised her hand to stop him. "Don't answer me now. Think on it, pray about it. Give it time."

He looked out at the road again, his head in turmoil. The last thing he needed was yet another thing to think about.

CHAPTER TWENTY-TWO

SUNDAY MORNING DAWNED BRIGHT AND COLD. The window across from Dan's bed was at the perfect angle to catch the first rays of the sun. As they bathed his face in light he sat up and swung his legs over the side of the bed, planting his feet on the cold floor. Since he hadn't been able to sleep, he might as well get up. It was early enough that he had hours to go over his sermon for that day, and he'd need the prep time. After dropping Beth off at her apartment he'd come home and mindlessly watched the news trying not to think about what had happened with Erin. Every time he let his head go back to that scene, he felt sick. He'd gone to bed at ten thinking sleep would come. It hadn't. His mind kept replaying the look on Erin's face as she told him to go.

His relationship with Erin was the one thing in his life he had no doubts about, and he'd taken it for granted, treated her like an afterthought, and lost her. Not only did he lose Erin, he lost James and Seth too, unless a miracle occurred and she gave him another chance. "She shouldn't." His voice echoed in the silent room. It was the truth. She was the smart one. She'd figured out what a mess he was and rightfully told him to get his head straight. If only he could. After all his promises to her it seemed he'd failed at the first test. She deserved better. Her kids deserved better. Maybe he wasn't cut out to be a husband and father.

He stood up, disgusted with his train of thought, and took a shower. Once he was dressed he headed downstairs to his office and tried to banish Erin from his mind. He prayed for clarity and discernment. When he was done he felt steadier, but his gut was still tight. Simply not thinking about her wasn't going to work. He needed to resolve to do the right thing and leave her alone. As much as the thought killed him, he had to do what was best for Erin.

Flipping through his Bible to check that he had bookmarked the right spots for today's sermon, something he'd highlighted a while ago leapt out at him. It was what he considered his life verse, Isaiah 6:8 *Then I heard the voice of the Lord saying, "Whom shall I send? And who will go for us?" And I said, "Here am I. Send me!"* He'd highlighted that passage in every Bible he owned as a reminder of his calling. Closing his eyes, he prayed aloud. "Here I am."

The guilt, pain, and conflict in his heart and mind were too loud. If there was an answer to his prayer, he didn't hear it. Instead, he reviewed his sermon notes. He re-read the verses until he was sure he had them down and wouldn't be tripping over his words in his fatigue. It wasn't the first sermon he'd be delivering while exhausted, but this was the first time the reason for it was hardly a noble one. He hadn't stayed up all night comforting a grieving parishioner or praying with a sick friend. No, it was his conscience that had robbed him of sleep. He deserved a sleepless night after the way he'd treated Erin.

Hours later he was standing in the pulpit, looking out over the assembled people thinking he wasn't worthy to be there. Then he remembered that he was the vessel. God would use him even if he was a conflicted mess. He concentrated on the verses before him, the words of the Being that gave his life purpose, and he delivered the sermon. It wasn't his best. At the end of the service he stood at the exit and shook hands with parishioners and managed small talk at coffee hour, all the while feeling the turmoil inside him simmer.

"Hey." Beth tugged on his elbow. "You look about a million miles away."

Dan shook his head. "Lost in my thoughts. I'm sorry."

"Ah, well, that's understandable. You've got a lot to think about." She cocked her head to the side. "My offer for one, but considering how distracted you are, I'm thinking it's something else on your mind."

He realized that he hadn't been thinking about her offer, but he should. Wasn't this the sign he was waiting for? Erin broke it off with him, rightly. He was reluctant to sign the contract with Calvary, and now Beth had offered him a way back into missions. With his mom on the mend, maybe this was God's will, working at Lodestone, building a new mission.

"Honestly, I do have a lot on my mind, but I'm considering your offer. I might just take it, but there's a lot to consider. I'll need a few days."

"Of course. I always assumed you'd need time." Beth smiled brightly. "This is good though, you thinking about it. I'm really pleased." She seemed almost relieved as she began going over the time line she was hoping to follow and when they'd be leaving. That made it feel real. If he did this he'd be getting on a plane for Africa, and he wouldn't be back for months. Once they got there he'd be working so hard there wouldn't be time to feel the loss of all he'd left behind. It would be a clean break and that was really appealing.

He said goodbye to Beth and headed back to his office. Once there he sat at his desk and tried to write a list of the pros and cons in taking the job with Lodestone. But, it was as if Erin was on every line, in every calculation. This wasn't going to work. How could he determine if he was really supposed to take the job if all he could think about was the pain he'd feel in leaving her behind? He knew the only way forward was to do the right thing and put an end to the hope that she could be his. He pulled his phone out of his pocket and opened their text thread. The last message sent had been from her before the apartment incident. It was a heart. Sometimes she did that, sent a single heart or a smiley face. It was as if she wanted to reach out to him in a way that didn't put the burden on him to reply. It was her giving to him and expecting nothing back. That was Erin and he didn't deserve her.

Erin pushed off with a foot and set the rocking chair in motion. She had maneuvered the chair into the perfect spot to catch the late-afternoon sun coming in through the front window of Mac and Katherine's house. Her whole family had joined them for Sunday dinner, and Erin was happily in a post-dinner doze with her granddaughter snuggled in her arms, her silky head pressed against Erin's shoulder. Looking down at the sleeping baby, her pert little mouth slightly open, her long lashes resting against her chubby cheeks, Erin felt a kind of contentment that was as close to perfect as could be. The baby reminded her of Brittany when she was small, but the child definitely had her father's hair and his solid structure. Brittany had been a tiny thing. Erin remembered holding her like she was spun glass, so afraid of hurting her that she rarely went out. Brittany was proving to be a far more confident mother. Even now, instead of hovering nearby she was out with her brothers and her husband playing soccer with Mac and Katherine on their big lawn.

Pete and Lauren had joined them for dinner and were sitting by the fireplace nearby, their quiet conversation gently lulling Erin into a deeper stupor. There was nothing like a peaceful Sunday afternoon to help banish her fear over the impending hearing. She felt safe with her family and friends around her. If only it could heal the ache in her heart left by breaking up with Dan. No amount of good food and friendly company could untie the knot in her stomach whenever she thought of him. She had no doubt she'd done the right thing. He needed to get his head on straight before he was ready to be in a serious relationship, and she wasn't going to waste her time on him playing house with her as some kind of practice run for the real thing... But part of her wanted to find a way to still be his friend, to help him through it. There didn't seem to be a way that didn't involve a lot of pain on her part and confusion on his.

She felt her phone vibrate in her pocket and managed to pull it out without waking the baby. As if thinking about him summoned the man, a text from Dan was on the screen. "You were right." She opened the conversation and read more. "I'm not sure I am the man you need me to be. You deserve someone who is." Her stomach dropped. She couldn't read the rest.

"Erin, is everything all right?" Lauren was staring at her with a concerned expression.

Erin couldn't respond. Her heart was racing, and she felt sick.

"Did you get bad news?" Pete was on his feet and coming near. She didn't know how to answer him. Yes, this was bad. It sounded like Dan was giving up. He wasn't going to even try to work out what was going on in his head so he could be with her. It was as if she wasn't worth the effort. Her heart felt the crushing disappointment for a second before it turned into something like grief. Looking down at the screen she read the last. "I am so sorry for hurting you. It was the last thing I wanted to do. God bless you, Erin."

Pete took the phone out of her hand as Lauren stood up and joined him, pulling his hand with the phone closer to her and reading along with him.

"That boy." Pete looked up at the ceiling and handed Erin the phone, his lips pressed together, his expression angry.

"In a text?" Lauren gasped. With a hand she flung her long, silver-blonde hair off her shoulder and held out her arms. "Let me take little Katie for a few minutes." She took the baby into her hands and with a practiced maneuver snuggled her into her shoulder. "Now you can feel free to throw things if you'd like."

Erin huffed out what should have been a laugh, but sounded all wrong. She looked up at Pete. "He's not even going to try, is he?"

Pete shook his head slightly. "I'm not sure what to tell you. I know he has deep feelings for you, but he's locked in his own head right now."

"You warned me." She swallowed the urge to burst into tears. "I didn't listen."

"Oh Erin, the open heart is rarely a cautious one." Lauren sank into one of the chairs by the fire and motioned for Erin to join her.

She got up from the rocking chair and slumped into the cushy armchair next to Lauren. "I was definitely not cautious."

"No one would have been in your shoes." Lauren gave her a guilty look. "I'm afraid I make Pete tell me everything. I hope you don't mind."

"No, not at all." Erin waved a hand as if to dismiss any awkwardness. The whole town knew the story. "It's not like the Lowdown hasn't covered it anyway." She tried to laugh again and failed.

"It's a beautiful story. He's a man of God, a good man by all measures. I can see it." She smiled at Erin. "You, admiring him from afar for years. Him, not realizing the treasure you are since you hide your light so well. Then one day, he sees it shining, and he falls for you. It's so romantic. But the course of love rarely runs smooth. Shakespeare said that, or something like it, in the 16th century so you know that's a universal truth." Lauren reached out and squeezed Erin's hand. "Your regard for

Dr. Connors says a lot about the woman you are. If I can be so bold as to offer you advice, tell him how this makes you feel. It seems he's concerned about your feelings, but he isn't considering them with this text."

"Relationships are new to him. He doesn't get what's okay and what's not when it comes to this stuff. He wouldn't understand that this isn't something you should say in a text."

"Don't feel the need to defend him." Pete took a seat on the ottoman opposite her.

"She's defending him because she's in love with him." Lauren pushed Pete's shoulder playfully. "It's what we do with people we love."

Love? The truth washed over her like a wave. She was in love with him. For years she had crushed on him, but what she felt now was soul-deep. Even if he didn't return it in kind, even if he left the country, she'd still feel the same way. Her first marriage hadn't been a loving one. She'd been infatuated with Jimmy, wrapped up in the rush of emotion, almost giddy with it. By the time that infatuation had faded Jimmy had begun to use his fists to end an argument, and that killed any budding love before it had the chance to blossom. What she felt for Dan was so different. It felt like the real thing. How that could be in a few short weeks, she didn't know, but it was real all the same.

"We old folks know a bit about love." Lauren's words were quiet, her tone gentle as she looked at Pete. He was staring back at her, the expression on his face saying it all. They'd only had a few weeks too, and that's all it took for them. Love grew in surprising places. It was a beautiful thing to see, but she needed them to quit before she dissolved into a puddle of tears.

Erin pointed at Pete. "If you get any sappier, I'm leaving the room."

Pete chuckled softly, letting Erin use sarcasm as her shield while Lauren changed the subject. "Why don't you take a walk and maybe kick something soft, like a hay bale. That always helps me."

Erin wished she felt like kicking or throwing things. It would be better to be angry than to feel so wounded. "Great idea. I'll be back." She put her coat on and headed outside. She watched her boys playing with the others for a bit before she walked down to the barn to see the horses. A soft nicker reached her ears as she opened the door. Mac owned a pair of failed race horses named Misery and Agony. They were rescues, high-energy and high-maintenance. Recently he'd added a sedate mare named Belinda that was much more Erin's speed. She was a rescue too so Mac couldn't be blamed for her name. Erin called to her as she made her way to the stall. Belinda poked out her nose and snuffled her for a bit before pushing her whole head out of the stall and nudging Erin. Erin petted her soft coat. "That's a good girl. You are so pretty."

"Careful, she bites."

Erin looked over her shoulder and saw Katherine entering the barn and sighed. Today was not turning out to be the day for quiet introspection. If she wanted to kick hay bales, it looked like she'd have an audience.

"She only bites you because she's in love with Mac and wants you out of the way."

Katherine smiled "She bites him too."

"He probably deserves it."

Katherine watched Belinda snuffle Erin's hand. "So, are you out here for horse cuddles or are you hiding out?"

"Both?"

"I thought as much. What's wrong?"

Erin pulled her phone out of her pocket, pulled up the text conversation, and handed it to Katherine. "Remember how I told you that Dan and I were taking a break until he got his head together and decided what he wanted? Well, it looks like he's decided."

Katherine read through the message making tisking noises. The expression on her face said it all as she handed the phone back.

"It's not like he's angry at me or anything. It's not that bad." She shrugged. "But he is giving up and that kills." Even she could hear the pain in that last word. Katherine didn't reply. Instead she gave Erin a hug. Out of habit Erin held herself stiffly, then gave in and hugged her back.

"I still don't like hugs."

"Liar." Katherine let her go.

"I only tolerate yours because I know you're a softie. You can't help it."

Katherine laughed and then grew serious. "I don't want to tell you what to do, but I will remind you that there was a day you came to me when I had no hope that Mac would come back to me. He and I were definitely over and he'd left town. I was devastated, and you literally had to pick me up off the floor."

Erin remembered going to see Katherine and finding her overcome after having received a curt voicemail from Mac. Erin had been so angry with him that she'd called him and told him off for knowing Katherine was fragile and breaking her all the same. The situation with Dan was different. She wasn't fragile and good thing since he hadn't been careful with her heart, hadn't even known how. "I remember, but this is different."

"Every relationship is, but I guess what I'm trying to say is that there's still a chance this could work out. He obviously has feelings for you. I think he's confused and in a bad place. I was there once too." She reached up to pet Belinda, but the horse gave her a warning nip, and she jerked her hand back. "Meanie. Anyway, maybe it's wrong, but I hope that he comes around and realizes what he has in you."

"Not everybody gets a happy ending, especially not in love. I have three great kids, one beautiful granddaughter, and a son-in-law I no longer want to shoot. I have wonderful friends, and I have a Heavenly Father who loves me. That's a lot. That's enough."

Katherine nodded and they lapsed into silence for a few moments before she spoke again. "All the same, I'm still going to hope he gets a clue. You deserve happiness." With that she left the barn.

It was close to supper time when Erin, James, and Seth got home, but no one was hungry after the big meal Katherine had made that afternoon. Erin told the boys they could play outside until it got dark. The sun was setting earlier so it meant they'd only have an hour at most. They went bolting out the door, and she went upstairs to change into PJs and find something to read. Instead of a book, she pulled out her Bible and looked up a passage in Romans. Bits of it had been running through her mind lately, a kind of calm in the storm her life was becoming. *"For I am convinced that neither death nor life, neither angels nor demons, neither the present nor the future, nor any powers, neither height nor depth, nor anything else in all creation, will be able to separate us from the love of God that is in Christ*

Jesus our Lord." She got out a notebook and wrote out the verse so it would be written into her memory as well.

Dan looked up at the knock on his door. He was sitting on his couch in his office trying to read, but mostly spacing out. He was surprised he had a visitor. It was only five, but on a Sunday night he rarely had anyone stopping by. Getting up he went to the door and opened it, startled to find James standing there. "Hey, buddy." Worry bit him James had come alone. "Is something wrong?"

"Yeah, something's wrong." His voice was strained and Dan could feel the tension pouring off him in waves. His face was growing red, his hands balled into fists, and it looked like he was in the mood to swing at Dan.

"Come in, let's get this sorted out." Dan stood back and James stepped inside.

"Now, can you tell me what's going on?"

"You dumped my mom." James pointed a finger in his face. "You acted like you liked her, acted like you wanted to be a part of our family, and then you dumped her!"

"Did she tell you that?"

"No." The look on James's face was disgusted. "She's pretending everything is fine, which is what she always does even though she's sad. I heard Mrs. MacAlister talking, and she said you broke mom's heart."

Dan absorbed that kick to the gut and tried to explain. "Buddy, it's not like that."

"You sent her a text? What is wrong with you? You're supposed to be a good guy!"

"James, let me explain. Please, sit down a second." He reached out to him, but James pulled away.

"No. I'm never listening to anything you have to say. You're a liar!"

"I'm not, James. You mom broke up with me."

"What?" The boy leaned back as if shocked.

"This isn't something you and I should be talking about, but as you've already got the wrong end of the stick, I'm going to set you straight. Your mom broke up with me because I've got a lot going on. She didn't want us to get more serious until I was free to take our relationship seriously. And she's right. You guys all deserve my best, and if I can't give it to you right now, I don't belong in your life."

"I don't understand. Why is she worried about that?"

"She's trying to protect us all from getting hurt. I have feelings for your mom, and I've really liked being part of your family. I don't want to damage that. With what I have to work out, if I'm not careful, I could end up hurting her. That's the last thing I'd want."

"What kind of stuff do you have to work out?"

Dan wondered how much he could or should explain. James might be bright and savvy, but he was still thirteen. "I've got a few job offers to consider."

"Would you leave Sweet River?"

"That's one option."

James seemed to consider this information, but Dan couldn't tell what his feelings were.

"But if it's just about jobs, why is my mom sad?"

"Because she has feelings for me too. Neither one of us really wants to be apart, but it's the best thing for right now."

"I guess I get it." James shrugged and stuffed his hands in the pocket of his hoodie. "But if someone's important to you, like if you feel things for them, what kind of job would stop you from being together?"

Dan was speechless. He had no answer for that question. It wasn't a job that was stopping him from being with Erin, it was his inner turmoil. Erin deserved a man who was uncomplicated. How could he explain that to a teenager who only saw things in black and white? "Sometimes, with adults, it gets complicated."

James rolled his eyes. "I've heard that before." He headed for the door.

"Are we good?" Dan waited while James slowly turned around, his hand on the door knob.

"I don't know." He paused for long enough that Dan began to feel deeply uneasy. "For me, it's no big thing because I don't get my hopes up, but Seth thought you were awesome. He thought you were sticking around, that you might end up being our dad." James opened the door, likely unaware his words were like a knife in Dan's heart. He couldn't know that was exactly what Dan had wanted as well. But if he could fail Erin so easily, he could fail the boys too, and there was no way he was going to do that.

"I guess we weren't enough for you after all." James slammed the door shut behind him before Dan could tell him how wrong he was.

CHAPTER TWENTY-THREE

FOR THE SECOND TIME SINCE COMING to teach at Sweet River Christian Academy, Erin sat in a chair in front of the board of trustees and waited to hear her fate. The first time she was there as a parent, and it was her current son-in-law Jake on the hot seat. Today she was in the hot seat and she was on her own. Katherine had been asked not to attend. In fact, no one other than Erin and the board were in attendance. At first this made her panic, and then she remembered that God was in attendance and that's all she needed. She didn't feel calm, but a kind of peace had filled her. Maybe it was resolve. Whatever it was, she didn't want to crawl out of her own skin anymore. When Will Thomas, the chairman, spoke she was ready for the decision regardless of what it was.

"Erin, the first thing I'd like to say is how we all have admired your work here. You took a department in chaos and brought it into order in a remarkably short time. Truly, you exceeded our expectations." He shifted in his chair and pushed a hand through his short, gray hair. She knew the 'however' was coming. "Despite your excellent work, there was a great deal made of the events last year. Even though you withdrew your daughter when it was discovered she was pregnant, there were parents who objected to the fact you stayed on as faculty."

She nodded. They hadn't just objected, they'd protested with letters to the board and snide messages in her inbox.

"Now that James has violated the code of conduct, we have heard from these parents again. Their concerns aren't without merit. If we go easy on James they may interpret that as bias. The other student was suspended as per policy, but James was the instigator which complicates the situation." He picked up a piece of paper in front of him. "And we've read your appeal to us concerning the appropriate consequences for this incident."

Erin glanced around the room. Most of the faces were friendly, although a few didn't make eye contact with her. She wasn't sure if that was a good or bad sign. Pete met her gaze, but he didn't give anything away. She knew this had to be awkward for him, and she was sorry she'd put him in this spot.

"We've made a decision." Will looked around at his fellow board members. "And it is unanimous. We will accept your resignation as of December 31st. That will give us enough time to find a replacement for your position as well as give you time to find another. James will serve an additional week of suspension, and when he returns he will be on probation for four semesters. Any infraction during that time will result in immediate dismissal."

Erin breathed a sigh of relief. She was going to have to work with James on his temper to keep him from violating that probation, but this outcome was better than she'd hoped for. Having the rest of November and all of December to find another job was a boon she hadn't been expecting. "Thank you." She couldn't think of what else to say.

"Thank you for offering to resign. It made this decision easier." Will answered and a few heads around the table nodded.

"Should I write a formal resignation and give it to the director?"

"Yes, that will be fine. We'll have you meet with HR as well and sort out the details." Will stood and held out his hand across the table. She stood up and shook it. "Thank you, Erin."

"Thank you, Will." She left the room, shutting the door behind her. Instead of feeling sorry or anxious, she felt nothing but relief and gratitude to God for the outcome. She jogged down the stairs and into the administration office, looking around to see if Katherine was still there. Spotting the door to the director's office slightly ajar, she knocked on it and then entered.

"You don't need to tell me." Katherine was stuffing a stack of papers into her briefcase. "They told me right before you went up." The papers weren't fitting, but she shoved them in anyway. "This stinks."

"No, it doesn't. Not really. What choice did they have?"

Katherine sighed as she tried to flip the cover of her briefcase down over the papers, but couldn't get the clasp to close. The papers were still sticking out, their edges mashed. "I guess in the end they had no choice, but I don't have to like it." She looked up at Erin. "I'm going to miss working with you."

"It's not like I'm moving away or something."

"With all the changes coming, this is one I didn't need."

"Ah, so all this." She pointed at the abused papers in Katherine's bag. "Isn't about me? Are you worried about taking on the kids?" She took a seat in the chair in front of Katherine's desk. "I thought you were all set."

"Me? No. Mac is. He's all…" She waived a hand in the air, and Erin wasn't sure exactly what that meant, but she guessed that Mac was being his usual stoic self. He rarely let his emotions show. He was probably nervous too, but he'd never burden Katherine with his concerns.

"Have you talked with him about your worries?"

"What? No. I don't want him to worry too."

Erin chuckled. "Man, you two are bad at this stuff, aren't you?"

"Bad at what?"

"Trusting. Leaning on the person God gave you to see you through problems. Mac would want to know that you're worried. He's probably got worries of his own. You need to talk to each other. What is it you're concerned about, though? All your preparations are good to go. Your mom has moved in so you've got back up right there. It seems you've got it all together."

"The details, yes, but this is such a huge change, and I am so afraid of failing. I'm worried I'll do it all wrong and end up making these kids hate me."

"Katherine, you're good with kids. You'll be even better with these because they're going to be your own. The biggest job of any parent is to love their children. The rest you improvise."

Katherine rolled her eyes. "I'll take your word for it. You're an awesome mom."

Those words felt like a blessing. Being on her own, handling every crisis alone and hoping she was doing the right thing was tough. She'd been at it for a decade, but it didn't seem to get any easier. The problems grew along with the kids. Although she was confident in her instincts at this point, it still felt good to hear someone else say she was doing a good job. "Thanks." Her throat felt scratchy, and she quickly changed the subject. "I'm going to write up an official letter of resignation and hand it over this week."

Katherine gave her a long, searching look. "I'm glad to see you're at peace with this. It will be a relief to tell Mac you're okay. He's been worried about you."

"No need. But remember, that I'm here for you both. Whatever you need."

Katherine reached across the desk and took Erin's hand in hers. "You're here for me, you're here for Claire, and you were there for Dan. Who's there for Erin?"

"God is. Someday I might have a flesh-and-blood person in my corner too, but even if that doesn't happen, God isn't leaving. Whatever road I walk, He's walking it with me. It took me a long time to figure that out."

"When did you get so wise?" Katherine squeezed her hand and let it go.

"It's a recent development." Erin gave her a quick grin then got up from the chair and headed out. "See you tomorrow."

"It's not too bright, is it?" Dan set the brakes on his mother's wheelchair so she could enjoy the sun if she wanted to. The light was streaming in through the glass. November in Maine usually meant gray skies and clouds. Some years it seemed like the whole month was somber, but today there wasn't a cloud in the sky. He would have liked to take her outside, but no way was she ready for that. Instead he decided they'd sit in the atrium, the next best thing. Dan watched as she raised her face to the sun, and he decided to interpret that as an okay.

He sat down next to her and looked out the windows and over the lawn. It wasn't an awe-inspiring view, but it was far better than the four walls of her hospital room. Now that she was showing some small signs of recovery there was the possibility that she'd be moved to the semi-independent wing where they might be able to work towards eventually leaving altogether for a senior apartment with an aide. He knew he was letting his hope run amok, but he was so relieved to see any improvement. It made him want to build a better future for her, one where she'd have some kind of independence. As much as he enjoyed sitting in the quiet with his mom, he didn't want to let the silence stretch.

It had been days since he'd sent that text to Erin, since James had confronted him and said those devastating words. He'd been struggling since then. Sleep had become almost impossible. He'd realized something last night when he was staring at the ceiling, a lead weight in his chest. Despite his careful control, despite his years of practice separating and governing his emotions, he'd managed to fall in love with Erin. She had his heart even if he didn't deserve hers. There was no taking it back. He didn't want it back. It was causing him too much pain. Longing and regret were his constant companions.

He needed to take Beth up on her offer, needed to dedicate his life to God's work and His work alone. Everything else he touched seemed to go wrong in some terrible way. In Africa, it would all be new again. He could start over. The thought of it made him feel hollow, but all the signs were pointing to leave. There were details to be taken care of, not the smallest of which was to tell his mom, but there wasn't any real impediment to leaving anymore.

"Hey mom." He turned to face her. She looked uncomfortable. "You okay?"

She pushed herself upright a bit and took a deep breath. "Okay."

"You sure?"

"Can I have tea?" Her voice was still pretty weak, but a full sentence of it sounded like an angel singing to him. After the years of damage from her stroke, any words she managed to string together in sensibility were a triumph as far as he was concerned.

"Sure, I can wheel you to the cafeteria if you'd like?" He stood and she looked up at him, a little frown on her face, her bangs falling into her eyes. He reached out and took the barrette out of her hair, brushed the locks back and re-fastened it. "Better?" Her lips tipped up into a shaky smile. He wheeled her chair out of the room and down the hallway to the cafeteria. When they arrived, the place was half-full of residents with assistants or family. Dan found a table near center and parked his mom there while he made her tea. It took a minute to find hot water among the many coffee carafes. As he was pouring he heard a commotion behind him. He spun around when he heard a loud, female voice call, "Mrs. Connors." A nurse was looming over his mother's wheelchair. "Mrs. Connors, are you okay?" Dan started to push his way through the maze of tables and chairs. As the nurse turned to shout over her shoulder for assistance Dan could clearly see his mother's face twisted in pain, her mouth agape. Her hands were clutching the gown at her chest, her fingers twisted in the fabric.

"What's happening?" He reached out to his mom, but an orderly came to her side, bumping him out of the way.

"She's in arrest." The nurse nodded to the orderly who sprinted to the far side of the room and hit a button. An alarm sounded. Dan heard the speakers blare the announcement of a code blue.

"What is going on?" Dan was shouting now. The nurse looked up at him and started to speak, but was interrupted as a crew of staff rushed in and began taking his mom out. The orderly held Dan by the arm to prevent him from following.

"Please, that's my mom. What's happening?"

"I'm sorry, sir, but they got to have room to work. C'mon to the doors." The man was huge. He had to have a foot on Dan and maybe fifty pounds as well, but Dan still yanked his arm away as he ran out of the room. In the hallway, he was stunned to see his mom already laid out on the stretcher, a nurse was straddling her and pounding her on the chest while another had a mask over her face, pumping air into her lungs. Another nurse came running with a cart with wires and paddles. He knew what that was for.

The orderly grabbed hold of him again and dragged him back a few feet. "I know that's your mama, but you can't get in the way." He had a slight Dominican accent as if years in Maine had worn off its edges.

"What's wrong with her?"

"She's in cardiac arrest."

"How?"

"I don't know, sir, but we're going to do our best to get her heart beating again." He turned Dan to face him. "You don't want to watch this."

Dan turned back and watched anyway. It was surreal. One moment he'd been pouring her tea and the next she'd been in agony. What they were doing to her now was supposed to save her life but it looked savage. The orderly was right, no son should watch this, but he couldn't pull himself away. Finally, a nurse shouted that they had a pulse, but that barely stopped them. The cart was wheeled away and the sides of the stretcher were lifted up and locked in place.

"This is her son. Can you help him?" A nurse called to the orderly, pointing at Dan.

The orderly nodded. "Okay, we got her heart beating again." He was using a gentle tone. "And next door?" He pointed his thumb at the nearby walkway over to the hospital the rehab was attached to. "We got the best cardiac department in the state. She's in good hands."

Dan was in such a fog that his mother was taken through the doors and out of his sight before he understood. "Where are they taking her?"

"They gonna take her next door to emergency and probably up to the cardiac wing. I can get you there."

Dan looked down at the orderly's name tag and then back up at him. "Thank you, Engel."

"You say it like a native." He seemed impressed as he guided Dan through the doors and down the walkway to the hospital.

If Dan had been himself he'd share that he'd spent a year in the Dominican working at a missionary school and had met several Engels, but he wasn't himself. Instead he tried to keep up with Engel's long strides as they entered the hospital and navigated the series of reception desks to see where his mother had been taken. They ended up in the cardiac wing. The waiting room was large with multiple banks of plastic chairs mostly facing two flat-screen TVs mounted to the wall showing a cable news station.

"I'll be sure they know you're waiting here. The doctor should come out shortly and talk to you about what's going on."

Dan held out his hand and Engel shook it. "Thank you." It was all he could say.

"No worries, you'll be okay." He clapped Dan on the shoulder and headed down the hallway and out of the wing. Dan sat in one of the few banks of chairs not facing the TV. He didn't need any additional stress right now. Mercifully he didn't have to wait long. A woman clad in surgical scrubs emerged from the double-doors off to his left. He stood up as she neared him.

"Dr. Connors?" She held out her hand and he shook it. "Dr. Burke. I am one of the team working on your mom right now. I know this is all a shock and everything is moving pretty fast, but since she's already a patient there's protocol for how we make decisions in case of a medical crisis. We needed to move fast in your mom's case or we were going to lose her." She went on to explain about how they'd already done the scan to see the damaged valve in her heart and went into detail about the operation they were about to do and the risks involved. Dan grasped the basics, but his head was stuck on one question.

"Dr. Burke, I trust you to do whatever is best. I don't understand what happened though. She doesn't have heart disease. She has no history of heart issues. She was sick a few days ago, but she finally got better. What happened?"

"We think it was the virus. Viruses can damage heart tissue, and it's usually a valve that is affected. The symptoms were likely mild at first, cloaked by her recovery. We'll probably know more after this crisis point has passed. Right now we need to get in there and replace that valve."

"Can I see her first?"

The doctor shook her head. "She's sedated. I'm sorry, but it was necessary."

Dan took a step back. "Of course. I understand. Please do whatever you can for her. Thank you."

"We'll update you as soon as possible." The doctor turned on her heel and rushed back through the doors to what he assumed was the operating theatre.

Dan sat again and began to pray. He couldn't believe this was happening. Why would God allow a virus to give her back her mind only to take her heart? It couldn't be. She'd just started talking to him again. He felt like he was trapped in a nightmare. He took his phone out of his pocket and sent a quick text to Beth canceling their meeting that evening. She texted back almost immediately offering to meet him at the hospital, but he declined. He didn't want to be around anyone right now. Actually, there was one person he wished he could have with him, but he'd blown that. He wasn't going to be so selfish as to call Erin for support when he'd failed to be there for her.

Instead he called the elders and asked them to pray for his mother. He also got permission to clear his schedule for the next few days not knowing what was ahead. Eventually he had nothing left to do but to mindlessly stare at the TV, reading the scroll running on the screen. The first hour passed quickly. The second dragged its feet. Halfway through the third Dr. Burke pushed through the double-doors and headed his way. She didn't need to open her mouth. Dan had seen that look before. He'd been in her shoes often enough after cars skidded off roads, or snowmobiles fell through ice, or someone OD'd. He stood slowly as she approached him.

She paused and he wondered if she was trying to find the words. There were never any good ones. He'd found it was always best to say it straight. She sighed, folded her hands in front of her, and in a gentle tone let him know what he had already guessed. "I am so sorry Dr. Connors. We were not able to save your mother."

"It's Dan. Please call me Dan." He offered his first name more to put her at ease than anything else. She was young, probably not even thirty. He could hear the tremble in her voice as she spoke. Maybe she wasn't used to this yet. Time would cure that.

"Thank you, Dan."

"Did something go wrong?"

She shook her head. "We were able to replace the valve. We were closing the incision when she went into arrest again and despite every effort, we couldn't get her heart started."

Dan nodded. "I understand. Thank you for doing what you could." He was numb all over. He couldn't feel anything.

"Is there anyone we should call for you?" She reached out to him tentatively, her finger tips brushing his arm.

"No. There's no one."

CHAPTER TWENTY-FOUR

"OKAY WE'VE GOT WHAT LOOKS LIKE tuna casserole, some kind of chicken and rice dish, and I don't know what this is, but it smells good." Pete was standing in Dan's kitchen with a casserole dish in his hand, the lid pried up and his nose an inch from the rim. "If it was me, I'd pick this one."

This was the second night since his mom died that Pete had showed up at his house with casseroles from the various ladies of the church and insisted on staying, probably to ensure he actually ate something. If he hadn't, Dan probably wouldn't have bothered. He was still mostly numb, still in disbelief that she was dead. The world went on around him, and he was stuck in the same place. He knew that the feeling was likely to come back all in a rush when the reality of her death finally hit him. Intellectually, he knew all sorts of things about how people process grief, but this was his mom and his life and suddenly he didn't know a thing.

"Sure." Dan got up from the table and took the dish from Pete's hands, pried the lid the rest of the way off and set it on the counter. "Do I microwave this?"

"No, son, you put it in the oven and you bake it."

"Ah, right." He slid it into the oven.

Pete set the oven at 350 degrees. "Every casserole goes in at 350. I don't know why, it just does." He set the timer before gesturing to the table. "Have a seat." Pete sat down and Dan joined him. The table was tiny, but so was his loft. It had never bothered him since it wasn't like he entertained. Pete was the first person he'd ever had up here. The table was big enough for the two of them at least.

"So, you wanna watch the game?"

"Hmm?" Dan looked up. "Yeah, sure."

Pete walked over to the little TV in the corner of the room and turned it on. The only places to sit in Dan's loft were the bed and the kitchen table; luckily both were in line with the TV. For the next twenty minutes, they watched the Celtics lose while their dinner heated. The timer rang and Pete got up and took the casserole out, serving them both on paper plates. Whatever the casserole was, it was probably good, but it tasted like nothing to Dan. It was hot and filling so it served its purpose. Pete kept up a steady stream of small talk with nods or monosyllabic responses from Dan. Eventually he gave up and ate to the sound of the game on the TV.

When Dan was done he laid his fork down and pushed his plate to the side. Pete must have picked that as a sign he was ready to talk.

"I cleared some time so I can go with you to the funeral home tomorrow."

"You don't have to do that."

"I know that. I'm choosing to. You've got no family here to help. That's what's friends are for." Pete looked back down at his plate and continued to eat.

"Thanks. Speaking of friends, I called one of mine to see about him doing Mom's service for me. He's got a church in Augusta so it's not too far. I wanted to do the service, but I know I can't."

"Yes, that's probably for the best." Pete shifted on his seat. "I had thought you might ask your friend Beth to do it for you, but I guess she's not ordained?"

"No." In truth, Dan hadn't even considered Beth. He hadn't seen her since his mom died. He hadn't seen anyone. He'd come home and hadn't left.

"Well, she's been busy anyway." Pete pushed his fork around his plate. "She worked with the hospitality committee to make sure you would get food delivered that you'd actually eat. You know how those ladies like red meat."

Dan huffed out a laugh. "I do. Beth's a good friend."

"I assumed she was. After all, she'd have to be since you broke it off with Erin for her."

"What?" Dan looked up so sharply he got a crick in his neck. He raised a hand to rub it. "Erin broke up with me. She was right to. She deserves someone who's got their act together, and that's not me. I certainly didn't break up with her for Beth. Beth offered me a job."

"Did she now?" Pete put down his fork and sat back.

"Yes. Co-director of Lodestone. With everything that's happened I was considering taking it."

Pete stared at him for a long moment before responding. "I guess I understand the draw. Mozambique is a long way from your troubles."

Dan's hackles rose. "It's not about escaping difficulty, Pete. There's nothing left for me here. I came home for my mom. I stayed for my mom. She's gone. There's nothing left to stay for."

Pete's eyebrows shot up. "Really? Nothing? Not a thing here in this town to stay for?"

Dan realized how that sounded and guilt washed through him. "No, that's not what I meant." He rubbed his face with his hands. "Or maybe it is. I don't know anymore."

Pete got up and took his plate and Dan's to the trash, putting their forks in the sink. When he returned, his face was hard. Dan had a feeling he was in for a lambasting. But Pete only stood there as if considering him for a long moment. Then he spoke. "I'll be here tomorrow at five. I've got some nuisance beavers I'm removing, and I could use a hand in checking the traps. There's nothing like a little manual labor to clear your head. It will take about two hours. You'll have some time to be quiet and reflect. This will be good because every time you open your mouth lately I get the urge to do something I'll regret. After that we'll go to the funeral home." He started to walk away.

"Pete, I—"

"Get some sleep." Pete patted him on the shoulder as he left the room. Dan could hear his boots on the stairs and then the door downstairs shut.

He got up and went to the counter. Picking up the cover he slapped it back over the remains of the casserole and tossed the dish in the fridge a little harder than he meant to. It broke. He stared at it thinking it was the perfect metaphor for what he'd done to Pete. "Great Dan. Go ahead and get everyone else to hate you too." He shook his head at his own stupidity and went to the bathroom to brush his teeth. He might as well call it a day, even if it was only seven. He wasn't sleeping normally anyway. He looked into the mirror over the sink and the fluorescent light made the dark circles under his eyes look sinister.

"You're a sorry excuse for a man, buddy." He brushed his teeth and turned off the light. Climbing into bed he tried to pray, but his head and heart were cloaked in black. The words wouldn't come.

"I'll get it!" Erin heard Seth call from upstairs as the doorbell rang. She didn't like him answering the door after dark, so she jumped up from where she'd been sitting on the couch and raced to cut him off in the hallway.

"Denied." She shoved him playfully aside while he laughed and checked the window to see who it was. Since it was Pete standing there she opened the door and stood back, giving him room to come inside. "Hey, what brings you by?"

Pete stepped in and shut the door behind him. He looked a bit haggard. "I wanted to check in with you and see how things were going. I was in town anyway and figured this was nicer than a phone call."

"Always. You know you can drop by anytime."

Pete glanced at Seth beside her and then up the stairs where James was now standing. "I see everybody's up."

"It's only seven, Pete. Bedtime is at eight." Erin smiled, but he didn't return it. She took the hint that whatever he wanted to talk about was serious. "Uh, Seth, can you and James hang out upstairs for a bit?"

Seth moved to the stairs, but James came pounding down them. "What's going on?"

Pete sighed and looked at Erin as if asking for permission. She nodded, trusting Pete that if it was news they couldn't hear, he wouldn't tell them, even if they asked. "I was in town because I was at Dan's place making sure he was okay."

Erin felt her stomach drop. "Why wouldn't Dan be okay?"

"His mom died yesterday."

"What?" She reached out and grabbed Pete by the arm to keep herself upright. "How?"

"Heart attack. It was sudden, nothing they were expecting. Bad luck or maybe it was from being sick, they don't really know. Dan was with her when it happened. From what I understand it was pretty difficult and he's having a hard time."

Erin closed her eyes, unable to imagine what it would have been like for him to see his mother have a heart attack right in front of him. "Is he okay?"

"Honestly? No. He's alone in this and feeling like there's nothing left here for him. He's talking about taking some job with that friend of his."

Erin took two steps to the door and had her coat in her hand before she remembered she had no business running to comfort him. He'd let her go. They weren't even friends anymore. It took a lot, but she put her coat back on the hook. "All I want to do is run over there." She said it softly hoping only Pete would hear. "But it's not my place anymore."

'I know." Pete sighed.

Erin heard a soft sound behind her and realized it was James. She swung around. He was crying. She felt her mouth drop open. The last time James had cried was when their cat got hit by a car and died seven years ago. He hadn't cried since. Not ever. "Honey." She reached out to him, but he stepped back.

"I've got to go over there."

"Oh, that's a nice thing to do, but—"

"No! You don't understand. See, I didn't know his mom was that sick when I said all that stuff to him."

"What?" Erin was completely confused. James hadn't said anything about talking to Dan, but she noticed Seth looking both worried and concerned. "Seth, do you know what he's talking about?"

Seth shot a look at James, then back to her. "I should've gone with him. I can usually keep him calm, but he told me not to so I hung out in the back yard until he got back." Seth's words tumbled out almost too fast to comprehend. "And he yelled at me like it was my fault. He was really mad. I told him we should've talked to you, but he told me to shut it. We should have talked to you first, but James was ticked."

Erin shook her head. "I'm still not getting it, boys."

James wiped a hand across his face. "I went to Dan's house after dinner at the MacAlisters. I heard them talking and they said he'd dumped you, that he'd broken your heart. I went over to Pastor Dan's when we got home and I said some stuff to him. I was so mad." His voice broke. "But I didn't know his mom was so sick. I didn't know he was alone and didn't have anybody. Now his mom is dead? How am I going to make that right? If he leaves we'll never see him again."

"Oh, James." She reached for him again and this time he let her hold him. "You take too much on yourself. You don't need to defend me."

"Who's going to do it? You let people walk all over you!" His face grew red, and she could feel the tension in his wiry limbs. "You gave up your job for me!"

"I did that because I decided it was for the best. I'm the mom."

"Yeah, well I'm the oldest son. And protecting you is my responsibility."

"James." She had to stop right there or she was going to cry. She pulled Seth into her arms as well and held them both. "We'll be okay." She looked at James. "You'll find a way to say what you need to Dan before he goes. But, my brave boy, you need to control that temper. Even if what you've done has been for a good reason, it was wrong."

"I know." He sounded devastated, but she wanted to be sure he was getting it.

"You can't go through life letting what others say or do to people you love make you respond with anger. If they get you to throw a punch or to scream at them, then they've won. Worse than that, you've done wrong. Nobody cares if your motives were pure when you punch someone or attack them with words. You've got to learn that now while you're still young and the consequences are light."

James nodded and Erin hoped it had sunk in. She was so worried that the patchwork of male role models she'd provided her boys since their father died hadn't been enough to show them how a good man behaves. She saw Pete staring at James, a thoughtful look on his face. Letting the boys go she squeezed James' shoulder trying to communicate that it was all going to be okay.

"Hey." Pete jutted his chin out at James "You're still serving your suspension, right?"

James nodded and Erin wondered where Pete was going with this.

"Tomorrow, five AM. Be ready. I'll come pick you up. Dress warm."

"Uh, okay."

"I've got traps to check and I could use a hand."

"What about me?" Seth looked between Erin and Pete as if one of them would cave.

"You'll be in your bed and then you'll be at school. Speaking of which, upstairs. I believe you haven't laid out your clothes or brushed your teeth. Get on it." She pointed to the stairs, and Seth sulkily climbed them mumbling something about wishing he was suspended too. James followed him up.

"Boys." Erin rolled her eyes to the ceiling.

"I wouldn't know. I had all girls. That was a challenge of another sort."

"You're not wrong." Erin smiled, but it faded quickly as thoughts of Dan returned. "Pete." She shook her head. "He has no one."

"Dan has friends and a church that loves him. He needs to see that he has a community here who cares. Right now, he's in shock." He leaned closer. "I know you're done with him and I know why, but he could use a friend."

"I can't, Pete. I'm in love with him. I can't be his friend. My heart won't let me, and it's not fair to him either. I can't draw close to him now only to go ghost on him once he's on his feet. It would be wrong, and it would likely do more harm than good."

"I understand." He turned away and opened the door.

"Keep me updated though, okay? Since I'm not going to Calvary anymore I never hear anything. I'd like to know if he's okay."

"Will do." He gave her a little salute and left. Erin shut the door behind him and locked up the first floor before heading upstairs.

"Mom?" James was waiting for her in the hallway.

"Right here, kiddo."

"Are we okay?"

"We are. God loves you, James. God loves this whole family. He'll see us through."

"He needs to see to Dan."

"I have no doubts he will." She brushed a curl off James's forehead. His big, brown eyes were still watery, and it reminded her of when he was small and still ran to her when he needed comfort. How quickly those years had flown by. Her little man was determined to grow up as fast as possible.

"I love you Mom."

"I love you too, so very much."

Hours later the house was quiet and she was still awake. Her heart was aching for Dan, and she was formulating half-insane ways to manage to bump into him so she could tell him how sorry she was, how much she missed him, how much it hurt that he didn't want to even try to make it work, which was all a huge mistake. Rolling over she gave up and grabbed her phone off the nightstand.

"I'm so sorry to hear about your mom." She typed into a text. "I know nothing I say will make it better, but please know that I'm thinking of you and praying for you." She hit send before she added anything more of what was on her heart. Tossing the phone back on the nightstand she lay on her back staring at the ceiling and prayed for Dan. Before long the tears formed and fell, one after another.

It was late and he was wide awake. He looked at the clock and realized at this point it was probably best to get up since he wasn't going to sleep anyway. He heard his phone chime from the table where he'd left it. He got out of bed and picked it up off the table. There was a text waiting. It was just two sentences, but it was both exactly what he needed and not near enough.

CHAPTER TWENTY-FIVE

PETE PULLED THE TRUCK TO A stop. Dan looked out the window in the early-morning dark and felt a moment of alarm when he saw they were outside Erin's house. "Why are we stopping here?"

"We're picking up James."

"He's coming to help?"

"Sure is. He's a woodsman in the making. Had him shadowing me and Alex the other day. He did a great job. A real natural."

Dan didn't doubt he was. He also didn't doubt that James would not be pleased to see Dan waiting in Pete's SUV. As much as he'd love to spend time with the kid, he knew the feeling would not be mutual. "Uh, Pete, I should let you know that's not a fantastic idea. He's not my biggest fan at the moment. More like he thinks I'm —"

"A horse's backside. Yes, I got that. But he's coming anyway. Sit tight. I'll get him."

Dan sent up a quick prayer for both patience and guidance until Pete returned with a sleepy-looking James.

"Hey, Dan." James climbed into the backseat.

"Hey, buddy." Dan figured that wasn't a bad start. The drive to the river Pete had the traps in was a short one. The hike to where he'd left the traps was not. It took a while and they were all silent for most of it. There was something about the early morning in the woods that made him quiet. It was as if he was trespassing on nature and needed to mind his manners. When they finally reached the spot in the river where the beaver had built their dam it was easy to see why Pete was moving them. The trail was getting washed out.

"You two stay put. I'll take a look to see if we have any guests."

"Okay." Dan leaned against a tree as Pete walked away. The sun had begun to rise slowly, filling the forest around them with a weak light. Erie and beautiful, it made Dan glad he'd gotten up early. It was soothing, almost peaceful.

"I'm sorry."

Dan turned around to see James standing there, hands stuffed into the pockets of his puffy coat, eyes on the ground. "About your mom."

"Thanks, buddy." He knew he should say something else, but his sluggish brain was out of ideas.

James wasn't done. "And for the other night. I said some stuff I shouldn't have."

Dan caught up, realizing he was trying to apologize for having told him off for hurting his mom. "You might have said it the wrong way, but you were speaking from the heart and I knew what you meant." Dan held out his hand. "All's forgiven."

James shook it, squeezing a bit too hard. It reminded him of when he was a teenager trying to figure out how to be a man, how hard to shake hands, how to talk to the older guys and not sound like an idiot. How to shave. He looked at James' upper lip and sure enough he had the classic dirt 'stache already coming in. He'd have to find a non-embarrassing way to tell him to get on that. That thought dropped a lead weight into his gut. Dan wouldn't be around to give James any advice on shaving or anything else. He'd be in Mozambique.

"It was cool, having you around."

"Yeah, it was." Dan smiled, but his heart wasn't in it. It hurt to think that he'd end up being a faint memory to Seth and James and a painful one for Erin. It was so far from what he'd wanted as to be in another reality altogether. With his heart in pain, his head went into problem-solving mode. Maybe he could stay? He could find a way to sort out his conflicting feelings about his calling on his own, he didn't need to leave. He could sign the contract and find a way to get Erin back. But that ship had sailed. All his plans evaporated in the face of the truth. He hadn't changed, and Erin didn't want him as he was. It was best for all of them if he left even though right now, that was the last thing he wanted to do.

James's eyes were narrowed and focused on him. It felt like the kid could see right through him. "You love her, my mom, don't you?"

Dan stared at James in disbelief. The kid was sharp, but this was ridiculous. He'd been careful never to show too much emotion around him.

"The look on your face whenever I mention her." James pointed to Dan's head. "You look cut up."

Dan laughed. "It's—"

"That's okay." James put up a hand. "You're gonna tell me it's complicated. I get that." He shrugged. "But I'm thinking maybe Seth had the right idea. Maybe it's better to get your hopes up. Sometimes, stuff works out."

"James." Dan closed his eyes.

"You're good for her. She was happier when you were around. Mom deserves to be happy."

"She does. She definitely does."

"If you two are done talking." Pete popped his head up over a pile of brush. "How about you get up here and help me drag these traps to a new spot. These beaver appear to be the clever sort. Didn't get a single one."

"Let's go." Dan headed up and James followed.

It took another hour, but they got the traps moved and Pete drove them back towards town, then detoured up the mountain to drop James off at the MacAlisters where Lauren was planning to give him a painting lesson. "She loves teaching, and she was bored waiting for the foster kids to arrive. She keeps telling me she's got nothing to do and a bored woman is a dangerous woman. They get ideas about projects you can do for them. Even if they're not married to you. Yet."

Dan spotted the contented look on Pete's face which belied his words. "Somehow I don't think you're all that concerned about Lauren burdening you with a honey-do list. Seems like you're looking forward to it."

"Maybe." Pete gave him a grin before turning back to the road. "I never expected to love another woman after my wife died. Lauren is night and day different. When I met her the first time I knew there was something there. I felt guilty at first, and I tried to ignore what I was feeling, but she wouldn't let me. She breezed into my life and knocked me off my feet. Never met anyone like her."

"I know that feeling."

"You would." Pete didn't elaborate. They drove into town and to Maria's where they stopped for breakfast. They sat at the counter and Dan ordered a bagel and coffee while Pete ordered what seemed to be the entire left side of the menu. While they waited, various neighbors and friends filtered in. They stopped to offer Dan condolences before talking with Pete or complaining about Alex, the new warden, who was getting a reputation for being a stickler.

"I keep telling you." Pete waggled a finger at a stocky man in a NASCAR cap. "Every good warden starts off being all about the letter of the law. And don't forget Alex was a cop first. Give him time to settle in."

The man left and Dan hoped what he'd heard had helped. "When are you officially retired, Pete?"

"Soon. I've got a month left."

"Wow. That is soon. What are you going to do with yourself?"

A slow smile spread across Pete's lips. "I got a few ideas."

Dan chuckled. "I don't know what the town will do without you."

"Oh, they'll get along fine."

After breakfast, they drove the short distance to the funeral home. It was near the church and only a few blocks from Dan's house. Pete parked in the lot out front. "You ready?" Pete had his door open.

Dan nodded and then got out of the SUV and followed Pete inside.

He stood in the funeral home and tried not to feel overwhelmed. The place itself was bland, probably on purpose. Beige carpet, beige walls, plain wood chairs in front of the funeral director's desk. He wasn't prepared for this. It felt like there were a thousand small details he had to make a decision on right there. The only guidance in his mom's will was that she be buried with his dad back in Lewiston, Maine where Dan had grown up.

"I don't want it to be a big thing." He shifted uncomfortably in his chair. He was worried it made him sound like a bad son to say he didn't want his mom to have a huge funeral, but he couldn't imagine that was what she wanted. "She had a lot of friends though. They're going to need something." He looked at Pete for help.

"I think you're right about the big funeral." Pete's expression grew thoughtful. "How about a private burial and then a memorial service later?"

"That's an excellent option, Dr. Connors." The funeral director was as bland as his surroundings—from his plain gray suit to his politician haircut. "We can do the burial as soon as Thursday if you wish?"

"Uh, I guess so."

"I'll see if the church can schedule the memorial service a bit out, like the first Saturday in December." Pete leaned forward to get his attention. "Would that work for you?"

"Yes, that's smart. Gives us enough time to announce it in the paper, make sure all her friends know."

The rest of the meeting slid by in a blur. He picked a coffin trying not to imagine her laying in it. He gave all the info that should go in the obituary and announcements and okayed a dozen other fine details until his head was swimming.

"I think that we've got everything we need." The funeral director looked at Dan. "I believe there is only the matter of her personal possessions. The hospital is holding them for you."

Pete nudged Dan's booted foot with his own. "Do you want me to give you a ride up there?"

"No, I appreciate the offer, but I'm going to try to catch a nap first and then head up later."

He walked home from the funeral home feeling overwhelmed. He tried to sleep, but he could only doze in fits and starts. After an hour of that he got up, drove to the hospital, and headed inside to the front desk. They handed him a bag with the things his mother had in her room or on her person when she died. Dan planned to sort it out and then store it with the rest of her belongings.

The first year she was sick he'd moved her out of the house she'd rented and put her things in a storage unit. The second year he'd gone through and set aside anything that looked personal and had an auction outfit sell the rest. The third year he'd put her few personal items in a box at the barn. Now these things would join them. He didn't want to see any of it, but there was no escaping the task. He drove home feeling exhausted both emotionally and physically. His heart and soul felt ragged.

Once he was home he stood at his desk sorting through his mail, tossing most of it in the 'in' basket Erin had set up for him that day she'd helped organize his desk. Looking at it only increased his melancholy so he decided to sort through the bag of stuff and get it over with. He stared at the bag in front of him trying to ready himself to see what little remained of his mother's life on this earth. He slid out the contents of the bag onto his desk in front of him; a necklace, her rings, a small picture of him and his dad. He felt an object at the bottom of the bag and shook it out. A few barrettes danced across his desk.

A wave of pathos, strong as anything he'd ever experienced, flooded his heart. It chased out the numbness and the feeling, all of it, rushed back in. He was consumed by a grief so heavy he couldn't take a full breath. His chest seemed to be caving in. He backed away from the desk, his hands pushing through his hair, trying to get a grip, but he wasn't in control. The grief had him, and wasn't letting go. He needed to go somewhere, do something to distract him from the emotions he wasn't ready for. Rushing upstairs he changed into his running gear. There was a trail behind the church that led into the state park. Usually he avoided it since it was rough, but he didn't want to see anyone he knew and be forced to stop and talk. He couldn't be around people right now. All he could think of was escaping into the woods and running until he couldn't feel anything anymore.

He ran south, behind the church, to the trailhead, and then into the woods. The trail wasn't well used in the off-season, so bracken had crept up on both sides and reached out to cling to his pant legs as he passed. He welcomed the pain of a thorn ripping into his skin, the burn of his lungs in the cold air, the pounding of his feet on the packed dirt; it all soothed his ragged heart. His brain was stuck in fight-or-flight and, with no flesh and blood enemy to take on, he ran instead. The roots tripped him, but still he ran. He knew he was probably losing his way, but still he ran. The setting sun all but disappeared as the thick canopy of branches closed overhead, and still he ran.

Some semblance of self-protection reemerged, and he finally stopped. He was deep into the woods and not sure if he was on the right trail. The trees and brush closed all around him as he stood and panted. His lungs were burning, his legs were stinging, and he was glad. He'd burned through the horrible weight of sadness, but fury chased it. The adrenalin now pumping through his system only egged it on. Why? The theologian in him could have pulled up a dozen answers and they'd all be right, but it wasn't the rational, learned pastor who was in control now. It wasn't the passionate missionary either. The all-too human man raised his face to the canopy of leaves overhead and cried it out at the top of his lungs. "Why?"

Around him he could hear the startled reaction of the birds that had been preparing for dusk. Nature was disturbed, but Dan didn't care. He wanted God to be disturbed. He wanted his heavenly Father to feel his anger and do something. He wanted God's reaction. "Why did You bring me home just to watch her die?" The sky was silent. "Why did You let the mission fail? What was the point in any of it?" There was too much inside him clawing to get out. His reason was gone and he was ravaged by emotion. "Wasn't I serving You? Wasn't I doing Your will?" Tears clogged his throat, and he couldn't go on. Silently he threw every last bit of it at God. Every resentment, every doubt, everything he'd been holding inside, holding against God. "Wasn't I good enough?"

Spent and broken, he fell back to the soft moss of the hillside and wiped his eyes. The noises of the woods returned as he lay there, unable to feel anything. It was almost as if he'd torn his own soul open and nothing was left. Empty and exhausted, he listened as night fell around him. The sky overhead darkened and one by one the stars slowly began to appear. Being so deep in the woods and so far from street lights, the stars and planets filled the heavens. Even in his state, he couldn't help but feel a sense of awe at the sheer number of them.

A memory began to surface in his mind. When he was ten, he'd convinced his parents to let him sleep outside so he could watch a meteor shower. He'd headed into the backyard with his sleeping bag and Coleman lamp, fully prepared to camp out under the stars and wait for the show. He'd fallen asleep staring at the sky and would have missed it if it hadn't been for his dad coming out and waking him up. He had stretched out with him, and they'd watched the sky put on a show.

Dan smiled. Of all the memories of his dad, that one was sweetest for being the example of the everyday way his father loved him. Henry

Connors was not a demonstrative guy. He didn't hug, he rarely praised, but he showed his love in a thousand other ways: the swing set he built, the bike he fixed, the old beater of a car he bought Dan the moment he turned fifteen, the dents he fixed in that car when Dan decided to practice hand-brake turns. There were other, smaller gestures too; the glazed donuts from Jan's Deli his dad would buy every Sunday morning knowing that only Dan liked them, the saved crossword puzzles, watching Celtics games with him even though Dad only cared about baseball. That night in the backyard he showed his love in making sure his kid got to experience something he'd been longing for.

"I blamed You for that, too," Dan whispered to the sky. "You took him from me too soon." Almost the moment the words were out, he regretted them. He'd never said that aloud; never let himself believe it before. Had he been holding that against God all this time? He remembered those first few months after Dad died. His whole focus was his mother, making sure he did everything he could to support her, so she wouldn't feel the loss any harder than she already did. He'd nearly killed himself to make sure he did all his dad's work around the house as well as his own, and as much of hers as she'd let him do. He'd felt the weight of the world on his shoulders. He alone was the man of the family, he was the only support. What a lie. What a terrible lie.

Like a movie reel spinning in his mind, images were flashing through his thoughts; the faces of all those who crowded around his family as they grieved his father. Had he not seen them at the time? Then came the faces around him now, the hospitality committee with their gentle words and the ridiculously huge casseroles they'd been dropping off at his house, Pete showing up and taking charge when Dan was feeling utterly lost. And then there was Erin. Even though she wasn't with him now, he knew she was praying for him, thinking of him, even though he didn't deserve her consideration. He knew it was God all along, providing what he needed when he needed it, moving people into his life at the right times, God was with him every step of his life. In his selfishness, in his pride, he'd ignored Him.

A tidal wave of regret rushed through him, and he didn't fight the tears when they came. All the years of resentment, all the years of working and toiling in the mission field as if he could buy his way to heaven, as if God, the Author of the universe, needed anything from him. No wonder the mission failed—had he built anyone up? Had he shepherded anyone or discipled a single soul to replace him? No, he'd done it all thinking he was the author of his success, he was bringing souls to Christ, and he was earning his salvation. How could he have been so blind to his own pride?

Dan willed his mind to be silent. Empty of thought, empty now of feeling, he listened to the soft sounds around him. It wasn't long before he felt the compulsion and into the dark he spoke the words that were on his heart, words that he should have been following all along. "Not my will, but Thine."

And he waited.

Softly, the words crept into his thoughts. "Be still and know that I am God."

There, surrounded by God's creation, feeling like a new creation himself, Dan truly felt God's presence, and it overwhelmed him. Who was he to question the Creator of the universe? Who was he to question God's will for his life? Hadn't God given him blessing after blessing? Yes, and he'd counted it all as glory for himself, not for God.

"Forgive me." The words were too small for what he felt pouring out of him. He got to his knees and emptied his soul, repenting of his pride, his anger, his bitterness. When he finally stood, he felt light as if a weight he hadn't known he had been carrying was gone. Praise and wonder filled his heart.

Erin pulled her coat around her as a strong breeze swept over the small group gathered around the grave. Dan seemed not to notice the wind. He wore a black suit with a large overcoat he hadn't buttoned. If she was cold with all her layers, he must be freezing, but he didn't shiver, didn't move to close his coat. He stood at the head of the casket alone. Beth was here, but she was standing with Rachel and people Erin recognized from

Calvary. Dan wasn't officiating. She didn't recognize the pastor, but assumed he must be a friend of Dan's. The brief service was lovely. She suspected Dan had written it and wisely chose someone else to deliver it. The passages in the Bible, the other readings, it all sounded like something Dan would choose. When the pastor was done speaking Dan took a single rose from a display beside him and laid it on his mother's coffin, his hand lingering for a moment before he backed away. Each attendee laid a rose as well. Erin waited until they were all done before approaching and doing the same.

She hung back and waited for the mourners to finish paying their respects. She watched as Dan seemed to say goodbye to Beth. Maybe she was helping with the gathering back at the church. Erin didn't intend to go to that part of the service. This was hard enough. When Dan was alone she caught his eye and gave him a small smile. His hair was a tousled mess, but the dark circles under his eyes and his gaunt cheeks alarmed her the most. He looked terrible. And being the dork she was, that was the first thing out of her mouth. "You look terrible."

Dan chuckled softly. "Thanks."

She felt her cheeks grow hot. "That came out all wrong. I'm so sorry."

"Don't be. I do look horrible."

"Are you okay?"

"I am now. God had a talk with me a few days ago. I've been doing a lot of reading and praying since then."

"Good, but do more eating and sleeping, okay?"

"I will. I promise. Something tells me it will be easier to sleep now that this part is over. It was important." He nodded his head at the coffin. "Having her buried here with Dad. They were so close in life it's right that they're together in death."

"Did you write the service?"

"I did." He seemed surprised she spotted it.

"I've always loved the way you write, how you put things together." She wanted to say more. If this was another time she'd tell him how much his preaching had meant to her in the years she went to Calvary and how much she'd learned, but this wasn't the place for that. "It was beautiful."

"Thank you." He looked out across the rows of headstones, and she wondered if he felt the strangeness like she did. All she wanted to do was to throw her arms around him and tell him it was all going to be all right, but she couldn't.

"Thank you for driving all this way. I didn't think so many people would come."

"There's a lot of people who love you, Dan. We don't mind a few hours in the car to support you."

He pressed his lips together and nodded.

"It was no trouble for me. When you're out the door in a few weeks anyway, the administration is much more flexible about personal days."

Dan frowned. "I'd heard about the board's decision. I'm sorry about your job."

"I'm not." Erin shrugged. "James gets to stay and he needs to be there. I can find another job. I always land on my feet."

He shook his head slightly and for a second she thought he was going to reach out to touch her, but he didn't. It was as if in the two feet of air that separated them there was a brick wall, an invisible one made up of unspoken words.

Dan sighed softly. "James is a great kid. I'm glad he gets to stay. Seth's a kick too. You've got two wonderful kids."

"Thanks. James is so..." she stopped herself from unloading her worries on him. That wasn't who they were anymore. There was a time she was hopeful he might be the one to share her life, her struggles, but that time was over. "Anyway. It's good to see you. I'm sorry for the reason, but glad to see you. Take care of yourself." She reached out, took his hand, and held it for a moment, unable to leave without at least that gesture. Then she turned her back on him and walked away.

"Erin."

She slowly spun on the spot. Dan's gaze was filled with emotions she couldn't interpret. They stared at each other, neither saying a word.

His shoulders slumped. "I miss you."

A thrill moved through her. Part of her was so glad to hear him say it, but the rest of her knew it didn't change anything. "I miss you too, but nothing has changed."

"Maybe..." He stood and stared at her, apparently unable to find the words.

"Let me know when it's not a maybe." She turned away feeling like she'd just kicked a puppy, but it had to be done. Love wasn't a maybe kind of thing. Either he was all in or he was out. Her heart couldn't take anything else. She walked to the paved pathway and headed for her car. It took everything she had not to look back. On the long drive home her conscience poked at her. Had she been too harsh? With Dan occupying most of her thoughts she decided she had no brain-power left to come up with a decent dinner so she decided it was a Nugget Night.

After dinner, the kids headed upstairs and Erin decided she had to do something with all she was feeling. She missed Dan. Seeing him had been hard, especially with how tired and sorrowful he looked. Her heart ached to comfort him, and she felt guilty for keeping him at arms-length even though she knew it was for the best. Opening the basement door, she flicked on the lights and headed down to her workbench. Picking up the crate of supplies she kept on her shelf she riffled through until she found what she wanted. She ran the brown leather strip cord through her fingers testing the pliability. It was high-quality, so soft instead of stiff. It would be able to take a lot of wear and age well. She took down another box and rummaged through it to find a brass cross. It was thick and rough-looking as if already an antique. She cut two lengths of the cord and wrapped them together, using the brass cross to bind them. It didn't take long to secure the cross and then add a simple clasp in brass as well.

She held it up in the flat of her palm, looking at it from every angle. It would suit him. The color, the style and materials were all a match for him. She grabbed a small box from the stack on her shelf, packed the bracelet, and tied the box shut with a length of twine. Jogging up the stairs, she switched off the light and grabbed her coat. "Hey." She called up the stairs. "I'll be right back. Running a quick errand." Normally she didn't leave the boys at night, but this would only take a few minutes.

As she headed down her front steps she noticed the temperature had taken a dip from that afternoon. Before long it would be snowing. Winter wasn't her favorite season, but it meant Thanksgiving and Christmas, two of her favorite holidays. She hurried down the sidewalk and seeing that there were no lights on, headed up the little path up to the side door of

Dan's office. Standing at his door she almost lost her nerve. This was an impulsive gesture, and she wasn't a spur-of-the moment sort of person, but it felt right. She took the box out of her pocket and hung it by its string from a hook in the trim of the door that was probably for a wreath. Giving it a little tug she decided it was sturdy enough, and she left the way she came.

Dan parked his car and grabbed the bags of food the ladies at church had insisted he take home. The small gathering had turned into more of a church supper. The congregation had surrounded him with their love and care, and he was humbled by it. It showed the depth of how selfish he'd been that he'd taken these loving, kind, and faithful people for granted. Sitting and sharing a meal with them felt blessed. Or maybe it was that he finally saw how God had blessed him with the call to Calvary. It had also solidified his decision to sign the contract and stay. The moment he'd done so a deep sense of peace had filled him. In many ways, he felt like he'd found his home after having been in the wilderness.

Juggling the bags of food and his briefcase in one hand he used his keys to unlock the door. When he looked up he saw he was eye to eye with a little box tied to a string hanging from a hook in the wood. "What's this?" He opened the door the rest of the way and put the bags down on the floor inside. Reaching up, he freed the box and shut the door. He brought it over to his desk and turned on the lamp there. Once he had the twine untied he lifted the cover. Inside, a man's bracelet sat in a nest of tissue paper. He lifted it out and held it up.

There was only one person who could have left this for him. He recognized her work. She'd made Mac a bracelet like this years ago, but that one was black and silver in a Celtic design. This? This was made for him. He opened the clasp and fastened it onto his left wrist. He ran his fingers over the two leather cords twined together and held with the cross and inside his heart a spark of hope flamed to life.

CHAPTER TWENTY-SIX

DAN TOOK HIS SEAT AT THE table and tried to quiet his thoughts. Ralph Wilson, the head elder, had opened in prayer, and that had helped to settle Dan's nerves, but they were ramping up again. He intended to add an item to the business they were about to consider and, even though he'd thought long and hard about what he was going to say, he hadn't written it down, hadn't rehearsed it. This was going to be direct from his heart, and he prayed that God would give him the words.

He raised his hand as Ralph began to read off the list of pending business. He had a thick Maine accent and a booming voice. Dan had to lean close to get his attention. "I'd like to add an item for immediate consideration."

"Okay, Dan, whatcha got?" Ralph picked up a pencil as if to add something to his list.

"I'd like to address the matter of my contract. I know this is a bit out of order, but I'd like to do this with all of you present." He looked at the small group of men and women. Pete was among them, and he gave Dan a sharp nod like he might know what was coming and approved. Ralph quickly called for a vote; it was seconded and carried and they told him he could speak. One of the things he liked best about the board of elders at Calvary was that they were all 'elders'. The youngest among them was probably fifty. They had that gravitas that leaders should. He could practically feel the wisdom and experience when he walked into the room. It made what he had to say a little easier to get out.

"Some time ago, Calvary offered me a generous contract for five years. I balked at it. Five years seemed like forever to me, and I wasn't sure I was ready for that kind of commitment. Or at least that's what I told myself. The fact is that I have been struggling with resentment, not at

Calvary, but at God for my mother's illness, for being pulled away from the mission I considered my life's work, for it failing after I left, and for being put in a place I didn't think needed me. I was wrong, and I would like to ask your forgiveness." There was a sort of shocked silence, but it only lasted a moment.

"You have it," Ralph looked around the table at the other elders. "I think we all sensed your reluctance but didn't know the source. Does this mean you're leaving?"

"No. After my mother died I was a mess. But I finally took that mess to God, and He opened my heart so that I could see all the ways that I had been ignoring my call to Calvary. These past few weeks I've spent a great deal of time thinking about missions because I've been helping Beth Russell with her fundraising. I can see now that the decisions I had been making were about my need to feel like the work I was doing was important, that *I* was important. My pride got in the way of seeing the value of the work I have right here. I'd like to apologize for that as well, for feeling resentful of the everyday duties that come with this job as if my *gifting* was above them. I have failed to honor my calling. Besides your forgiveness, I'd also like the opportunity to sign that contract. If it's still available."

"Of course it is, Dan." Bill Lewis spoke.

Dan looked up in surprise. The man rarely said a word during the meetings. In fact, he rarely spoke outside of them either. Dan knew him mostly from the few talks they'd had during the planning of the funeral for Bill's father. Bill had shared that his dad had believed that church and faith itself were a civic duty of sorts. His moralism had never bloomed into what Bill believed was a saving faith. He had told Dan that there was no pain as poignant as he'd felt standing next to his father's bedside after he'd died knowing the likely fate of his soul.

Bill's voice grew gruff. "I think I speak for all when I say we appreciate your confession, and we support you in your decision. We all know how important the gospel message is right here in Sweet River." He tapped his finger on the table. "I'm glad you're going to stay. We appreciate your preaching, and we appreciate you."

"Thank you."

When the meeting was done Dan stood, collecting his papers into his bag. He was looking forward to going home and picking one of the many casseroles the parishioners of the church had delivered to him and heating it up. He was also thinking about Erin. Thoughts of her had accompanied everything he did in the days since the funeral. He was getting his act together. All that remained was to let Beth know he wouldn't be taking her up on her offer to co-direct Lodestone with her. That was not going to be a fun conversation, but it was one he couldn't delay.

On the walk home he removed his phone and took a picture of the bracelet on his wrist, then texted it to Erin. Right before he reached his driveway she texted back in emoji, a fist-bump and a smile. He laughed, thinking that was so her.

"Hey, history repeats."

He looked up to see Beth waiting on his stoop, and his gut tightened. It was good that she was there, though. He had to get this over with, and it was better to do it now than to stress about it. "Hey. Hang on a sec, and I'll get the door." He let them in, dropping his bag on his desk and turning on the lights. He sat in his chair, and she took a seat across from him.

"I wanted to let you know that I'm done. I plan to wrap things up tomorrow and head out."

"A day early? That must mean you have new events planned?"

"New York. I have a handful of churches that signed up on the web site. It's going to be tricky to work them in, but I feel like I need to take advantage of every opening."

Dan nodded. "Definitely. It's the safest bet, but don't go driving all night. You've been running on empty for a while. Keep that in mind as you go. If it gets to be too much, take a break."

She sighed, visibly sinking into the chair. Dan wasn't sure how to read that, but he could tell she had something on her mind, something she was reluctant to share.

"What's on your mind?"

"I haven't wanted to bother you, what with all you've been going through, but I'm really hoping you've had time to make a decision about my offer. It feels selfish to ask you to hurry, but if you are interested in coming to Mozambique with me, there are things we should probably start discussing."

It was his turn to sigh and sit back. "No, it's good that you brought it up. I've made my decision. I've signed the contract at Calvary. I'll be staying. I really appreciate the offer, but I know this is where I should be." Beth was silent for a moment. "That was quick. A few weeks ago you were questioning your calling and now you're all set? No more doubts?" A look of comprehension slid across her expression. "This is about Erin, isn't it? You're choosing Sweet River because you're really choosing Erin."

Dan took a breath before he answered because he wanted to be clear. Beth was one of his oldest friends, and he didn't want this between them. "No, I might be choosing Erin as a wife, but my decision to stay at Calvary was based—"

"As a wife?" She sat upright. "You're getting married?"

"Not right this moment, but that's the end game, yes. I wouldn't have ever dated her if I hadn't planned to eventually marry her."

"So you're not actually engaged?"

"No. We sort of broke up. She wanted to be sure that I knew what I wanted before things got serious. I know what I want now. Calvary is my calling and after a lot of prayer, I believe it's truly God that brought Erin into my life to be my wife."

Beth looked away, shaking her head. "I waited too long. I should have come here over the summer. I meant to, but I got caught up."

"What does that have—"

"Because I need you, Dan. Not as a co-director. I need you as a husband."

"What?" Dan was floored. She'd never betrayed the slightest romantic interest in him in all the years they'd known each other.

"Even Rachel thought we'd make a good couple. She's your church secretary so she'd be a good judge."

Dan felt himself start with surprise.

Beth shrugged. "Think about it. We've got the same background, we understand each other. You used to joke about how we'd be two old people sitting around the nursing home swapping stories of all the places we'd seen, the people we'd known, the work we'd done."

"Beth . . ." Dan was finally seeing why she was in Sweet River, and it made his gut twist with guilt. He should have seen it in all her affectionate touches, that kiss on the cheek when she'd first arrived. He should have put a stop to it, explained that there was no chance they'd end up together, not in that way. Now he had no idea what to say. He didn't want to hurt her. They'd always been friends, but there'd never been so much as a spark of anything else.

"You're the perfect director, and I'm the perfect director's wife. I know what I'm doing; I've literally written the book on missions, I speak three languages for pity's sake. I'm the perfect choice for you."

He shook his head in disbelief. "If it was a position seeking fulfillment I'd agree, but we're talking about a sacred union." He was floored by her blunt dismissal of his love for Erin and the calculating way she was talking about what was far more than a partnership. "Marriage isn't an equation you can plug details into and get the right result."

"But how is this" —she gestured between the two of them--"not a sacred union of sorts? We're two people, evenly yoked, doing God's work. I can't think of anything more 'sacred' than that."

"A sacred union requires love. I don't love you, Beth. Not like that."

"But that's why this is perfect." She slid forward to the edge of her chair. "Love is messy. So if we don't have love, we have something better, friendship and a common goal. We're good friends, we've worked together for years, if something develops later that's great, but even if it never does, we have each other to lean on in true friendship. That's a lot more than either of us have had separately."

That might have been true during his years in India, but now he had a community of believers he had come to love as brothers and sisters and, with Erin, the chance at a family of his own. "Beth, I signed a contract with Calvary, and I'm going to honor that. Even if I hadn't, God is not calling me to Africa. He's not calling me to go back to India or to anywhere else. I have a mission now, right here. When you arrived, I was waiting for a sign, utterly confused. Things have changed. I know God's will for my life, and what you're offering isn't it."

"Right now, I may have the better read on what God's will is, Dan." Beth spoke slowly as if he was an overly emotional child. "You've been struggling here. Is it any wonder that while you're having all these doubts about your calling you happen to start a relationship with a beautiful woman in need of a husband and a father for her kids? After years of being content in your singleness, suddenly you develop feelings for someone who is obviously not meant to fit into your life, but is certainly available?" She was using her patient tone, as if she knew better. "I honestly believe you'll see as soon as you decide to go to Mozambique that it's the right choice. That's where you belong. That's where we both belong."

"I belong where I'm called. He's called me here." He tapped the desk with his index finger. "To this church. I've never felt surer of anything. And I believe He's brought Erin into my life because that's also His will, even if right now that relationship is gonna take work." He drew in a breath and said aloud what he'd known for a while. "This isn't some misplaced sympathy for her situation or me giving into lust. It's love, the real thing. I've fallen in love with Erin, and it isn't a mistake. I'm finally home. I'm sure. No Reserves, No Retreats, No Regrets."

Beth winced as if the words he said hurt. He didn't want to hurt her, but he had to be sure she understood.

"This conversation is so crazy." He sighed. "You never once acted like you cared what I did with myself and now you want to get married?"

"Married is the only way we can work together at Lodestone." Beth lifted her hands in a helpless gesture. "The foundation has made it clear that they are not interested in funding a single woman. They want a couple. They will never okay us working together unless we're married."

"Is that why you had me sit in on the video conference with them?"

"I'm sorry." She cringed. "Yes. I didn't lie to them. I said you were helping me, nothing more, but I was hoping they'd jump to conclusions and that would stall them for a bit while I tried to get up the courage to tell you what I really needed."

"Beth—"

"I know, this is awful. But I have been working on Lodestone for the last two years. Finding stable funding has been a nightmare. If the foundation walks away I will have to start all over. Again." She flopped back in the chair and put her head in her hands.

"That's a really bad reason to get married. And I think you know it."

"I do." Her face was still in her hands.

"If the foundation won't fund you, find another."

She looked up at him. "That's easier said than done."

"Easier than finding a husband when you don't want one."

"If I could get them to stay with the project I can be in Mozambique in two months. If I have to start over . . ." She shook her head.

"God will provide another way to fund you. I hate to say it, but have some faith." He watched while Beth's expression went from defeated to annoyed. That was a good sign. If she was irritated with him she wasn't sad about his refusal. It might mean they could move forward as friends and not have this be awkward. "You seriously asked me to marry you so you wouldn't lose your funding. You're nuts." He shook his head and chuckled. "No one else but you would be so dedicated to the cause they'd try to survive being attached to me. I drive Erin nuts, and we're only dating. You were risking your sanity."

Beth sputtered, but then she groaned and rolled her eyes to the ceiling. "This is mortifying."

"No." He reached across the desk and held out his hand. She hesitated, and then she took it. "We're not going to let it destroy what is a perfectly good friendship." He shook her hand and then let it go.

"Erin probably hates me."

"She's a woman of strong opinions, but she's a forgiving soul."

"Maybe someday I'll be over the extreme embarrassment I've caused and am currently enduring, and I can come for dinner or something." She got up as if to leave then sat back down again. "Aren't you bored here? I don't get the draw."

"If you think every man, woman, and child who sits in those pews" — he pointed out the windows towards the church— "is already saved then you are sorely mistaken. Every soul that enters through those doors is hungry in some way, and a lot of them don't even know it because they never got past reciting a sinner's prayer and hoping it was enough fire insurance to get them out of hell. Believers and unbelievers of every stripe sit out there. This community, the school, they need God. He chose me to be His instrument, and I'm not second-guessing that."

"Wow." Her lips quirked upward like she wanted to smile but couldn't commit to it. "I was wrong. And I'm sorry. I'm sorry for taking up all your time while your mom was sick."

Dan tried to wave her apology away since it opened a wound that was busy healing.

"No, let me say it. If I had known how precious your time was, please believe I never would have wasted it."

He could see her regret. It covered any resentment he might have held onto.

"Forgiven and, really, Beth, it's forgotten. You came up here when I was in the middle of a spiritual crisis. Your timing was terrible." He gave her a smile. "But God ordered it this way. My mom . . . I know better than to question why He chose to take her now and not when she had the stroke, or why it was only after I finally saw improvement in her condition. My faith is in the Father."

"That's a bit convicting. I think my faith has been in me, to be honest."

"If it makes you feel any better your enthusiasm for your work convicted me for my lack of it."

"Well, at least there's that." She laughed.

"Don't forget all the connections you made while you were up here. If those turn into donations, you may not need the foundation's funding."

He stood and she followed suit. "I'll be praying for you, and if I hear of any millionaires looking to donate excess cash I'll send them your way."

"Make it 'billionaires'."

"You got it." He walked to the door and held it open for her.

"I'll pray for you as well." She paused a moment. "Thanks Dan, for everything."

Dan shut the door behind her as she walked away. He shook his head, still a bit shocked by their conversation. Hopefully that was the last surprise life had for him for a while.

CHAPTER TWENTY-SEVEN

"HEY GUYS!" ERIN CALLED UP THE stairs and waited until she saw both James and Seth appear at the top. "Let's get going. We're dropping by the Murphy's to see if they're settled in."

"Awesome!" Seth punched the air. "We can see if they set up their PS4."

"Right, because that's why we're visiting. Get going." Erin herded her boys out of the house and into the car. On the drive to Claire's new apartment the boys argued over which game they wanted to play first. Erin had to remind them they were visiting friends, not an arcade. When they arrived, Claire cheerfully buzzed them up. The Murphy boys seemed to be genuinely excited about their new place. After they gave James and Seth a brief tour they sat down with them in front of the gaming system, and that was the end of any meaningful conversation. Claire offered Erin a coffee and the two of them headed to the kitchen. "So . . ."

"So, what?" Erin asked over the rim of the cup she'd lifted to her lips.

"Okay, the story thus far is that you faced off with Beth that day we were moving in, then with Beth and Dan, then you told the crew to do what I said or else. Then Beth left in a huff. You and Dan had a private chat that had him leaving in a huff. The entire work crew was abuzz. Whenever Pete wasn't near anyway. That man does not gossip."

"And neither should you!"

"Oh, come on, that was all too good not to listen to. Besides, I was worried I had caused a rift between you and Dan. I know you said it was fine." She held up a hand as Erin tried to interrupt. "And you said you and Dan are on a break while he sorts his head out, but I know for a fact that Beth is long gone. Now what does that mean?"

"It was never about Beth." And Erin realized it was true. Even if the woman was tempting Dan away with an offer to return to the mission field—something she knew he'd wanted before—it didn't matter. It was Dan who had to decide she was what he wanted with no reservations, and it was him who had to treat her as if she mattered to him. She had to be able to trust him and right now, she didn't. "I can't be with a man I can't trust. Years of a very bad marriage taught me that lesson."

"It's hard to imagine Dan not being trustworthy."

"It's not about him being worthy of trust, it's me being able to put myself and the boys in his hands and know that he's going to take care of us. He's too conflicted about what he wants in life, where he's going. He needs to sort that all out before we can be anything to each other."

Claire sat back and shook her head slightly. "Right now, I want to be you. All in command and knowing what you want." Claire snapped in the air. "Me, I'm a mess. But I did get a job."

"Wow, that's great." Erin was relieved. She'd been concerned that Claire would have trouble finding a job after so many years of not working. "What's the job?"

"At Annie's coffee shop. She needed someone during school hours. Voila!" Claire waved her hand with a flourish. "She now has me. It's a perfect fit, and I didn't even have to apply. I was at the school volunteering in the library, and I heard her mention she needed help. Just like that." She snapped her fingers. "I had a job."

"God is provident." Erin set her cup down. "Whenever something like this happens I remember we aren't in charge, He is. I was thinking you'd have to look for a while or end up working at some chain place up on the highway, but no, without an ounce of drama, a job comes to you. That's awesome."

"Well, I did have to tell her I was interested."

"I'm sorry." She didn't want to take anything away from Claire's win. "I mean, without any crisis to be endured, your need has been met. How's the money?"

"Above minimum, which is nice, and we have a tip jar. I will have to come up with something else on the side to get by."

"I was thinking about that the other night since I'm looking for a job as well."

Claire's face fell, and it seemed she was about to apologize again for the fight between their sons which led to Erin's resignation.

"Not your fault. Remember that. We've been through this."

"I still feel horrible."

"You're going to need to let that go. Anyway, I was thinking about something Katherine mentioned to me ages ago about artist collectives. I know it sounds kind of pretentious rather than profitable, but there are grants available for women setting up shop to sell their art. Like pottery?" Erin said it suggestively. Claire's eyes lit. "Every time I set up at a craft fair I have to pay for the table. At the good craft fairs it can get pricey. With a grant covering work space and web site hosting we could go into business together, maybe even recruit another crafter and consider retail space. That would mean no more weekends spent at craft fairs for me and money on the side for you."

"Let's do it!"

"Hold on, there's a lot of work involved so we should think it over carefully. I'll get something formal together, a real business plan, and we can review it."

"That sounds so professional."

"Professional and profitable go together. I'm thinking I can go back to taking on personal training clients and teach a few classes at the Y or something like that and then have this on the side. Either way, God will provide."

"God will provide," Claire echoed. "I want to believe that."

"I've struggled with that. A lot, actually. I've spent years worrying instead of walking in faith. I've tried to outthink every possible outcome, like I had any control over it." Erin realized that something had changed. She hadn't panicked over having to resign, hadn't felt the fear like she normally would. She'd trusted in God and the reward was a good night's sleep and a whole lot less anxiety. "You know, I'm done with bracing for the worst. Yes, I lost my job, but that might be because God has something better for me. All my effort, all my anxious thoughts got me nothing but a headache." She shook her head. "I've been doing it to myself for years, and I think I finally understand that having faith in God's Providence is a whole lot easier than fretting over the worst possible outcome on my own.

I guess it's only been recently that I've realized He has us in His hands no matter what happens so all the worrying in the world is useless."

"Yeah!" Claire's face broke out in a smile and Erin was reminded how lovely her friend was. She couldn't understand Scott Murphy's faithlessness. He had a beautiful wife and two boys that needed him.

Claire cocked her head to the side. "What are you thinking?"

"That you are a beautiful person, inside and out, and that your husband is a fool."

"Ex-husband now." Claire ducked her head. "Court says it's official."

Erin reached out her hand, thought better of it, and hugged her instead.

Saturday came and with no fishing available and a light snowfall overnight preventing him from running, Dan decided to visit Pete to see if talking with him might bring clarity. Now that he'd sorted out his head, as she'd requested, he was trying to think of how best to approach Erin. He didn't want to blow it. Pete was always at home on Saturdays and rarely picked up his phone that day so Dan drove up the mountain to his cabin. He knocked on the door and waited, but it wasn't Pete who came to the door.

"Dan!" Lauren swung the door wide and beckoned him in. "It's so nice to see you." She had her long, silver hair in a bun with a pencil stuck through it. The clothes she was wearing had small spatters of paint on them that matched the spatters on her hands. "Excuse the mess." She waved a hand to her clothes. "I'm helping Pete repaint his living room. It's remarkable that I can paint a watercolor, oil, or acrylic and not spill a drop on me, but give me a can of interior latex paint and I end up covered."

"It's a very nice shade of blue." Dan stepped inside and she shut the door behind him.

"Why thank you. I picked it." She led him inside and Dan looked around, but didn't see Pete.

"Is Pete home today?"

"You just missed him. He got called out. Some kind of emergency." She shook her head. "He's sixty-five and supposedly retired, but when you love what you do." She left it there.

"I get that." Dan smiled. "Well, I'm sorry to have missed him."

"Did you have church business?"

"No, I was hoping he might have time to talk."

"Oh?" She sat down at the kitchen island and patted the stool next to her. "You're in luck. I do."

"Uh, well." Dan sat down, not wanting to offend her, but not ready to discuss his love life with her either.

"Feel free to ask me anything." She sat patiently. When Dan didn't speak she guessed the cause. "Is this about Erin?"

"How did you know?"

"It's awful to be in a small town where everyone knows your business, isn't it?" She leaned back and chuckled. "You can't blame us though; we're all rooting for you. Erin is such a lovely person, and you are so clearly in love with her."

"What?"

"It's written all over your face every time you look at her."

Dan wasn't sure how he felt about that. She hadn't been the first person to guess his feelings, but he didn't realize that he wore them on his face for all to see. So much for thinking he was in control of his emotions. "Since you've already guessed, yes, I wanted Pete's advice."

"What this requires is a grand, romantic gesture." Lauren clapped her hands together. "Grand and public. It has to be something that removes all doubt about your feelings for her. Considering all the gossip she has to put up with, she deserves something impressive."

He frowned, not sure about that advice. Erin wasn't showy at all. She might not be the shy, reserved woman he used to think of her as, but she definitely wasn't dramatic. "Impressive?"

Lauren nodded sagely. "The big stuff. Like start off by sending her a huge bouquet of flowers every day for a week. No note, only the flowers." Lauren seemed to be warming to her topic, her hands waving as she spoke.

"Um, okay."

"Then, I have the perfect idea." Lauren was practically beaming. "The senior center is having a dance."

"Okay."

"The Civics Club at the school sponsored it. The kids are going to decorate the gym and serve snacks and things. I know for a fact that Erin is going to be there. Half the PTO is helping out."

"Okay."

"So, don't you see? You show up in a suit and sweep her onto the dance floor and off her feet. Metaphorically, of course. Better yet, have a ring in your pocket and propose!" She pressed her palms against her cheeks. "But that ring better be pretty since you're dealing with a woman who has the soul of an artist."

"Right." *No pressure.* Dan wasn't sure about any of this, but Lauren seemed to know what she was talking about, and Dan knew absolutely nothing about how to get a woman to take you back after you'd been an idiot. He didn't really have a reason to be at the dance, but it's not like they were going to card him on his way in. "This will really work?"

"Oh, she will be delighted."

"Okay. I guess I'll go ring shopping."

Erin stared down at the punchbowl filled with pink liquid and slowly melting blobs of sherbet ice cream spreading out on the surface like disintegrating islands of green, orange, and red. Below the mess on top, lights flickered. "Is the punch glowing?"

Claire poked at one of the mounds of melting sherbet with the ladle. "Yes, although surprisingly, not from the sheer number of chemicals it contains." She filled a paper cup and tried to hand it to Erin, but Erin shook her head. "It's plastic glow cubes. Apparently, they're a 'thing'."

"So is diabetes. I hope we have water to offer anyone sane enough to

244 | AT THE CROSSROAD

avoid this sugar coma waiting to happen?"

"Of course. Ms. Grumpy-pants."

Erin was grumpy and she knew it. This wasn't the place for her rotten attitude either. She looked around the gym decorated from beam to post and back again. The club had done quite a job in transforming the place. There was barely an inch of it that didn't sparkle or glow. "I'm glad you talked the girls into the white lights."

"For sure. Can you imagine this place if those risers were wrapped with twinkling colored ones? Ghastly." Claire made a face. "Anyway, I suppose that's my lot in life now. I'm embracing my new role." She sighed tragically.

Erin resisted the urge to roll her eyes. "And that is?"

"Matriarch." Claire told her with a perfectly straight face. "I'm the giver of wisdom. Like you." She gestured to Erin. "I've passed through my girlish youth, my young womanhood as well, and now I embrace my matronly role, doling out advice to these innocent girls among us." Her eyes fell on Annie who was manning the laptop connected to the giant speakers playing the music for that night's dance. "Like Annie. She's . . . I don't know, but she needs wisdom. When I asked her to volunteer—"

"You mean 'shanghaied'."

"Oh, shush." Claire fluttered a hand at her. "She might be my new boss and a good deal younger than me, but she needs some words of advice. She opens that coffee shop at the crack of dawn, and every day there's a certain gentleman that comes in, and I can tell they're meant to be." Claire narrowed her eyes. "I'm going to go—"

Erin grabbed her arm. "How about we leave Annie to herself?"

"She's too shy."

"No, she's reserved; there's nothing wrong with that."

"Maybe, but I think she has secrets."

"If she does, she gets to keep them."

"Oh, all right. You are such a nag." Claire settled in behind the drink table and Erin left her to it, crossing over to the snack table. She had to remind herself it was only for a few hours since she was crossing from grumpy to sulky and that wasn't a good look on anyone. But her memories weren't helping her in the effort. The last time she'd been manning a refreshments table Dan had pulled her out onto the dancefloor. That had started a dance of a very different kind between them, one that had her thrilled one moment, heartsick the next. She missed him. The last time they'd talked face-to-face it was at his mom's service. He texted her that picture of his bracelet, but that was about it until a giant bouquet of flowers appeared on her porch. There was no note, but she knew it was him, and she supposed he was replying in kind although that was weird. He didn't call, didn't drop by, didn't text, just kept sending flowers. She didn't understand what he was up to.

Feeling uncertain and unsettled was not conducive to keeping a good mood. Neither was pining for a man. Her longing for him wasn't a small thing either, it was bone-deep. Her crush had turned into admiration, which had given way to love. She hadn't planned on it, and a good portion of the time she'd resisted it, but her heart fell anyway. Dan now occupied a permanent spot whether she wanted him to or not. She'd taken to praying for him when she noticed she was missing him. That felt like the right thing to do, a way to still care for him even if he wasn't ready for her love.

Tonight seemed purpose-built for moodiness. It was cold and dark. The recent snow had turned into brown slush, and she'd had to wade through it to get there. She looked out at the couples dancing and felt a pang. Pete was out there with Lauren. She'd heard that they had an understanding, and that as soon as Mac and Katherine were settled with their foster kids, they were going to get married. The love practically beaming out of them left Erin with a hollow feeling, although it was good to know happy endings actually happened.

"There you are."

She turned to the voice and there he was. Dan. In a suit, no less, and either someone had helped him with his hair or he'd seen a barber in the time they'd been apart. It was almost tame. Her eyes raked over him, taking in his carefully knotted tie, and his shoes, polished and shiny. He must have been eating and sleeping again since the circles under his eyes were gone and his cheeks were no longer sunken. He was smiling at her, and she realized he'd been speaking and she hadn't heard a word. "What?"

"I asked if you saved me a dance." He sounded amused.

"With you?" She looked around, her mind trying to catch up since Dan was neither a senior citizen, a student, nor a parent. "Why are you here?"

"To see you." He seemed uncertain, as if he didn't expect her to ask that question.

"But this is for the seniors."

"I know that, but—"

"I'm working."

"I know that too." Now he sounded exasperated.

"I can't be dancing."

"Sure you can." He held out his hand, but she didn't take it. Instead she came from around the table, grabbed his elbow, and towed him to a corner of the room where everyone in the room wouldn't be watching them.

"What is up with you?"

"What's up with me?" He pushed a hand through his hair, messing it up. "I'm trying to show you that I love you. I'm trying to be romantic. This is supposed to be my grand, romantic gesture where you're swept off your feet and take me back."

Erin felt her jaw drop open. "Take you back?"

"This is turning into another huge fail." He rolled his eyes to the ceiling.

"Okay, second lesson in romantic relationships. No grand gestures when you're not actively dating."

"What?"

"Dan, this display is sweet, the flowers were sweet, but we need to treat this relationship like it's serious and worth working on. You waltzing in here like this." She gestured at his suit. "Doesn't work. I don't want any grand, romantic gestures. I want to know I can trust you, that you're the real deal."

He fumbled in his pocket and pulled out a small box. He dropped to his knee, and she gasped.

"Does this look like the real deal?" He held out an exquisite ring. It was either platinum or white gold with a huge diamond surrounded by filigree. It was gorgeous, but it wasn't anything she'd ever wear. It was ostentatious, a show piece. This was all a show. This was all too fast, too much, too soon.

"Erin, I know this is all wrong, but my love isn't. It's real. Will you marry me?"

She looked down at his face full of hope and answered the only way she could. "No."

His eyes slowly closed, and he dropped his hand. He got up off his knee, not looking at her. Once again, she felt like she'd kicked a puppy. "Dan," She reached out and touched his arm. He raised his eyes to hers. She almost drew back at the misery she saw there. "We should talk."

"Yeah." He agreed, sounding as unhappy as he looked.

She heard her name shouted and turned around to see one of the club members waiving frantically at her. "Seriously?" She turned back to Dan. "I've got to go."

"I can see that."

"The timing—"

"I know. It's all wrong, isn't it?" He smiled, but it was a half-hearted effort. "Go, I'm sorry for this. I promise, no more grand gestures from me." He put his hand over his heart.

"Okay, but we should talk. I mean that." She started to walk away, looking over her shoulder at him, trying to tell if he understood that she wanted to try again, just not like this. "I'll call you."

"Sure." His voice still sounded despondent, and if it wasn't for the student practically bouncing up and down in anxiety, waiting for her, she'd have stopped and explained to be sure he understood. He raised a hand in a wave goodbye as she turned around to find out what, exactly, the emergency was.

"Oh my goodness, Mrs. Sullivan." The girl said in a rush. "I am so sorry, but Wendy said we're out of seltzer and two of the seniors can't have punch because of the sugar and don't want water, and we don't know what else to give them."

This was their emergency? She spun on the spot to see if she could stop him from leaving, but Dan was gone.

CHAPTER TWENTY-EIGHT

DAN WAS ANXIOUS. NOT ONLY ANXIOUS, but unsettled, unhappy, and irritated. It wasn't Mac's fault, but he couldn't help taking it out on him a bit. Mac had called him first thing in the morning and insisted Dan help him tune up his snow machines. Dan was antsy because although Erin said she'd call, it had been three days and she hadn't. Yesterday he'd caved and called her. Twice. He'd had to leave voicemails both times. He was unsettled because she hadn't called back, and he was unhappy because he was beginning to fear that he'd blown it so spectacularly that she was done. The irritated bit was all Mac. Why the man needed to get the machines out after the first decent snowfall, he didn't know.

"Okay, I think this one is all set." Dan stood and wiped his hands on a rag.

"Yeah, this one's good too." Mac wiped the machine down and stood back, looking it over. "I'm glad I traded up to these. The old ones I had were fine, but these are better suited to two riders and with the kids coming, I have a feeling I'll be riding with a passenger more often than not."

"Okay. Well, glad I could help."

"Oh, we're not done yet. Gotta take one out and test the trail." Mac said, grabbing his jacket and zipping it on.

"You don't need me for that."

"Gotta have two people on the sled. Get your helmet." Mac gestured to a helmet on the nearby workbench.

Dan sighed and grabbed it and his coat. "One pass over the trail, and then I've got to get going."

"Why, you got plans?"

For a moment he was tempted to lie. He had planned to visit Rob's kids today at their group home, but the social worker had called with the news that Dylan and Kyla were meeting a couple that might end up adopting them. "Honestly? No. But this is about the last thing I feel like doing at the moment."

"Ah, heartache will do that to you. Climb on. We'll make this quick."

Dan got on behind Mac and put his helmet on. The second seat had a bit of a back to it, and Mac was driving slowly enough that Dan was able to relax and take in the scenery. Mac's property was beautiful–half fields, half forest and on a plateau of the mountain so it wasn't all on a pitch. The trail they took was pretty sedate although the fresh snow generated a lot of dust as they skimmed along. It looked like another sled had already been out. Dan could see fresh tracks. That wasn't unusual though. The snowmobile trails in Maine often went over private lands. Large landowners like Mac gave access unless the traffic got to be too much or too many ATVs cut it up in the mud season.

Eventually, they came to a small clearing and Mac stopped. Dan could hear the other snowmobile in the distance. "What are we stopping for?"

Mac lifted the visor of his helmet. "Hey, can you hop off?"

Dan climbed off, lifting the visor of his own helmet, and brushed some of the snow dust. He heard Mac gun the engine. "Wha—"

The sled took off, showering Dan in snow. He stumbled back and pulled off his helmet, wiping the snow out of his face. "Hey!" But Mac was already up the trail and over a rise. "What is wrong with that guy?"

"Nothing a swift kick wouldn't cure."

Dan spun around and spotted Erin leaning against a tree across the clearing. She was dressed for snowmobiling in ski pants and parka, with white, fluffy mittens on her hands. Those hands were now on her hips, and the expression on her face was thunderous.

Erin watched Dan's face visibly pale, and she almost laughed. "I assume this was not your idea?" When James and Seth had talked her into taking a snowmobile ride on the sleds Mac had bequeathed them when he bought his new ones, she assumed they wanted to cheer her up. She hadn't suspected a thing until they'd stopped in the clearing so Seth could try driving. Once she was off to change drivers, Seth took off. James did too, shouting over his shoulder not to worry because Mac had taught them both how to drive.

"Oh, no." He held both hands up. "You asked for no more grand gestures. I promised and I intend to keep that promise."

"Did you tell the boys that?"

"No." He lowered his hands. "You think they attempted this, uh, parent trap?"

"Yes. They recruited Mac it seems. The jerk." She couldn't help but smile. "Those kids. They've been nagging me for days about you. 'Is Pastor Dan coming for dinner soon?' 'Maybe Pastor Dan can come help us shovel the walk.' They really like you."

The change that came over Dan's face was remarkable. He first looked pleased, then regretful, and finally resigned. "That means a great deal to me. Especially coming from you." His voice was sorrowful.

She took a step closer to him. "So, you think they marooned us here hoping we'd look into each other's eyes and realize that we belong together?" She waved a hand dismissively. "They watch too much TV."

"No they don't." He stepped closer to her. "You don't let them."

"Too many Disney movies then." She trudged through the snow, closing the distance between them to a few yards.

"Maybe that's it." He copied her steps until they were standing only feet apart. The slow smile that crossed his lips was the sweetest thing she'd seen in ages, and it was making her heart beat faster. She needed to think of something sarcastic to say to cut the tension, but she was all out of snark. She felt the tell-tale flutter of the long-dormant butterflies in her stomach.

It looked like he wanted to reach out for her, but he stuffed his hands in his pockets. "I think they were counting on us taking this time to talk. No audience, no grand gestures. The two of us alone."

"That's all I've been wanting. When I said we should talk, this is what

I had in mind." She looked around. "Okay, not being dumped in the snow, but being alone and having no distractions."

"No party-supply emergencies?" He laughed.

"No students, no parishioners, no crises, no old friends popping in." The wind kicked up a bit and began to blow her hair around along with a fine mist of snow.

"Beth's gone." Dan's tone had a slight edge to it.

"I know." She pushed the hair off her face with a mitten, but it blew back.

"You were right." He reached out and tucked her hair behind her ear. She tried to ignore the very pleasant shiver that caused. "Beth was up here to fundraise, yes, but also to." He stopped and laughed a little. "She hoped that I'd not only help her run Lodestone, but do it as her husband."

Erin felt her mouth drop open. "I knew it! Okay, I didn't, but at least my instincts weren't that far off."

"Yeah, I was blind. And that's the thing." He took a step nearer. "I was locked up in my head, consumed with my problems, my concerns, my wants. I never thought about what you needed." His eyes searched her face. "And I am so sorry." He dragged the words out, and she heard the depth of feeling in them.

"It's good to hear you say that, but I need to apologize for not calling you after the other night. I picked up the phone a dozen times, but I lost my nerve. You need to know that I love you, Dan." She watched his eyes widen in surprise and as he moved to reach for her, she grabbed hold of his arms intending to keep him where he was so he'd really listen. "But I want to be sure that the love you say you have for me is the real thing, not an infatuation all dressed up."

"It took some time, but my head is straightened out. I signed the contract at Calvary. I know this is where God has called me. That had to come first, before I could understand what I was feeling for you. It all started that day in the gym, at the beginning of the school year, when I saw you dancing. You had this carefree joy that I'd never seen. I knew then that you had depths you didn't show the world, and I wanted to know them. I wanted to get to know you. I've been falling in love with you ever since." He reached out and took her hand. "This is yours." He pressed her hand against his chest over his heart. "Has been for a while now."

"Dan . . ." She wanted to believe him, but this was so crazy. They'd known each other for years, but had only dated for what—weeks? And half that time was spent on misunderstandings and crises of epic proportions. "I can't help feeling that this is an emotional decision, not a sound one."

"If this wasn't the right decision at the right time, then when I spent a week praying about it I think God would have clued me in."

"You prayed about this?"

He let out a short bark of a laugh. "Yeah, I did not wake up one morning and suddenly decide I wanted to marry you. After my mom died I finally realized what a self-absorbed jerk I'd been and all that it had cost me. Not only your trust, but James and Seth's too. That was a blow like nothing else. I spent a lot of time in prayer because I wanted to be sure this was His will, not only my hope. Once I felt certain it was, I didn't know how to fix what I had broken. I didn't even know where to start. I should have called you and we could have had this talk a week ago, but Lauren said you'd appreciate a grand romantic gesture, and I guess I went a little overboard."

"You got advice from Lauren?"

"I went looking for Pete at his cabin, but she was there instead. Painting. It was a nice blue color."

Erin laughed. "Artists. They like dramatic."

"Well, you're an artist too so I figured she wouldn't lead me astray."

"I've never thought of myself that way. I make jewelry."

He lifted up his wrist and pushed the sleeve of his coat up to show he was wearing the bracelet she'd made him. A happy glow filled her chest. "You make art."

"I'm so glad you like it."

"I've barely taken it off. It's perfect. When I look at the two cords being held by the cross I can't help but think it's the perfect image for marriage. I know you probably didn't mean it that way, but for me it was a sort of sign. The two become one. It's both profound and uncomplicated."

Erin felt her cheeks get hot. "Still, I'm not an artist."

"No. I know who you are." His voice was soft, barely above a whisper. "You are a good mother, a patient teacher, a faithful friend, and the most generous soul I have ever met." He took her hand in his again. "I deeply want to add wife to that list."

She started to speak, but he raised a hand and gently placed his fingers on her lips. "I know. I have some work to do to earn your trust again. I made it hard on you, didn't I?" His words were contrite and Erin wanted to object, but she let him go on, sensing he needed to say these things. "Starting a relationship in the middle of a spiritual crisis was not the best timing on my part."

She pulled his hand away from her lips. "No, but I'm glad you did start it. I do love you, Dan."

He raised her left hand to his lips, and he kissed her ring finger. "Will you keep that as a promise from me?" His eyes searched her face. "I'll wait for you. If it takes a lifetime, I'll wait until you're ready."

Erin felt her heart swell with emotion. She'd been here before. The first time she'd said yes to a marriage it was such a mistake, but it was nothing like this. Dan had thrown the doors of his heart and soul wide open for her to see that his love was real. It wouldn't be easy, they'd make mistakes, but Dan had given her his heart and she'd given him the same. They'd acted in both faith and trust. It might be new-born, but it was real.

"Ask me again."

His eyes slowly widened. "What?"

Her lips twitched with the urge to smile. "Ask. Me. Again."

He took a breath and let it out slowly. "Erin, love of my heart, will you marry me?"

"Yes." The second that word was out of her mouth he pulled her to him. She reached her arms around his neck as their lips met. His love, his promise, all his hope was in that kiss. It made her weak in the knees. It felt like the start of something truly beautiful. This man she had admired from a distance for so long was holding her in his arms. Their love was in spite of her past, his mistakes, and all the strikes against them. God had picked them for each other, and now here they were. He lifted his head and smiled down at her. He was about to speak when the whine of an engine sounded in the distance.

"Typical." She rolled her eyes and sighed.

The sound got louder until two snow machines appeared, her sons driving them. They stopped and the boys each lifted their helmet visors. Seth was the closer of the two and he waved. "Uh, we're here to pick you up. So, how's it going?"

"Just fine, thank you for asking." Dan jerked his thumb from Seth to James. "How about you ride with your brother?"

Seth climbed off his sled as Dan grabbed Erin's helmet and then his own. He got on the snow machine and motioned for her to climb on behind him which she did. She slid up close to Dan and wrapped her arms around his waist. The sled took off, and she turned her head in time to see James pulling away with Seth riding behind, his fist raised triumphantly in the air. She held on tight to Dan as she laughed out loud.

EPILOGUE

"LINDA? HI, IT'S ERIN."

"Oh, hello sweetness. It's so good to hear your voice."

Erin felt the same. Linda's gentle southern accent communicated her love regardless of distance. "I'm glad you called. Your father has been in a mood all day."

"There's nothing wrong, is there?" Erin felt a stab of panic. She hated that Linda and her dad lived so far away. If something did go wrong she'd be hearing of it long past the point she could be of any help. Maybe she could convince them to come north again.

"Oh, no." She laughed lightly. "You know your dad, he's watching politics again. I keep hiding the remotes so he can't turn the TV on, but then he goes on the internet and gets even madder. I may have to make it like prairie times in this house to get him away from the news." She paused. "Of course, then he'd read the paper. You know how he is."

"I do, and I do want to talk to him, but I was hoping to talk to you first."

"What's wrong?" Her voice was both stern and concerned. Linda was as bad as she was, always assuming the worst.

"Nothing's wrong. I have news." Erin paused hoping this was going to go over well. "I've been seeing someone, and I didn't get a chance to talk to you about it because it kind of happened fast."

She could hear Linda's deep intake of breath. "Do not tell me you've hooked up with one of those online men. They're dangerous. All killers, liars, and thieves."

"No!" Erin had to get it out quickly or Linda was going to get into lecture mode and hand off the phone to her dad and this would take all day. "Not a killer." She snuck a quick look at Dan to see he was trying not to laugh. She'd put Linda on speakerphone so they could both talk to her when the time came. She should have warned him what her step-mom was like. "We've known each other for years; he's the church pastor for pity's sake."

Linda gasped again. "The pastor, you say?"

"You've actually met him. When you were up for Brittany and Jake's wedding. He's the pastor at Calvary."

"Sweet-looking boy, blond hair?"

Erin shot Dan a warning look in case he felt like laughing out loud. "Yes. That's him."

"Oh, and he had his doctorate, didn't he? Yes, he did. Dr. Connors, right?" Linda's memory was as sharp as always. "Well, it certainly has been a long time you've been a widow. I'm glad you're dating a nice man. Maybe we can all go to dinner when we come up this spring."

"That's the thing. Um, it's progressed a bit beyond dating."

"Do not tell me you got married!" The phone crackled as it tried to handle the sheer volume of Linda's voice. "I don't care if you did. We'll have a vow renewal when we get up there. I didn't get to see you married the first time, since you slunk off to city hall with that Jimmy, but I'm going to see it this time, y'hear? I'll get the dress and handle the reception. I am not missing my only baby's wedding for the second time."

"Linda, wait." Erin was thrown by 'my only baby' since Linda had never said that before. They had been close, but when Erin eloped with Jimmy, to say things were tense was an understatement. "We didn't get married yet. I want to wait for you and Dad to come up." Linda started praising Jesus. Erin figured it was best to wait her out. When she looked at Dan he wasn't laughing, but he was smiling wide.

"Okay," Linda began in a much calmer tone. "You tell your friends that they better not so much as show you a wedding magazine until I get there." Her voice became muffled as she called for Erin's dad. "Bill! You need to come to the phone. No, I don't care if it's breaking news, it's going to be bad either way. Come hear some good news from your daughter. She's getting married to a pastor." It sounded like she uncovered the phone's mouthpiece. "Okay. Did you pick a date yet?"

"Not quite. Dan's voting for sooner rather than later."

"They all do."

"We don't want to wait until summer because it can really get crowded here."

"Third weekend in May would be about right. Skips Mother's Day and it's before Memorial Day. Weather will be a bit cold, but not too bad. Won't have the usual tourists, and I bet we can get that golf course place for the reception, the one up by the ski resort? It won't really be in season so we'll get it nice and cheap. They do the prettiest events. Oh, this is so exciting!"

"Linda, I have Dan here with me; if you'd like to put Dad on, he'd like to talk to him for a minute."

"Oh, of course he would." They could hear shuffling noises and then her father's voice.

"Erin." Her father packed a world of affection into two syllables. "My girl's getting married?"

"Yes, Dad, and he's right here." She picked up the phone and switched modes so that Dan could talk to her dad directly. He took the phone from her and got up, wandering into the hall. Erin sat on the living room couch and hummed so she couldn't hear them talk. Her dad could be hardheaded. She didn't think he would be hard on Dan, but he might make him sweat it a bit. The minutes passed and Erin became concerned. She got up and found Dan had wandered from the hall through the kitchen and out the back door. He was standing in the yard, still talking on the phone. When he spotted Erin at the door he motioned for her to join him.

"Bill, I have to disagree with you there. The flat tax sounds great in principle, but in practice—" Erin wrapped her arm around Dan. It sounded like her father had suckered him into talking politics. "Well, no sir, I do consider myself to be a principled conservative, but when it comes to—" Dan rolled his eyes. "Sure, I vote in every election." Dan put his hand over the phone. "He's asking who I voted for. I'm guessing this is a trap."

"Don't fall for it. Give me the phone." Dan handed her the phone, and she put it up to her ear. "Dad, stop torturing Dan with politics."

"Hey, I gotta ask the important questions." Then her dad chuckled.

"He seems like a nice guy."

"He is." Erin looked up at Dan. "Very nice."

"Listen, little one, there's something I want to say. Something I should have said when you eloped, but with Linda losing it, I never got a chance." Erin braced for maximum emotional impact since her father never said a word about her late husband. "We weren't happy with your choice. I didn't like him, I think you knew that. I didn't like that he slacked off and let you carry the burden of the finances. I really didn't like his drinking, but that didn't matter in the end. He was your husband, and we were prepared to support you both, no matter what. I regret that you never felt that from us, that you took so much on your own shoulders. We should have butted in more, visited more often, insisted on getting involved. But you always seemed to be handling it. I'm sorry, honey. What I want you to know is that we're here for you, and we'll be praying for you and this new man you've found. We're here no matter what."

"Thanks, dad." Erin managed to speak around the lump in her throat. She felt Dan's arm slide around her shoulder and then he drew her against him. She leaned on him while her dad called her stepmother back to the phone to finish making plans.

Long after they'd finished the phone call, after Dan waited while she made sure the kids were in bed, they sat out on the front porch, and said a long goodnight. "So we finally have a sort-of date." Dan held Erin a little closer. "Five short months and I won't have to say goodnight outside in the cold." He leaned his forehead against hers. "Not from the moment they introduce us as Mr. and Mrs. Connors."

"Hearing that, it's so weird."

"Yeah, 'weird'. That's what I was thinking."

"Oh, you know what I mean. It's thrilling and strange, but not in a bad way. I don't know what the word for that is."

"All I'm feeling is impatience."

"Men . . ." Erin slipped out of his arm and pushed him towards the stairs. "Besides, it will be 'Dr. and Mrs.' I'm pretty sure Linda will insist on it."

Dan smiled as he backed down the stairs. "I don't care if it's 'this shlub and this princess' so long as it's us and we're together." Dan blew a kiss to her as he walked down the walk towards his house. Erin took in a deep breath of the cold, December air and reflected that for once, she wasn't braced for the next shoe to fall. They were both on the floor, and she was looking forward to tomorrow.

A Sneak Peek at Book Three

The Redemption Road

CHAPTER ONE

THE JINGLE OF SLEIGH BELLS RANG out as the door to the shop swung open. A blast of cold air swept inside along with a swirl of snow which twinkled like fairy-dust in the overhead lights. A man in an olive-green parka shut the door and stood on the welcome mat stomping his boots to shake off the new-fallen snow. Annie watched him push back his hood and unwind a long scarf from around his face. Even with the wintry camouflage she knew who it was. There was only one person who ever arrived almost every morning rain, shine, or snow right after she opened. She started up the espresso machine and took out the coffee beans, knowing his order by heart. A minute later she looked up to see him standing at the counter in front of her, and she felt her lips form the smile that his presence always conjured. "Good morning, Alex."

He closed his eyes and sniffed the air. "What is that baking?"

"Gingerbread men. But you can't have any yet." Her smile broadened at his perplexed look. "They'll need time to cool so I can decorate them."

"I'll have to stop in later." His eyes fell on the glass case under the counter where sheets of scones, muffins, donuts, and other treats sat ready to tempt her customers. "What's the special today?"

"You'll love it." She walked into the back room for the tray of today's special. Most of her baked goods she bought from a wholesaler one town over, but she liked to add a few things of her own every day. They were in limited quantities, so regular customers knew to ask to avoid missing out. She grabbed the tray, and when she returned his face lit up.

"Cinnamon rolls? I thought you said you hated those."

"I hate making them. They're a pain, but I love eating them, and it's the Christmas season so I'm feeling generous." She took a sheet of bakery paper and pulled a roll off the tray, then placed it on a plate. "Here you go." She slid the plate across the counter to him then scooted back over to the espresso machine to finish his double macchiato.

"Speaking of Christmas, are you going to stay open over the holidays?"

She shrugged. "I'm not going anywhere. Business should be good with all the shops staying open. I'll have regular hours on Christmas Eve, but I'll close on Christmas Day. No one is likely to be out."

"You're not going home to your family?"

Annie managed not to wince. If there was one topic she could erase from every conversation she'd have until the end of time, it was this one. She'd had a pretty good run with Game Warden Alex Moretti. They'd talked about books, his job, even politics, but she'd worked hard to avoid the family topic altogether. The reason being, she didn't have one. Not a real one.

"My parents are traveling, so I'll be here. How about you? Are you headed home for Christmas?" She finished his drink and slid it across the counter toward him.

"No." He gave a brief shake of his head, his short-cropped hair unmoved by the gesture. His tone didn't invite a follow-up question, and she had no intentions of asking one, but for what was probably the hundredth time, she wished she was his real friend. She wished she could reach across the counter, take his hand, and say 'Hey, if you ever want to talk about it...' But that would never happen. Instead, she changed the subject.

"If you're going to be in town anyway, you might want to check out the candlelight service at Calvary Church. The music will all be carols from medieval times through the twentieth century. It's supposed to be beautiful."

"I might." It was same answer he'd give her any time she told him about stuff happening in Sweet River. Didn't matter if it was an all you can eat BBQ fundraiser for the firehouse or a farmers' market or a church service. He always said he might go, but he never had. Annie wondered if his seclusion was by choice, a product of his nature, or something else. She didn't think he had a girlfriend, but she assumed he had plenty of offers. Handsome and kind, he wouldn't be alone for long.

Annie had been alone most of her life, something she'd been trying to change. In fact, she was going to the concert at the church, and she'd go to the Christmas Eve service too. If she was brave enough, she might even sit in a pew instead of staying up in the balcony by herself. It had taken a while to feel comfortable going somewhere new and she wasn't quite ready for the awkward small-talk of sharing a pew or going to the coffee hour. Strangers placing orders for coffee she could handle, people wanting to get to know her, asking her questions about herself, that was another matter.

Small talk with Alex was something different altogether. He'd made small talk easy right from the first time he'd come into the shop. Do you have any plans for Christmas?" Annie almost regretted asking a moment later when Alex's expression clouded over.

"Pete and his new wife invited me over for dinner. If nothing comes up, I'll probably go."

"Oh, you definitely should! Lauren's a great cook. What I wouldn't give for her talent."

Alex lifted an eyebrow and pointed down at his cinnamon roll.

"That's baking–it's totally different. Baking is science. I follow the recipe, and it comes out every time. Cooking is an art. It takes a certain degree of creativity to be any good at it, not to mention a level of courage I apparently lack."

He shook his head. "I don't believe it."

"No, really, I can do eggs and a decent stir-fry, but sauces or the fancy stuff? No way. I can't even make chili. It always come out lackluster, watery, or off somehow."

"Bland chili is the worst. I use my mom's recipe, but I add a few things."

"See?" She held up her hand. "That's the creativity and courage part. I wouldn't know what to add."

"You need somebody to teach you the basics, that's all."

Annie huffed out a laugh and lifted a shoulder in a half-hearted shrug while her mind spun through all the possible responses. This was the moment where she could spin that opening into a witty reply about how if he was offering, she'd be happy to let him teach her. In her imagination, it wouldn't be a weird self-invite at all. He'd get it, and he'd give her one of his rare, real smiles and they'd set up a time. Maybe it would even turn into another date, but instead of responding she stalled. The moment had all the time it needed to become awkward. Alex ended it by sliding a five across the counter to pay. As she rung the order up he took his coffee and his breakfast then gave her a little salute before heading to the corner table where, if it was like every other day, he'd sit and read while he ate. Annie tried to bury the disappointment like she had a dozen times before.

The door to the shop swung open again as Claire Murphy, her only employee, swept in with another flurry of snow. "It is so pretty!" She pulled off her coat and hung it up. "The world is frosted over, not a scraggily brown bush or blade of grass to be seen." Claire pulled off her knitted hat and fluffed her long, brown hair.

"You're early."

"Hockey practice. Normally I drop the boys off and then go back to bed, but it took so long to dig the car out of the snow I didn't feel like doing that twice this morning. I figure I can help you with prep or whatever."

"There's always something." Annie quickly reviewed all she had planned for the week. There were probably a half-dozen tasks she could hand off to Claire. Coffee by the Book was a pretty simple business. Coffee was her mainstay, the baked goods a nice addition, with the books lining the shelves more of a lost leader. She bought books she liked, old friends and new favorites, and she didn't try to stock based on what was popular, so they sold slowly, some weeks she'd only move ten or so. Claire called them 'ambiance', and she wasn't wide off the mark. When Annie had bought the shop it utterly lacked charm. She'd torn down the dropped ceiling and wallboard to find original brick and huge, wood beams in the ceiling. She'd been thrilled but decided to add books to make it feel cozy instead of industrial.

"I see 'tall, dark, and broody' has arrived." Claire's eyes slid to where Alex was sitting.

"He's not broody, he's reserved. There's a difference."

"Whatever he is, he's in need of something to smile about." Claire gave her a long look then gestured from Annie to Alex with a quick jerk of her head. "Maybe you could go discuss books or something. Don't you both read mysteries?"

"No. He likes suspense, I read mystery. It's two different things."

"If you say so." Claire dismissed her answer with a vague wave of her hand. "But he really is a bit too serious. It's probably why he's had trouble getting the locals to like him."

Game wardens in Maine were always the most popular with hunters since they were out in the woods to enforce the law, but Alex seemed to be especially disliked. It might be his strict adherence to the letter of the law, but he'd had to deal with more pushback and attitude than the previous warden. Annie admired Alex's dedication, but she was pretty much alone in that. She wished he'd go to more events in town so others could see what she did.

"If people would give him a chance, they'd find out he's actually really nice." Annie turned to see Claire staring at her with narrowed eyes. This was not good. Claire had a habit of puzzling things out of her, things she didn't want to share. Annie's feelings for Alex were top on the list of things she did not want to share. It was time to find Claire something to do to distract her from asking questions Annie didn't want to answer.

"Hey, since you're early, can you mix up some royal icing? I've got gingerbread men on the menu today, and they'll be cool enough to decorate soon."

"Yay!" Claire cheered as she headed into the back. "I love decorating!"

This was something Annie already knew. Claire was very outgoing, which was good since Annie wasn't. And she loved making things pretty, which Annie wasn't great at either. With Claire happily mixing icing in the back, Annie made a plan to buzz by Alex's table and offer a refill. As she got ready to come around the counter she saw he was in motion already. He had his phone up to his ear and was heading for the door. His coat was on before he whirled to face her.

He pulled the phone away from his head "Thanks." Then he waved to her as he ran out the door and into the swirling snow. She looked at the coat rack and realized he'd forgotten his scarf. She left the counter and grabbed it, but when she looked out the glass door she could see him pulling away in his truck. It was no matter. He'd be back tomorrow. As she rehung it on the pegboard she could smell pine needles, wool, and bergamot. She wondered if he drank Earl Grey tea like her Aunt Delia or if it was his after shave; another puzzling detail to Warden Moretti. Despite his daily trips to her store she felt like he was still a mystery, one she longed to solve.

Roger Cook stood about a foot too close while he stuck his index finger an inch from Alex's face and continued to shout. His face was a spectacular shade of red, beyond florid and headed for heart-attack scarlet. Alex waited for the man to either run out of steam or throw a punch. It could go either way. The facts of the situation were undeniable. His snowmobile wasn't registered, and he'd been operating it on private land. Alex had gotten the call from the landowner during the hour he usually reserved for Annie's, and he wasn't happy about it. About all that was saving Roger from being slapped into cuffs and sitting in the back of his truck was the fact that Alex knew Roger wasn't really angry at him.

Snowmobile registrations were a grand total of forty-six dollars. From the scattering of previous years' stickers on the sled, Roger knew that he could have avoided this drama by registering it as usual. Alex had stopped Roger at the mouth of the trail and let him know the landowner had closed this and it was posted, but he was prepared to acknowledge it might have been missed and let him off with a warning. But the unregistered snow machine turned this into another situation. Roger was angry at himself and taking it out on Alex. Knowing this made Alex calm. He was content to let the man scream himself hoarse if he needed to.

A car pulled up and Roger spluttered to a stop. A woman got out from the driver's side. It looked to Alex like she'd thrown a parka over her pajamas. As she stomped closer he saw the pajama bottoms had little bunnies on them. Her feet were stuffed into a pair of sloppy boots and a knit hat was shoved down over her long, brown hair. She rolled right up to Alex and got in his face despite being about a foot shorter. She had fine lines around her eyes as if she laughed a lot. The pom-pom on the top of her hat bobbled as she yelled at him.

"What's going on? Roger called me saying you're towing him?"

Between her getup and the way she was defending what he assumed was her husband, it was hard not to smile.

"Lucy, chill. I thought the snowmobile was registered this year, but it's not. No big deal."

Alex turned in surprise to find Roger completely calm.

"My fault, babe." Roger's tone was placating.

"I told you to get that thing registered." Lucy wasn't chill. She didn't seem interested in being calm either. She had her arms crossed over her chest, her anger directed at Roger now.

"I know, I know. I forgot."

Instead of telling him off, Lucy seemed to deflate slightly. Her shoulders slumped a little, and her tone changed. "Like you forgot to order oil yesterday?" Her head tilted to the side and her face softened. "I told you to let me take care of this stuff for you. You're working killer hours, Roger. You can't do it all."

Roger glanced over at Alex and pulled his wife away a few feet. Alex pulled out his notebook and mindlessly scribbled trying to make it clear he wasn't going to listen. He watched though, and after only a minute or two he saw Roger nod as if agreeing to something, and Lucy reached up to him and placed her hand against his cheek. It was a small gesture, but Alex was moved by it all the same.

"Hey." He called over. "Do you live close by?"

Roger looked up and nodded. "Seven Oak. Two streets over."

"Okay." Alex radioed in and canceled the tow. "Here's what we're going to do. I'll pretend that I didn't see you today. You go home and get online to this web address." He wrote it out, tore the page from his notebook, and handed it to Roger. "And get this machine registered. Then you will email me a screenshot of it." He handed him another piece of paper with his email address.

"Oh, man, thank you!" Roger seemed both shocked and pleased. Alex wasn't surprised by his reaction knowing his own reputation for being uncompromising.

"You get that done, and we're good. You don't, and I'll write you up." Alex nodded first to Lucy and then to Roger and headed back to his truck. He drove around the corner and up the long driveway to the house of the landowner who had called about Roger zooming over his fields. Once out of his truck, he waded through the snow that had yet to be cleared from the walk and up to the front door. He didn't need to knock since the homeowner was right there, waiting for him.

"I assume the situation is resolved?" The landowner was older, probably in his sixties, dressed in a cardigan sweater and wearing slippers. His accent hinted that he wasn't a local product. He sounded like a transplant from Massachusetts.

"I know you said that the land is posted, but there's no signs at the head of the trail or at the exit at the road. I can help you with that if you'd like. I've got a few signs in my truck and can hang them for you. That would go a long way to keeping the ATVs and snowmobiles out."

The man waved. "No. Thank you. I just wanted Cook to know he has to stay off my land. I can deal with the occasional trail rider."

"Uh, okay." That was odd, but Roger was this guy's neighbor, and if there was one thing Alex had learned in his six months on the job it was that neighbors made the best enemies. "Give us a call if you need us again." Alex backed away, and the man shut the door in his face. He brushed off the insult since it was a rare one. Most of the time landowners were glad to have help. As Alex got in his truck and drove away he thought over the call. He rarely gave anyone the kind of pass he had given Roger. For some reason, seeing his wife pull up and defend her husband had stirred something inside him. He wondered what it would be like to have someone on his side like that. A 'ride or die' partner for life.

Annie would be that kind of partner. She was everything loyal and good. Like Lucy she was petite too, but she was built, a perfect hourglass in miniature. Her eyes were far prettier, a kind of lavender blue. The first time Alex had seen them he'd been rendered speechless. It was a good thing that his reputation as a quiet guy had covered for him. Her eyes weren't even her best feature; it was her hair, a pure black that circled her heart-shaped face with curls. He often wondered if it was natural or if she walked around her apartment in curlers. He smiled at the thought. Alex knew it wasn't likely that he'd ever get to know. Someone like him didn't deserve someone like Annie. That thought was followed by a stab of regret.

He'd told himself a hundred times that it was probably stupid to keep showing up every morning, ordering coffee, and eating whatever she'd made pretending she'd made it for him alone, but he couldn't stop. It was the one comfort he allowed himself. Every day he'd wait at the table until she came by with a refill or with a book recommendation. She'd sit across from him, and he'd pretend that they were really friends, or something more, something infinitely better. It never lasted, but if life had taught one lesson, it had taught him that nothing good ever did.

AUTHOR NOTE

Motherhood is not for the faint of heart. (Fatherhood either) Whether you've given birth to your kids, adopted them, or acted as a mom for kids without one, it's a hard job. It requires you to be both tender and tough. But, I believe that the nature of a woman is exactly that – soft yet strong, compassionate yet resolute, quiet until it's time to be loud. As great as we are, we're not super-heroes. We need support. I believe that's why God designed it so we'd have a partner to rely on. But, this is a fallen world and many of us end up going it alone.

Erin Sullivan is a single mom who suffered through a bad marriage to an abusive man addicted to alcohol. It would be nice to be able to write that after her husband's death Erin was supported by her community, but if you're familiar with my writing you know that I try to make my characters, settings, and plots as real as possible. So, like so many single moms, Erin doesn't get the support and understanding she needs. She deals with rumors about her husband's death being her fault, that somehow she failed him. Too often it's the partner of an abuser who is saddled with the responsibility of their actions. It's wrong, but it happens.

If you've read my first book, The Broken Trail, then you may have noticed a common subplot in this one – foster kids. It's another aspect of the real world that doesn't get the light shone on it often enough. While most states do their best for kids in difficult circumstances, the foster system is often a dehumanizing experience for children. In general the system is as good as any government could make it. What it needs is more loving families willing to participate. If you have a heart for fostering, do it! There are kids right now who need your love. In the book Rob's kids, Dylan and Kayla, are placed in the system following his death. I was going to leave it there since the fate of kids who enter the system is often never known by those in the communities they were removed from. But, my publisher rightly pointed out that readers do not like loose ends and neither do I so in the last chapter we see that they are about to be placed with adoptive parents.

The fostering theme will continue in book three when we see Katherine and Mac with their new foster children. Oh, and if you haven't read the teaser chapter for book three yet, can you guess who the main characters will be? If you already read it, were they who you were thinking they'd be? Book three is underway as I write this author note and if you'd like updates and extra content, visit my website. You can join my mailing list there and keep up to date on all things Sweet River.

Thank you, dear reader, for picking up this book. I hope you enjoyed it. Reach out to let me know what you thought, and if you're able, please do leave a review. They are a great way to support an author and I deeply appreciate every one as I appreciate every reader. Thank you!

Connect with Christa
Website: https://christamacdonald.com
Facebook: https://www.facebook.com/groups/1538432676468229

DISCUSSION QUESTIONS

1. Early-on in the book Erin could almost be described as pessimistic. She's always waiting for the other shoe to drop. What happens to change her outlook?

2. The Providence of God can be a difficult concept for some believers. How would you describe it?

3. When Pete tells Erin that Dan is at a crossroad in his life, what two paths was Dan considering? Which road did he take and do you think it was the right one?

4. Church pastors face challenges that their parishioners often don't see. What kind of challenges did Dan face? How can a church better support their pastors?

5. Both Claire and Rob have a spouse leave them. Rob spirals into drug and alcohol use, ignoring the needs of his children, and ends up overdosing. Claire is able to get back on her feet despite being devastated by her husband's betrayal and financially ruined. What made the difference for Claire?

6. Single parents often face difficulties that married parents do not. How does your church, school, and larger community support single parents? Is there something they could be doing that they're not?

67175635R00156

Made in the USA
Middletown, DE
09 September 2019